life
before

July 1993

Northam

It was four-thirty in the morning when Senior Sergeant Des Robinson emerged from the Northam police station on Grant Street and made his way across the road to where his car was parked in a gravel lay-by overlooking the town. He stood for a moment in the no-man's-land somewhere between the driver's door and the low crash barrier that rimmed the edge, hugging his jacket close against the cold. The sky was black as pitch. No moon. No stars. Only the streetlights below creating an abstract map, an ethereal representation of the place, drew his eye as he fumbled in his pockets and found his cigarettes and lighter.

It was quiet, too, he noted. No hum from the highway on the far side of town. Not this morning. This morning the air was cool and still and there was a heaviness to it, a metallic scent that told him it was about to rain. He felt a passing gratitude that it had held off, that they'd had time to do their work and clear the scene without having to grapple with the weather. The only thing worse than having to deal with fatals was having to deal with them in the wet.

He took a cigarette from the packet and lit it, taking the smoke deep into his lungs, feeling the rough sensation on the back of his throat. What was it, this need? A conditioned response, half reward, half punishment. Probably mostly punishment if he was ever to analyse the situation. The pointless waste of life was something he always found hard to take; even after all these years he hadn't found a way to make any sense of it. It wasn't so much death itself. He'd become used enough to that and could largely cope with its physical reality. It was something deeper that affected him. The sense of futility, of some unfulfilled promise. What might have been and would now never be. An existential chasm that yawned before him and left him wondering why he, now looking fifty in the eye, was still here while golden youths with everything in front of them did not live to see their twentieth birthdays.

He ground the cigarette out in the gravel and got into his car. There was an opened bottle of water on the passenger side. He rinsed his mouth then took a peppermint from the compartment between the seats as he started up the engine. From the station he drove along the ridge and down towards Main Street, looking up to his own house as he went. He noted the lights were off and was glad of it. Mary had stirred when he had been called out and he'd hoped she'd settle back.

'Where're you going?' she'd murmured.

'Don't know yet, love,' he'd said softly, even though he did know, had been told by the dispatcher that there'd been a single car accident out on Allens Road, twenty minutes out of town. Telling Mary might spill her out of sleep, leave her wakeful and wondering until he got home. It was like that in a small town. An accident out on the highway could just as easily be a visitor passing through. An accident on one of the back roads meant a local, likely someone known.

He turned right at the bottom of the hill. The town centre lay directly in front of him. Main Street, still and ghostly under spare electric light, looked like a disused film set. A light rain was starting to fall now and the droplets formed a misty white curtain across his line of sight. He turned right again into Longmuir, noting the first stirrings of the day. Life going on. A truck was backing into the loading dock at the supermarket. On the other side of the road there were lights on at the bakery.

He drove on, down Longmuir Street towards the bridge. Here the houses were newer and more compact than those on the hill. In the dark they were barely visible, but he knew them, could see them in his mind's eye, their blank 1960s weather-board exteriors, plain front fences, overgrown, neglected gardens or patches of dirt. Much of his daily police work centred on the streets that ran either side of this stretch. The Flat they called it colloquially. He'd been summoned here more times than he could remember to deal with domestic disputes, noisy drunken parties, firearm offences and, increasingly these days, drugs. But the early hours were a great democratiser. At this time of the day the Flat was as peaceful as anywhere else in Northam and he had no need to stop here. This morning his business lay further out in the new part of town, across the river.

The estate was the town's answer to a rising population and growing affluence. It was not middle class, not rural establishment like the Hill, but there was a certain air of prosperity. Large houses with even larger garages, V8 sedans, utes and trail bikes littering the driveways. The garages themselves held the prizes: hot rods, vintage vehicles, works in progress, even the occasional boat, despite being so far from a good body of water. At the end of a cul-de-sac he pulled up next to a long, low cream-brick veneer, not unlike most of its neighbours. Neat as a pin. A concrete driveway led up to the double garage from the street and another narrower parallel path ran up to its front door.

He turned off the engine and sat for a moment in the darkness. It was one thing to attend accidents but another to take the news to the family. Mary had been on at him for a while to give up what they called the death messages. If he was on duty, and often even if he wasn't, he invariably delivered them, despite the fact he could have given the job to one of the constables, especially now that there were more personnel. There was nothing about doing it that he liked, yet he believed it was the part of his work that needed the greatest care. He felt obligated to take responsibility, he'd told her. He knew what these people were going through, how they needed to be treated. She'd replied that his real obligation now was to pass on his skills, his understanding of people, to younger officers. And she was right, of course, as she was always right. Still, this time, he thought he had made the correct decision. This time, given what he knew about this particular family, it was best for it to be him.

Thunder rumbled behind the hills and the rain began to beat down. He cursed and leaned across to the glove box, hoping to find an umbrella, a plastic file, something to hold over his head, but there was nothing useful that he could see. When he straightened in his seat again sheet lightning lit up the street, and it was in that second of illumination that he saw a figure. Someone standing on the driveway, directly in front of the double garage doors, rain-drenched, dripping, staring at the car. At him. Des couldn't clearly recognise who it was through the streaming window, but he knew anyway and felt a thrill of adrenaline run through him, a grab of apprehension. Had he been there the whole time? Had he watched him pull up?

Splinters of frozen rain fired at him as he opened the door, causing him to pause for a moment, shocked by the assault. In the dull glow of the interior light, with his arm outstretched to the handle, he noticed something dark on his sleeve. Smears of blood across the cuff of his shirt. How had he failed to see this before? But of course it didn't matter now. Couldn't matter. Like everything else, it was too late to do anything about it. In seconds he was out of the car, running up the drive, thinking only of what needed to be done next.

April 2016

Melbourne

She was closing the front door behind her when the white and blue squad car drove past. She noted it slow, turn into a driveway up the street and circle back as she herded the kids down the path and out the front gate.

'Look, Mum. The police,' said Cody, who at five was highly skilled at stating the obvious.

'Yep,' she said. 'No time to gawk, bubs. We need to get a move on.'

By then the car was crawling along almost opposite them, the two officers—a man in the passenger seat, a woman behind the wheel—clearly observing her, checking the house. She paused for a split second by the gate as the kids ran on down the street, saw the female officer register them, and felt something flutter inside her, that residual fear, sense of guilt. There was something about cops, the way they had of looking at you, wary and observant as though they had X-ray vision and could see what was in your head. Or worse still, what was in your heart. Would they be able to tell there was a distinct possibility of law-breaking this morning? Speeding in a forty zone. Running a red light. They usually walked, she and the kids, but this morning she'd overslept and the kids had been groggy and slow to wake. Now they were going to have to drive, and even then they might not make it on time.

She followed her children along the footpath towards their car, glancing back only fleetingly at the police, who had now stopped a little further up on the other side of the street, perhaps scrutinising something or someone else. Without as much as a traffic ticket to her name so far, the likelihood they were looking for her was low. Her attention shifted instead to Sophie, who had run across the grass verge to their ageing Toyota and was yanking at the back doorhandle. When it failed to yield she turned sharply and gave her mother the look, the one that spoke of thinly veiled impatience in the face of adult incompetency. They were in a hurry (hadn't she been harassing Sophie for the last twenty minutes to get a move on?) and now the car wasn't even unlocked. Sophie hopped from one foot to the other as though the ground was too hot to stand on, her body suddenly, annoyingly, alight with childish energy.

'Hold on,' she said, dropping Cody's backpack on the ground and patting her jeans pockets for the keys, before finally retrieving them and pointing the remote control at the door. The locks clunked open, but Sophie had turned and was now frozen in position, her arm bent back gymnastically against the door, her attention taken with something over her mother's shoulder down the street. Sophie lifted her hand and pointed. 'Mum.'

She turned to see one of the cops, the woman, striding towards her, wisps of hair escaping from under her cap, seemingly eager to waylay her before she got into the car.

'Excuse me,' she called. A few more steps and the woman was upon them, police training clearly having kicked in. 'Off to school, are we?' she said in a tone that approximated friendly but still held an interrogatory edge.

'Yes, running a bit late. We have to be—'

The cop nodded as she cut her off. 'Sorry, but we're looking for someone. You might be able to help. Someone who we believe lives at number fifteen? A Loren . . . ah . . . Green?'

'Green!' piped Cody, appearing suddenly beside his mother and looking up at the stranger in uniform. 'She's not green.' He issued a sharp little I-cracked-a-joke laugh, and the officer glanced down at him and smiled, momentarily indulgent.

In those few seconds when she'd seen the cop striding towards her she'd thought the worst. That something had happened to Jason at work. There was always a fear at the back of her mind that he could have an accident. His job might not be high risk, but his workplace was. All that machinery. The chances of walls collapsing, cranes toppling sideways, a girder swinging loose just as he crossed the site. A thousand possible catastrophes. But, in the way the woman had addressed her, she had realised quickly it was not about him. If it had been, they would have known what her name was now; there would have been a different, more solicitous set to the woman's face. Still, the wave of quiet dread didn't quite abate, old reflexes remained. Cops never came bearing good news.

'Hop in the car with Sophie, sweetheart,' she said, reaching down and angling Cody's head in the direction of the Toyota.

'Sophie's not in the car,' he countered, pointing towards his sister who was still standing next to the open back door, looking expectantly at her mother.

'She's getting in, aren't you, Soph?' she said in a louder voice, then quieter again, but more sternly to Cody. 'I want you in there too. Now, please.' She turned back to the woman. 'I was Loren Green, before I got married. I'm Loren—Lori—Spyker now. What's this about?'

The woman glanced briefly at the children as Sophie opened the car door. 'Mrs Spyker, I'm Constable Leonard. We're here about your brother, Scott Michael Green?'

Scott.

Of all the small inchoate notions that sat at the edge of her consciousness, none of them involved her brother. She looked at the woman then, searching her face for a trace of recognition (what did she know?). There didn't seem to be anything behind her query other than the obvious, the current circumstances, whatever they were. 'Are you sure? I mean, it's a common name. There must be hundreds of Scott Greens.'

By now, the other officer had parked the car and was coming towards them. He nodded to her in acknowledgement, mumbled something that her mind was too busy whirring to catch. 'We found your name and address,' Constable Leonard said, her eyes searching Lori's face. 'We—'

Lori held up her hand. 'Sorry. Hold on.' Behind her she could hear the kids' voices. She swivelled around to check them. They were in the car, but the door was wide open. She took a step closer to the police, reducing her volume to almost a whisper. She wasn't sure where to start. Questions queued haphazardly. 'Look, I haven't seen him for a long time. Years. Has he done something? What's happened?'

'I'm afraid your brother has been injured in an accident,' Constable Leonard replied.

'What?' She could see the officers looking at her, noting her reaction. That ingrained observation. 'How? I mean . . .'

'Perhaps we should go inside?' the man suggested.

'I really need to get the kids to school, we . . .' She looked from one to the other, unsure of what to say, what she could say. Did she sound odd? Heartless? Perhaps they would put it down to shock. Well, it was a shock. Definitely a shock.

'I think it might be a good idea for you to sit down for a few minutes,' the policeman said.

'Mu-um.' Sophie's voice rang out behind her. 'We're going to be late.'

The policewoman took the initiative, walked over to Sophie, now half out of the car, and crouched down. 'We're all going to go back inside for a minute or two. We need to talk to Mum for a while. School won't mind, promise.'

Sophie nodded, overwhelmed by the uniform and the moment. She took an uncertain step forward, skirting the woman. 'Mummy?'

Lori put out a hand, and Sophie lunged at her, wrapping her arms around her mother's thighs. 'It's all right, hon. Don't worry. This won't take long.'

Lori felt Sophie's head move against her leg, nodding in acqui-escence. She wasn't about to protest in front of the police. Even at her age she understood the power of authority. But her fingers dug into her mother's flesh in mute protestation. Lori stroked her shoulder as they hobbled back to the house, Sophie attached limpet-like to her leg, Cody following, unnervingly quiet.

Inside, Lori sat with the constables at the wooden table at one end of the L-shape that was their kitchen-dining-living area. She had parked the kids in front of the TV and glanced over at them as they sat motionless on the carpet, staring at actors wearing aprons and pretending to bake a cake. It was stuff for younger children, preschoolers, but they could still be enticed into watching. They leaned close into each other, unconscious of their ease, happy enough to be at home for the time being, perhaps even hoping there might be a reprieve from classes for the day.

Constable Leonard, sitting directly opposite, leaned forward and spoke quietly. 'Look, I'm sorry to have to tell you this, but Scott was knocked from his bike by a car at about eight last night. It looks like a hit and run. At this point we have few leads, but obviously we're working on that. He was unconscious and taken to St James's, where he is now in critical care.'

Lori shook her head, finding it difficult to take in their words; feeling only a strange hollowness, a sense of disbelief that she was sitting here with these people, uniformed strangers, having this conversation at all. 'Is it bad?' she managed at last. 'Will he be all right?'

'They'll be able to tell you more at the hospital. While we don't believe he's in any immediate danger, he's not in the best shape right at the minute.'

She took a deep breath, felt a sense of foreboding creep in. Something niggled at her. 'You said you found my name and address? Scott and I haven't seen each other for a long time.'

'He had his home address and a key on him. We went to his flat this morning where we found your info.'

'Really?' She regarded them silently for a moment. 'This address?'

The woman looked curious. 'Yes. Is there a problem?'

'No.' Lori shook her head vaguely, half smiled. Not a problem, she wanted to say. Just a huge mistake. Maybe that was a problem? The officers went on, offering information about the accident, the scene, but she found it hard to concentrate on what they were saying, her mind drifting to her brother and how this could have happened. Or, more precisely, how she had never imagined that something like this could happen. But, of course, she had known the possibilities. She just hadn't chosen to recognise them. She thought of the kids, covering their eyes and saying 'you can't see me'. What was that? Naivety, or simply wilful ignorance?

'Are you all right?' The male cop speaking now, the one whose name she hadn't caught, a small frown on his face. 'Do you want some water? I can make a cup of tea if you like. Or coffee.'

'No, no. It's just, like I said, I haven't seen him for a long time. It's weird, that's all.'

He nodded. She was sure he'd seen plenty of weird. This wouldn't even count as weird from his perspective. Just another routine notification. Another disconnected family. Nothing whatsoever to see here.

'The Major Collision Investigation Unit will be looking into this. They may want to speak to you,' he went on. 'There are a number of questions, such as where he worked.'

She shook her head. 'I can't tell you anything. I have no idea about him or what he does.'

'What did he do before, when you last saw him?'

'He didn't have a job back then. He was a kid. Eighteen. Still at school. He liked cars.'

The cop raised his eyebrows.

'I really know nothing. I didn't even know he was in Melbourne.' I didn't know he was still alive, she might well have added. 'Where does he live?'

'In Prahran,' said Constable Leonard.

A couple of train stops. That close. 'Is that where he was hit? Where the accident happened?'

'No, in the city. Top end of Flinders Lane.'

'Do you know . . . ?'

'No witnesses that we know of as yet. Might be some CCTV footage. There's a bit around the area. Waiting on that.'

The two officers got up. The man gave her a card and contact information and Constable Leonard called a goodbye to the children, who managed a half-hearted glance in her direction from the mesmeric screen. Lori followed them to the front door, walking behind them up the hallway. In the confined space she suddenly became aware of them as intruders in her house, the bulk of them, their uniforms, the cluster of paraphernalia at their waists. She sensed them making assessments as they passed the bedrooms with unmade beds and her studio with its substantial desk facing the window—not disordered, but covered with piles of paper, jars of pens and brushes, a shiny computer monitor.

From her bedroom she watched them walk away along the footpath, then waited for the few minutes it took before their car glided past again. The male officer was now driving, Constable Leonard in the passenger seat, her head turned towards the house. Lori swivelled back against the wall behind an open wardrobe door, uncertain if she'd been seen and wondering, even as she did it, why it would matter. She wasn't even sure why she was there. Perhaps she simply needed to see them go, see them gone from her sphere. Only wishing that they could take the information they brought with them back too. Banish the knowledge to the place it had been for the past twenty-plus years. For a moment she stayed pressed against the wall then she turned and pushed the door closed, her head following her hand to rest on the cool laminated surface, and she let out a slow, jagged breath.

It was close to ten when she finally bundled the children into the car and drove to school. The implicit promise of a day off (now clearly denied) had spoiled their mood, and both sat glumly in the back looking stupefied from the effects of too much morning TV. They drove along tree-lined local streets, through the car-congested shopping strip and on to the main road, where thankfully at least the peak-hour traffic had abated, before turning into the street that led down to school. At home they hadn't mentioned the police again. It was as though, when the kids looked away from the screen, the two officers had simply disappeared in the same way that the actors had. But in the car, perched on her booster seat with nothing better to do than stare out the window, something came back to Sophie.

'Are you in trouble, Mummy?' she asked.

'What? No, darling. Not at all.'

'So why did the police come?'

'They wanted to ask me about someone.'

'Who?'

'Someone they believed I knew.'

'Your brother?' Sophie had obviously heard more than she thought.

'Oh sweetheart, I don't think the police . . . I think they made a mistake.' In the rear-vision mirror, she could see Sophie mulling this statement over, her face mobilised by thought, trying to make sense of her mother's response.

She summoned her conspirator's voice. 'Hey, what about a visit to Game On after school? Daddy has to work late. Again! We don't have to come back early.'

Cody sparked up, perhaps sensing her overenthusiasm, the very oddness of the suggestion. 'Can we get burgers?'

'And chips too?' added Sophie, in on the act.

'Sure,' she said. 'Let's go the whole hog.'

'Cool!' shrieked Cody, who proceeded to babble, filling the space with amiable non sequiturs, unable to believe his good luck at the prospect of games and normally forbidden foods on a weeknight.

At school she parked and walked with the kids to the office to get late passes before delivering them to their classrooms. When she returned to the car, she sat for a few minutes staring at the empty playground, glad finally of a moment alone. A cigarette. That would do the trick. If only she still smoked. What was it that cigarettes did? Sedate and stimulate, depending on how you smoked them. Slow drags as opposed to frantic puffing. If she had a cigarette right then, she thought she'd go for both. Something like Dutch courage; that's what she needed now. She checked the car clock. An hour to get across town. An hour to get back before the bell sounded again at three-thirty. Enough time.

———

Going to a hospital—any hospital—was a challenge. There was nothing Lori liked about hospitals. The look of them. The smell of them. She hadn't been to one since she'd had the kids, and even then she'd gone reluctantly. She'd wanted a home birth for Sophie, but Jason had been resistant. He worried for her, wanted to protect her. 'It's an unnecessary risk,' he'd said, shaking his head in frustration. (She'd wondered if he might add, 'For a family as unlucky as yours.') Then, joking, cajolling, 'Come on, just for the sake of a few days in a sterile green room? It's no big deal, is it?' He couldn't comprehend her aversion, although

when he pressed her on it she could see some glimmer of understanding on his face. 'I'm sorry,' he'd added, not an apology in
the end, but a sign of his implacability. He saw them, hospitals,
as places of safety, but she saw them as places of suffering. Her
feelings so ingrained that even the joy of two healthy newborns
hadn't erased her sense of foreboding on stepping through the
front door of St James.

If the lobby had seemed depressing, with its eighties ice-blue
leather couches and its kiosk display of flaccid metallic balloons,
the seventh floor, where ICU was housed, felt like something
from a sci-fi film. After negotiating a security door she'd followed a short corridor into an open space where a panoptical
nurses' station looked onto a dozen glass-fronted rooms. The
place appeared freshly-minted, unworn. Walls, beds, cupboards,
machines: everything white except the floors, which she noted
were a pale striated grey.

A woman at the nurses' station took her across the space to a
partially curtained room on the opposite side of the ward to
where she had entered. The woman instructed Lori to put on
a paper gown and wash her hands with antiseptic lotion from a
dispenser on the adjacent wall. She rapped gently on the glass
door and a nurse appeared, slid it open and beckoned Lori inside.

The nurse, a no-nonsense woman with cropped dark hair,
introduced herself as Rebecca. She said this was her second
shift with Scott. She'd been there when he came in.

'Has anyone talked to you about your brother's condition
yet?' she asked.

Lori shook her head. 'No.'

Rebecca turned slightly to regard Scott, and Lori turned
too, her eyes skimming the contours of the room, taking in the

monitors, the tubes and leads, the elevated bed—but somehow avoiding looking directly at the body under the draped sheet—before coming to rest back on the nurse.

'As you might be able to see, Scott has some bruising, a few cuts. There are no internal bodily injuries. Nothing broken. Apparently he was wearing a helmet, but still . . .' Rebecca inclined her head a little, implying that she couldn't say whether this had worked in his favour or not. 'His brain has suffered a traumatic assault, and there has been a bleed, which is being monitored. On the positive side his responses are generally good. I'm afraid I can't tell you much more. You'll need to talk to the doctors for a fuller picture. The neurologist, especially, will be helpful. We'll arrange a meeting for you as soon as possible.'

'So, you don't know how he'll be? If he'll recover? Or how quickly?'

Rebecca's face was sympathetic. 'Brain injuries are difficult to predict, and to understand. As time goes on we'll know better. I would say we're cautiously optimistic, but I don't want to lead you on. It's very early days.'

Looking at the nurse, Lori felt a sudden sense of panic, a terrible uncertainty. 'I'm not sure what I can do.'

Rebecca smiled gently, taking the query at face value. 'The difficult thing is that there really isn't a lot you *can* do. Sit for a while. Talk to him.' She pointed to the far corner, past a box-like machine that was most probably a respirator. 'You can bring that chair closer if you like.'

Lori nodded. Of course, she could, should, do the obvious. She was here, had made the choice to come, and that was enough for now. She didn't need to overthink anything, worry about a big picture. She walked around the bed, pulled the chair forward under the window, where narrow strips of natural light entered between half-closed slats, and sat down.

Beside her, Scott lay disconcertingly still. She could have believed he was dead except for the rise and fall of his chest, almost imperceptible under the hospital gown and sheet. These last few minutes she'd avoided looking at him because she had anticipated that the sight of him would be overwhelming, but her first reaction was that he didn't look quite real. It was something about him being so inert, his face slightly slack. He could have been a modern art installation; some kind of conceptual curiosity.

'Can he hear me?' she asked.

Rebecca, who had returned to the monitor, glanced over at her. 'We believe so. Although it's doubtful he'll remember anything later. These early days always seem to be lost to patients. We do feel though that they respond to voice, to touch. You can't underestimate human contact in the healing process.' Rebecca made a final tap on the keyboard, smiled across at her. 'Listen, I'm going to leave you for a while. There's a buzzer there if you need anything.' She pointed to a red button just to the side of the bed.

With Rebecca gone, there was a sudden quiet in the room, and for a while all Lori was aware of were the small sounds that interrupted it. An indecipherable hum like a fridge running, occasional voices, the syncopated squeak of a trolley wheel from the ward outside. She'd had no real idea of what to expect before she got here. What would she see? How would she feel? What struck her most now, apart from the unreality of it all, was how little Scott had changed, or perhaps her idea of how he might possibly have changed was so close to the way he actually appeared. Familiar, yet unfamiliar. There was the essence of the boy, but the image of a man—a man she did not know—that lay like a semi-transparent veil over him. His hair, still golden blond, dulled only by a hint of grey, cut short close to his skull, revealed a face that had changed little apart from the lines around his eyes and mouth. He had always been good-looking. She'd forgotten that. How the girls loved him, loved that impossible surfer-boy appeal (especially exotic given they lived nowhere near the sea) and his strong, spare physique. He was still lean, she could see, almost to the point of gaunt, but she could tell from the shape of his shoulders and arms under his gown that he had a force to him too, that he worked hard somewhere, did something physical.

A hint of bruising on his cheek and a thin gash along the side of his scalp above his ear were the only visible signs of what had happened. What his real injuries were, remained to be seen. Such a mysterious organ, the brain. Like an iceberg, so much invisible, unknowable. She thought of who he'd been all those years ago. Loose, carefree. Funny. She'd forgotten that too. What had he become, she mused. Who had he been all this time when she hadn't been looking? She knew she should talk to him. But what could she say? Once there had been blame to apportion, rage to hurl. Now she no longer had a sense of that. Who knew what the facts of them being here together like this meant. What was she to make of the situation? Scott lying unconscious here in this bed, unknown to her in almost every way. She a wife, a mother, but in her mind no longer a sister. Not a sister for a very long time now.

She looked down on him, saw his breath and the pulse at his neck. A wave welled inside her, a surge of emotion that took her by surprise. She felt her lip quiver and pressed her teeth together as though she could set her face like a dam and stop the tears. Before she'd had time to even consider what she was doing, she reached out and laid her hand on his arm, felt his warmth under her fingers. When was it she'd touched him last? She struggled to remember. Perhaps because for so long she had simply sought to forget.

March 1993

Northam

The one thing that Pam Green had realised living in Northam, which subtracting her four years at boarding school in Melbourne amounted to almost thirty-eight now, was that, in essence, it wasn't too different from anywhere else. There was a myth abroad about country towns, that they were somehow better, more wholesome places than the greater metropolises to which they always seemed to play second fiddle. But Pam believed in another reality: they were a microcosm. Not that she would have used that word to describe them, but she would certainly say they were a cross-section of what you could expect in any larger place. There were people with money, and people who did it hard, go-getters and underachievers, those with kind hearts and others with dark souls. She thought of all the different types you mixed with, at school, through work and business. Crossing paths with almost all of them, at some point at least, was unavoidable. But it had its divides too. Like anywhere, especially as you grew older, people tended to gravitate to others like them. If you lived on the Hill (Northam's equivalent of establishment—the lawyers, the doctors, the accountants, heaven bloody forbid!) you didn't socialise with the inhabitants of the Flat, those who lived on the land down below. (Like feudal serfs, she'd heard someone say once, although given half of them were unemployed she wasn't sure it was an apt analogy.) She thought sometimes this was changing, social mobility being what it was, but essentially she felt there was a divide. Something that set certain sectors of the town apart from each other, separated them into tribes. Forced them to take sides when sides had to be taken.

It wasn't that Pam saw any of this as a particular problem. It was simply the way things were. Her reflections on the town were not judgemental, merely evaluative. She would probably never have even bothered to ponder too deeply on life in Northam had it not been for the comments she got from outsiders, those people who told her how they envied her idyllic life. A few of them had even moved here from the larger centres to take advantage of the peace and quiet and what they perceived to be a community more cohesive and nurturing than the one they came from. She could see right off the bat that half of them were going to end up leaving again. It was one thing to live on the edge of the mountains, to enjoy the vistas and inhale the clean, fresh air, but another to have to endure small-town gossip and backbiting, conservative politics and the enmity and suspicion of a community that didn't believe you could be a part of it until you'd been here at least a generation.

Pam didn't have to trouble herself with that. Her own family, the Temples, had lived in and around Northam since the 1850s. Her great-great-grandfather had come for the gold and like so many had found none, or at least not enough to make him wealthy. When he gave up on the idea of instant affluence he managed to acquire a little land in the area, where he ran cattle and sheep and gradually expanded his operations. By the time her father was born, three generations had made a living from the undulating terrain, prospered even, considered themselves local establishment. Her brother, Peter, now ran the farm, a sizeable acreage these days, and she had relatives across the district. Her cousin, Hugh, was one of the handful of solicitors in town. Another, Andrew, owned Northam Farm Supplies and, like her, they both lived on the Hill.

She sometimes wondered what it might be like to live somewhere else, in a place where she was more anonymous. When she first met Mick she had played with the idea of moving to Melbourne, even Sydney, and starting afresh. But leaving her parents, or not having help when she had children, that scared her off. She'd never thought a lot about working, so that wasn't a factor. As for Mick, he didn't want to move. He hadn't grown up in Northam, but was from another town, a little bigger but not dissimilar, across the border, and it felt comfortable to him, he wanted to stay. Unlike many, he'd found a niche, and marrying into a local family had boosted his status sufficiently for him to feel at home. It was 1971 and the old order was starting to crumble. The fact that he was an outsider, the fact that he was a Catholic, these perturbations were not as serious as they would have been even ten years earlier. Still, they weren't ideal as far as her family, her father in particular, was concerned. She wasn't sure he'd got over it, even now.

Pam had just come back from school for the summer holidays when she'd first met Mick. She'd finished form five and it had been decided somehow or other that she wouldn't be returning the following year. She wasn't highly academic and she had no desire to teach or nurse, the default positions for girls in those days. Her mother suggested she could work in the office at

Northam Farm Supplies, then owned by her uncle; the subtext being until she married. They'd had high hopes of a pairing with John van der Bandt, son of the town's only legal practitioner (before her cousin Hugh graduated from law school) and a boy she'd had a lukewarm affection for in her early teens. But, as fate would have it, she'd only been in the office two days when Mick Green walked in the door and any thoughts of a more advantageous union were dashed.

The situation had seemed so dire to her parents that they talked about sending her back to school to do sixth form. She wasn't really the rebellious type, but she did have a streak of stubbornness and that 'bugger you' trait which ran in a strong vein through the Temple family. The same one that kept them on the land all these years, through wars, depressions, drought and various family dramas. The thought of being separated from Mick was too much. Once her parents had voiced their concerns, she upped the ante. She and Mick were barely apart. At nineteen she was engaged. By twenty she was married. People who didn't know Pam well (which almost certainly included her parents at this point) might have believed the couple were doomed to failure, but Pam knew from the start that there was something special about Mick Green. He might have been brought up in the wrong religion and he might not have much money, but Pam knew that he would always adore her, that he would be a wonderful father and that he would work hard for his family.

'Till death us do part,' Mick had whispered mischievously (but without a hint of irony) as they lay down on the bed on their wedding night. Since then, he had never wavered. For him, Pam was and always would be the centre of his universe. And, despite some moments of frustration, he hers. While they had their disagreements, they always talked, worked things through, in their own way at least. Miraculously, nothing of any real consequence had come between them in more than twenty years.

———

Mick was standing over the mower, pulling the cord, wrenching at it, attempting to muster the force to bring the damned thing to life. Pam watched him from the kitchen window with a twitchy smile. She wanted to go out and tell him to give it a rest. He'd probably flooded the motor, or maybe the sparkplug needed cleaning. But she wasn't game to get in his way when he was obsessed. After another violent jerk the engine burst into fitful rhythm and she saw him bend down and make a quick adjustment.

She picked up a tea towel and dried off the last of the dishes from the draining board. Somewhere behind her a door opened. One of the kids was up, her guess was Scott. He didn't often sleep in. He'd got up with the larks since he was a baby, and even after a late night he didn't tend to stay in bed long. He emerged as she put the last of the breakfast dishes away, a long stringy swipe of tanned skin and tousled blond hair. She sometimes wondered where it came from, this perpetual summer look. Mick had a touch of olive but it was a darker, muddier version. Scott was gold. Her golden child.

'Morning.' He walked to where she stood, threw his arms around her from behind.

'Oh god. What were you doing last night?' She pulled away, mock grimaced. 'You smell like a brewery.'

'Just a couple of coldies, Ma. You know me.'

'I do, that's the problem. I hope you weren't driving.'

He grinned and turned to the fridge. 'What's to eat?'

'Did you eat last night?'

'Yeah, we got burgers on the way back.'

'What time was that?'

'When we got burgers? Dunno, about two-thirty. Didn't you hear me come in?'

'No. Thank god.'

She used to lie awake waiting for him. Friday and Saturday nights were lost to her, she'd wake and drift. Sometimes it was close to five when he'd get in the door. Occasionally he'd stay at a mate's, but she insisted he ring her if he did, if he was able to call. She just needed to know he was okay. She and Mick had a philosophy (built on late-night conversations, cobbled together in small exchanges) that allowed certain freedoms. They had to learn and grow, even if it had meant sleepless nights for her. Although not usually both of them, as Mick seemed to be immune from this kind of worry. Now Scott was eighteen and they couldn't stop him if they wanted to. He was old enough to drive himself, join the army, vote, get married. Old enough to do whatever he bloody well liked.

'I'll make you some bacon and eggs.'

'You are the best, Mum. You know that, don't you?'

She gave a little snort. The mower broke into full throttle and the noise filled the kitchen. She leaned across the sink and pulled the window closed.

'Isn't Dad working today?' Scott asked as he took some milk out of the fridge, poured a large glass, carried it to the table.

'Not at the shop.' She raised her eyebrows. It was a long-standing joke in the family that Mick Green could not keep still. If she'd ever wondered about where Scott got his energy from she only had to look as far as his father. In so many ways they were nothing alike, but in terms of their energy and their constant urge to be doing, to be engaged, they were cut from the same cloth.

Mick used his energy to keep order, but Scott couldn't be accused of tidiness. His room was a sea of clothes, the clean and the dirty (frequently greasy and stinking) fraternised on the floor and lounged over the bed. Periodically Pam would go in and sort the them out, or just wash the lot if she was short on patience. When he was a kid he built models—aeroplanes, trains, cars, engines. There'd be small bits across the table, on the floor under the dining room chairs, along with half-built Lego castles and fortresses, little people loitering in the most unexpected of places. As he grew, so did the scale on which he worked. On his grandfather's farm he rode motorbikes and drove the truck along the quieter local roads. He turned his hand to fixing them when they broke down. He pestered them for a bike of his own, even though he was only fifteen. This thing with vehicles, with engines, was puzzling to Mick. He was handy, adept at all kinds of household repairs, but he'd always been a middling mechanic. Pam's father, although host to a shed full of mechanical delights (truck, ute, tractor, quadbike, motorbike) was not much better himself. He'd always had hired help to do most of his work. Yet there was Scott, somehow able to perform miracles with machines, to train his frantic energies to perfect intricacy.

Pam had waited for Scott to declare he was going to leave school and do something practical with motors, but he never once mentioned such an idea. Pam wasn't sure if this was simply because he knew they expected him to stay at school or if he actually liked it. He was bright enough, that was certain, but he didn't work hard and his marks were mediocre. She knew he liked the social life at least. A lot had changed since she was at school. Kids were expected to stay on longer if they had even an ounce of aptitude.

Simon, three years older than Scott, was at university studying accounting. He'd been a scholar from the start. At four he could be found buried in the depths of a beanbag with a book, while Scott buzzed around him, barely able to walk but already starting to run, tripping, bouncing up, raiding cupboards, pulling books and ornaments from shelves. Pam liked the fact that she had three children, loved to see their differences, and their similarities. She felt an utter contentment that was hard to fathom when Loren arrived. Pam had had the name waiting through three pregnancies and finally she'd come, her beautiful baby girl, a tiny carbon copy, everyone said, of her. Pam had loved to dress her up when she was little, but as Loren grew she took a dislike to all things pink and frothy and, in complete thrall to Scott, began running wild, climbing trees, riding bikes and generally colluding with him on almost everything. It wasn't what Pam had expected, but then Pam was a little older by then, heading for thirty, and she'd come to realise that much of life wasn't what you expected. Much of it was mundane and ornery and capricious. You just had to be grateful for what you had, especially when in truth you had nothing whatsoever to complain about. Which she didn't. Three beautiful children. She really didn't.

The mower spluttered and died again and for a moment there was only the sizzle of splattering fat in the pan.

'What's happening today?' she asked.

'Homework.' His sniff indicated that he wasn't giving it high priority.

She had her back to him, affecting nonchalance. 'You given any thought about what you'll do next year?'

Somewhere out of sight Mick was swearing, odd words filtering through the closed window.

'I was thinking engineering.'

She turned and looked at him. 'Engineering?'

He shrugged. 'Makes sense, doesn't it?'

'But don't you need good marks?' (Was that too tactless?)

'I might do it. Anyway, I can go to TAFE. My marks'll be okay for that.'

She piled the eggs and bacon on top of four slices of toast and slid them across the table. He started on the food as though it was a job to get through, his knife and fork poised, his elbows high.

She didn't like to push the kids, make them feel like they were being scrutinised. Simon had just found his own way, worked out where he wanted to be, but with Scott she wasn't sure. It wasn't that he lacked passion and drive, but he had no focus, no sense of danger or trepidation. No foresight she would have thought either. But suddenly he's telling her he's thinking of engineering and she feels like there's been a radical shift. Growing up, just like growing, can happen in strange little bursts.

In a couple of minutes he'd polished off everything on the plate. She took it from him, ran some hot water into the sink.

'Thanks, Ma. I'm going to have a shower,' he said.

'Put your clothes out to wash. I haven't seen any for a while.'

The mower was still quiet but there were voices outside—Mick talking to someone. She slid open the back door and walked onto the deck, hearing Mick's joking tones, then the kick of the lawnmower again.

'You beauty!' he exclaimed as it burst into life.

Rounding the corner of the house, she saw Troy standing next to her husband, patting him on the shoulder as if he'd done something amazing. She wanted to laugh. Of course. Troy would have fiddled with the motor for a second or two, got it working and still managed to make Mick feel as though he'd done it.

Troy looked up. 'Mrs Gee,' he said. Only he would call her that and not make her feel like an old bag.

She smiled, not bothering to shout over the mower, and turned back into the house. He followed, closing the door behind him, pushing the sound of the mower out.

'Scott's just hopped in the shower. He won't be long. Do you want a drink or anything?'

'Nah, I'm right. Thanks.' Troy sat on a kitchen chair as she put the kettle on. She could see him out of the corner of her eye picking at his fingernails. A nervous tick. He wasn't the sort of kid who seemed nervous. He had a confidence to him that belied his seventeen years, that made him seem more respon-sible than some. But she knew this to be mostly a facade. She'd seen him drunk more than once after a party, staggering home, held up by Scott. She'd heard—and overheard—the stories that Scott and Loren told about him, his sometimes daredevil antics. According to Scott, Troy's family, his dad particularly, was pretty strict with him. There were nights she found out later when he had supposedly stayed at their place or another friend's but instead had done god knows what. Crashed at a party house. Driven to Wangaratta or Shepparton. Scott had shrugged as though the list could be endless. She'd given Scott her version of a lecture and said she didn't want to be held responsible by another parent for their child's wellbeing, or, more precisely, safety. Scott had nodded, looked vaguely contrite. She was sure it would happen again.

'You have plans for tonight?' she asked him.

'Yeah, there's a party down at Nipper's.'

'Someone from school?'

'Nah. A guy who works out at the abattoir. I mean, yeah, he used to go to school, left a couple of years ago.'

'I know that guy. The one with the purple seventies Monaro. Classic.' Loren walked through the living room and into the kitchen. She was already dressed. The weather was warm, a prolonged summer, and she had on cut-off jeans and a t-shirt. Her hair, long, golden brown, tousled from sleep, fell over her shoulders in a way that suggested a sensuality that Pam had not quite seen in her daughter before and made her take a quiet breath.

Troy turned towards Loren's voice, grinned again. 'Morning.'

She opened the fridge door, leaning forward so that she appeared all legs, and took out a tub of yoghurt. 'I might come along.'

'Might you?' said Pam half sarcastically.

'Well, if Scott and Troy are okay with it. They can look after me.'

'Scott and Troy, I do believe, are not capable of looking after anyone.'

Loren laughed. 'You're right. I can look after them.'

'Still, those places down on the Flat. A bit rough, aren't they?'

'I know those guys from school. Some of them are all right. Anyway, it's the boys who fight. The boys are more likely to get into trouble.'

'Great,' said Pam, pouring the boiling water into a cup with a tea bag. 'Put my mind at rest.'

There were always parties on. Pam didn't remember as much activity in her youth. But then she had been at boarding school for the bulk of her teenage years and her family had lived out of town, out of the loop of action when she was home. At sixteen, seventeen, she was far too young, her mother often reminded her, to be out gallivanting. Perhaps it had always been like this. Her friend Cathy, who was six years her junior, said she was always at some party or other. There was constantly something going on down on the Flat. There had probably been parties at Nipper's place for thirty years for all she knew. That was their entertainment. She was sure there was a lot of alcohol, and even a bit of pot, but that's what young people did these days. The excesses concerned her, and the driving, of course. But what could she do bar lock them up? They were teenagers. Invincible. On the law of averages they would make it through.

'Do you want tea, sweetheart?' she asked Loren.

'Yeah, thanks.'

Pam turned back to Troy. 'How's your mum?' she asked.

'She's okay. Better, I think. Cooking again, which is good.' He laughed.

'What's the matter with her?' Loren asked.

Troy shrugged. 'Dunno. Ladies' problems.' He lowered his head and dark curls fell across his eyes.

Loren looked to Pam who screwed her face up in a way that was meant to indicate she'd tell her later. Of course, there wouldn't be a later because Loren would have forgotten by the time they got to talk again (what do teenagers care about the middle-aged?) and, really, Troy's parents weren't anything to her. She hardly knew them. In reality, Pam herself hardly knew them either. Just a few conversations here and there, snippets picked up from Troy on his visits. Enough to form an impression, but not a relationship.

Scott emerged from the bathroom.

'You ready?' Troy greeted him.

'Where are you off to?' Pam asked as Scott pulled on his socks.

'Going down to the workshop,' Scott told her, referring to the huge shed at the back of Troy's place.

'Don't know if Scott told you, Mrs Gee. Dad got this old Ford that we're going to start doing up.'

'I remember. So will you be back for dinner?'

'Might get something to eat in town before the party. Dunno.'

'You've got to come back to pick me up,' said Lori.

'Yeah, okay. I'll give you a call later.' Scott was heading to the door, pulling it open, Troy right behind. Troy turned and grinned a goodbye, but Scott's head was already somewhere else. He didn't look back as he pushed past the flywire door and let it bang behind him.

———

After lunch, Pam changed into footless tights and a baggy t-shirt and drove down the hill to town. Except for the supermarket, which stayed open until six on a Saturday, the shops had all shut and Main Street was largely devoid of cars and people. She drove into in a dusty open area behind the town hall and parked next to a dirty dark blue Holden.

'I'm tempted to write "clean me" on this poor old bomb of yours,' she said as she got out, addressing the occupant, a woman in her mid-thirties with an unlikely shade of blond hair and a significant amount of eye make-up.

Cathy climbed out of the car and opened the back door to claim a rolled up piece of foam. 'Well, I don't have boys to clean my car like you do,' she said over her shoulder

'Boys? I think you're getting me mixed up with someone else. I clean my own car. Mostly. And what is that you've got?'

'My mat. Didn't you bring one?'

'Bugger. I forgot. I knew there was something. Not that I have one. I would have brought a towel.'

Cathy sighed. 'Don't worry, there'll be spares. A towel would be useless. Scrunched up in a minute.'

Pam followed Cathy around the side of the solid old sandstone building that was their civic hub, through the open back door and along a short hallway. Inside, three women stood talking, their voices high and sharp, bouncing around the bare, timber-floored space. Pam had spent many hours here over the years. Community meetings, toddlers' groups when the kids were small, rehearsals for the annual gala. She knew it well (might even have thought of it as part of her natural domain) but felt a pang of anxiety as she stepped through the doorway this time, not quite sure of what to expect. Right now it felt like foreign territory.

Not for Cathy, though, it seemed. 'Pam has forgotten her mat,' she announced, striding into the room. 'Is there one she can borrow?'

'Of course,' said one of the women. She turned away from the two others and moved towards Pam, smiling. 'I'm Aurora. So glad you could come.'

Pam had heard a lot about Aurora from Cathy, who had been talking about her yoga classes for months, trying to persuade

Pam that yoga sessions with Aurora would be the best thing she could do for herself. Mind, body, spirit, Cathy assured her, all benefited from the weekly regime of stretching and deep breathing. Hippie stuff, Pam had thought, feeling an immediate unease. Thoughts of Ananda Marga, Hare Krishna and Divine Light flooded through her head. Didn't they trade on yoga? And run by someone called Aurora. What kind of a name was that?

'She'll be one of those blow-ins,' Mick had said dismissively when she'd mentioned the idea of going along. She'd pointed out that he was a blow-in himself. 'Yeah, but I'm a blow-in who's like everyone else,' he'd countered. 'You won't catch me teaching yoga.'

'Thank the lord for that,' said Pam, who found it hard to think of Mick in any position that required stillness for longer than five seconds—except on the couch.

But she took his point nonetheless. It was a hard for locals not to feel suspicious. Some people fitted in better than others. Hippies, or alternative lifestylers or whatever you wanted to call them, seemed harder to like, harder to integrate. Most people didn't make any waves. But hippies were like aliens, bringing with them a whole new set of values and ideas about how life in the country should be, as opposed to the way people actually lived it. Their very existence seemed to be an inherent criticism, an affront to the natural order.

But Aurora turned out to be quite ordinary really. She certainly looked like a card-carrying member of the counterculture, with her wild hair tied in a bunch on top of her head with a strip of purple cloth and her multicoloured baggy harem pants, but she came across as rather earnest and genuine. In fact, there was something surprisingly engaging about her, a kind of warmth and directness that Pam had not expected.

Aurora put her hand out and Pam felt hot, rough skin against her own. 'Gardening hands,' she said with a grimace. 'No amount of cream ever works.'

A gardener. Pam smiled, liking this woman even more. 'I know what you mean.'

'Yours feel all right. What's your secret?'

'Gloves,' said Pam.

Aurora laughed and turned to the women behind her, beaming an appreciative smile. 'This is Reggie and Janice. My wonderful regulars.'

Reggie and Janice smiled back, puffing themselves up a little at the description before sliding their eyes across to Pam, saying hello. Pam didn't recognise them, but if they were blow-ins they were definitely of the variety that fitted Mick's familiarity criteria, although what that truly was Pam would have struggled to say. (You know them when you see them.) One thing she would have betted on, though, was that they were not from her side of town. Northam was small, but not so small that everyone knew everyone else. If they lived on the Hill she might have known them by sight, but the fact that she didn't and the fact that they were wearing bright-coloured and obviously expensive lycra leotards, one in red and pink, the other in blue, and matching headbands made her think they were from the estate across the river. They looked around her age. Fortyish, give or take. Probably with nearly grown children and a little time on their hands, a sliver of anxiety at their core, worried about staying fit, keeping off the weight. Friendly enough it seemed, but eying her up surreptitiously. Just as she eyed them.

Aurora retrieved a mat for Pam and handed it to her. Pam realised she must have looked a little tentative as Aurora leaned forward and said, 'Don't worry, I don't do anything too hard. No headstands. We're all beginners here. I want you to enjoy this. I want you to come back.'

Pam laid her mat out next to Cathy's a little behind the other women. She didn't want what she knew would be an inadequate performance to be centre stage. Cathy had assured her that yoga lessons were not about performance, but she didn't really believe her. Everything was about performance in a room full of strangers. And as they had been doing it longer, they would undoubtedly be better. Which all in all would be no big surprise for Pam who was used to being no good at anything sporty, the category in which she thought yoga more or less belonged if it wasn't being used for cult purposes.

As it turned out, the yoga class was everything that Cathy had promised, and really not at all sporty. Something else altogether. Although the others had been coming to classes for months, Aurora was true to her word and concentrated on simple poses. There wasn't anything that Pam felt she couldn't try. Stretching, though, had never been her forte. Her hamstrings protested as she attempted to hold a forward bend, despite the fact that she could barely touch her toes. It was going to be something she'd need to work on, she thought, suddenly realising she was already making a commitment to coming back, and feeling almost excited at the prospect. At the end, in counterpoint to movement and pain, they practised a small meditation, lying on their backs. Deep breathing and no stretching. Heaven. By the time it was over, Pam felt more relaxed and clearer than she had for a long time. She hesitated to call it rejuvenated, but it was something close to that. Was this the road to brainwashing? she pondered. If so, perhaps joining a cult wasn't such a bad thing after all. The thought of giving up day-to-day responsibilities, handing everything over to someone or something else, was suddenly immensely appealing.

'Hard to get up, isn't it?' said Reggie or Janice, whichever one was wearing red. 'I am totally addicted to these classes now. Always leave feeling super relaxed. Never would have imagined it. Mind you, they can be a bit of a workout too. You might be sore in a few places tomorrow.' She laughed the throaty laugh of a smoker.

Pam propped herself up on an elbow, then to full sitting position with a small grunt. 'Cathy's been at me for ages to come along.'

From behind her the woman in the blue leotard said, 'You want a lift home, Reg?'

'Yeah, that'd be great, darl,' the now identified Reggie replied, looking across to her friend before returning her gaze to Pam. 'I know you. You're very familiar.'

Pam cocked her head to one side in a gesture of studied concentration, not wanting to offend with a lack of recognition. 'Maybe at school?' she said as she got to her feet. 'My two youngest are still at the high school.'

Reggie shook her head. 'I've only got Robby still at school. My baby. Afterthought, as they used to say. He's at Eastside Primary in year six. What's your last name?'

'Green. I'm married to Mick. He works at Coghlans.'

Reggie's eyes widened. 'Oh, of course. I know now. Your boy's Scotty.'

Scotty, thought Pam. 'You know Scott?'

'Yeah, well, I'm Troy's aunty. Aunty Regina.' Pam opened her mouth to say that Troy had just been at her house, but

Reggie issued a little self-referencing cackle and continued on. 'Not that anyone calls me that. Aunty or Regina. Mum and Dad were obviously having some kind of a moment when they named me. My sister's almost as bad. Max-ine.' She drew out the last syllable.

Pam nodded, thinking of her own name. Pamela. Not a name she'd ever really liked either. When she was a kid she'd thought she should have been Anne, or Elizabeth. Something more simple and elegant. (Or royal as Mick had once jokingly suggested.) Perhaps her parents had been having a moment too. Probably half the population was having a moment in the postwar euphoria of 1950, embracing modernity and the new world order for all it was worth.

Reggie went on. 'I live next door. To Max and Ray, I mean. I guess you know them.'

'I've met them,' said Pam. 'But I don't really—'

'They're good people, you know,' Reggie said almost defensively, as if Pam had said something against them. 'They work super hard for those kids. They want the best for them, always. They can be a bit full on, a bit strict, but they have high expectations. I think it's worked.'

'Yes,' said Pam again, nodding, agreeing to something vaguely implied but oddly undefined. Had there been some threat of the kids turning out badly? She didn't know much about the family. She wasn't sure she wanted to.

Reggie ploughed on. 'They've done a lot for the kids. Moving here, all that. It's been good for me too, to have Max close. When I split up with Brian, my ex, that was tough. Really tough. But it's always family first with those two. I never would have thought it when I was younger, but blood is a powerful thing.'

'Mm,' said Pam, trying to think what she might do for her brother, or what he might do for her. She guessed he'd probably step up if he had to.

Reggie seemed to run out of puff. She regarded Pam, as though seeing her for the first time. 'Scotty's a wild one, isn't he?'

'Wild?' said Pam, somewhat surprised. 'Well, he's full of energy, I suppose. He's always been like that.'

Reggie leaned forward conspiratorially, eyes narrowed. 'Compared to Troy. You know, just between you and me, I think Max worries about them sometimes.'

'We all do, especially when they're out late at night.'

'Yeah. More, well, you know . . . Troy's had a sheltered upbringing in some ways. What he gets up to now with—'

Reggie was interrupted by Janice. 'I need to get back to pick up Nathan from tennis. I don't want to be late,' she said. 'You ready?' She leaned around Reggie to look at Pam. 'Sorry.'

'No, not at all,' said Pam, feeling slightly uneasy, not sure if she'd just missed out on something important or been given a reprieve.

'See you next week then,' said Reggie brightly, to Pam, the room, anyone in earshot.

Pam nodded goodbye. She watched Reggie go, her attention diverted like a puppy with a new toy and focused now on her friend, words bubbling into the atmosphere around her as they walked off together, a blur of fluoro colour against the dark wood panelling of the room. Soon they had disappeared through the door and into the hallway, but the last vestiges of their conversation echoed until they reached the back entrance. Then merciful silence.

On the other side of the room Cathy was sitting on one of the chairs lined up around the perimeter, pulling on socks and shoes. She'd already put a t-shirt and jeans over the leotard she'd been wearing. Pam went and sat next to her, grabbed her own bag from under the chair and slid out her sandals. On the other side of the room Aurora was stacking her mats into a large tote.

'Do you want to come to my place? Have a cuppa, Cath?'

'Tea?'

'What? Is there something wrong with my tea? I can probably rustle up a bit of cake to go with it,' Pam said, dropping a sandal on the floor. She'd known Cathy for ten years. They'd met when she'd gone back to work at the local council offices after Loren started school. Cathy was one of those people who filled up a room, had energy enough for four people. Pam's boss at the council, Roger Figan, called them the dynamic duo. Not that Pam thought of herself as being as lively as Cathy, but she was, as others often said, a people person. 'You have the common touch, my dear,' her mother used to tell her, which sounded more insult than compliment to her. In truth, though, she knew that her mother was really referring to the fact that the rest of the family found it hard to relax around other people. They were all a bit uptight. Pam in contrast seemed to have benefited from some recessive gene that allowed her to meet and greet, make quips to people she hardly knew, elicit confidences. Connect.

'Well,' Cathy was standing now, 'I was thinking more about going down to the Royal for a glass of wine.'

'You really want to spoil all that good work?' asked Pam.

'Not spoil. Consolidate. The icing on the cake of relaxation.'

Pam raised an eyebrow. As if Cathy needed to be more relaxed. She led the most stress-free life of anyone she knew.

Aurora appeared beside them, a towel around her neck, the tote hauled over her shoulder.

'All good to go?' she asked.

'You're off to Melbourne?' said Cathy.

'Yeah.' Aurora sighed. 'I'm not sure I really feel like it now. Four hours of driving. I might just want to go to bed when I get there. But we have this dinner party happening. Old friends. You know how it is.'

'You and your husband?' asked Pam.

'Yeah. Noel.'

'How long have you been here now?' asked Pam as they walked out the door.

Aurora looked almost apologetic. 'Eight months. But all of my, our, friends are still down there. I feel like I haven't properly settled here yet.'

'Eight months really isn't long,' said Cathy. 'You need to give it a while.'

'It feels like quite a while to me,' said Aurora, turning the key in the lock of the community room.

'What about Noel?' asked Pam.

'He's a builder. He's getting a bit of work here and there. We're not completely skint at least. And he's okay enough with that. He probably survives better without friends than I do. He's happy to potter at home. Make stuff.'

'Like most men,' said Cathy. 'Honestly, I think Clem wouldn't bother to leave the house if he could. Just sit around eating and drinking and watching sport on the goggle box.'

'So did you come from out of town yourself?'

'Me?' said Cathy. 'No, I've been here all my life. But I've seen other people come. And go. I guess it depends on who you are, what you expect. Country life isn't for everyone.'

'Kids,' said Pam.

'Kids?' Aurora looked nonplussed.

'Having kids can make a move easier. I guess it's having things in common, isn't it? Kids can do that. School. Sport.'

'No kids.' Aurora looked apologetic. 'None planned.'

'I don't have kids,' said Cathy, sounding a little huffy. Kids were a bit of a no-go area for her, Pam had found. 'I know people.'

'Yes, but you've always lived here. So has Clem,' said Pam.

'I suppose that's true. Well, I guess you'll get to know people through your classes, Aurora,' said Cathy as they emerged into the late afternoon light.

'It's slow, ' said Aurora, a little flatly, turning to lock the second door. 'I'd really love to see a lot more people than I do. And not just for social reasons. Unfortunately, I do need to make a living as well.'

'I'll put the word out,' said Pam. 'I really enjoyed today.'

Cathy flashed her a look, a smug smile crossing her lips, and perhaps the thought too that she'd put the word out months ago and had only now finally managed to drag Pam along. Northam was a hard nut to crack.

The three of them walked across the car park and said their goodbyes. Pam and Cathy stood next to their vehicles as they watched Aurora get into her car and speed off. Behind her a cloud of yellow dust lingered in the late afternoon heat.

'I don't know how she's going to go,' said Pam. 'I'm not sure this town is ready for a yoga craze.'

'You never know.'

'If she was a vet she'd get lots of work.'

'Well, she's not. Which really is much better for us, as I don't plan to get brucellosis or myxomatosis anytime soon,' Cathy said. 'But I do get stress headaches from processing too many rates notices.'

'What about bloat?' said Pam. 'You can't rule that out.'

Cathy gurgled a laugh. 'Well, I'm glad you liked it anyway. I was worried I was going to lose face.'

Pam huffed. 'I didn't think that would be possible for you.'

Cathy surveyed the now empty car park then turned to Pam. 'So, a drink?'

'I'm not sure about the class.'

'What? You just said you liked it.'

'Reggie and Janice. I don't know . . .'

'Reggie and Janice? They're all right. I saw you talking to Reggie after class. You looked like you were having a good old chat. Well, as much as you can with her, she is a bit of a motormouth.'

'That's an understatement. Do you know who she is?'

Cathy let out a little shriek. 'You're about to tell me she's connected to the mob, aren't you?'

'She's Maxine Druitt's sister.'

'Maxine Druitt? Who's that?'

'You know, Scott's friend Troy? His mum.'

'Oh, right.' She paused. 'And that's a bad thing because?'

'Well, you mentioned the mob.'

Cathy half smiled. 'What's the problem?'

'There's something about those people. I don't know. I think she was about to have a go at me.'

'Have a go?'

'Oh, I don't know. Accuse me of bad parenting. They're sort of . . . self-righteous. I can't really put my finger on it.'

'Don't worry about Reggie. She's a bit of a talker. But I'm sure her heart's in the right place. And you're a great parent.'

'And how would you know that?'

'Just because I don't have kids doesn't mean I don't see things. Anyway, this conversation is getting boring. What about that drink?'

Pam spread her arms wide to indicate her clothes. 'I'm not going anywhere looking like this.'

'What about I get a bottle of something and come up to yours then?' said Cathy.

Pam smiled. 'It's getting late. Come up and have dinner. Ring Clem. Will he want to come?'

'A reprieve from my cooking? Course he'll want to come.'

'Good,' said Pam decisively. Saturday night settled in the way she liked best, with food, wine and good company.

April 1993

Northam

It was hot for April. Warm enough for shorts and a t-shirt. Warm enough for a light summer frock. A day before the end of term and Pam was standing in a makeshift queue waiting to talk to Miss Keenan, Scott's English teacher, wearing an expensive yellow summer frock and feeling a little self-conscious. It was her best dress, or the dress she liked best at the moment, and she'd worn it to have lunch with her father at the Saltram, the only local pub with a bit of class and a dining room with food worth eating. It was the place that he liked to take her when he had something serious to celebrate or discuss. (Truth be told, he was always looking for an excuse to go.) The only place around about where she might faintly be expected to dress up. She hadn't had time afterwards to go home and change for parent–teacher interviews, where no one seemed to care much at all about what they wore. As a consequence, she now found herself surrounded by a hoard of women sporting flimsy skirts and shorts, tank tops, t-shirts and thongs, some even in track-pants. Overdressed felt like an understatement

She knew a lot of people in this room, the library, with its shelving pushed back to make way for islands of chairs and tables. She might have known more of them better if she'd gone to high school here, but having been sent away to board, there were many who remained at the periphery of her knowledge: some ghosts from primary school, others not known at all. Newcomers even. Was it odd then that she'd sent her kids to the local school? She was sure many people here thought it was a strange decision. Her father had certainly found it hard to believe. 'If you want to pay for the three of them to go to boarding school, be my guest,' she'd said when he brought it up a few years before, sometime after it became clear she hadn't enrolled them at her or her brother's alma maters. Predictably that had shut him up. He wouldn't want to be saddled with that expense, or the possible accusation of playing favourites when Peter was paying for his daughter Justine's schooling at the ultra-exclusive Clearton all by himself. Instead it was she who had had to pay for her outburst by suffering the unspoken condescension he was so good at. The sense of 'I told you so' that still hovered between them for marrying Mick. For not having the money to do what she should be doing. For not upholding the family name. Lucky then that she'd changed hers, although everyone knew who she was anyway.

But, even besides the cost, she couldn't see the point of boarding school. The insignia embroidered on Scott's uniform pocket read *Industria et probitate*. By diligence and integrity. Not too different from her old school motto. *Scientia et industria*, if she remembered correctly. Yet despite the science (substandard as it was for most girls' schools in the 1960s, she was fairly sure) and the industry (homework only done by virtue of the stand-over tactics of the boarding house matron) she certainly hadn't walked out with a deep knowledge of physics (or metaphysics, for that matter) or history or poetry. Only in geography could she claim some advantage. She could still recite capital cities (border changes notwithstanding), highest mountains and longest rivers at the drop of a hat. That and a few phrases in French. But, all in all, considering the money her parents had spent, what good had it done her—or them? She hadn't moved far, hadn't done much, had married a impecunious mick called Mick. She wasn't even in touch with her old school cohort, although letters arrived every year suggesting she join the old girls' network. Her brother, similarly packed off, had spent a year at university then simply returned to the farm. He could have cut out the middle man, Mick observed once, and just stayed at home. She speculated now that if her father had come with her today, he'd have seen only the hoi polloi.

'All the good people send their kids away,' he told her during one of their verbal tussles.

'Depends what you mean by good,' she'd responded. I'm good, aren't I? she'd wanted to say, but thought better of it. Did she really want him to answer that?

She was ruminating on this as she stood awkwardly, shuffling from one foot to another in strappy sandals that really were too high for queuing, watching Scott fidget beside her. She hated the process—all the waiting around and the evaluation—and thought if Scott was at boarding school at least she'd have the excuse of being too far away to come down for the ordeal. Simon had been dux of the school. He generally worked hard and got on with the teachers. Loren likewise made few waves. But, with Scott, she'd had six years of being told how much better he could do. How he needed to concentrate more, work harder, stop talking, wear his uniform with pride. Of course, that wasn't every teacher, but at least one or two per semester complained. She'd learned to shut most of it out and only listen to the positive. What else could she possibly do? He was completely beyond retraining now. And perhaps, more to the point, so was she.

Pam was also tired. She would have loved to just go home, but she was the parent who always went to these meetings. Mick never came along. He didn't like anything to do with school. It was almost a phobia, which she understood knowing his relationship with educational institutions and the limits of his patience. So here she was in her role as family representative, standing in the queue having rushed here to make the four o'clock timeslot only to find that Miss Keenan was running way behind. She glanced at her watch and looked around the room. Lori was near the door in a huddle with her friend Katie and another girl Pam couldn't quite place. Was it Julie Roth? She had an appointment in fifteen minutes with Loren's maths teacher and she didn't want to miss that either. She'd never expected to be stuck here like this but, if push came to shove, talking to Scott's teachers was more pressing; VCE year was as important as it got, and Scott making it this far seemed like some monumental achievement. It was going to be the last time they would ever have to bend her ear and what they had to say about these last few months was significant.

'There's Troy,' said Scott, straightening up. She saw him tilt his head in the direction of the door on the far side of the library where Troy had paused to scan the room, looking, Pam knew, for Scott. In seconds his face lit up and, as though some invisible electric current connected them, she felt Scott's body charge a little beside her and return the greeting with a grin.

Behind Troy, his parents, Ray and Maxine, were still orienting themselves to the unfamiliar layout of the room, searching for teachers among the throng. She looked away quickly, picking up her bag and poking at its contents so she wouldn't have to greet them from afar, make them look like movie stars when they turned in her direction and she was forced into a smile or, even worse, a wave.

She'd first seen them in this very room at a parent–teacher meeting three years before. The boys were in year nine then. The Druitts had only just moved to Northam, and Troy and Scott had struck up an immediate friendship. She had met Troy a couple of times before she met his parents, and her surprise when she first clapped eyes on them was palpable. She'd liked Troy from the first. He was a sparky kid, she'd thought, wiry and lively with black curls that fell across his face, like one of those adolescents from a Renaissance painting. 'He looks like Marc Bolan,' she said to Loren, who had stared at her blankly.

'Who's Marc Bolan?'

'A bit of a sex symbol in the seventies,' Pam had replied.

Loren, then aged thirteen, had made a face of disgust (which probably encompassed the gamut from the ridiculous idea that her mother could ever have been young, a vague notion of the prehistoric 1970s, and the fact that her mother could even dare to have this thought about a teenage boy) and countered, 'Oh gross, Mum.'

Looking at Ray and Maxine, it was hard to see where Troy had come from. Where Troy was dark and angelic, they were fair and raw. Not unattractive, not uninteresting, but, especially in Ray's case, so different in looks as to pose the question of adoption in Pam's mind. Ray was the sort of person your eyes would light on in a crowd. He was big, not fat, but tall and imposing, muscled, like a strongman in a circus, with a large head that sported the double whammy of luxuriant blond mullet and a thick russet moustache. Commanding was a word that might have been used, except there was another layer to the man. A sense of something rigid and unyielding and entirely self-possessed. An air that suggested sergeant major, but with more than a touch of sergeant-at-arms.

Beside him, Maxine was what Pam's mother, always a sharp observer (with the emphasis on sharp), would have called a bottle blond. Mid-height and mid-build—a good figure, Pam grudgingly conceded—and blessed with an even-featured, although somewhat coarse, face that was neither good-looking nor plain. The only feature that seemed to link her to Troy was her dark-lashed blue eyes. Mostly she was made interesting by her choice of make-up and clothes, which served to give her colour and expression that probably didn't exist in the rough (and arguably could never exist in nature). In another incarnation she would have been brassy, but she didn't quite have the confidence. She was too much in Ray's shadow to run her own show, yet as Pam came to believe perhaps that was because Maxine was not so different from Ray; in truth, she too had a kind of steeliness at her core, hidden by this outer layer of adornment, an almost exaggerated politeness and, most of the time, a devotional deferral to her husband.

That first time Pam had met them, Ray had stepped up to her and shaken her hand. His grasp firm and his stare, a fraction short of challenging, seemed to sum her up in an instant, although what that summation might be was hard to guess. She had a feeling that Ray wasn't the sort to be in thrall to

anyone, that most of his assessments might not turn out particularly favourably for the subjects of his scrutiny. But there was
something else about him. A whiff of sensuality that made her
wonder, just a little, if he might have tried something on if the
circumstances had been a little different. It made her wonder
too if that was why Maxine always stood so close.

She soon learned that Ray liked to talk. He was a mechanic
and had moved from Karatta, a town about fifty kilometres
north, to become head mechanic at Gary Alderson's Holden
dealership in town. Pam had almost said Gary was a friend of
theirs, but somehow she didn't think that would be appropriate.
With Ray, it felt like pulling rank, which was not who she was,
and something she sensed he'd be sensitive to. Defensive about.
Ray had filled her in on their philosophy on life, told her one of
the reasons they had moved here was that the local secondary
school had a good reputation. (At least someone held it in high
regard.) They wanted the best for their kids, opportunities he
and Maxine hadn't had or hadn't grasped when they were young.
Their children were not going to miss out.

And there was Maxine, right next to him, nodding mostly,
quietly scrutinising. Occasionally Maxine added something of
her own. A small, seemingly humble line that was in reality a
quiet boast about each of the boys under the guise of how lucky
they were to be here. They'd been told by the teachers within
a few weeks of their arrival that Troy had the capacity to do
whatever he wanted, and Kyle, only in year seven and young for
his class, hadn't quite found his direction yet, but at least he
was fitting in, having already been chosen for the junior football team. Pam didn't recall that they'd asked her about her
kids, or herself. Either they already knew enough, didn't care,

or didn't want to know. She told them a few facts anyway, just to get her point across, but not enough to make them feel she wanted to be their friend.

They mixed in different circles, the Greens and the Druitts. (Well, to be honest, Pam didn't know if the Druitts had a circle, but if they did it wasn't hers, not even a Venn diagram. She didn't count yoga classes with Reggie.) While the boys grew to be inseparable, they, the parents, rarely saw each other. When they did, Pam was often struck by how differently Troy behaved in his parents' company. She thought of him when he was at her house, half slumped across the table, conspiring with Scott, teasing Loren, and couldn't imagine him being like that at home. Couldn't imagine him less than bolt upright, sitting to attention, waiting for his father to signal the commencement of the meal. She never heard a word of complaint from Troy about his family life, nothing that signalled any dissatisfaction, but she often wondered about their relationship. She'd heard from Scott that the Druitt house was the neatest place he'd ever seen. The kids' rooms were *really* tidy, he'd said incredulously after his first visit.

'Why can't our place be like that?' she'd muttered and he'd looked at her and rolled his eyes, as if his own logic could not stretch to such an eventuality, could only see tidiness as a negative and not a positive.

She'd reasoned at the time that Maxine had probably tidied the boys' rooms because she knew that a new friend was coming over. But sometime, much later, when she'd mentioned it to Scott again, he'd looked at her wide-eyed and said nothing had changed. 'That place is like a museum. We can't go inside if we look a bit scruffy. No boots, no dirty clothes.' He shook his head in mock disbelief. What he didn't tell her for a long time was that the kids helped to keep the place tidy themselves. There was a regimentation, a system that everyone followed. Their rooms had to be spotless and both boys had chores to do as well. Scott wasn't about to set himself up for similar hardship by announcing such facts to his mother. Not then at least.

In retrospect, despite their lack of questions for her, Pam had felt severely vetted at that first meeting. It was more as though Ray and Maxine were reading her character as she stood in front of them, evaluating her reactions to them. Her approval or disapproval sucked up and sieved through their own filtering system, then spat out again as a judgement for or against her. She was part of a bigger picture, some way of working out if Scott was a good enough person for their son to be spending time with. This would have made her laugh if it hadn't been more than a touch insulting. She could feel the spirit of her mother taking up residence inside her. 'Nothing worse than being patronised by a social inferior,' she incanted. Subsequent meetings seemed to acknowledge a status quo. Perhaps there was some kind of trade-off. Her family might not meet the exacting standards of the Druitts, but they did live on the Hill. Her father had been shire mayor through the 1970s and was still president of the golf club. They were viewed as good people in the district. They still had some clout.

'Mum.' Scott nudged her and she looked up from her bag.

Maxine Druitt stood next to her, smiling. Pam wondered for a moment if Maxine had had her teeth straightened. They seemed so regular and white. Had they always been like that? 'Reggie says you've been doing yoga together. Small world,' said Maxine.

Pam smiled, hoping not to seem as stiff as she felt. 'Small town.'

'She said I should do yoga.' Maxine let out a nervous laugh as if the idea was clearly preposterous.

Pam's first reaction was *God no*, but she realised Maxine was being quite abstract, her real question was about yoga, not about her presence in the class. 'Well, it's probably not for everyone.' Feeling that the short summation didn't seem like enough, she went on. 'I didn't actually think I'd like it as much as I did. The teacher is good.' (Why had she said that? She really didn't want to encourage her.)

'Reg told me about her. Aurora. That's her name, isn't it? I don't think I could do that. Reg is a bit more adventurous than me. You know. She's the sort of person who gets divorced.' Maxine laughed nervously again, then cast a glance over her shoulder.

Pam followed her gaze and saw Ray talking to a man she didn't know, but whom she assumed was one of the teachers. Beside her she was aware of Maxine stiffening. Ray had what she thought of as his bonhomie face on—mouth smiling, but eyes cold. His feet were planted firmly apart, upper part of his body leaning into the other man's space.

'Do you know him?' asked Maxine.

'No.'

'Ryan Gall. Teaches woodwork. Kyle nearly took his finger off last week. Ray was beside himself. I mean, Ray knows about how to be safe in a workshop. He came down to school the next day. Had a word with Mrs Clarke. You can't have this happen. You've got to let people know when they step out of line, don't you?' Maxine turned back to look at Pam. 'You waiting for Miss Keenan?'

'Yes. She seems to be popular,' said Pam, still half digesting what had been said.

'Mmm.' Maxine nodded and cast an eye around her, most probably wondering how long she would have to wait. She looked back at Pam as though seeing her for the first time. 'You're all dressed up.'

Pam felt a flush of embarrassment. Why she had no idea, but she found herself stuttering a response. 'I had lunch with my father. He—we—it was a business lunch, I suppose you could say.' Pam found it hard to explain to some people (people like Maxine) why she would get dressed up to have lunch with her father, the kind of code they had between them that dictated lunch at a certain place wearing certain clothes. Perhaps more to the point it gave her licence to get dressed up once in a while. Odd, really, because if anyone else in the room had made an effort of sorts it was Maxine, whose tight-fitting skirt and shocking-pink top marked her out from most of the others.

But Maxine didn't seem to care why she was dressed up. Pam suspected that she was just filling in space. She looked over at Scott. 'And did you go too?'

Scott looked momentarily puzzled. 'I was at school, Mrs Druitt.'

'Oh yes. Of course you were.' Maxine glanced over her shoulder again.

'Mum,' said Scott. He pointed towards Miss Keenan's table. 'It's us.'

'Sorry,' said Pam, edging away from Maxine.

'No, it's all good. Means we won't have long to wait either.'

Out of the corner of her eye Pam could see Ray approaching. Miss Keenan's summons had been perfectly timed.

———

Mick was sitting in an armchair in the living room with a beer, the newspaper in his hand and Pink Floyd on the stereo. He got up and turned the volume down when Pam came in. 'How'd it go?'

'They are both geniuses,' said Pam, stalking past him. 'But you knew that.'

'Yeah, well. It's the genes, isn't it?'

'Mine, you mean?' she called over her shoulder. 'Did you get the stew out?'

Mick walked into the kitchen and stood next to Pam, who was now holding open the fridge door, surveying its contents. 'I wasn't sure what time you'd be back,' he said.

Pam reached forward and grabbed a wine bottle with one hand and a stew-filled glass container with the other, and placed them both on the bench. 'Veggies would be good too. Want to give me a hand?'

Mick, biddable as he often was, fetched his beer and stood beside her, cutting up carrots and potatoes while she topped and tailed beans then put the stew in a pot.

'You've got your good dress on,' he said.

Pam sighed wearily, as though she had only just realised. 'I thought I'd get home to change before the interviews but I ran out of time.'

'You could change now.'

'I really want to get dinner on.' She sounded peevish.

'Hungry, huh?' She didn't acknowledge him so he continued. 'How long did that lunch go on for?'

'Long enough.'

'And?'

'I'll tell you after dinner.'

'Hmm,' he grunted. Then he caught her eye and saw the look on her face. 'You all right?'

She shrugged noncommittally. 'It's been a long day.'

After dinner, Pam did the dishes. It was a solitary act that attracted little interest from anyone else. Mick had become distracted with something on TV. Scott and Loren had disappeared into their bedrooms. Loren had ruefully declared she had homework to do after a bruising assessment from her maths teacher about her waning numeracy skills. Scott had simply disappeared, as he could do. The stealth bomber, Simon christened him once long ago, half disparaging, half admiring his ability to create havoc, then exit without trace. Pam noted that at least on this particular occasion he had taken his plate to the sink. Somewhere between the food heating and the food eating she herself had managed to slip out of the yellow dress and into a shirt and cotton pants. She stood barefoot at the sink now, her wrists in suds, staring out the window. Daylight saving was over and night had closed in early. The glass in front of her was a mirror in which she could see the outlines of her face, her hair in its unchanging wavy cut always managing to make her look upbeat and cheerful, as though she was about to walk into a 1950s whitegoods ad. She didn't mind doing the dishes. Occasionally she hassled Mick and the kids about helping with the washing up and occasionally they did. But it was usually just her—cooking, clearing, washing. Mick had said the solution was to get a dishwasher. But she didn't want a dishwasher, just an occasional helping hand. There was something restful about the doing of dishes, something almost meditative.

She thought of what Aurora had said in their yoga session last week as she carefully ran the dishcloth around the rim of a glass, then up and down its sides: that every act done mindfully could be an act of meditation, a giving over of her 'self' into a simple activity, making the best job of it she could. It took her away from herself, and yet it had a purpose as well. She liked that idea. Two birds with one stone. No just lying on your back and breathing in and out, in and out, dishes still piled up at home.

'A penny for them.'

In the window reflection she could see Mick behind her. At the moment she registered him he put his arm around her. She felt the warmth and weight of it and bent her head to one side and briefly rested her cheek on his shoulder.

'No thoughts,' she said. 'Just washing.'

He picked up a tea towel from the oven handle and started drying. She saw him glance tentatively at her. He wanted to know about lunch. He couldn't help himself, wasn't going to wait for her. 'Okay, so what did the old bastard have to say?'

'He asked me why I married someone so uncouth.'

'Uncouth? What the bloody hell does that mean?'

By now she had finished the last of the washing and was scrubbing the sink down as it drained. 'Want a cuppa?' she asked, although she didn't know why she bothered. She'd never known Mick to turn one down.

They sat at the table. Background sound from the TV wafted from the living room to the kitchen, not impeding conversation but softening it, giving shape to the aural space.

'He wants us to move up there,' she said.

'What?' he said, although it wasn't really a question.

She inclined her head slightly, flattened her mouth in a pantomime of 'I know, how ridiculous'.

'What did you say to that? And why the hell wasn't I there?' Irritation flared briefly in his eyes. 'That gives me the shits.'

She put her hand out across the table. 'Hey. Come on. He was only sounding me out.'

'He thinks he can get to you.'

'What are you talking about? Besides, you don't even know the offer yet.'

'Offer? Yeah, right. Of course there's an offer.'

She made a small disparaging noise. 'He's only trying to think of our future. With Pete already up on the farm, I mean. Dad wants to see everything shared equally. I can see where he's going with this.'

'So what's the deal?'

'He wants to split the land up. Pete takes one half, we have the other. We can have his house.'

'And you think this is a good idea?'

'No.'

'No?'

'You're not a farmer, Mick.'

'So you said that on my behalf, did you?'

'Yeah.'

He laughed then, and took a gulp of his tea. 'So what's the reasoning?'

'Oh, I don't know. Avoiding tax somehow. Making a partial gift of something or other. We talked about a few other ways it could be done. I said you were too old to start farming now. Forty-five, you'll be retiring in a wink.'

'Bet he laughed at that, the old bugger. He'll never bloody retire. Which is why I can see that even if we wanted to take the land over he'd never be out of our hair. He's never out of Pete's.'

'Mmm.'

'Anyway, why now?'

'Old age. Fear of being alone. Who knows? It's been a while now since Mum died. Perhaps he thinks he could pop off anytime. You know his heart's not great. He's seventy-nine. I reckon secretly he thinks Scott might want to be on the land one day.'

'Scott! You've got to be joking.'

'Well, he is the one who goes up there.'

'Only to ride the quad bike around. Use the shed to tinker with bloody motors. Do god knows what with his mates.'

She sighed. 'It makes the old man happy. To see someone, I mean. To see someone enjoying the place in some kind of way. Not that I'd know, really. It's not like he's ever going to tell me what makes him happy. I don't think he knows himself. But that's my guess.'

'He's short-changed with Pete only having one girl.'

'Dad doesn't have anything against girls,' said Pam. 'He's always supported me. Well, you know, in his own way. I think he's only thinking about who might want to make a future on the land.'

'Pete's doing it already.'

'Yeah, but Pete can't have it all. Once Dad goes it has to be divided up. He does have two children, you know.'

Pam thought suddenly of her brother, realising she hadn't seen him for a while and that she should give him a ring. They had never been close, but then they had never been entirely distant either. When their mother had been alive they were constantly being brought together, following her summonses. But since her death, their relationship had disintegrated into something more occasional, seasonal and obligatory. Birthdays, Christmas. Fathers' Day. A perfunctory, odd familiarity.

'What are you guys up to?' Loren appeared at the kitchen door. 'You didn't tell me there was a cup of tea going.'

'It was for the dishwashers,' said Mick.

Loren made a grumpy face. 'That's not fair.'

'Fair?' said Pam. 'What's fair got to do with it? If I was using fair as my benchmark I would say it wasn't fair that you weren't helping with the dishes.'

'You know I had homework to do. Remember what Mr Watts said, Mum. I need to put more time into maths. Which means I can't do everything. Not all at once, anyway.' She smiled charmingly as if that might make her sound more reasonable.

Pam sighed. 'What's in the pot is probably still warm enough.'

Loren moved to the bench, poured a cup and sat down with them. Pam thought again, as she seemed to do a lot of late, that her daughter was becoming an adult before her eyes. She could vaguely remember the age herself, being sixteen, and sometimes it shocked her to realise that Loren was only now three years younger than she had been when she met Mick. Scott was only a year off himself and Simon, at three years older again, was in fact the age that Mick was when they met. Surely that couldn't be right? She tried to imagine her bespectacled, industrious son about to settle down to domesticity. He was barely an adult, still had to finish his course and start a job. Mick had already been working for six years when he was twenty-one. The times were different. Did it mean they were more mature in her day? She had a feeling that in all likelihood they just had a different focus. She had probably been just as naïve, just lucky to have had the support system (as they called it these days) of family.

Nowadays education was starting to mean a lot more. Kids aimed for professional jobs. She didn't remember the word 'professional' being bandied about much when she was young. People were just what they were: doctors or lawyers or accountants. Farmers, businessmen (even if they happened to be women, which of course was a rare occurrence). There was an invisible scaffold that it all hung on, knowing that some people had more money, were better educated, more powerful. Still, despite this current notion that professionals were going to inherit the earth, she wasn't a stickler for her kids going to university. She certainly expected them to finish school, because that gave them options, but overall she felt that education was something you could gain in all sorts of ways. She was happy to support them as best she could. She was only getting used to the idea that Scott might take up some post-school study when she'd been quite convinced he would find his own way to doing something useful with his life. She hadn't really talked to Loren about her future, but she could see she'd have to start making some decisions soon with her final two years of school looming.

'You okay?' she asked.

'Sure,' replied Loren, a brief flicker of puzzlement crossing her face. 'Oh, you mean after that bollocking from—'

'Language,' Mick interjected, a tone of mock sternness.

'From Miss Hicks?'

'And your English teacher, what's her name again?'

'Callahan. She didn't say anything bad, did she?'

'No, but I got the impression she thought you could do a little better.'

'Well, that's the way they think, isn't it? Always critical,' said Mick, a little huffy.

Pam sighed. If only Mick went to school once in a while he would see that it was no longer like his Catholic education circa 1960. 'I felt she thought you were capable of more.'

'Yeah,' said Loren slowly. She gazed into her teacup as though she was reading her fortune. 'She probably does. I probably am.'

It had always been art that had held Loren's interest. She'd been drawing since she was old enough to clutch a crayon. At eight she'd told Pam that she was going to be an artist. A year or two later they had bought her an easel and a set of acrylic paints. Since then she'd moved through watercolour, gouache and oil phases. She set up a kind of studio space in one half of her room close to the windows that looked out onto the side garden, where the camellias and the rhododendrons had taken over and formed a kind of mini Himalayan forest and created a diffuse, soft light for painting. Loren's bedroom door was opposite Pam and Mick's and the putty-like scent of linseed often filtered out into the hallway. Pam hadn't considered fumes when she'd suggested the studio situation. In retrospect she hoped they weren't toxic.

'Have you thought about when you finish school? What you might work towards?'

'Si says there are painting courses I can do in Melbourne or Sydney. He knows someone who's doing one. Thinks it's pretty cool.' She shrugged uncertainly.

'What would you do with a painting course?' asked Mick suspiciously. 'What kind of a job would you get with that?'

'What is wrong with you tonight, Michael Green?' Pam scolded. 'So negative.'

Mick shot her a look that told her she should know the answer to that question. The business with her father had put his nose out of joint. There was no way around it. She was going to be in a dog box of kinds for a day or so for having gone off by herself; although, in her defence, she didn't know her father's mission when he'd ordered her to lunch.

'I want to be an artist,' said Loren. 'I think I'm okay. I can work hard. I want to. It's not even like work when I'm painting.'

'Well, people with art degrees can teach and work in museums and art galleries. You know, if you need a back-up plan,' she heard herself say, but thinking at the same time why shouldn't her daughter be an artist, do something she was passionate about. In two minds. That's what she was. She wanted so much for her children, maybe Loren in particular. And yet she wanted to keep them safe as well, not to suffer for their choices. How to encourage, but keep a lid on things? Keep perspective? It was so much easier when they wanted to be accountants or engineers. Or mechanics. She seemed to be in luck with the boys.

Then it occurred to her that this conversation wasn't about the future, that she had missed the point entirely. This conversation was about right now. Loren was opening up in a way that she hadn't done for a while. Shifts that had been happening since Lori started high school. A little less information, a little more distance. Almost imperceptible. And now, almost imperceptibly again, a shift back, a slow welcoming in.

April 2016

Melbourne

Brunswick Street, just north of Johnston, lunchtime. The narrow pavement was choked with pedestrians following the north-south route in search of food and drink, something quirky, a bargain if they were lucky. On the road, a long queue of cars was stuck behind a tram. Cyclists flew past, threatening to bowl over unsuspecting jaywalkers who had assumed now was a good time to cross while the traffic was stationary.

Lori had taken the last seat at an outdoor table, on the corner of one of the side streets, where cafés colonised the space. It was a sheltered spot, guarded by a fledgling tree that was just losing its leaves and enclosed by a hip-height planter box, full of rosemary and thyme. Quieter here too, away from the main action but close enough to the buzz to still see what was going on but not get caught up in it. She pressed her back against the metal chair and felt its reassuring warmth, absorbed from the heat of the midday sun. All around her diners sat eating and chatting, reading, gazing at their phones. The usual urban tableau.

On the corner opposite, a young man sat hunched on a grubby-looking blanket, a wiry-haired dog curled up against his leg, a cardboard sign with a scrawl indecipherable from this distance but one she knew would be asking for money for food, or offering up the story of how he had fallen on hard times. When she was last over this way there hadn't been any beggars. Now they were everywhere. In the city, in Balaclava, in St Kilda. A constant reminder of the fragility of life. The thin line so easily crossed; what might have been, what could become, just a few metres away.

A waiter appeared and slid a menu in front of her, asked if she wanted a coffee to start. She looked up, glad of distraction. He was young, early twenties, but with a world-weary demeanour that took her back. She thought it was a thing of the past, that insouciant, detached attitude. These days waiters all seemed so friendly, almost American in their relentless desire to charm the customer. This guy reminded her of the old days. The Fitzroy of the nineties, full of wannabe actors and artists all trying to make ends meet, working in cafés, looking down their noses at those who might have (given a chance, and for entirely different reasons) looked down their noses at them first. The eternal battle between the bourgeoisie and the counterculture, or whatever you wanted to call the ninety-nine percent of creatives who'd never work in their chosen fields. She could have almost included herself in their numbers, and would no doubt have fitted the bill with her incessant scribbling and sketching and obsession with art and design, but she'd cleaned houses for a living then rather than waiting on tables. It was better for her. The job satisfaction, the pay, the freedom that came from not having to constantly deal with people face to face. A level of anonymity.

Lori put her hand up to shade her brow from the sun that threatened to bounce over the top of her sunglasses and blind her. 'Is Schiller still here?' she asked the waiter.

He hesitated, surprised by the question. Not the usual 'Do you have gluten-free bread?' variety. 'Schiller? Sorry, I don't think so.'

'He used to own this place.' She fanned her hands either side of her head. 'Long hair.'

'Ah, you mean Chris?' he said.

Gazing up at the waiter, she thought about how she'd once been a part of this place. Once she would have come here and known people. Today she could almost believe she'd never been here at all but was simply looking at the set of a familiar TV show, now with a brand new ensemble cast. Except for Schiller, who it seemed was still here but had taken on a new role. They'd never called him by his given name. It took her a moment to connect the two. 'Yeah, Chris. Is he here?'

The waiter shrugged the shrug of the terminally incurious. 'He's usually in at some point. Haven't seen him today.'

She ordered a long black and resigned herself to the idea that she wouldn't meet up with Schiller after all. Perhaps that was for the best. It had been a long time and there were no guarantees that he'd even want to see her. She joined the ranks of those around her, took her phone out and checked the time, scanned her emails and glanced at *The Onion*, in the hope of distracting herself both from the thought of meeting Schiller and the very reason she was in Fitzroy in the first place, while she waited for her coffee to arrive.

She had woken that morning in a fog of uneasiness, those strange few seconds of knowing something wasn't right before remembering exactly what that not-right thing was. Jason had left early, crept silently out long before dawn so as not to wake her, and then she was alone in bed, the grey morning light filtering into the room, trying to think about what to do, to make sense of what had happened the day before. But ordered thoughts did not come to her, only the notion that she was bound to do what she had agreed to yesterday, which was to return to the hospital, take some kind of responsibility. It felt like a hangover—the hollow head, a vague sense of nausea, the feeling of being held captive to a spur of the moment decision.

At the hospital Lori had found Scott in much the same condition as he had been in the day before. She wasn't able to see the neurologist until later in the afternoon, so all she could do was to sit with her brother. She'd been advised to talk to him, but she knew nothing about him, about what he liked. (Was he into sport, did he read books, binge watch box sets or Netflix?) About what made him tick. (Was he religious, interested in politics; a lover of art or a science buff?) She had imagined telling him about her kids, but realised she couldn't, didn't want to bring them into the picture. Would they ever know him? Did she want them to? Who was he, this man? And then there was the fact of simply being with him, something that gave her stage fright. Sitting beside him and reciting fragmented pieces of her life to him, all in a vacuum. No response, no acknowledgement. Beyond the perfunctory, there was little she could say without self-consciousness disrupting her thoughts, strangling her words.

A nurse had told her he'd had periods of stirring earlier in the morning, but he showed no signs of movement in her presence. She had waited, half hopeful, half dreading, but he had remained still, eyes closed and shut off from the world. Yesterday she had marvelled at him, had seen that it was him, despite the changes of the years. The fact that he existed seemed to be a kind of miracle. Today the connection felt tenuous. It was too much to bear to have no idea of him and who he was. Looking at her brother gave her no new information, only a deep sense of inadequacy and unease. After an interminable ten minutes she had headed out the door.

Soon after she had found herself on Brunswick Street, on automatic, crossing Gertrude, the autumn sun on her back, around her the cacophony of trams and cars and passing conversations. She hadn't been thinking of Schiller then. Not immediately. Her only thoughts had been to escape, but once outside she had been struck by the fact that she was on familiar territory. Two blocks on she had seen the café, the logo above the front door that she had designed twelve years before. Her first 'proper' piece of work. She had stopped in her tracks. It was a funny thing, seeing that. If she was superstitious she might see her own sign as being a sign. God knows she was desperate enough for direction. But there was something else too, a kind of hunger she didn't realise she had. It had been a long time since she'd seen Schiller and she had felt an odd yearning for his company. For someone to talk to. For an old familiarity that she didn't have with anyone else.

She sat on her coffee for twenty minutes and was almost at the point of getting up to pay when she saw him, Schiller (or was it Chris?), striding down the street towards the café. He looked the same, she thought—still the flowing Jesus-like hair—but he was somehow different too. Older, she supposed. A little less energy to his stride, his face a little less firm, hair dulled with imperceptible grey strands. As he neared the café he must have felt her eyes upon him because he turned suddenly and stared at her as she sat, perched sideways on her chair. He was wearing sunglasses too, sleek Ray-Bans with dense, dark lenses, so that there were two barriers of darkness between their eyes. Two levels of anonymity. She put her hand up, as though she were summoning the waiter, and he frowned. It wasn't until she called out his name, his last name, that there was a jolt of recognition.

'Lori?' He stepped around a table to where she sat. The lunchtime crowd had thinned now and there was a space next to her. He didn't bend to hug or kiss her and she didn't attempt to get up to do the same. 'Wow. I wasn't expecting to see you here today.'

'When are you ever?'

'Hah! No, never. It's been a long time. You look great.'

'You too. Just the same.'

He made a small cynical snort. 'I'm going to grab a coffee. You want one?'

'No, I already did.' She gestured towards her cup. 'I was just about to leave.'

'Oh.' His voice had the downward inflection of disappointment. 'So what brings you here? Not your part of town these days, is it?'

'I was up the road, at St James. Visiting.'

'Nothing serious, I hope?'

'Hard to tell just yet. He's in intensive care.'

Concern crossed Schiller's face. He pulled a chair out and sat down opposite her. 'Shit, that's no good. Not . . .' He hesitated. 'Not someone close?'

'My brother.'

'Your brother?' He scowled fleetingly. 'I'm really sorry to hear that.' He signalled to the young waiter. 'Sure you don't want another coffee?'

Lori shook her head and, turning in her chair, she held her hand out towards the front door of the café. 'You're still here.'

'Yeah, I am. My life now. Who would have guessed?' He shrugged one shoulder in a way that suggested this was as much a surprise to him as anyone. 'I reckon they'll have to take me out of here in the proverbial box. Can't see me branching out into anything else now. But the place is doing pretty well, and I've got a manager so I'm not tied here. And I have to say that, thanks to good ol' Grandad Leo's real estate foresight, no astronomical rents for me.'

'I'd forgotten about that. Your grandfather, the slum landlord.' She twisted her mouth into a sly smile. 'Lucky for you, given the cost of real estate these days.'

'Ah yes, very true. I've always been pretty lucky with money. Or lucky enough. Something's always come along at the right time, saved me from penury.' He looked past her to some point across the street and sighed. 'Sadly, though, I've never had the same kind of luck with love.'

An update or a rebuke? She looked at him for a few seconds, unsure, unable to read his expression, so much lost behind the glasses. He'd always had a deadpan self-deprecating sense of humour. It had been his saving grace, back in the day. 'So you're telling me there's no one special? That truly surprises me. You always did all right. Popular with the ladies.'

'Well, you know me. Good for a good time, but not for a long time, hey?' There was a flicker of a smile then. 'But what about you? You've done okay, got your business going. Still married to that guy, right?'

That guy, she thought. It didn't seem possible that Schiller had forgotten Jason's name. But maybe. It was a long time ago. A long time for him to keep her and the accessories to her life in his mind. 'Yeah. Two kids now, a girl and a boy. At school already.'

'Wow, I'm impressed. I can't imagine kids. I mean, every-one's having them. Had them. Shit, we're all getting old!' he exclaimed as though the thought had just hit him. 'But it's not for me. Hard enough running a café, managing people all day. At least they go home at night. I go home at night. Couldn't think about dealing with kids twenty-four seven. They being able to tell you to fuck off and you not being able to fire them. Tragedy.'

She laughed. 'Most of us muddle through. It seems to work well enough. Helps if there're two of you, I guess. People've been doing it for thousands of years. That's what I told myself when Sophie was born and I had no idea what to do. You're not the first dummy to do this. Besides, you love them. They love you. It makes it worth it.'

Schiller turned distractedly as the waiter placed a coffee on the table next to him. He reached for a jar and spooned in two sugars and stirred, before looking back at her. 'I don't remember you having a brother.' He paused momentarily. 'I thought your brother had . . . had passed away.'

She looked across the street, caught sight of the homeless man again and thought of Scott. Where had he been all these years? What had he been doing? 'That was my brother Simon,' she said. 'Simon who died.'

'In a car crash? With the family?'

'Yeah. Well, there were two. I had two brothers. This is . . . this is the other one. His name is Scott.'

He nodded, contemplative for a moment. 'So why is it I don't remember that there were two?'

'I didn't see him, Scott, for a long time. I don't think I talked about him to you. We didn't get on. You know . . . my family. It was all weird after everything that happened.'

'Sure. Every fucked-up family fucked up in their own unique way. I know that one all right. My brother, Max, remember him? He's a corporate lawyer these days.'

'Wow,' she said, remembering the nerdy law student who used to hang out with them sometimes, who talked about changing the system and volunteered at legal aid. 'That's really fucked up.'

Schiller laughed, threw her a bashful look. 'Sorry.'

She waved a hand at him dismissively. 'I always liked Max.'

'Me too. He's still all right. Just moved a little closer to the tree than I expected.'

'Yeah, well. We all do that,' she said. 'In one way or another.'

'So, I guess it's just you responsible for your bro?' he said. 'Given that your parents aren't . . . around.'

'Yeah.' She let out a long sigh. 'I've been struggling with that. What do you owe someone you haven't seen for twenty years? Blood ties. Family. What do they mean?'

'Hard.' He paused. 'He doesn't have a partner? Or friends? Kids?'

'I really don't know. Isn't it crazy? I don't know a thing about him. I seemed to be the only contact the police could find. I don't know what that means.'

Schiller stretched his legs out in front of him and looked down at his boots. 'I can't imagine being responsible for my brother. Although, the way things are, chances are he'll be the one responsible for me. But this is different—he's a stranger, essentially. That's tough. So what does your husband say about all this?'

She was silent for a moment. 'We're just taking it day by day.'

'Yeah, guess you can't do much else. Life's a bitch, ain't it?'

She pushed her coffee cup away and it made a sharp scraping noise on the metal table. The waiter hadn't bothered to pick the cup up when he'd delivered Schiller's coffee and she wondered how long he'd last here. Not that she'd know what kind of a boss Schiller was, whether he'd care much. He was only beginning on that journey when she saw him last, a funny sideways diversion she'd thought at the time. 'Do you miss the old days?' she asked.

She saw his eyebrows rise above his glasses. 'Old days? Which old days are those?'

'Oh, you know. The squat. Here. Kerr Street. Collingwood. Those old days. Do you keep in touch with anyone?'

'Those days when we were young. All that time ago. Huh! Well, I guess the beauty of owning a café in the heart of sunny Melbourne is that people drop in occasionally. A lot have drifted. Coupled up, had kids, moved interstate, overseas. Got fucking Arts Council grants. Carl, Perry, Rosie. I see them sometimes. Rosie's living with a woman called Bette. She's blond now, well, actually they both are. Platinum as. They run a bar in Northcote. Always a good sort, Rosie.'

'Yeah, she was.' There was a note of wistfulness in her voice.

Schiller cocked his head thoughtfully. 'Don't tell me that you're feeling nostalgic, my friend? I mean, it never struck me that you were particularly happy a lot of the time back then. You had the weight of the world.'

'What do you mean?'

He looked suddenly serious. 'You're kidding me, aren't you?'

Weight of the world. She didn't remember that, but then she wasn't particularly good at remembering. She'd cultivated the art of forgetting so well that her past was like a piece of Swiss cheese. There were moments though. Many moments, really, if she was being honest (not remembering being quite a different thing from having no memory). Fragments, whole scenes, chunks lifted out from the fabric of what had gone before that acted like a rough guide to the past. Some of these came to her crystal clear, even now. Like the morning she got off the bus at Spencer Street Station and walked out onto the pavement with her bag and looked up and down the street and felt an incredible rush that somehow managed to blend loss and exhilaration into one sensation. Freedom, the possibility of a limitless, unfettered and pain-free future. It was this feeling she remembered more than the weather conditions, the traffic, who she'd sat next to on the bus.

She'd caught the tram that day to Darren's place where she'd stayed for several weeks in a tiny spare room with a window that was painted shut and felt suffocatingly hot and stuffy in the late summer warmth. Darren was working for the same big accounting firm that Simon was going to work for—would have been working for already by then—and he shared the house with two students. They all came and went like ghosts. No one cooked or cleaned. Darren had been a good friend of Simon's—not to mention the only person she really knew in Melbourne—and she thought she'd find it comforting to stay with him, but instead it was an unwanted reminder. For them both. He avoided her, she avoided him. She found a job selling t-shirts in a shop in Fitzroy frequented by goths. The job itself wasn't particularly exciting and she didn't last there long, but she did meet Rosie.

That meeting was a stand-out vignette too. Rosie sported pink hair and a nose ring and lived in a squat nearby.

'Come stay at mine,' Rosie had said the second day they worked together. 'We're looking for people. There's heaps of room. It's cheap.'

'But you don't know me,' Lori replied, trying to disguise her shock that Rosie, five years her senior, so hip, so worldly, had even deigned to speak to her let alone was offering her a place in her home.

Rosie laughed. Lori still remembered Rosie's laugh and her endless enthusiasm for life, a sense that nothing could ever affect her. It was something Lori hadn't even realised she envied until she came face to face with it. 'Come and meet the others, but I know you'll all be cool.' She gave a little half shrug that told Lori there was nothing to consider in this decision.

The next day Lori had stood outside the old terrace and experienced something like a homecoming. The metre-deep garden at the front was a tangle of weeds and spindly neglected shrubs. The front verandah was home to an old couch, multiple bicycles, a pile of wood and some pieces of machinery that had long lost any connection to their origins. It was Perry, dread-locked hair tied on top of his head, who opened the door and led her through the house, showing her each room off the hallway, remarking on the period features like a seasoned real estate agent. In the kitchen Rosie was cooking a chickpea stew on the stove. Kaz was making a salad at the old wooden kitchen table. Two other people were living there at the time as well, but she'd forgotten their names now, what they looked like. Faint blurs at the periphery. She didn't think they'd stayed long.

A troupe of people went through that house over the years. Towards the end of her time there, Schiller was one of them. At first he was just the guy that Rosie and Perry bought their drugs from. ('Nothing hard,' he'd declare, hands up in the air as though he'd just had a gun pulled on him. 'Mostly weed and ecstasy. I like people to be happy.') Later he was the house-mate who wasn't a housemate. He never moved in, but he often stayed, usually in someone's room, frequently Rosie's. Lori hadn't thought about sleeping with him. After all, who could take someone who'd slept with almost every other woman who'd stayed in the house, and sold drugs, seriously?

It was a few years later, after she'd moved to Kerr Street and he'd moved into a flat in Brunswick Street, a place that she only found out later was owned by his family, that she did just that— took him seriously (enough) and slept with him. She remembered that first night as a moment too. She and he hanging out at his place, slumped on sagging 1950s chairs, surrounded by beer cans and ashtrays overflowing with butts, watching the opening cere-mony of the Sydney Olympics. Laughing at the Australiana themes, the lawnmowers, the flora and fauna, the potted history of the wide brown land. They had bonded in a way that sur-prised her. She stayed over. It became something of a habit.

Weight of the world. Had it been like that? Those memories she had were enough to situate her, but didn't tell her anything about how she'd been perceived, how she'd fitted in. She never thought about what Schiller had seen all those years ago. Even what he was seeing as he looked at her now. He put up a palm. 'Sorry, I didn't mean that to sound harsh. What I did mean is, well, that you must have found some stability.'

A sensation went through her, something akin to shame. She sat back a little in her chair. 'Are you saying you thought I was unstable?'

'No, not unstable, Lore. I'm not meaning you so much but your situation. What happened. You were troubled. I knew things had been bad for you, but I was young and stupid and I never knew what to say. And you never wanted to talk. I mean, losing your family and . . . you know. It was obviously huge for you. Traumatic.'

Her heart was pounding. She hadn't envisaged this kind of conversation with Schiller. If anything, she'd thought it would be a comfort, a quick rave about old times, something that would anchor her in the past, not mire her in it. 'Funny, I really don't remember things being that bad. I remember being wild, that's absolutely true. Running amok. Like I'd finally found my freedom.' She looked down at the table, ran a finger around its edge. 'Frankly there are a lot of things I'm not so clear on anymore. Blocked out the shit, apparently.'

Schiller took off his glasses and pinched the bridge of his nose. He appeared strangely vulnerable, a little tired. Definitely older, although he still had those beautiful pale eyes, dark lashes and brows. He looked over at her, shook his head slightly, smiled. 'You did a lot of mad stuff, that's for sure. Especially when I first knew you, but I didn't *really* know you that well. You and your skateboard. Those random graffiti strikes you did with Perry. Caving in the sewers—that was crazy. I was kind of in awe of you, to tell you the truth. Everyone we hung out with was a bit mad, but you seemed fearless somehow.'

'Fearless?' Had she been fearless? She had a vision of being on a skateboard, feeling the juddering of the wheels under her feet (like being eleven again), the thrill of careering helter-skelter down the pavement, the slight decline heading north on Brunswick Street. Was that fearlessness? Or numbness?

79

Simply a need to feel something? She gave out a small cynical snort. 'I don't think it was all down to me and my superpowers. There were a lot of substances. I seem to remember many of those were supplied by you.'

'Yeah,' he bowed his head as if in contrition. 'It was all a distraction of one sort or another. For all of us. I am the first to admit that now.'

'When I look back I realise how young I was then. It took a while for me to grow up. Find my way.'

'And heal, I guess.'

'Heal?'

'Well, you know. The disturbed sleep, the crying. That was still happening when you left. Maybe not so much, but . . .'

'What?' She shook her head slowly back and forth, her face creased with disbelief. 'What do you mean, "disturbed sleep"? You never said anything.'

'Actually, I did. Well, I tried to, but you never wanted to . . . I seem to remember you accusing me of being a liar at one point.'

There was a part of her that felt like saying it now, getting up and knocking over a chair, shutting him down for good. The other part felt strangely suspended, as if she was watching someone putting the final pieces of a jigsaw into place. As if she was outside herself, seeing herself, aware of herself in a landscape of others.

Schiller was leaning closer now, his voice soft. 'Listen, by the time we were together you'd settled down a lot. You'd started your course, had somewhere to put your energy. But, when you were sleeping, something else kicked in. It wasn't every night, but often enough. Everyone had their shit to deal with back then. We were young, all of us. Even me. But over the years,

I thought about it more. I can see now what I couldn't then. That you went through big stuff. I'm sorry that I couldn't do more for you. You were alone and lost and I didn't help. I feel bad about that.'

She shook her head, felt the sting of tears behind her eyes, was grateful for the dark glasses. Was that what she'd been like? Thrillseeking? Attention-seeking? Despondent and isolated, frequently failing to connect? She thought of those times as the opposite, as formative, exciting, creative. Rosie had introduced her to books and film, with Schiller she'd gone to see every decent band who'd ever played in Melbourne. Perry graffitied half of the north side when he wasn't organising shifts at Friends of the Earth or welding sculptures out of scrap metal and barbed wire. They'd all talked philosophy and politics, and loads of complete and utter bullshit. She was who she was now because of them, because of all that. But she hadn't kept the friendships. She'd walked away from those people when they were no longer in her orbit. Let them go completely.

'All I'm saying is it's great you have the man and the kids. That they have given you something that, I don't know, you didn't have before. I can see it just looking at you.' He might have been doing counselling, or a Gestalt course, all these new-found (or perhaps not so new) insights. She certainly hadn't been expecting this.

A tram passed and she followed it with her eyes, trying to take in what had just been said, feeling agonisingly exposed. What was he implying? That she was a fuck-up who'd been miraculously repaired? It was true that being with Jason, having the kids had changed everything, made her a part of something bigger. She had a family again. But was she really so different now to the person Schiller knew, or at least the version he was recounting to her?

'Are you okay?' he asked, leaning forward towards her. 'I'm sorry, bringing up old shit. I didn't intend to make anything harder. I'm sure you have enough on your plate.'

'It's okay,' she replied. 'It seems to be what the universe wants from me right now. Time for some deep self-examination.'

He looked across at her, shook his head and laughed. 'The universe, huh?' Then she laughed too. A point of connection still, a fundamental understanding.

Schiller pointed to the sign. 'See I've still got your design here.'

'Might be time for a change.'

'Still works for me,' he said softly. 'Maybe when I need something new I'll be in touch.'

He pushed up his sleeves in the face of the warmth. Brushed his hair back from his face. She noticed his lean, sinewy arms and saw that the left one was now completely covered in ink, swirling interlocking designs of blue, green and red. She felt the pull of distraction, the very thing that design had always done for her, taken her into a different space. So different, tattoos now. So much more skill in them than twenty, thirty years ago. These days they were body art, considered acceptable, even in polite company. There wasn't the stigma that they had when she was young.

'Speaking of work, that's beautiful,' she said, gesturing towards his arm, the sleeve, fighting the desire to lean across and touch it.

He looked down as if considering it for the first time. 'If you'd been around I would have consulted you on this too.'

'No. That would have been a bad idea. This person has done an amazing job. Not my thing, images on the body.'

'You mean to do them or have them?'

'Both. But that doesn't mean I don't appreciate good ones.'

The other arm had fewer tattoos; they were older, more discrete, accumulated one by one over the years. A rose, an angel, a spider, the ace of spades. There was one she remembered running her finger over, searching its form over and over again, higher up on his bicep.

She looked up at him. 'The bird,' she said.

'What?'

'You had a little bird tattoo, a swallow, on that arm.'

'Yeah, a bird, but not a swallow. It's an eagle.'

'An eagle,' she repeated dubiously. Could that be right?

'Yep, an eagle with outstretched wings. Soaring high above it all.' He tugged his shirt sleeve up higher and showed her.

Lori felt a little jolt as soon as she saw it, wondered why on earth she would ever have thought the swallow belonged to Schiller. 'Wow, my memory playing tricks. Again.'

After a moment she ferreted out her coin purse from her bag. 'Hey, I need to get going. I have to get back to meet the neurologist.'

'Don't worry about paying for the coffee,' he said, reaching towards the hand that held the purse but too far away to touch it.

'Thank you,' she said simply, glad that he hadn't wanted more, encouraged her to return, asked for something she couldn't give him. She got up, grasping the coins for her coffee and walked past him then, across the street to where the man sat with his dog. He didn't look up when she dumped them in his cup. With the hood pulled low over his face, he could well have been asleep.

When she turned around, Schiller was at the front door of the café talking to the waiter but looking her way. Lori walked towards him and he smiled a small smile. She remembered that look. The last time she'd seen him, just before she got married, when she'd last come here to tell him the news and she'd seen what she'd thought then was indifference, cynicism, disguised behind that enigmatic smile, but she realised now was actually sadness. Loss. For a long time she hadn't believed that she was worth much. She thought he thought the same thing. That she wasn't worth the effort of trying to keep, trying to love. And perhaps that was true too, just as it was true that he had cared for her. She knew now that emotions and their impulses were never singular. Thoughts never simply pure or impure, motivations never crystal clear. You could love someone and hate them in the same breath, wish them the best and the worst, help and sabotage in one sweeping motion. Reading it all was a skill, perhaps an art. One that she knew she still hadn't managed to fully understand, let alone master.

May 1993

Northam

It wasn't until Pam put the washing on that she noticed. Spots of blood on the top of his shirt sleeve. She might have thought it was a cut or a scratch if it hadn't been for the strange shape, suggesting something of a circular outline. She went into his room and pulled back the bedclothes. There was a smear of something dark against his pillow and a piece of gauze lying at the side of his bed.

Pam looked at the amassed evidence like a detective. There was only one conclusion, and a shocking one at that. A tattoo. He'd got a tattoo. Why the hell would he have done that? After her brief moment of satisfaction a few months before (the revelation that he was indeed thinking about his future, and seemed intent on continuing in the right direction, well, any direction), this came as a slap. A neat reminder that he was indeed still impulsive, perhaps still easily influenced. When had he done it? she wondered. Last weekend? She thought back to the account that he'd given himself, but it seemed to be exactly the same sort of thing he'd say on any weekend. Mick said the kids recounting what they did when they were out reminded him of making his confession when he was a child. 'I was disobedient and told lies' was his staple for a good ten years. The other question was why? There were silly things you could do, but nothing so irrevocable, so indelible, as a tattoo. She was rarely angry with Scott, but today she felt that surge of emotion fill her, make her want to scream at him. She hated the thought that her children were going to ruin their lives in some way. With Simon she had always believed that everything was shipshape, but with Scott she really should have known by now that nothing was ever going to quite go to plan. For every step forward there would always be several back.

Outside the day was bright and sunny with a sharp little breeze. She pegged out the clothes on the washing line. Scott and Loren's items not too different from each other. T-shirts, flannel shirts, jeans. Only the underwear and gender-defined school uniforms betrayed the fact that they belonged to different people. To make matters more confusing there were shirts of Scott's that Loren had taken over. Pam would routinely receive admonitions from her daughter about putting articles of clothing into the wrong pile. Surely she should know by now that Scott was no longer the owner of the yellow t-shirt, or the brown and blue check shirt. The underpants seemed safe enough, though. For now.

In Scott's room, she removed the bedding and hauled it to the washing machine before remaking the bed. She'd check his arm tonight and make sure it was healing properly. Who knows what he had been doing to look after it. They'd have a good talk, preferably before Mick came home and started World War III. She'd get to the bottom of what was going on. A momentary youthful indiscretion she hoped, and not the beginning of an extensive collection of ugly ink. Mum, Dad, on each arm. Love, Hate, across the knuckles.

Loren's room was not quite as untidy as her brother's. Pam pulled the sheets and quilt to an approximation of a made bed, picked up a tangle of clothes from the floor and hung them on the open rail that stood in for a wardrobe. Mick told her she shouldn't bother with their rooms, but she couldn't help herself. She hated walking past to see the clutter and the mess, it disturbed her. Why she couldn't quite say, but it seemed to tip some equilibrium inside her into low-level agitation.

'They are grown up enough now to do things for themselves,' he said.

'Grown up,' she scoffed. 'That is hardly even technically true.' She felt confident that Mick hadn't been tidy at their age. Or if he had been it was because he had nothing to be untidy with. He certainly wasn't when they got married and that hadn't changed, for all that he might think he was now. Four kids, that's what she had. Well, three live-in dependants. The other one was away at university.

After hanging out the sheets she checked her watch and swore in a way that her mother would definitely not have approved of. She had to be at work by ten and it was five to already. She ran a comb through her hair, smeared gloss across her lips (no time for foundation and blusher today, they'd just have to deal with that) and changed her shoes. She was grateful that she could wear pants to work now. When she'd first started in the late sixties, skirts were mandatory for women. She'd never thought that was fair. Skirts, pantyhose, an uplifting bra (not that uplifting bras were mandated, it was just the state of them back then before they went all natural and formless in the seventies). The whole catastrophe. Worse than her school uniform, which was pretty awful. That starchy shirt and tie, the gloves, stockings and suspender belt, the boater hat. Cripes. It incorporated the worst of men's suits, and added restrictive undergarments to boot. What kind of special hell was that? In hindsight, though, perhaps that uniform had inoculated her against putting up with discomfort. If she could live in jersey knit, she would. She was gradually moving towards it, season by season. Imagine what she was going to be like at eighty? An ageing member of the Starship *Enterprise*. Not so bad perhaps if those suits were antigravity.

At work she sauntered past the main desk in an effort to look as though she wasn't racing. No one seemed to notice the time. The two receptionists greeted her as they always did. 'Morning, Pam. Lovely day.' When she reached her office she discovered that Roger was in a meeting somewhere deep in the bowels of the council chambers, so she was accountable to no one for being ten minutes late. Cathy simply raised her eyebrows as she looked up from her screen and made a grunting noise that indicated she was in the middle of something and they would speak in a moment. Leeanne, the junior, was, she assumed, on her tea break.

The office had recently been fully computerised. She and Cathy had done a course on the new Windows operating system and another on a special program that generated rates notices tailor-made for the shire. This was supposed to make their lives so much easier but they had both agreed was really going to load them with much more work. Not that she really minded, as long as she had a job. Work meant time out of the house, time with people she mostly liked, and money. The trifecta really. But, still, she was sceptical of technology. It wasn't like anything came at the press of a button without some trade-off.

There was always so much to learn and so much to go wrong. Simon said that mobile phones (devices Pam had only seen on TV) would take over the world. They would get smaller and smaller and cheaper and cheaper, and everyone would have one that they'd carry all the time and be able to communicate in new ways. She sighed. Not for her. Imagine being able to be contacted twenty-four hours a day, being at everyone's beck and call. (Weren't mothers at the coalface already?) Just the thought of it all was exhausting.

'Sorry,' said Cathy, looking up from her computer. 'I just had to finish this batch of payments before Roger got back. He wanted everything put through. Now that you're here you can hold the fort and I can go and get a cuppa.'

'Sure,' said Pam.

'Everything all right?' asked Cathy.

Pam threw her hands up. 'Scott! He got a tattoo.'

'What? When was this?'

'I don't know. I just found the evidence this morning. I ended up doing some extra washing, which is why I was late.'

Cathy swotted the air in a 'who cares' gesture. 'But you haven't spoken to him yet? Have you seen it? What is it?'

'Not a giant skull and crossbones at least. Something small on his arm.'

'Up the top? That's not too bad, is it? No one will see it.'

Pam sighed. 'But it's what it represents, isn't it?'

'What does it represent?'

'Oh, I don't know. It just . . . it just doesn't *seem* right. Tattoos say something, don't they? He's only eighteen.' Pam's voice wavered.

Cathy stood up and walked around to her desk. 'Don't worry.' She put a hand on Pam's shoulder. 'It's no big deal, really.'

'You reckon? I don't know. It feels like it is. I can't imagine why he'd do it. He just seemed to be going along so well and now he's done this stupid bloody thing.'

'Oh Pammy. It's really not so bad. I mean, he hasn't hurt anyone. Or himself. A few inches of skin notwithstanding.'

'No,' she conceded. 'You're right. It's just . . . oh, I don't know. It's off kilter.' And it wasn't just Scott's action she meant. It was how she felt about it too, how it had affected her as if by contagion. Like a giant hand had just come along and knocked everything ever so slightly out of place. Hard as she tried, she couldn't shake that feeling all day. There was plenty to do at work, plenty to keep her busy, but her mind kept shifting, settling in some strange space around Scott, as though the tattoo was a harbinger, a sign that something more would come out of all of this.

Back home from work just after four, she took the washing off the line and folded it while she sat on the couch in the living room with a cup of tea watching *Wheel of Fortune*. It was Loren who came in first, appearing at the door of the living room as she walked past to the kitchen.

'There's tea made if you want one,' said Pam, patting the left side of the couch which was washing free. 'You can come back and take your clothes away.'

Loren returned in a moment with a mug in one hand and two biscuits in the other.

'Crumbs,' said Pam.

Loren eyed the screen. 'Why are you watching this?'

'I'll turn it off. I want to talk to you anyway.' Pam jabbed the mute button on the remote control.

'Why? What have I done?'

'Nothing. Nothing. I just need to . . . to talk.'

Loren sat up abruptly and the tea swirled and threatened to spill in its mug. She placed it carefully on the coffee table and gave her mother a sheepish look.

Pam had felt calmer folding the laundry, but now that Loren was here she could feel the anxiety bubbling to the surface again. She didn't worry about preliminaries. 'Did you know about Scott's tattoo?'

Loren's eyes widened. 'Did he tell you?'

'Well, he was going to have to some time, wasn't he?'

'So he didn't? Hasn't?'

'That's why I'm talking to you. I want to know what the hell is going on.'

Loren sucked in her bottom lip. Pam knew that gesture, it made her feel guilty about asking, about making Loren the teller of tales. The dobber.

'He got it last weekend.'

'There aren't any places to get tattoos in Northam, are there?'

'We went over to Shep.'

'We? Plural?' Pam's voice rose.

'Calm down, Mum.'

'Don't tell me to calm down. I am calm, for god's sake.'

'I didn't get one, if that's what you're worried about.'

'Worried? Just the idea that you are hanging out in a tattoo parlour, with god knows who.' Pam shook her head and sighed loudly.

'The place was fine. The guy is an artist.'

'An artist! Oh, really.'

'Mum.' Loren stood up. 'I didn't do it, don't blame me.'

Pam put out her hand and clasped Lori's skirt. 'I'm sorry, sweetheart. I'm just a bit . . . a bit rattled by this.'

'You don't need to freak out. It's okay. It's just a little thing and no one will see it and it's actually pretty cute.'

Pam had to control herself to not let out a small scream. 'I just don't understand why he did it, that's all.'

Loren sat down again. 'They were drunk.'

'They? And *they* drove?'

'Well, Scott was drunk. Troy drove down. I don't think he was so drunk.'

'You are making me feel so much better about all of this. Especially as Troy is still on his Ls.'

'The boys had been talking about it for ages. Troy had all these cool ideas for designs. He'd sketched out loads of them. But when they got to the place, he kinda chickened out and . . . well.'

'Of course he would chicken out. He has a father who would make anyone think twice.'

Loren made a face. 'Yeah, that's so true. He's a bit of a weirdo.'

'And Scott has parents that let him—and you!—do whatever you like.'

'Oh Mum. He's not a kid anymore.'

'He's still at school. And you. I've let you just tag along with those boys. And you definitely are still a kid.'

'Mum!' Loren was halfway between sympathetic and outraged. She was waiting for the next sentence which was going to entail a curb on her activities. 'Don't you trust me?'

'I trust you, but you are still young and sometimes I forget that. I'm sorry. I think I've asked too much of you.'

They were silent for a moment, Loren not wanting to make herself the focus of a conversation that was threatening to turn against her.

'I don't get why a tattoo is such a big deal.'

'Tattoos are, well, let's just say that nice people don't get tattoos. Rough people get tattoos. People who commit crimes and go to gaol. Those are the people who get tattoos.'

'Mum. That's so old-fashioned. Besides, it's crazy to think that Scott's one of those people.'

'When other people see tattoos, they get ideas.'

'So that's what you don't like? You're worried that people will think Scott's a loser?'

Pam shook her head vaguely. 'Was it Troy's idea?'

'No. Why would you think that? Both of them were going to do it.'

Pam searched Loren's face. She wasn't sure she could be relied on to give a balanced account of anything to do with Troy. She'd seen the looks, the change in her manner whenever he was around. For years Troy had just been her brother's slightly irritating friend and she'd just been the baby sister. Lately there had been a change, a different dynamic between them.

'I thought you liked Troy.'

'I do,' said Pam, a small smile crossing her face. 'But I know he can be, well, impulsive.'

'Troy wanted to get a tattoo too, right? It was strange. He'd been raving on in the car but when we got there, he went quiet then. Sobered up, I guess. He told Scott we should go home. But Scott was kind of pissed off. Said Troy was chicken. Troy went, yeah, he was. Scott said that he, meaning himself, wasn't.

I don't even think he wanted the tattoo then, but he couldn't not get it. You know what I mean?'

Pam exhaled sharply. She knew exactly.

Loren's voice softened, like she was telling her mother a secret. 'So he ended up getting this little bird with blue wings. So pretty. Honestly, Mum it's okay. You won't freak out when you see it.'

'Dad might,' said Pam. 'Your dad, I mean. God, mine too.'

'Are you going to tell Dad?'

'No, I don't think so. Not for now. You know what he can be like. Give me time to get over it first. At least it's not summer. Scott'll have a bit of time before he has to own up.'

Mick came home from work before Scott got back from school. Pam realised then that Scott had come home late on Monday as well. It occurred to her that he had been avoiding her. But perhaps not. He certainly hadn't bothered to cover any of his other tracks. He might not have thought there were tracks to cover. He was so oblivious to the outside world some-times, to how he might be seen. There was that innocence about him that she loved in many ways, but it was something that she feared would make him vulnerable too. By dinnertime he must have guessed that she knew. Either he'd noticed she'd changed his sheets and tidied his room (perhaps) or he'd spoken to Lori (more likely). There was a look on his face, a failure to meet her eyes. He was so quiet at the table that even Mick frowned and made a comment about him being under the weather.

'I'm fine,' he'd said somewhat defensively, and soon got up and took his plate to the kitchen sink. Mick looked at Pam and she shrugged vaguely, feeling a tinge of guilt about not talking to Mick, pretending she had no idea. Then again, maybe she didn't. Maybe he was troubled by something else entirely. She hadn't spoken to him so there was no way of really knowing.

Once the dishes were done and Mick was ensconced in front of the TV, she went down the hall to Scott's room and knocked on the door. There were no sounds from inside, but he didn't reply and she thought that he was listening to his Discman, earphones in. She didn't want to knock again louder and alert the house to her visitation, so she turned the handle of the bedroom door, hoping she wouldn't catch him in the middle of something that might embarrass them both.

Scott was on his bed, earphones in as she had imagined. His head jolted up as hers peered around the door. 'Sorry,' she mouthed, pointing to her ears, indicating, really, his. He quickly pulled one earphone out and looked at her without a smile. Unusual for Scott. Lack of expression was more of a Loren thing. But, then, Pam didn't tend to invade Scott's privacy as much as she did her daughter's. This thought went through her head in the second she pushed open the door and slid into the room. What was that about? Did she feel more ownership of her daughter? Was it because she was still young? Perhaps she'd been pushier, more present, with the boys when they were smaller, too? She couldn't quite remember. Not that she'd ever completely articulated it to herself, but she didn't want to put it down to the kind of attitude that said boys were okay by themselves, but girls needed guidance. She wanted all her children to be caring and self-reliant in equal measure. She wanted her boys to be better than her generation of boys, Mick included. She wanted them to be more loving, more demonstrative, more involved. Times were changing. Had changed since she was young. Surely these weren't unreasonable hopes.

'Can I have a word?' she asked.

Scott was under his quilt. The bedrooms were cold at night now and he hadn't bothered to turn on his heater, but instead had pulled the bedding up to his chin. He removed the other earphone and looked at her, his mouth twisted into a small smile that suggested he thought he was going to get a talking to, but maybe it wouldn't be so bad, because it never really was. This was Mum after all.

Pam perched on the edge of the bed. A book slipped to the floor and she picked it up. 'You've been studying,' she said.

'You sound surprised.'

'Was that surprise in my voice? I don't think so. Gratitude maybe.'

He laughed.

She flicked through the pages. 'Further Maths. I never got past grade ten.'

'In Maths?'

'Yeah. I could never get Maths. All these numbers.'

'You can add up. That's all you need.'

She made a face. 'Only just.'

'So.' He looked at her appealingly, as if she might offer him something.

'So,' she echoed, 'let's have a squizz at that arm.'

'What? What for?' He seemed slightly taken aback. But surely he'd been expecting this.

'I found the evidence this morning when I cleaned up.'

'I told you that you don't need to do that, Ma.'

'Well, I wouldn't if you did it, but you don't. I don't want a major infestation in this house.'

He grunted. 'God.'

'Come on,' she said, her eyes fixing on his left shoulder.

He pulled the bedding down and yanked off the jumper he was wearing, then flipped the edge of his t-shirt up. She remembered how thin his arms were when he was a small boy, sticks of bone with knobbly elbows. Now they were covered in if not muscular then sinewy flesh. She could see the definition of them, the rounded deltoid, the narrower biceps, with the image of the small bird, a scroll flowing from its beak, engraved at the intersection of the two. It was pretty, well executed, small and tasteful. She had to admit all that. While it had a slight redness to it, it didn't look to be infected.

'I went to the chemist and got some cream,' he said, angling his arm outwards and looking down at the image. 'I think it's okay. The tattoo guy said that it might weep and be a bit gross for a day or so, but I think it's already dried up.'

She wanted to touch it, but somehow she didn't dare. She just gazed at it for a while, observing how it had changed the contours of his arm, made what she had always known look so different, so foreign somehow.

'Are there meant to be words on that scroll?'

Scott laughed sheepishly. 'Yeah, I guess.'

'They didn't have a line already set to go you could have used? Death before dishonour? Carpe diem? Wind beneath my wings?'

'Are you taking the piss?'

Her lips twisted into a half smile. 'You know, I've had all day to get used to the idea that my child has a tattoo. I've been through the seven—or is it five?—stages of grief. Some stages anyway. I read about them somewhere. Anger, denial, what have you. Now I am at the abandonment of all principles stage. Perhaps that's acceptance?' Scott was staring at her, still frowning, with clearly no idea what she was talking about. She sighed. 'What's done is done.' She snorted. 'That might have worked on your scroll too.'

'Look, I didn't say anything because I knew you and Dad wouldn't like it, but I like it. It wasn't just because I was drunk. I mean, I wasn't really drunk. I wanted it.' He put his hand to the tattoo and gingerly touched the empty scroll with his middle finger. 'I didn't get anything put in here because, I don't know. I wasn't sure what I wanted to say. I didn't have the right words. I'll fill it out sometime. When I do.'

Pam looked at Scott and thought how young he still was, in many ways still her little boy. She thought of him as a toddler, the sweet round earnest face, not so round now, but still remarkably earnest. She wanted to put her arms around him and hold him close, but they didn't have a relationship like that anymore. 'So does it mean something without words, this tattoo? Apart from bugger off, parents and society.'

He glanced up at her quickly before passing his finger over the image. 'The bird, it's a swallow. The guy at the tattoo parlour said swallows stand for peace and safe journeys. You know, like a guardian angel.'

She wished it could be so. Of her three children, Scott was definitely the one who needed someone to watch over him. 'And Troy?'

Scott looked at her, his eyes narrowed slightly. 'What about Troy?'

'He didn't get a tattoo?'

'You've been talking to Loz?' There was a hint of accusation in his voice.

'I asked her about it. She just mentioned that the three of you went together. No state secrets.'

'Yeah, well, he wants to get one too. He had a rad drawing of a dragon he'd done. But it was going to cost too much.'

She raised an eyebrow. 'Really? I don't imagine his father would like it, either.'

Scott snorted. 'Funny that, 'cos he's got a few.'

'He has?'

'Yeah. He was a bit bad when he was younger. Well, that's what Troy and Kyle say. Now he's a hard arse. Everything by the book. "Do as I say, because I know what's best."'

'Maybe he made some mistakes he doesn't want Troy to repeat.'

Scott shrugged.

'There is a stigma attached to tattoos, in case you haven't noticed.'

Scott looked heavenwards. 'Mum. I promise I will not show off my tattoo in front of your friends. Or your enemies. No one will see this unless I'm wearing a singlet. I'll even be safe for job interviews. Believe me, it's not going to be a problem.'

Pam sighed. Believe her teenage son? Really, who did he think he was kidding? 'It's cold in here,' she said, standing up. 'Do you want me to turn your heater on?'

'Okay.' Scott looked up at her. He had that expression that he used to have when he was tiny, something that always melted her heart. He was never going to tell her voluntarily that he loved her. If she said it first he'd say, 'Yeah, me too' back. This look though was the closest she'd ever get, a silent message of adoration. She took the plunge and leaned down and put her arms around his shoulders. His own arms remained under the covers, but his head leaned into her neck and she moved her hand up to the back of his head and ruffled his hair. Her boy, her darling boy. 'Just concentrate on your studies,' she whispered. 'Let's get through this year. Then the world is your oyster.'

April 2016

Melbourne

Lori slid open the glass doors and stepped out onto the deck. A sharp, salty breeze had whipped up. Reflexively she pulled her cardigan close around her. In front of her lay the expanse of the bay; blue-grey sky and sea framed by the dusky green of tea-tree and she-oak that grew up alongside the house. Only the container ships sailing in and out of the bay gave a sense of perspective, offered an idea of where air ended and water began. She wasn't used to the openness and it took her a moment to get over a sense of vertigo, a feeling that there was nothing much to anchor her here at the edge of the land, at the edge of the world. If she didn't know better she would have thought she was somewhere wild and remote, but in truth, here, not more than a hundred kilometres from the city, there were neighbours all around, other similar weathered houses nestled in among the bushy growth dotted across the side of the incline that looked out over the water.

The rest of her family were somewhere down below, past the vegetation and the road, most probably on the beach by now. She imagined Jason and his father walking shoulder to shoulder, that soft intimacy they had, deep in conversation. The kids running ahead, zigzagging across the glossy sand to play chasey with the waves, screaming as the frothy water threatened to douse their shoes. She had told them to go ahead without her. Go out for a walk. She had a slight headache. Once she'd conquered that she'd organise dinner.

'No, no,' Niels had protested. 'You don't come down here to do that.'

'I want to. I like cooking,' she'd countered. 'We did some shopping. I have food.'

He'd given her a quizzical smile before throwing his hands in the air in a gesture of capitulation.

'Don't worry, I plan to get out a bit later.'

'Yeah, yeah,' he said, laughing now. 'I know you.'

The words caught her unawares, and she felt a tiny sting of emotion. A sensation of shame that made her look away.

When they left she lay down for a few minutes on the couch and waited for the tablets to kick in. The whole morning had been a rush, everything decided at the last minute, all pivoting around the kids. Cody being ferried to and from a party. An outing to the supermarket with a whining Sophie in tow. She'd had broken sleep for two nights in a row and had seen virtually nothing of Jason, who had been on some ridiculous overtime regime and stressed about something at work which he'd fleetingly explained and she'd barely taken in when he had spoken. And then there had been the hospital visits. Twice in two days, the trip across town, which felt to her now to have never happened. Or perhaps had happened to someone else, as though she had watched a movie of it and the import was already starting to fade.

Outside she felt an unexpected sense of calm. The clear air, the lack of visual clutter, a sense of everything having been stripped back. She hadn't been sure she'd wanted to come down. It was Jason who'd insisted, who'd said he had to get out of town, and she was glad in the end to be away. It felt like she could get some perspective here, work something out. But standing on the deck, the fresh breeze on her face, headache lifting, it seemed rather that she could simply forget.

She sat down on the timber bench, the hard slab of wooden railing at her back. It offered a different perspective, sitting. She was enclosed here, the trees tall against the railing, the sky receding from view unless she looked up. Her eye followed the pattern of the wooden decking into the house through the glass. She'd been surprised when she first came here, over ten years ago now. The house was more stylish than she'd envisioned. A modernist vibe of open spaces and unfussy furniture. Inside, a sleek blond dining table, a stone chimney in the American rustic style. Lots of glass. She soon found out that Niels had put the place together himself, for himself. He was not an architect, not a designer, but he had a natural feel for spaces, was mindful of the kind of space he lived in, and the creating of it came easily. Jason said that when they'd all lived together—he, his mother, father and brother—it was his father who defined the place, chosen furniture, painted walls. Not that his mother hadn't had a say herself, but she'd ceded a deal of the usual territory to her husband, understanding his affinity, perhaps grateful not to have full responsibility. Who would know now that she was no longer around to give her side of the story. Lori just had to take Jason's word. But Niels, although at times single-minded, wasn't a bully. She could imagine it could have been that way.

'Dad claims it's because he's Dutch,' Jason had told Lori wryly. He hadn't thought that the Dutch had any particular credentials with design, but she, the designer, disabused him of that notion. The Dutch had a long history of producing estimable art and architecture, she'd said. Even though she'd never been there and he had. 'Only to visit relatives when I was younger,' he clarified. It was rural and flat and dull in his recollection, with the odd windmill here and there. Strangely, she thought, he hadn't gone back when he'd done his European stint in his years before they'd met. He hadn't wandered the canals of Amsterdam and Utrecht, visited museums, seen the van Goghs and the Rembrandts, reflected on De Stijl. 'Maybe one day we can go together,' she'd suggested. He laughed. 'For sure,' he'd replied, but that was before the renovation, the kids and the daily grind got to them. Thoughts of travel slid under the horizon.

In her pocket her phone buzzed. She didn't recognise the number when she pulled it out. A landline, a city number. The hospital? She braced herself for news and was taken by surprise when a male voice asked for her, then identified himself as Detective Sergeant Levandi from the Major Collision Investigation Unit.

'I'm trying to find out a bit more about your brother. I understand you hadn't been in touch with him for some time. I wondered who might have been?'

She got up and went to the edge of the balcony, checked the driveway below and the little of the street she could see through the trees. 'My uncle could still be in Northam. His name is Peter Temple. There's a chance they're in contact. I can't think of anyone else.'

'Okay,' he said slowly, as though preoccupied. 'Look, I'm wondering if you could meet me at your brother's apartment? Perhaps this afternoon.'

'Meet?' This was unexpected. 'No, I'm not in the city right now. We're away for the weekend. Why? What do you need me for?'

'What about Monday morning then?' He was persistent, she had to give him that. She hadn't expected to have to be involved in an investigation. It was starting to feel intrusive.

'Ah.' She paused. 'I could do nine-thirty. I have to drop kids off at school.'

'Right. Good.'

'You'll need to give me the address.'

'Yes, yes, of course.' She could hear the shuffling of paper. 'Let's see. Forty Quin Street. Flat eight.'

'You haven't said what this is about. I'm not . . .' She faltered.

'Look, I know some of your brother's history. I know he served time. I gather you no longer have a relationship. But any help you can give us would be appreciated. We have some reason to believe that his injuries may have been intentional. There's the possibility that he's crossed someone or that someone may be still be seeking to settle old scores. I can only speculate at this point. But if you can accompany me we can have a look through his flat. You might be able to assist us in some small way.'

She tried to keep her voice even. 'What makes you think it was intentional? Did someone see what happened?'

She heard him take a breath. 'This is a part of an overall investigation. I can't talk to you about the details at this stage. I might be able to in a day or two,' he said, as though he was reciting a well-worn script. 'Of course, he may well regain consciousness by then and help us himself. But in the meantime . . .'

She agreed to the appointment time and rang off, then sat for a moment, aware of the suddenly darkening sky. Billowing grey clouds threatened not just rain but the imminent return of the family. She got up, went inside and surveyed the kitchen. Unlike her kitchen at home with its seemingly never-ending mess of plastic containers, compost bucket, bowls of fruit, fortresses of stacked bills and random toys, here the only thing out of place was the squat green reusable bag that held the groceries she'd brought down with her. She retrieved a bottle of red from the bag and opened it, pouring a glass and taking a gulp, then another, before amassing the ingredients she needed, the pots and utensils.

She knew the kitchen well after all these years. Niels was a good cook but he wasn't averse to her, or Jason, making food when they came down. He appreciated the escape from the monotony of his own food. Yet, as he'd said to her once, if it was the worst price he paid for living alone, in the scheme of things it was not too much of a price at all. Food could be many things, he'd discovered—tasty, evocative, creative—but primarily it was fuel. He found that out, he told her, as a small child in the 1940s. It was a commodity that was short in the Netherlands during and after the war; people made do with little, and living like that had made an imprint. He kept to the same fairly spartan regime all his life, and not just with food. Jason's only complaint about his father was his somewhat minimalist lifestyle. It might be admirable in many ways, but when he was a child the stoicism was little hard to live with.

'Is that why they split up, your mum and dad?' Lori asked in the early days.

'They were different people. The way they lived their lives was different,' Jason had replied. 'Politics. She never cared as much as he did. When you live with someone who does care it can seem, well, you know, that you aren't quite as worthy.'

The warmth of the wine began to flood her body. She hadn't eaten since breakfast. Not wise, but it worked in her favour now, the quick rush of alcohol buoying her, pushing her to get through food prep before the others returned. Indeed, it wasn't long before she saw the tops of Niels's and Jason's heads bobbing along the path leading up to the deck. Soon they were at the door, the children behind them, shrill and chorusing and not quite ready to drop, but in that heightened state of needing food and rest.

'It's brisk down there,' announced Niels, rubbing his crossed arms with his hands. 'Nice. I think it's made us all a little hungry.'

Jason, the circus master, took Sophie and Cody into the living room, raising his eyebrows at Lori as they marched past as if to say *is there no end to this?* In his wake, Niels assembled cheese and biscuits, juice for the kids, beer for himself and Jason.

'Need a hand?' he asked Lori when he returned.

'No, nearly done.'

He settled onto a stool at the bench, held his beer aloft in a gesture of a toast. '*Proost.*' She could feel him looking at her. 'So,' he said after a few seconds, 'you all right?'

'Just that headache.'

'Ach. I could have cooked.'

'No, no. I'm fine. It's gone now.'

He was still looking at her. 'Sure? Nothing on your mind?'

She scraped seeds from a small chilli, stopped. 'Why do you say that?'

'Just what Jason was telling me. I thought you might be a bit concerned.'

'Concerned?' Her stomach gave a little twist.

He hesitated. 'You know, at work.'

'Jason's work? *Should* I be concerned?'

'Oh no. I thought it was conceivable you might be. That's all.' He offered up a small, unconvincing smile as a reassurance.

She found herself staring at Niels. Was there something she'd missed? Most assuredly, yes. After the last few days, of course she'd missed something. She kept her voice as neutral as she could, tried not to let panic filter out. 'I know it's been hard for him recently. Delays or something. Is that what you were talking about?'

'Yeah, yeah. It's nothing really.' Niels waved his hand dismissively. 'Sorry, I didn't mean to worry you. I just thought . . . I don't know what I thought. Maybe that you were worrying unduly about something. You look a little tired, but as you say, the headache . . .'

Niels had been in the construction industry himself. Not the management side, but working on building sites. Tough physical work, a lot of it. He'd endured it for years. When he first arrived in the country, he laboured on the Snowy Mountains Scheme, the mother of all huge projects. Despite his obvious fierce intelligence, he never moved beyond construction. He was a reader, a lover of music and nature, and that gave him another life in the hours outside work. Then he married, somewhat later than many of his generation, became father to two boys. In the end he worked for the union. He'd retired by the time Lori met Jason, so it always seemed something of a mystery to her that he'd had this life before, full of hard work and confrontation. His experience now translated to be both a boon and something of a censure to Jason, who had never envisaged he'd be working in construction himself one day, especially not on the other side of the (hurricane) fence.

At the dinner table they talked politics, as they often did. It was an easy conversation, really. Despite their circumstances, Jason and Niels had a similar outlook on political parties, the system. Both of them hated the current government, agreed on the environment, the worry of climate change, the changes that were being wrought on the planet. Loren joined in their banter. She was used to it now after all these years, knew the right rejoinders, which wasn't to say she didn't agree wholeheartedly but testified more to the fact that she loved the atmosphere, the camaraderie, the repartee. The sense of being immersed in it all. Embedded.

Her own family had never talked politics that she could remember. Her grandfather had been the mayor of Northam for some time. Whether he stood for election on any ticket, she didn't know. Even if he had, she thought that any political party affiliation would have been more social than ideological, assumed values, not overreaching vision. At home, politics was rarely mentioned, apart from the occasional word to the television from Mick, usually at the sight of a Labor politician. But then, not always. Unlike many, her parents had never seemed to be particularly partisan. The Liberals and the Nationals could be given a serve as well. She sometimes wondered what their reaction would be to the Greens. Would they be open, like some of the old cockies she'd seen on TV in recent times, to turning their backs to genetically modified crops, fracking and selling out to mining companies?

She put the kids to bed while Jason and Niels cleaned up. When she returned to the kitchen it was as pristine as it had been when she'd started. The three of them sat down with a cup of tea in the living room and talked briefly about plans for the next day. Niels offered to look after the kids if they wanted to go for a walk or out for breakfast. A part of her drifted away from the conversation, and in the quiet of the evening, with kids in bed and the television off, she was aware only of the faint rhythmic sound of the waves breaking down below. The weight of the night closing in around her. She felt a sudden fatigue— the fallout from the headache, too much wine before eating. The need to lie down seemed overwhelming.

In bed Jason put his arms around her and said, 'You realise we haven't had any time alone for weeks.'

'Months, maybe,' she murmured.

He pulled her to him and nestled his head over her shoulder. 'So what were you talking to Dad about in the kitchen?'

'About you, actually.'

'Yeah?'

'He asked if I was worried about you.'

'Oh? And are you?' There was a note of wariness in his voice.

'Well, I wasn't. I mean you'd said a few things about work lately, but I didn't feel too concerned. Now I'm speculating if I should be.'

'No. You shouldn't be.'

'So this stuff at work isn't preying on your mind?'

'Well, it is, if you want the truth. I don't know. We never seem to get the time to discuss anything. I'm home too late. The kids. Really, it's stuff you don't need to know.'

'Like what?' she felt that twinge of anxiety again, a spike of adrenaline pulling her back to alertness. 'Why don't I need to know?'

'Well . . .' She could feel him shrug. 'There's nothing you can do about it, that's why. There've been some things that have happened at work. Frankly, some of it is a little shady. But . . . Look, I wanted to talk to Dad because he knows exactly what some of these guys are like. The kinds of things they get up to.'

'Are they dangerous?'

'No. No.' He answered quickly, but there was an edge to his voice. In the dark she couldn't see his face, read his expression.

'Tell me about this shady stuff.'

He exhaled slowly in a way that seemed to indicate that it was unimaginably tedious to have to explain. 'There are some guys on site who are very difficult to work with, making excuses, using complaints about work practices to extend the contract out to get more money. There could be some theft involved too. Nothing I can prove until I do a full inventory. It could cost the company a bit if it was the case though. There's a guy, Mike, I've worked with him on a couple of projects—'

'I remember you mentioning him.'

'Yeah, well, I've always trusted him. He's helped me a lot, but I'm beginning to wonder if he's been white-anting me. He's done some odd things of late. Now's he's pissed off somewhere, left me in the lurch.'

'Really? Oh Jase, that's terrible. But what do you mean left you in the lurch?'

'Look, I'm probably just being paranoid. It'll sort itself out. I don't really want to keep talking about it. But . . .'

'But?'

'Work could be a bit rocky for a while. Just bear with me.'

She shook her head in the darkness. 'I'm here, that's all I can say.'

'I'm sorry. I know it's hard for you with the kids. I don't even ask you about what you're doing. Divorce is probably imminent and I haven't even noticed.'

'Not so far, but if it keeps going this way . . .'

'Good to know. That it's not imminent, I mean. On that note, how's the week been for you, then? You had to do some illustrations. For McPherson's, was it? You done? I have to say, you've been a bit quiet. I did think that at dinner. Not your usual chirpy self.'

She made a huffing sound at his description. Ironic. She would never be known for her chirp. 'I had that headache. Maybe I'm a bit under the weather. Tired. The week has been . . . well, just the usual really.'

'Mmm.' Jason was quiet for a moment. 'You know, Sophie said something really funny when we were going down to the beach.'

'Yeah?'

'We were waiting to cross the road and a police car went past and she said the police came to our place last week.'

Loren turned over onto her back so Jason's head wasn't as close to her neck, so he wouldn't hear the thump of her heartbeat in her jugular. 'Oh yeah, they did. Just an inquiry about someone. But they had the wrong person. Me, that is. I couldn't help them.'

'Sophie said it was about your brother?'

'Crazy, yeah. Someone with the same name as my brother.'

'That's weird. I thought they would have databases with all that stuff. They'd know he'd died.'

'I suppose there're a lot of people with the same name out there. They don't know everything.'

'Why were they looking for him? This other Simon Green?'

'I don't know.' Her heart was pounding now. 'They didn't say.'

'I'm sorry, hon. It must have been hard.'

'It was just strange. That's all. Just strange.'

'I was thinking. How do you feel about going up there sometime?'

'Up where?'

'To Northam. For the kids. They might want to see where their family, your family, is from. They're getting old enough, and—'

'There's nothing to see, Jase. Nothing's changed. I don't want to take them to a graveyard.' Her voice was brittle, dismissive to her ears. 'And they're not old enough. They're still way too young to have any idea.'

He went quiet then and so did she. She heard his steady breathing next to her and wondered if he was falling asleep. But as she rolled away from his arm he stirred. 'You know, Dad loves you,' he said.

'What?'

'I don't mean like that.' He laughed quietly. 'I mean, he totally approves of you.'

'I approve of him too.'

'Ah, funny. What I'm saying is he's always liked you. I remember once he said you were the kind of person who got on with things. You're so alike you two. Kindred spirits. I've never been able to put my finger on it, really, but I think he feels you're more like him than me or Josh. His own flesh and blood.'

'You jealous?' she said teasingly.

'No! I guess I was trying to say that you have a family, babe. Me and him. The kids. I know it's a bit late in the piece to say this, I guess you've already figured it out yourself over the years. I hope it's enough for you.'

She rolled back towards him, pushed her face into his neck, felt the scratchiness of his stubble on her forehead. 'Don't say that like an apology. It's more than enough,' she murmured. And it was true. From the first time she'd met him she'd known he was the one. What 'the one' was she might have struggled to define. What was it that made it so? Love at first sight? Lust? Pheromones? Some other kind of deep and instinctual chemistry? Maybe just timing. There was a possibility that she was ready, after all those years, simply to take someone into her heart. To begin anew. A blank slate, but one with restorative possibilities; a real future. At twenty-eight she had been starting to contemplate settling down, making something good, constructive, in her life. And then there he was, walking in the door of that smoky pub. A guy who didn't have the word danger stencilled on his forehead. An ordinary guy she wouldn't have looked at five years before. One year before.

She wrapped her arm over his body and pulled him to her, feeling his cock grow suddenly hard against her stomach, the boundary between them slipping away, and she thought of that first night, when he had told her that his mother had just died. He'd come back from overseas for the funeral and was in a fog of grief and jet lag. She was there with her empathy and understanding and there was all that heightened intensity between them. She knew he needed to talk, so she let him. She didn't say then that she'd lost her mother. And father. And brother. She didn't want it to overshadow his own loss, compete with it in any way.

It was only later that she told him about the accident. The car accident that had wiped out her family. It was a brief sketch, an outline of how she came to be here. And that was enough. He, preoccupied with his own grief, had simply accepted her reluctance to talk much about her own—by then—long ago past, and as time went on he would only sometimes ask, bring family up. Mostly she managed to deflect deeper questions, offer up broad brushstrokes rather than details. She'd been surprised at how little people (loved ones and acquaintances alike) needed to know; how easy it was for them to disregard what had gone before. How most of life was simply lived on a day-to-day basis with only a glancing regard to history.

Lying in bed now, listening to his even breathing, she thought of the times, especially in the early years, when she had turned suddenly to see him looking at her, wondering she guessed if perhaps he should ask more, attempt to know more. And now, having seen Schiller, she realised that he must have noticed something in her, recognised tells that she wasn't even aware of herself. Once he'd described her as self-contained and self-reliant. 'You make that sound like a criticism,' she'd countered, and he'd tilted his head in that way he did when he wanted to make a point without having to use words. 'Mysterious,' he'd said lightly, reaching out and brushing the backs of his fingers down her hair. 'That's what you are. My own international woman of mystery.'

July 1993

Northam

P am was half awake when the knocking started. She'd roused around four needing to go to the loo and was finding it difficult to get back to sleep. Loren's door was open when she got up, and while she didn't panic, a little seed of concern lodged itself in her gut. Late nights weren't unusual for the boys, but Loren tended to come home at a reasonable hour. Still, given they were all together, it was probably just a question of logistics. Easier to wait for Scott than to get a lift back. And they all knew how Scott loved a late night.

Loren hadn't been going out with the boys as often as she used to. This was probably due to the fact that the boys themselves had been leading quieter lives these last couple of months, part of some small concessions being made to study. Pam suspected the slowdown had a fair bit to do with Troy's parents. That parent–teacher interview in April had been a little bruising for them too, by all accounts. Troy's social life had been somewhat curtailed since then. This had had a domino effect, which Pam conceded wasn't entirely unwelcome. Perhaps she had something to thank the Druitts for after all.

But tonight had been a departure from all that. Tonight was the beginning of the mid-year break, and the spectre of early mornings and daily academic assessments had disappeared for the next two weeks. For the first time in months there had been a bunch of kids at the Greens' for dinner. Pam had sat at the head of the table and had looked contentedly at the gathered throng, her family and their friends. Troy, Mike, Scott's friend since kindergarten, Lori's friend Katie, and Melissa, who may or may not have been Mike's girlfriend at the moment. (There were questions Pam realised that you just didn't ask.) The dining room had buzzed with life. Mick had decided on some quiet Rolling Stones (if you could call *Goat's Head Soup* quiet) to accompany the meal and the conversation levels had raised a decibel or two. The buzz had made Pam feel energetic. There was something about young people. She wondered once if she hadn't missed her calling, if perhaps she should have been a teacher. But then she'd have to chase them up for homework and tell them off for talking in class, smoking behind the bike shed. Being what she was, whatever that was exactly—the coolest mother, she'd like to think—gave her a much better feeling. She remembered her mother's comment from years before: 'You want to be liked too much.' 'What's wrong with that?' Pam had responded. She thought everyone wanted to be liked. (Apart from her mother perhaps, who wanted to be respected, even feared.) It was a part of human nature, wasn't it?

During the term Troy had turned eighteen and got his driver's licence. His father had bought him a Falcon ute, about ten years old but still in good nick. Despite the timing, it hadn't truly been a birthday present. Ray was big on responsibility. Something like a car shouldn't just be given away—it needed to be earned, valued. Troy would pay it off by helping out part-time in the workshop, which in all honesty wasn't really that arduous for him because what didn't he love about labouring over cars? So now there were two drivers and two vehicles, and when they had left the Greens' that night they had driven in convoy: Troy and Mike in the ute; Scott, Loren and Melissa in the car. Pam had stood at the front door and watched the red tail-lights disappear down the road and around into Grant Street and had thought warmly, as she knocked back her fourth wine of the night, how lucky these kids were to have each other. They were a nice bunch, good-hearted. People often complained about the youth of today, but if this lot were anything to go by the world would be fine. Funny, kind, caring. Just normal kids who liked to let their hair down from time to time. What was wrong with that?

When the pounding roused her the clock was glowing five am. Pam hadn't realised she'd fallen back to sleep and would have thought she'd been awake for the last hour except for the fact that she'd been speaking to her mother, who had been admonishing her for something. No surprises there except that her mother had been dead for five years now. Beside her Mick murmured something she couldn't quite catch and swung out of bed, flicking on the light at the same time. She looked at his face and saw a reflection of her own. Puffy with sleep and full of foreboding.

They opened the front door to a young, unfamiliar-looking constable, pale and nervous under the porch light. For a moment her spirits inexplicably lifted. She realised that he, this policeman, was not Des Robinson, which made her feel that the situation might not be dire. She knew Des. Had known him a long time, since he'd arrived in town over twenty years ago. She felt he would have come to them if it had been something truly catastrophic. Beside her Mick stood straight and tall, braced for the worst. She never thought anyone could look dignified wearing striped pyjamas, skivvy and socks, but somehow Mick managed to. He stared at the boy who'd come to tell them the news and took a small step forward, his hand shaking as he gripped the edge of the door.

The constable seemed nervous too, but he could see what needed to be done. Probably drilled by Des, Pam thought. 'To put your minds at rest, they're okay. They were in an accident but they're okay.'

'Jesus fucking Christ.' Mick bent forward as though he was going to throw up.

'But you're not just here to tell us they're okay,' said Pam.

'No,' said the constable. 'They're both at Belandra hospital.'

The forty-minute drive to Belandra seemed more like two hours. It felt to Pam that Mick was driving like a ninety-year-old and she had to restrain herself from telling him to put his foot down. But the roads at this time of the year, this time of the morning, were dangerous, treacherous with black ice and the slime that formed on sheltered stretches of bitumen. All made worse by the rain they'd had, which by now had mercifully eased to the occasional splatter on the windscreen. The constable had been able to tell them very little. He hadn't attended the accident and had scant information. As a consequence, they didn't know whose car the kids were in or who they were with. He'd assured them that someone else from the station, 'probably Sergeant Robinson', would join them at the hospital shortly to fill them in. But, in the meantime, at least they knew that Scott and Lori were not seriously injured, were actually okay. That was all that mattered to Pam. They were alive. They were safe.

At the hospital a registrar told them Scott had a shattered ankle, which required urgent repair and the insertion of a plate, and he had just been taken in to surgery. A stroke of luck, he said, that the visiting orthopaedic surgeon was up from Melbourne and had a scheduled operation that morning. They had to get him out of bed slightly earlier than usual, which seemed to amuse the registrar, who had the look of a man who had spent far too little time in bed on this night, or in general. Loren was physically unharmed, he'd continued, but they wanted to keep her in for a few more hours, possibly the day, for observation. She was clearly in shock. But she had been sedated and was resting.

The registrar was a tall man, and Pam, who was not terribly tall at all, stared up at him. The emergency ward was so quiet she could almost hear the molecules of air moving around them. She watched him, it seemed, in slow motion turn towards a curtained cubicle and an odd sensation ran through her. The part of her that had just felt a rush of relief was beginning to shrink. Something didn't feel right.

'Was anyone else admitted?' she asked suddenly. 'Are they okay, the rest of them?'

The registrar stopped just short of the curtain and turned, pausing for the briefest moment as if having to recall the details. 'Yes. There were two others. One with a few cuts and bruises. He'll be fine.' He saw their quizzical looks. 'Josh Friar his name is.'

Mick and Pam glanced at each other. There had clearly been some personnel swapping during the course of the evening.

'The other was a young woman with more serious injuries who we sent to Goulburn Valley. Melissa, I believe? I don't have the paperwork on hand to tell you her last name.'

'Melissa.' Pam put her hand to her mouth. 'Was she badly hurt?' She thought of the tall, willowy girl who'd sat at her table earlier that evening. She hadn't met her before, but was struck by her poise, her polite, quiet, amused manner too. A hearty eater, which was always pleasing to see. Pam liked it when they devoured her food.

'We sent her down for specialist care. It's not good, but we think she'll come through.'

'Thank god.' Pam pressed her lips together. 'And that was all? No one else?'

Suddenly the doctor looked uncertain. He opened his mouth, then closed it again. 'I do understand there was a fatality at the scene.'

Pam gripped Mick's arm, felt a flood of anguish take hold of her. Someone had died. One of the kids they knew was dead, perhaps someone who had been at her dinner table that night. A friend of Scott's, or Loren's. Next to her Mick seemed as incapable of speech as she was.

When she found her voice she was barely audible. 'Who?'

The registrar shook his head. 'All I can tell you is that it was a young man. I'm afraid I don't know the name.'

To know and not to know. And yet already she had formed an idea of who it might be. Later when she thought back she couldn't believe that she had never not known, that it had only been this moment that a swirling universe had burst forth from a pinhead of information and changed everything.

'Mum.' Loren's voice, muted and husky, filtered from beyond the curtain. Pam pushed past the doctor and with hands shaking yanked the curtain back. Even after a morning of shocks she was taken aback by what she saw. Loren, looking like Loren, but not looking like Loren. A facsimile of her daughter. A broken doll propped up in bed, her back against the headboard with her knees bent in front of her making a tent out of the hospital cotton blanket, her face so pale that its only apparent features were two dark mascara-stained eyes. For the umpteenth time this morning Pam felt the temporal world shift and split into two. In the few seconds it took her to reach her child, the space inside her brain seemed to expand infinitesimally. Thoughts raced through her head. Impressions lodged in her mind. She could see the meaning of her actions and their futility too. Her one impulse was to hold Lori, comfort her, make everything right. But there was no making this right. Her daughter had witnessed—no, more than that—had been part of something terrible. Something that could never be changed. Never erased.

'I'm here,' was all she could say, all she was capable of. 'I'm here.'

For a few seconds Lori didn't move, stayed stiff and unyielding inside her mother's arms. 'Troy,' she murmured. Then her body seemed to crumble. She began sobbing, not hysterically but rhythmically, keening. A low call. 'Mum, mum, mumma.' Mick was with them by then, too, his arms around them both. In better times, when the children were small, they would have joked and said, 'Group hug.' But there was nothing comforting about this. It felt instead as though they were building some kind of fortress with their bodies. A pathetic attempt to prop up a crumbling edifice, to keep the world at bay. But in reality, there was no making good, making better. Only the dubious consolation of solidarity.

They sat with Loren for a very long time until her whimpering gave way to ragged breathing and finally to sleep. Mick got up to find the doctor, who came to check her and pronounced this all to be a good thing. The pills, he explained, might send her out for a few hours. But she needed the rest. Rest, thought Pam. Respite perhaps. That was about all her dear child would get. She imagined the intensity of waking up. Remembering. That's how it would be now, for a long time to come.

In a daze, she left Mick with Lori and went to get a cup of coffee. She hadn't eaten, but food wasn't what she wanted. By now there were a few more staff around, the cafeteria was open. Almost as if she'd conjured him, Des Robinson appeared near the cafeteria door. Like everyone she'd encountered this morning, he looked exhausted. His eyes were bloodshot and his cheeks bore the trace of yesterday's stubble. Even his uniform seemed somewhat rumpled, adding to the effect of a man down on his luck. Perhaps he thought the same of her: that she looked down on her luck as well. God knows she hadn't looked in the mirror all morning. He gave her what she thought of as the long look. The one where his head was tilted downwards, as though he wanted to angle his eyes to the level of the person he was speaking to. It was interrogation meets sympathy, and it could have come off badly, but with Des it always seemed avuncular, had the effect of making you think he cared. And she was fairly certain he did. That was his saving grace as a small-town cop. That he had a true concern for the people he lived among.

'How are you?' he asked quietly.

She could feel her eyes filling with tears. Her jaw began to quiver. Des quickly placed his hand under her elbow and guided her into the cafeteria, to the nearest table by the door. He told her to sit while he fetched them a drink. When he returned he spooned a couple of teaspoons of sugar into the coffee before passing it to her.

'We didn't know until we got here,' she said. 'I thought every-thing was going to be all right. How stupid is that?'

'I apologise. It took me longer than I thought to . . . How's your lad doing?'

'He's in surgery. His leg. Ankle. I'm not quite sure. They're putting in a plate.'

'Yeah, I saw it. Smashed up. Might take him a while to get the full use back.'

'God, really? You were there?'

Des nodded and took a sip of his drink. Mr Laconic. That's what Mick had called him after years of running into him, rubbing shoulders at community functions and working bees. 'Getting conversation out of him was like getting blood out of a stone,' Mick once said. Well, who could blame him? Town cops had to stay neutral, out of the fray. The less they said the better, she supposed.

'What happened?'

'There'll be an investigation. Hard to say exactly. But I think you could put alcohol and speed into the equation. Inattention.'

She didn't want to ask who was driving, she felt too raw to know more, but somehow the words escaped her lips anyway, and she knew from his split second of hesitation that the driver was Scott. 'Oh my god,' she said, staring at the half-empty cup in front of her. 'Did you go to the Druitts' place? You know, they were at our house last night for dinner. Not the Druitts. Oh god, not them. I mean the kids. A few of them. I was thinking how great they were, how lucky to have each other. Everything they had ahead of them.' She looked up at him. She was babbling. 'Oh god,' she said again, frustrated at her lack of vocabulary, incredulous that she wasn't crying.

124

'Is Mick here?'

'With Loren.'

'We'll take him a coffee.'

Mick was sitting in a chair, hunched over the bed, his head resting on his forearm. He might have been asleep too but he looked up quickly when they came in, alert enough but saggy-faced.

Des cast a glance at Loren. 'It was hard for her this morning. Seeing her boyfriend like that. Terrible for these kids.'

'Boyfriend?' Mick squinted.

'The Druitt boy.'

'Troy wasn't her boyfriend,' said Pam, slightly defensively, as if it mattered. 'He was a friend. To all of us. We've all known him for years. We . . .' She turned to Mick, delivered the news like she was ripping off a bandaid. 'Des just told me that Scott was driving.'

She watched Mick's face. The import of it all settling in. 'No,' he said firmly, looking up at her as if she'd told him the damnedest lie. 'No.'

Pam put her fingers to her lips and glanced at Loren.

Mick closed his eyes for a few seconds, then stood up. 'I'm going to get some air. Des, you want to join me?' He gripped Pam's forearm as he turned to leave. 'We won't go far.' His eyes were moist and raw-looking and she nodded, giving him the tacit approval to leave that he hadn't actually asked her for. He needed to talk to Des now, perhaps he would be braver than her, find out more.

Pam moved into Mick's chair and gazed for a while at her daughter. When the kids were little she'd loved watching them sleep. It filled her with an exquisite contentedness of the sort that she had never experienced before. Parenting was like that.

Incredible highs, and occasionally awful lows. Joy and anxiety. And now she discovered there was also abject misery. The worst misery she could imagine, apart from one of them dying. And, even then, she wasn't sure if that would be worse, because this particular misery came from a death and was served with extra helpings of second-hand guilt, terror and grief. Everything mixed up, what she felt herself and what she was feeling for her children. Especially Scott now. Poor, poor Scott.

Loren's breath grew patchy and rapid, and Pam leaned over her, touched her brow, whispered her name. After a little while her eyes opened and she stared up. 'Mum,' she whispered.

'You don't have to talk.'

Loren's face collapsed. 'I'm sorry. I'm so sorry.'

Pam took her hand and gripped it tight. All the things she could say suddenly seemed trite and false. She couldn't say it'll be all right. Maybe one day it would be, but not anytime soon. She couldn't say it's not your fault. That seemed to put the blame elsewhere. And, although there may be blame, she was reluctant to lay any.

'Troy.' Lori let out a small, strangled cry. 'Oh Mum.'

'I know. I'm here. I'm not leaving. We'll go home soon.'

Tears streamed down Lori's face. 'I loved him, Mum. I loved him so much. I can't . . .'

'I know you did.' Did she? She hadn't been sure before, but of course it was clear now.

'I don't know what to do. What am I going to do?'

'I don't know, sweetheart. We'll just do what we have to do. Put one foot in front of the other.'

Pam realised she was crying too. A tear dripped off the end of her nose and she wiped it with the back of her hand. She leaned back a little and her eyes followed the light to the window. The sky was beginning to clear, and she could see patches of blue above the rooftop of the building next door. The Earth was still spinning, morning morphing into midday, into afternoon. Her mind went back to the night before, Troy sitting opposite Loren at the table, balling up pieces of paper napkin and flicking them at her. She was pretending to be annoyed but laughing, basking in the attention. Troy was grinning, his teeth gleamed white against his fresh olive skin, his eyes fixed on her daughter. Then a distraction and he turned Pam's way, grinning still, met her gaze. 'Awesome food, Mrs Gee. As always.' He raised his glass in a mock toast that could have been interpreted as cheeky but was so warm and spontaneous that she felt quite touched. Manners were important in his family he'd told her on several occasions. He was always being raked over the coals for some social transgression (he didn't actually say that, she'd filled in the gaps). His parents may have failed to curb his personality in some ways, but they managed to instill politeness into him, and respect. That was one thing that Pam would give them: whether by accident or design, they'd brought up a beautiful young man. She couldn't imagine their loss. It was bad enough for her. They must be going through hell.

April 2016

Melbourne

The road ahead was a river of red tail-lights as far as the eye could see. They were late coming back from Niels's and the kids had fallen asleep quickly, Cody out like a light almost as soon as they got into the car and Sophie succumbing soon after to the rhythm of tyres on asphalt and the heater turned up full bore against the chilly night air.

'We should have left earlier,' Jason said irritably. 'Look at this bloody traffic.'

Lori's head was pressed back against the headrest, the lights in front mesmerising. She didn't respond.

'Don't tell me you're going to go to sleep as well?' Jason sounded about one quarter serious.

'Have you ever known me to fall asleep in the car?'

'Nah, guess not.'

She sat forward suddenly and turned to him. 'Do you want me to drive?'

'What? I'm fine.'

'Just thought it would save you being frustrated.'

'Me!' He laughed. 'I'm never frustrated behind the wheel. 'Specially not in traffic jams.'

It had taken her a long time to feel comfortable in a car. In the weeks after the accident she had insisted on walking everywhere until circumstances dictated otherwise. When she did finally take the plunge she was continually wary, on edge. Later, in Melbourne, there was no need to use cars. She lived in the inner city. Trams, bikes, skateboards, feet got her around. She didn't learn to drive until she met Jason, who was horrified that she didn't already know how. (A country girl who couldn't drive? Surely an oxymoron.) He taught her on the back roads of Mornington and the long sweeping Peninsula highways, the very place where they were now. Weekends spent learning to surf and learning to drive. She found she liked being in the driver's seat. There was a feeling of being in control that you didn't have as a passenger. It astounded her that she'd never really imagined that before she got behind the wheel. The freedom. The exhilaration. She saw a reason that people liked cars, other than a way to get from one place to another.

It was nine o'clock by the time they got back and hauled the kids from the car to their room. Sophie was half awake and Lori managed to run a toothbrush around her mouth and a flannel across her face. Jason carried Cody straight to bed.

'At least they'll have a good night's sleep,' he said, returning to the kitchen where she was putting away produce they'd bought at a farmers' market earlier in the day. A cabbage, some onions, carrots with long feathery tops, a solid chunk of deep-yellow cheese.

'Yeah, they'll probably wake me up at the crack of bloody dawn. Payback.'

'Speaking of which—dawn, I mean, not payback—I'm going to head off pretty soon too.' Jason started his working day before the rest of them woke up. He wasn't a natural early riser, but he'd learned to accommodate new diurnal rhythms. Lori envied the fact he was an easy sleeper. It was something she had never been good at. There had been long periods that she had used sleeping pills to soothe her into a pattern. Before kids she had a job at an advertising agency, and had to get to work on time, be alert enough to create decent artwork. Children had reintroduced erratic sleep, but they were also infinitely tiring. Now her sleep seemed to be controlled by them. When they woke, so did she. Whether she liked it or not.

Jason showered and Lori went into her studio to check the calendar on her computer. She'd had a nagging feeling she'd already scheduled something for tomorrow, the time when she'd agreed to meet that policeman. Sure enough there was a coffee date with Anselma at ten. Anselma was sparky and irreverent, larger than life. They'd made friends through their kids. Anselma's son, Mischa, and Sophie had gravitated to each other at kindergarten and the mothers arranged a play date, soon discovering a shared passion for art (she was a photographer, 'Prophetically named for Ansel Adams,' she'd declared on the first day they'd met) and a fellow outsider's disrespect for authority and decorum. Lori took her phone out of her pocket and plugged in a quick text. *Sorry, something has come up for tomorrow. Have to reschedule. Call soon.* Cancellations between them were not unusual. Work could be unexpectedly demanding and Anselma, self-employed herself, frequently had the same problem. Lori regretted it though. They had a lot of laughs together. She didn't see any laughs coming up tomorrow.

Lori looked back at the screen, scrolled through her calendar and emails, and quietly lamented that she'd gone away for the weekend. She should have put up a bit more of a fight, made some excuse. She could have even sent Jason and the kids away by themselves. But she didn't do that. She'd never done that. It would have been strange (very unlike her), and she was trying as hard as she could to make sure nothing was strange at the moment.

Jason appeared at the door dressed in a t-shirt and towel. 'Guess I'll see you tomorrow night.' He smiled wanly and, not for the first time, he reminded her of her father standing there in the half light, his hair wet and ruffled from the shower, his t-shirt snug across his belly. Growing into middle age, just as her dad had been when she'd last seen him. Bittersweet love and loss in one package.

She walked over and nuzzled into his neck. 'What time will you be back?'

'Hard to say. I'll text you tomorrow, let you know what's happening. Should be better this week.'

'Pity they don't pay you for the extra twenty hours you've been clocking up the last few weeks.'

'Ha, no hope of that. Do or die. If I don't fuck this up too badly I'll get another job out of them. Maybe a better contract.'

'And if you do?'

'What? Fuck it up? Well, I'll probably never work in this town again.' He smiled crookedly.

She looked up at him, scrutinised his face. Was he being serious? It was often hard to tell with Jason. In most ways he played life so straight—the very thing she'd always liked about him, his reliability, his rock-solidness. And yet there was just a little more to him than you imagined. A little something that undercut those expectations of convention. Subversive humour, a dry sense of irony.

'Hey. It'll be fine. Honestly. I just need to go to bed and get some sleep. A weekend away has tuckered me out. All that fresh air.'

'All those fresh kids, you mean.'

He smiled. 'It's the best time, the time with them. Oh, and you too, of course, my darling wife.'

She kissed him on the cheek and thought that ten years ago they could never have imagined being so domestic, so kid-centric, so tired, having so little sex (anything less than nightly would have been unimaginable). Her mind flickered to Schiller. Still in the thick of it, it seemed. Was that what she would have had instead? Sliding doors. Take one path and you'll never know where the other one would have led you. Perhaps just accept that none of them was ever going to take you where you might have once imagined you'd go. Most of life was down to sheer luck. Good or bad. Often indifferent.

She went to the back of the house and made a herbal tea. It was quiet there with the door closed. She could play a little music if she fancied. But she never really did fancy. It was the silence she craved above all else, silence and seclusion. She never explicitly articulated that need to Jason. Her usual shtick was that this time of the evening was when she could get things done. But the truth was that she rarely did *anything* with the time. Why did she need it then? She had no idea. All it gave her was a little while to sit undisturbed. Not to think, but to let her mind drift, float across a mutable landscape of knowledge and speculation.

The living room was almost in darkness. A small lamp gave out minimal light and allowed her to see the vague shapes of the garden overlaid with the reflection of the room. A double exposure. It was a simple, elegant space (when the floors weren't strewn with toys). One solid wall filled with shelves of books and objects, two walls of black-framed glass that looked out into the backyard. She and Jason had designed the back of the house themselves and even contributed at times to its building. They had made a space that felt like theirs out of something that had once very definitely not been, although it was most certainly a place of significance. The house had been Jason's family home and was where his mum, Jo, had continued to live after she split from Niels. The bedroom where Sophie and Cody slept now had been his. The one across the hall his brother Josh's. Their bedroom his parents' room. Her studio the living room. The back of the house, a basic lean-to, had housed a kitchen–dining room and laundry, renovated in the seventies with brown floor tiles, dark wood laminate and orange Formica benchtops.

'Do you miss your old home?' Lori had asked Jason, renovation completed.

'It's still in here,' he said, putting a finger to his temple, giving her a downturned smile. 'Just like all the other memories I have of places that still exist, or don't exist anymore. This house is different now. It's a new start. I'm pretty happy about that.'

Lori had first visited the house only days after the funeral. It was as though Jo had just stepped out for a moment. The cupboards and fridge were full of food. There were cigarettes on the bench and half-filled ashtrays in the dining and living rooms. Every free space around the house chock-a-block with knick-knacks that ranged from the almost stylish to the down-right kitsch. When Lori first saw Niels's house a month or so later she was shocked at the difference between them. His minimalism, she conjectured, must have been a response to Jo's excess. Jason laughed at that notion. 'No, he kept her in check while they were together. When he left, the ornaments started to move in. When me and Josh went, there was a mass invasion. Trinkets and fags right out of control.'

Lori had seen photos of Jo at different stages of her life. Pretty young bride in the seventies. Mother to small boys in the eighties. An older woman at a barbecue twenty or so years later. As time went on there was a growing seriousness about her, a maturity as she emerged out of the shadow of Niels. But a sadness too, Lori thought. Something unfulfilled. But perhaps she was just reading in too much from what Jason had told her. Between them they might have come up with an interpretation that wasn't really true. That she would never know.

Jason resembled Jo. The dark hair and eyes, round face, tendency to carry a little weight. Lori felt inexplicably close to her for that likeness to her son and she often thought about her in the house as she went about the day to day. What would Jo think of her? Their decisions? Jason found her once crying hysterically over one of the decorations she'd accidentally broken, one of the few they'd kept. ('I'm not sure what significance this one has,' Jason had said, 'but it does remind me that she did sometimes have good taste. Maybe it was a gift?') He'd been puzzled by her meltdown, but of course it really wasn't about Jo then but about Pam. Pam and Jo had been conflated into one absent super-mother. The perfect guardian angel Lori had never had, who'd love her no matter what, be ready with sage advice, dote on her children.

Jason had divined all this to some extent. 'You must miss your mum,' he'd asked her a couple of times when something had come up about his. She'd shake her head as if it didn't matter, tell him it was so long ago now that she couldn't really remember her mother very well at all anymore. 'You don't have any photos of her. Or you as a kid, either,' he'd stated incredulously once, when they'd been looking through, trying to sort, Jo's relatively vast collection, which featured many of Niels and of the boys at various stages of their childhoods. Jason grungy in the early nineties had made her laugh. A doe-eyed teen with shaggy dark hair. (He still had his Nirvana and Hole albums, a few Stone Temple Pilots, as if to say that it was more than a phase.) She told him that her parents hadn't been much into photography, and then what photos there were had been misplaced when their house was cleared out. She'd said she was grateful at the time, that she didn't want to ever look back, and that, for her, photos were only a reminder of what you didn't have anymore. She'd felt him observing her for a moment, weighing up her words. 'I guess we're all different,' he'd said at last.

Lori wasn't sure what had hurt more: his pity or her inability to be honest. There were photos, had been photos. Some in albums, most in a box. And she had taken one. Kept it close, secreted in various places over the years, hidden away like a precious relic, shown to no one. It was the only memento she'd allowed herself to take when she left her grandfather's house the morning after his funeral. A shot of her and her mother together at Scott's eighteenth birthday party on the back lawn that last summer—autumn really by then. Her mother beaming out at the camera, as was her way; Lori smiling too, a teenager's grin-and-bear-it smile. Her mother's arm was around her shoulder, bracing her, anchoring her to the spot. If Lori closed her eyes she could still feel the force of that hold, smell Pam's soapy scent, the mineral whiff of wine on her breath.

Lori used the photo like a knife in the same way that those who cut themselves might use a blade. The image held a visceral force that was completely overwhelming. In her first years away from home she employed it continually, often in the company of alcohol and pot. A tool in the constant roundabout of self-loathing and depression; the thing that could flick her out of numbness. The risk-taking adrenaline rushes of graffiti and skateboarding might have made her feel alive, but this plunged her deep into another sensation: the rawness of grief. It was, for a long time, the ultimate emotional trigger. When Jason arrived on the scene, the photo, time-worn now, had already lost a good deal of its potency, just as the drugs and alcohol, already then receding, had virtually disappeared too. But it was still there, at the back of one of her old notebooks, ready if she needed it. Not just to inflict pain but to remind her that she once did have that life. That it had been real.

In her pocket her phone buzzed. She pulled it out. A text from Anselma. *No worries. Talk whenever. Look forward to it. XX* It was late, she saw from the time on the phone, and she had to be up early. She picked up her cup and rinsed it in the sink, wiped down the bench, surveyed the kitchen, satisfied that the place was tidy enough. She thought of their old kitchen at home. Her mother's kitchen, really, it was so much her domain. Sixties cupboards painted a soft teal, a stainless steel sink and bench. Her mother had taken such good care of it, never complained about it being ancient, there being no dishwasher, not enough bench space or storage. Lori loved that kitchen. In her mind's eye that was the heart of her childhood, there at the kitchen table, with the back door open and a breeze blowing in through the flywire. A view out across the timber decking to the lawn, and beyond that the fruit trees tucked into the corner and then the bigger gums on the back road outlined against a clouded blue sky. If her dad was home he might have Led Zeppelin booming out in the background, one of the rock anthems he loved, the soundtrack to her childhood. This kitchen, her own kitchen, had everything she needed. She'd designed it, made it hers. But it wasn't the same. If they had to move tomorrow, she wouldn't pine for its polished boards and marble benchtops, its glass splashback and stainless steel appliances. If she could trade it in for the old model, if that could bring them all back to life, she'd do it in a heartbeat.

July 1993

Northam

The line of light around the edges of the curtains was all Des Robinson was aware of in the dim room when he opened his eyes. He wasn't used to waking here in daylight, or at least this broad midday kind of daylight. It was all wrong, not just the light but the warmth in the room. At this time of the year it was ordinarily freezing when he got up. He rarely found himself in bed after seven am. On occasion after a late night he might sleep in an hour or two longer, but to sleep through the day like this was not only unusual but discombobulating. It took him some moments to get his bearings, to understand the heaviness that pervaded his brain.

Waking like this reminded him of his childhood, of being an invalid, having to stay in bed for months with some illness or other. He thought it might have been polio. Or perhaps TB. He wasn't sure anymore and would never find out now. His parents and his only brother were long dead, all family knowledge gone with them. Whatever it was, this illness, it had laid him low for a long time, he did remember that. He'd spent endless days staring at the ivy-papered walls in his bedroom and then later in his parents' room, where his mother had installed him because it was closer to the living areas when it had become apparent he wouldn't be recovering quickly. The paper in their room was prettier, floral, stripes of pink entwined with red roses, but it was older too, the seams gaped open in places and its edges yellowed where the sun hit. He hated wallpaper. When they'd moved here Mary couldn't understand why he'd insisted on painting the whole house inside and not wallpapering. He didn't insist on much, but no wallpaper was one thing he was clear about. Idiosyncratic, Mary had said he was. That's a big word for a Greek girl, he'd teased, and she'd given him a filthy look and said it was a Greek word, but that was something that was clearly lost on the ignorant son of an illiterate coalminer.

He got out of bed and pulled back the curtains. The vast windows looked down on the street but also allowed, not unlike the police station just up the road, a panoramic view of the town right across to the hills on the far side of the new estate across the river. It was a handsome and rather modern house, one that had seemed entirely improbable to him when he'd first seen it in the summer of 1970. The place had been designed by an architect, almost certainly the only house in Northam at that time to have been, and had been owned by the town's doctor, a man who had come to live out his life in the mountain air but had decided after six years to move back to civilisation. Sometime in those six years he had built the house, which Des had thought must have been an attempt by the man to create something closer to his heart in this town, to make his own place there. In the end it only served to amplify his difference. After a protracted fight with council to have it built, difficulties finding builders to erect it and the sneers of many of the townsfolk, the doctor seemed to have thrown his arms up in despair and left. Des never met him. He'd departed before Des and Mary arrived and the town had continued to search for a doctor for the best part of a year before a new one appeared.

Des and Mary had inspected the house on their second day in Northam. It wasn't the sort of place he'd ever thought about, but devoid of furniture, all he could see were the generous angular rooms and the wonderful views. He fell in love. 'Fantastic place for kids,' he'd said, turning to Mary when they stood in the living room looking out to the hills. She'd laughed. 'Are you counting yourself as one of the kids? Let's have a proper look outside before you get carried away.'

They'd inspected the garden, which Mary conceded would be ideal for growing vegetables. She could see a place for some fruit trees in the far corner. There was enough lawn to drive Des mad with mowing on his days off and a good-sized shed to contain whatever paraphernalia needed to be contained.

'Nothing we'll want for here,' he'd said.

'Furniture? Children?' replied Mary. 'There're a lot of rooms to fill.'

'Well, I know how to fix at least some of that,' Des declared, grabbing Mary around the waist and swinging her in a clumsy tango-esque move.

They'd managed the furniture, eventually. But all the tan-going in the world had not produced offspring. They made some investigations over the years, but Mary didn't want to delve too far. 'It's God's will,' she asserted. 'We have each other. That must be enough for Him.' But Des felt guilty. Mary had come from Greece with her family when she was ten. It had been a wrench for all of them. Another trauma after the war and then the civil war. The hardship of establishing themselves in a new and not always welcoming land. They had expectations for her, one of which was to marry a good Greek boy, a boy who believed in God, their god. They weren't expecting this skinny, freckled, gingery kid, brought up in Gippsland, who'd somehow become a copper. (For them the words 'policeman' and 'respect' did not go hand in hand.) He was neither Greek nor god-fearing. And, as it turned out, probably not fertile either.

Des pulled on some old pants, a shirt and jumper and went into the kitchen. Mary had gone out. Being Saturday morning she'd had a small sleep-in and had only half surfaced as he climbed into bed at eight. When she turned over to check on him he pretended to be asleep. He hadn't been ready to talk then. He was exhausted. He still was, but at least he'd managed a few hours' rest, enough to keep him going. Just. Midday and already he was thinking about the stiff whisky he was going to have before dinner.

In the kitchen he found a packet of cigarettes and made a pot of tea. The local newspaper was on the kitchen table, but nothing about the accident, which had happened too late in the night for it to be reported. He grabbed a jacket and took the paper, a mug of tea and his fags to the back terrace. Flicking away the last of the raindrops, he sat down at the little iron table under a now naked trellis in the patchy sun. He read about the council's decision to grant, despite police objections, a liquor licence to a sports club in town (yet somewhere else to keep an eye on). A proposal to build a new Olympic-sized swimming pool in one of the old factory sites down by the river. The winners of the best scones, cakes and fruitcakes at Nilmkuk Primary's fete. Youth awards across the local high schools. He skimmed the names, alighting only on Melissa Smythe, year twelve Northam High, for sport. Netball. He thought of the girl in the accident and wondered. That poor child wouldn't be playing netball again anytime soon.

Mary's car pulled up at the back gate. He couldn't see her for the tall privet hedge, but he knew the sound of her car, the dull thud of its doors closing. Soon she was on the path, shopping bags in hand. He stood up to come and help her, but she called out, 'Don't worry. There's only this.'

'Tea's probably still warm,' he said, following as she went inside.

He poured her a cup while she put a few items away.

'What a terrible night,' she said.

'You heard?'

'Pat Mills down at the bread shop. She knows the Friars. Their boy.'

'Hmm.'

She shook her head as if it were all beyond belief. 'Just the one boy?'

'One fatality. One of the girls was pretty badly hurt. Don't know how she'll go.'

'Kids.' Her tone was neutral, but he knew she meant that they were just kids. Not grown yet. One dead. The others injured in ways obvious and not so obvious. That this was a tragedy of the most banal kind, one that had played out many times before, so much so that they had a shorthand between them now, an understanding. She never launched in with concern after he'd attended an accident like this. She'd learned that over the years. She knew he needed time to unwind, unfurl his emotions, or at least those he could deal with showing. He didn't want any fuss.

'You managed to get a bit of sleep?'

'Enough.'

She cut some bread, put out cheese and ham. They sat down at the table.

'You saw the family?'

He looked at the food. He wasn't sure if he was ready to eat. 'Do you know the Druitts?'

'I've heard of them. About them. They live over on the estate, don't they?'

'Yeah, moved here a few years ago. Two boys.' He looked at his plate. 'One now. They've been hit for a six.'

'So awful.'

'It was odd, though. He was waiting for me last night, their old man. Like he knew I was coming. It was coming. Standing there in the rain outside his house. There was this strange calm about him when I told him. It was very unusual.'

'The shock.'

'Everyone's different. I can still be surprised by that.'

'I've heard they're slightly strange.'

'What? The Druitts?'

'Mmm. They're a bit—' she searched for a word '—aloof. Don't mix.'

Des rubbed his chin, considered her description. 'Could be. They, well, I should say he, might be described in other ways as well. Intense was one word I've heard used. Rigid was another. I can't say I'm not concerned about him.'

'How so?'

'He wanted to know a lot of details about the accident. Who was there. Who was driving interested him most. I saw a look cross his face that made me worry a little.'

'He's angry. That's more than understandable.'

'It's usually the helplessness I see first. That initial shock, people break down, or they're numb. Takes a while for anger to kick in. I think anger, cold anger, might always be with that man, a permanent part of his personality.' Des took a bite of his sandwich, chewed slowly.

'Who was driving?' Mary asked after a minute.

'Mick and Pam Green's boy, Scott. Little Loren was there too, in the car. Although she's not little now really. Sixteen.'

'Oh lord. Did you see them?'

'Mick and Pam? I met them at the hospital. The boy was in surgery. He'll be all right.'

Mary sighed and looked out the window to the back garden. 'Sometimes I think we were blessed not to have children,' she said.

Des didn't reply. He wanted to say that love and pain were inseparable companions, but he didn't want to sound like a sanctimonious git, even to his wife who already knew him for one. But it would have seemed condescending too, and he didn't want that either. To his mind, Mary was essentially the most sensible woman he knew, but her adherence to religion still puzzled him after all these years. Her idea that there was some divine plan made him shake his head in wonder. God was important to her, he was like the other man in their relationship, in the background, never mentioned. Or perhaps, as Des had considered more than once, it was the other way around and that he himself was the other man, living in a permanent state of sin with a woman already wedded to Christ. Whatever it was, Des never talked about God with Mary. He knew that he might say something he could never take back. He might shout at her and tell her that he couldn't believe in a god who would allow the kind of suffering he had seen last night. What was the point of life for it to be thrown away almost as soon as it had begun? What was the bloody point?

Des looked at his half-eaten sandwich. Food had definitely not been a good idea.

'You should go back to bed,' Mary offered.

'No, the sun's out. I might pull some weeds out of the garden.' The truth was that he didn't want to pull out weeds. He'd much rather go to bed, but the time just before sleep was always the worst, images would come to him, movies playing on the membrane of his closed eyelids. He'd prefer to have to go through that just once in a day, not twice. And with luck tonight he'd be so dog-tired he'd drop off quickly and not be afflicted. He never told Mary about this. He never told her anything much about the scenes he had to attend. The road accidents, the suicides, the tractor deaths, the drownings, the occasional homicide. He had it good compared to many of his city counterparts, he knew that. A country cop's life was not usually as confrontational. He could go for months—once a whole year—without having to see something so terrible it would not leave him for days or weeks after. Over time he learned strategies for dealing with the flashes and the afterimages. He learned to switch his mind into another mode. But try as he would, he couldn't do it immediately. It was like a process, where with each assault he would have to relive what happened any number of times before it could be—he didn't want to say filed away—managed to some extent. Mary played a role in this. Her not knowing every little thing made it easier. He saw her as an unsullied part of his life, a neutral zone that he could come back to, find comfort in. Sometimes she'd look at him in an uncomprehending way and it did cross his mind that perhaps he wasn't being fair to shut off this part of himself from her. But surely it would be cruel to inflict the details of his job, to have her imagine what he saw, to have her thinking about it all too.

He remembered realising when he was about twelve that his own father had served in World War II. He would never have known if it hadn't been for a school project provoking the inquiry. His dad didn't go to the RSL or attend dawn services. When Des asked him about it he'd said it was better to put the past behind you, to always look forward, to focus on the better part of human nature and not the worst. Des was fairly certain army life had been more traumatic for his father than police life was for him (he'd never been shot at, never spent days dug into a tiny piece of ground not knowing if he'd make it out alive, never seen his friends die beside him), but he took his father's view as a template for himself. When he attended his first death—and he remembered it still, a dilapidated paint-flaking house in Malvern, an old woman dead a good few weeks—it was 1964. The bloke he'd gone in with was a senior constable a few years older who'd been around the block a few times. He didn't laugh when Des threw up in the kitchen, unable to get out of the house quickly enough to puke outside. But he did tell him that he'd get used to it, would start to see it as it was. The end of life. Nothing more or less. After their shift he took him back to his place for a beer (in the days of six o'clock closing) and they drank themselves stupid, while his wife cleaned up in the kitchen and took herself off to bed. Des fell asleep on the senior constable's couch and woke up in the morning to the faces of two small children staring intently at him and shouting to their mother that there was a strange man in the living room. She came in and unsmilingly offered him bacon and eggs.

'What will happen?' Mary's voice came to him as though from a distance. He wondered for a moment if he'd blacked out but Mary's face didn't betray any concern, or at least not for him.

'You mean to Scott Green? I'm pretty sure he'll be charged with culpable driving. Depends on whether he pleads guilty or not as to whether there's a court case. Mostly they get a prison sentence. A few years.'

'For a life. A few years for a life?'

'A year. Two. Could be up to twenty. But these boys were best friends. Scott Green will carry the burden of guilt forever, however long he spends in prison. If anything I think he might welcome it. A real punishment. Something concrete.'

'You really think so?'

'I know it. I've seen it before. I'll see it again. These moments of madness that lead to a lifetime of . . . regret, to put it mildly. Boys like Scott Green want to be punished. Remember Glenn Gannon?'

'Lord, Des. He killed himself, didn't he?'

Des got up and took his plate to the bench, looked out at the garden. It was only at times like these that he thought about retiring. When the prospect of a simple life doing simple activities seemed overwhelmingly attractive. He'd wondered sometimes if he'd stay in this town after he left the force, and he and Mary had discussed the idea but had decided they'd probably stay put. More than twenty-five years he'd been here, seen all sorts of comings and goings. He wasn't sure he could claim to have a lot of close friends, but Mary was well in with the community. In their own ways they both belonged here now. And they had each other. He couldn't imagine living somewhere else, but he also couldn't quite imagine what it would be like to live here and not be the local copper. Who would he be when he retired? What would he do?

In another ten years he may not even care. A lot of water could pass under the bridge between now and then. If there was anything he knew it was that he was no seer. The constant in life was the unpredictability of human nature. It was what made him love and hate his job in the same breath.

July 1993

Northam

P am woke in a sweat. She'd dreamed that she was being strangled. It wasn't clear who her assailant was, but she had a sense that it might have been a demon or a spirit rather than a person. She could feel the weight of the thing upon her, exerting all its force into extinguishing hers, pulling a tight band around her throat. When she opened her eyes she felt a sudden surge of buoyancy, a rising up, as though she could levitate off the bed. Her heart thumped fit to bursting.

It was still dark and it took her a few seconds to get her bearings, remember she was at home in her own bed. She lay panting, feeling the relief. Then a seeping heaviness. She tilted sideways to check the time. Six-thirty. She was surprised that she'd slept at all, let alone so long. It seemed absurd that she'd been able to, but she'd been so exhausted the night before that as soon as she'd eaten she'd hauled herself off to the bedroom— where the bed was still a mess from the morning—and fallen promptly into a torpid slumber. It was extraordinary the way the body demanded a level of normality, asked that day-to-day life be kept ticking over even under duress. That you continued to take part in those acts that kept you alive, nourished your body and soul (eating, sleeping, conversing), when death lay so close. She'd felt the same way when her mother died. How in the days that followed her death and burial Pam watched the world pass by in a blur, people going about their business just as they always did. Her included. Functioning in the most mundane of ways: washing, cooking, getting the kids off to school. Yet inside she'd been rendered in stone, ossified with grief.

When Pam's mother, Marjorie, had been diagnosed with cancer at the age of fifty-five, Pam felt as though the bottom had been torn from her world, as though nothing would ever be right, that no fact could ever be trusted again. After four years of treatments, of hope and then hopes dashed, Marjorie died and Pam came to the profound realisation that nothing *would* ever be right again. Marjorie was not what you would call an easy personality. She was old-fashioned (born just after World War I, the child of Victorian-era parents), middle-class, snobbish to some degree, and not given to displays of affection or effusion. But she was her mother; her constant, her compass. And then she was not. Pam saw in a blinding flash that for most of her life she had been living in a fantasy of existential constancy. She had never really believed that anyone close to her would die and leave her alone, at least until some point in the far distant future. Marjorie's illness had been a shock, but at least the unceasing concern for her mother had given Pam purpose. Her death though had left nothing but a huge gaping hole.

For a long time afterwards Pam was unable to make sense of it at all. This wasn't what was supposed to happen. Her grand plan of life (in reality more of a loose sketch, but still an expectation) had gone seriously off script. A few years before, a woman she knew had lost her husband (suicide) and her mother (stroke) within a few months of each other. Pam thought about this fact a great deal after Marjorie's death, prayed every day for a good year or so that she wouldn't lose anyone else she loved anytime soon. The idea of Mick or one of the kids dying filled her with a terrible anxiety; more than that, a bottomless ennui. She couldn't imagine how it would be possible to bear this terrible pain times two. How could anyone survive? Amazingly, the woman she knew had survived. Pam didn't know how; she didn't know her well enough to interrogate her, uncover the details. But then, she mused, there was survival and survival. A vast difference between existing and thriving, something often impossible to see from the outside. Some people were good actors, and perhaps that was the secret. Perhaps that was what resilience really was?

Next to her Mick lay snoring, testament no doubt to the beers he'd drunk the evening before. He hadn't thought he'd be able to sleep without the aid of alcohol. She on the other hand hadn't thought she'd be able to sleep if she imbibed, and she speculated briefly if she could ever drink again. The taste of alcohol seemed repulsive to her, but the idea of what it did still held an attraction. She pulled herself out of bed without turning on the light so she didn't wake him. She didn't know if he'd fallen asleep quickly last night or had lain awake for hours. He needed rest either way. So did she. But now she was awake she knew she wouldn't go back to sleep; the dream demon had put paid to that.

Slipping on her dressing-gown and slippers she went out into the hallway, closing the bedroom door behind her. In the hall she turned on the light and quietly opened Loren's door. The room felt cold and curiously silent. A tiny trill of apprehension ran through her. She tiptoed to the bed and stood stock-still, hoping to catch and then hearing the faint sounds of her daughter's breathing. There was just enough light in the room to see her shape in the bed, her hair pooling darkly across the pillow, her hands balled against her cheeks. 'My poor darling,' whispered Pam, resisting the temptation to reach down and touch her.

In the kitchen she turned on the heater and put on the kettle. Through the curtainless kitchen windows she registered that the sky had lightened fractionally. In another half hour or so she would be able to see the sun rise above the slope behind the house. It could have been just any other Sunday (although on most Sundays she was not up this early). It could have been an ordinary day in which she was looking forward to doing the kinds of things she usually did on the weekend: baking, gardening, having friends over for lunch, reading a book on the couch. Instead the day loomed before her—as though it were a part of her dream—unknown and threatening, like some monster, its mouth yawning open, waiting to swallow her whole.

The day before felt both distant and vivid. It too had failed to fit the weekend template and instead of shopping, cleaning and the yoga classes she'd been attending of late, she had passed the day waiting at the hospital. Some of the time spent with Loren in A and E, some spent on the ward with Scott post-surgery. She recalled almost every detail of the day and suspected that in years to come vignettes, whole scenes even, would stay with her, play out in her mind. The perspective she had of the room where she sat, the view from the windows out across the blue-green mountains. The odours of disinfectant and starched sheets, the feel of the stiff fabric under her fingers. A moment in the hallway when the surgeon who'd operated on Scott had said, 'There could be ongoing problems with the ankle, arthritis later in life.' Her noticing how the silver stubble on Des Robinson's face contrasted with the golden hairs on the back of his freckled hand as he spooned the sugar into her coffee cup.

When the registrar had given Loren the green light to go home, Pam's father, Jim, had come and picked them up. Mick was going to stay on with Scott, make sure he was settled for the night before he left. Pam and her dad had hardly spoken as they'd driven back. She was grateful that he wasn't a chatterer, didn't have the need to talk to fill up space. He'd only asked the basic questions when she'd phoned him from the hospital. There wasn't much more to say, or at least that's how she felt, exhausted from a day that seemed to have gone on forever. She suspected that he was more than a little shocked himself at what had happened and at Loren's state, and could sense it was better to stay silent in her presence.

At home Pam had made tea and assembled some food: a couple of corned beef sandwiches, biscuits, slices of lemon cake she'd made a few days before. She and her father had sat at the kitchen table while Loren burrowed in with her plate on the couch, staring mindlessly at the last few minutes of a Collingwood–Hawthorn game on television. The steady murmur of the commentary drifted between the rooms. Only the occasional excited outburst or the roar of the fans told her that one side or the other had momentarily triumphed. She was sure Loren had no idea at all of the state of the game. Even under normal circumstances she never cared much for football.

Pam glanced over at her father who seemed intent on his cup.

'It's a terrible, terrible shame. I liked that boy,' he said finally, not moving his eyes.

'He was a really nice kid.' Pam tried to sound neutral, at arm's length somehow. She hoped she wasn't going to cry. She seemed to have avoided it for most of the day and she knew her father would disapprove, as he did with all displays of emotion. He'd been almost unbearable in his stoicism (denial) when her mother died. His seeming bewilderment that there was anything he (or anyone else) should be upset about was corrosive. She knew it was his way of managing, but she'd felt it as a wilful dismissal of her, and her feelings. There was a part of her that found it hard to forgive him for this.

'You know, if Scott wants to come and stay with me when he gets out of hospital, he's more than welcome.' She was taken aback by this offer for a moment and felt passingly guilty about her negative thoughts. Perhaps in her stressed state, she had been doing him a disservice. Or perhaps he didn't think she and Mick were capable of dealing with the situation.

'He's got his studies to finish, Dad.'

'He might not though, might he?'

She looked at him. 'I don't want to think about that right now. There's going to be a lot to deal with.'

He gave her a tight smile. 'I don't envy you the months ahead. There'll be an investigation. Possibly a court case.'

She stared past his shoulder to the wall and a framed photo of Broulee beach on the south coast of New South Wales, where she and Mick used to take their holidays when the kids were young. They hadn't been there for years. She'd loved the place: the vast expansive beach, the scattered collection of old wooden houses unspoiled by development. Hours spent on building sandcastles, bodysurfing, beach cricket. The photo showed the five of them, a lopsided pyramid, with Mick holding Loren on his shoulders, flanked by her and the boys, everyone laughing at something: a joke, the wonder of being on the beach unencumbered, free to do whatever they liked. They'd never intended not to return, but one summer they just didn't. Funny how things come to pass.

'Thanks for bringing us home, Dad,' she had said as civilly as she could, standing up and gathering the cups from the table. 'I need to get onto a few things now.'

Behind her he'd cleared his throat as she put the dishes in the sink, but she didn't turn around until she heard the scrape of his chair.

'Keep me informed, won't you?' he'd said at the back door. 'We probably should talk to Hugh.'

Pam had stood in the kitchen gazing distractedly at the cups in the sink and the plate on which she'd eaten her sandwich. Three chocolate biscuits sat on a torn biscuit packet on the bench. Callous or not, he was right, her father. It was all a shock now, but soon they'd have to drag themselves out of that state for long enough to organise legal representation; whatever it was that had to be done for Scott. The fact that this wasn't something they could simply put behind them made her feel sick. This—this point they were at now—was only the beginning.

She thought about this again now in the almost-light of the morning as the kettle boiled. Organising practicalities. The first being to check the answering machine; she had a vague recollection of the phone ringing last night. In the hallway she saw its light blinking urgently off and on in the darkness. She flicked on the light, pressed the message button and listened. Five calls from friends, neighbours, wanting to know if the kids were all right, if she and Mick were all right, before Cathy's familiar voice, clear and resonant, a little audio beacon in an ocean of static. 'Call me any time,' she said. 'I don't care if it's two in the morning.' After that, a final message, largely indecipherable: muffled voices, loud cries of what seemed to be laughter. 'Jesus,' she said, and pressed erase.

She would have taken Cathy up on her offer but Mick got up then, woken by the light, the messages playing on the machine, his own internal agitation. He appeared in the hallway in his pyjamas, the same set he'd worn the night before to greet the young policeman. Pam thought absently that she should put them in the washing machine. Then she thought she might burn them. She would never be able to look at those blue and white stripes again without replaying the scenes of Friday night in her mind. She followed him into the kitchen and flicked the kettle on again, dragging another mug out of the cupboard.

'I didn't hear you come to bed,' she said.

'Read the paper. Turned in about midnight.'

'That was late.'

He'd sat down at the table and she went over to him and wrapped her arms around his head, pressing him to her, his nose between her breasts. He put his arms around her hips, and she said, 'Will we ever get over this?'

She could feel his head nodding against her ribs. Was that yes or no? One of those indeterminate head waggles that signified neither. The unknown.

Then a sound from behind them. 'Mum.'

Pam whipped around, embarrassed in the way that parents are in front of children, embarrassed for their intimacy at a time like this. Loren stood in the doorway, wearing yesterday's t-shirt. Barelegged and bedraggled, hair a bird's nest of clumps and starbursts. She hadn't had a shower before she'd collapsed into bed, for which Pam felt ashamed. She should have been more attentive, cleaned her daughter up last night. But then she hadn't even succeeded in it herself, only managing to pull off her clothes, dump the mess on the floor and slide on a nightie. This morning she was aware of her skin, grainy and greasy, her underarms clammy. She pulled her dressing-gown close and said, 'You want a cup of tea?'

Loren shrugged in acquiescence, then sat down at the table opposite Mick. Pam went up to the bedroom and fetched Loren's dressing-gown, returned and draped it over her shoulders. 'It's cold,' she said, feeling it necessary to explain her actions. She poured another tea and placed it in front of Loren, who was running her finger over the pattern on the tablecloth as if she had just discovered a secret Braille message in its folds.

'Should I go to school tomorrow?'

Pam and Mick exchanged glances. Mick's pallid face barely registered any expression, but Pam knew what he was thinking regardless, could sense his momentary panic.

'There is no school tomorrow, sweetheart. It's the holidays,' he said, keeping his voice even and low.

She looked blankly at Mick as though what he said hadn't sunk in. 'There'll be a funeral.'

'Yes,' said Pam. 'In a few days, I imagine.'

'We'll have to go, won't we?' said Loren, her mouth twisting in uncertainty. 'But I don't think I want to go. I . . .'

'You don't have to go,' said Mick.

Loren shook her head. 'Everyone from school will be there. I don't want to have to see them. See anyone.'

They sat silently for a moment. Pam got up again and started to put out breakfast food. Cereal, milk, tinned fruit, some bowls and spoons.

'Do you want the shower first?' Pam asked Loren. 'We need to head off soon.'

'What? Head off where?'

'Back to the hospital. For Scott.'

Loren straightened in her chair. 'I'm not going back to the hospital,' she said, a note of panic in her voice. 'I can't go there.'

Pam opened her mouth then closed it again. On reflection it seemed quite understandable that the hospital would be the last place that Loren would want to be. 'I'm sorry, darling. Of course you can stay here.'

Mick didn't seem as certain. 'What about Scott? He might do with your company.'

Loren shook her bent head twice, a swatch of her hair swayed from side to side in front of her face, obscuring her expression.

Pam held her hand out to silence Mick who she could sense was about to speak again. 'Listen, I can call Cathy and get her to come over and stay with you.'

Her head shot up. 'I don't need babysitting.'

'You don't have to talk to Cath. I just think you need some company.'

'I want Katie to come over then. I can call her.'

Mick interjected. 'Si's coming down today. Said he'd leave earlyish. I reckon he'll be here about lunchtime.'

Pam turned to Mick. 'You didn't tell me.'

'Sorry.'

'No, I'm not bagging you. I mean, I'm glad he's coming. God, glad—I don't know if that's the word. It will be good to see him.' Although perhaps not so good for him to see them, she thought, trying to imagine what it would be like for him to walk into this mess.

'Maybe we can play tag team till then?' Mick suggested.

'Hmm,' she grunted in reply.

———

Scott was sitting up in bed when she arrived, his plastered leg elevated, gazing out the window. His room had a view over the car park and Pam thought he had probably seen her pull up, watched her get out of the car, clumsily juggling her basket and the flowers she'd brought from the garden while locking the door. Nothing new. Her children had scrutinised her from an early age, made comments on the way she did things, the way she looked. Her little foibles. She had no doubt they knew her body and its movements better than she did herself. It never ceased to amaze her how observant they could be, yet in the same breath how oblivious. One moment noticing, the next ignoring. If she chose to hide things from them they were easily diverted. But of course, not always. The thing was, one never really knew what they may or may not pick up on. She was glad she'd never had anything more to hide than the occasional chocolate bar. No gambling addictions. No lovers in the wardrobe.

'Did you see me coming?' she asked.

'What?' He looked at her blankly. His mind had clearly been elsewhere.

She smiled. 'How's the ankle?'

'I've had lots of painkillers. I think that's helped. Kinda feels all right. You by yourself?'

'Your dad's stayed home to keep an eye on Loren. Simon'll get in at lunchtime. They'll probably come over then.'

'What's the story with Loz? Why didn't she come?'

'Oh, I don't know.' She paused, unsure how to go on. 'I think she's still in shock. After yesterday. I don't believe she can bear to be here. It's very, very hard for her.'

'You mean she's not coming at all?'

Pam wasn't sure if she was imagining her son's eyes glistening. She sat on the bed beside him and put her hand on his shoulder.

'Some of us can't fucking bear being here either, but we don't get a choice about it,' he said, his voice thick.

'A terrible thing has happened,' she said slowly.

'You don't think I noticed? Jesus.'

Scott didn't do bitter or sarcastic. It was a shock to hear him snap. Not that she was about to blame him, lord no, but the contrast with his usual sanguine self appeared so marked that she could have been talking to someone else. When she'd spoken to him yesterday he'd still been a little groggy and disoriented from the anaesthetic. He'd rambled like an old drunkard, and some of what he'd said hadn't made any kind of sense. Under the strain, her stable, constant, sunny-natured son seemed to have veered between two characters, neither of whom she'd ever glimpsed before.

'I want to see her.' He shook his head quickly and looked up to the ceiling. 'I need her to help me . . . talk to me . . . I . . .'

Pam shifted her arm around him and pulled herself closer so that their shoulders and upper arms pressed together. 'I don't think she can help anyone at the moment, sweetie. I don't think she understands anything herself.'

'It feels like a nightmare. It feels like I should wake up and everything is back to normal. It's so fucking terrible.'

'Shh.' Pam squeezed him tight, as though physical proximity could remedy his pain. (Only a mother could be so arrogant.) But this time he responded and leaned back into her, his head dropping on her shoulder. 'We'll always be here for you, you know. No matter what. Always.'

'I know, Mum,' he said. 'But . . .'

'It doesn't change a thing. I understand that. Still, here we are.' So trite, she thought. The script of life. A thousand clichés strung in a row like fairy lights to signpost the way. And yet what other words could she utter that would be more apt, more true? There was certainly nothing she could say to erase any of it, which is all she really wanted to be able to do. The only thing that could have made a difference.

After a while she took the flowers, a small bunch of camellias from one of the trees at home, and went to see if she could find a vase. She was hoping to find a doctor along the way as well, someone who could tell her how long Scott would have to stay in hospital. She returned to the room a few minutes later with a glass jar but no answers to find a policeman, his back to her, standing over Scott.

'Can I help you?' she asked.

The officer turned. He was from State Highway Patrol. A tall, heavy man, with moist red lips. Senior Constable Highett, he told her. Here to take a statement. 'You're the mother, I'm assuming.'

'I thought you took a statement yesterday morning?'

'We didn't have enough time before surgery. Just the basics. Got the tests done.'

'Tests?'

'Drugs. Alcohol.'

'And what did they show?'

'Results aren't back yet. Tuesday, Wednesday, we should know.' He addressed Scott again. 'Okay, as I was saying, I'm going to ask you a few questions. My colleague Constable Smit will be here soon with a tape recorder.'

Pam drew closer to the bed, her face lined up near Highett's. 'Should he have a lawyer?'

Highett took a slight step backwards, keeping eye contact as he did. 'It's an option. As are you.'

'I'm an option?' She could feel her cheeks smart as though she'd been slapped.

'He's over eighteen,' Highett continued blithely. 'He can make that decision, about who's here.'

'It's okay, Mum,' said Scott who had glanced up at his mother and could see the anger in her eyes. 'I'm just going to tell them what happened. I don't need a lawyer. I want you to stay though.'

'I wasn't planning on going anywhere,' she said sharply. Then turning back to Highett, 'Are you going to charge him with something?'

'No, we have to interview everyone at the scene. Look at the forensics. It takes a while for us to put a case together.'

'A case?'

'There has been a death, Mrs—' he glanced down at the folder in his hand '—Green. In all likelihood there will be charges. First we have to determine what happened.'

Still holding the jar of flowers, Pam walked to the other side of the bed and placed them on the bedside table. She leaned over, squeezed Scott's hand and sat down in a throne-like green vinyl chair by the window, a kernel of anger still simmering inside her. She stared at Highett as he flicked through some papers and pulled one of two smaller chairs closer to the bed on the other side.

Soon a second police officer came in, younger and friendlier-faced than Highett, with a folder, a pad, a small tape recorder and a couple of pens. 'Hello,' he said, smiling first at Scott then Pam.

'Smit,' said Highett by way of introduction.

Smit put the paraphernalia down on the small table and Highett looked over at Pam. 'As I said, you can be in the room, but you will have to remain silent during the interview.'

Pam stared at Highett and wished she had the power of the evil eye. He really was so bloody rude.

'Right,' Smit said, leaning down and pushing the record button. 'Ready to roll.' He recited the day and time and Scott's full name and read him his rights.

'Tell me about where you were that night,' said Highett.

'We were at a party just out of town. Raki Parry's place. We were there until about one in the morning.'

'Who's we?'

'Me and my mates. Troy,' Scott's voice faltered, 'Mike, Josh Friar, Tom Pickering. Some girls. Katie, Julie, Melissa, my sister. There were a few people there.'

Highett made him repeat all the names in full before continuing. 'All right. What about before the party?'

'I was at home. We had dinner.'

'You were drinking there?'

'Yeah, I had a couple of stubbies.'

'So you left your parents' house and went straight to the party?'

'We went to the Northam pub bottle shop and bought some beer.'

'And you supplied some of this to minors?'

Scott hesitated for a moment. 'Yeah, I guess I probably did.'

'What about you? In the course of the evening did you consume alcohol or drugs of any kind?'

'Yeah.'

'Can you tell me what and how much?'

'Don't know really. I was mostly drinking tinnies. I can't really say.'

'And drugs?'

'Some spliffs. A few tokes. Not much. Mostly booze.'

'So you might have had a dozen or so cans?'

'Maybe.'

'Over six or so hours.'

'Yeah.'

'And you got in the car at one am to go home.'

'Probably. But we weren't really going home. Just driving around for a while. I had to drop Mike off first.'

'Who was in the car?'

'Me, Troy, Melissa, Josh, Mike and my sister, Loren.'

'There seemed to be some confusion as to why Troy wasn't driving his car, er, utility.'

'He said he was too drunk to drive.'

'And you didn't think you were?'

Scott stared at the cop, bit his lower lip. 'I didn't think about it at all. I felt okay.'

Highett shifted in his seat. 'Orright. So where did you go?'

'Up the back of the hills.'

'Were you driving the whole time?' Smit cut in.

Scott paused then, clearly surprised by this question. 'Ah, no. Mike was driving for a short while. I was giving him a driving lesson on his way home.'

Smit's eyebrows went up. 'I meant did you stop, but okay. Mike was unlicensed I'm assuming. Was Mike intoxicated?'

'I guess. Everyone was. We stopped once 'cause someone needed a piss. Josh, I think.'

'So can you describe the driving you were doing? Were you speeding? Showing off?'

'A bit. Those roads are windy up there. Everyone does it. See how fast you can take a corner. It was a bit of a mix, I guess. Most of the time just cruising.'

'And then you dropped Mike off?'

'Yeah, Mike drove to his place. And then I drove.'

'You seem to remember this all quite clearly.'

'Yeah. I mean, I felt okay. Not blotto. I reckon I remember most of it, but then I wouldn't know if I didn't remember, would I?'

Highett looked at him for a moment. 'All right. So you remember the accident?'

Scott swallowed, exhaled. 'Yeah, most, I think.'

'Can you tell us what led up to the accident?'

'I was going too fast. Not super fast, just, I don't know, too fast at the end. I know that. I got a bit distracted. I think Josh was yelling something. The music was loud. I kind of turned around.' He stopped, a tear slid down his cheek. 'Then I went to floor it and the wheels got caught on the gravel. Felt like the car slipped away underneath us. It all happened so fast. And slow too.' He paused. 'There was a scream. I looked back and we were going sideways and then we flipped over and there was this enormous crashing sound. Like an explosion. I can remember everything tumbling over. Stuff falling like in those shaky snowdome things. Then it was super quiet. The engine stopped. The music stopped. But there was moaning.' He took several breaths, stared down towards his legs. 'Oh god.'

'Take your time,' said Smit gently.

'It was Melissa. I couldn't really see her. Like the car had collapsed between us. Steam or smoke or something rising around us. And I thought, I have to get out, but I realised then my foot was trapped. I couldn't move. I think I called out for Loz or Troy. I don't know exactly.'

Pam looked over at the two cops. They were both taking notes. Highett seemed strangely unmoved, but Smit's face betrayed his sympathy, or perhaps his inexperience.

'You managed to get out of the car?' asked Highett.

'I think Josh opened my door, tried to pull me out, but then he saw my leg.'

'You were wearing a seatbelt?'

'Yeah. I'm pretty sure.'

'But not everyone was?'

'I really don't know.'

'Not Troy Druitt.'

Scott made a small animal sound.

'He was thrown out of the car.'

'I didn't see him. Loren found him. I didn't see that. I heard her screaming. I was stuck and Josh tore his shirt off and wrapped it around my leg because of the blood. And he kept saying, 'Just stay calm, man.' He was helping Mel too. I think I passed out because there's some bits there I can't really remember. I do remember him telling me that he thought Troy was dead. I didn't believe him. He was just saying something in the car. Yelling something. He was so alive. He couldn't be dead.'

'What was Troy yelling at you, Scott?' asked Smit.

'I don't know.'

'Was he yelling at you to slow down, perhaps?' asked Highett.

'Maybe, maybe. I just don't know.'

'So you remained partially trapped in the car for some time?'

'I don't know how long. It felt like forever, but it also seemed like you guys, or the ambos, got there quick.'

Smit spoke again. 'You were lucky the neighbours heard the crash, called triple zero. That road might have been deserted till daybreak.'

'Didn't make any difference though, did it?' Scott sobbed. 'Troy died. I killed him straight up. There was never any hope for him.'

Pam heard herself utter a tiny cry, but neither of the officers nor Scott appeared to have heard.

Smit leaned forward. There was sympathy in his voice. 'But you and Melissa survived. That might not have happened if you'd had to wait two or three hours.'

Scott looked away, over Pam's shoulder out the window. 'Is Melissa going to be all right? Do you know? I asked the nurse here but she said she was at Goulburn Valley, and they didn't know anything.'

'She's been transferred to the Royal Melbourne now,' said Smit. 'She's undergoing some fairly major surgery.'

Scott made a gagging sound, his bottom lip shook. 'I didn't want any of this. I'm so sorry. So sorry.'

'I know, mate,' said Smit. 'No one wants anything like this to happen. It's no good for anyone. We don't like it either, to have to attend things like this. See you guys all beaten up.'

Pam realised Smit must have been there that night. Des Robinson had told her that Highway Patrol had reached the scene first.

'Well, I think that's about it for now,' said Highett after a short silence.

'You have anything more to add, Scott?' asked Smit.

Scott pinched his lips together and shook his head.

'Interview ended eleven-fifteen am.' Smit leaned forward and clicked off the tape.

Highett looked over to Pam. 'We'll be in touch in the next few days.'

Pam stared at him vacantly. 'Will you need to talk to him again?'

'At some point. But we need to interview your daughter. Apparently she wasn't in any state yesterday.' For the first time a small smile passed over his lips. She wasn't sure if it was sympathy or schadenfreude.

Pam hadn't been thinking about Loren. But of course she would have to be interviewed too, have to tell the police about her brother. Have to relive the whole event. After the police left, she got up from her chair, perched on the edge of the bed and put her arm around Scott again. After a moment he collapsed onto her shoulder and she held him close, like she did when he was a child, and felt his body heave with dry convulsive sobs.

April 2016

Melbourne

Quin Street was not what she had expected. In her mind's eye she'd thought Scott would be living in a cheap seventies walk-up plonked in the middle of a concrete car park. Instead she found herself facing a discreet block of twenties brown clinker-brick flats, complete with a cottage garden nestled behind a tall black-painted fence. She had walked up from the train station, not wanting to drive and try to find a park in the maze of tiny Prahran streets, and now here she was on the pavement double-checking the number, wondering if she'd got it wrong.

From a few paces away she heard the click of a car door opening. A man in a shapeless grey suit emerged from the driver's side holding a folder. It was clear he was the detective. There was something about the suits they wore, the way they held themselves, that rendered them almost as homogeneous as their uniformed counterparts. She'd had an impression of him from the phone call, imagined him beefy with a buzz cut. But he was lithe. Tall and rangy, with fair hair that fell foppishly to one side. Without the suit he could have passed for a university lecturer or a theatre director. The force had clearly loosened up since the last time she'd had to deal with detectives, a little more latitude than there used to be in the grooming department. Perhaps he too was sporting a tatt under his sleeve.

'Loren Spyker? I'm Detective Sergeant Daniel Levandi from the Major Collision Investigation Unit,' he said, hand outstretched.

She took it and nodded. 'Hello.'

He tilted his head towards the flats. 'Shall we go in?'

In front of them, a block of eight flats. Number eight, Scott's flat, was on the top floor. On the landing outside, Daniel Levandi hunted through an envelope in the folder he was carrying and fished out a key.

Inside nothing was as she had expected. Much of the flat was original, with dark woodwork and cream stucco walls. The living room, first door off the hallway, was furnished with an old deco-style couch and chair, a coffee table and two bookshelves thick with books. Behind the couch, large bevelled-glass doors were permanently opened to the dining room where an old oak table doubled as a desk, with a laptop and a pile of papers at one end. On the far wall a sideboard was stacked along the top with more books, spines out. Another door opened to a small kitchen. Across the hallway, a bathroom and two bedrooms completed the general layout. Apart from an abstract painting in the style of de Kooning above the fireplace in the living room, there was little in the way of decoration. The second room, something of a junk room, although a fairly tidy one, was devoid of ornamentation altogether. The main bedroom held a double bed, some drawers and a framed painting of a mandala. She'd noticed that there were prayer flags over the door to the balcony, and a buddha on a shelf in the dining room as well. She imagined a faint smell of incense lingered in the air.

'Seems like he lives alone,' observed Daniel Levandi coming out of the bathroom. 'No second toothbrush.'

She wondered how expensive it would be for Scott to live here in this part of town. He must have a bit of money. 'Have you found out what he does?' she asked.

'It's one of the things I'd like to establish today. I did manage to track down your uncle, Peter Temple. He hadn't seen Scott for about ten years, and even then briefly. Unfortunately he couldn't tell us anything about Scott's life now. Job, partner, et cetera. Seems no one has really kept in touch.'

Peter. She hadn't thought about him in a long time. 'Is he still in Northam?'

'No, he's on the Sunshine Coast. Said he'd been up there a few years. He was interested to hear about you though. Asked about you, where you were.'

She'd never had a lot to do with her uncle and his family. Her mother and he weren't close and, as a consequence, get-togethers were infrequent. She'd barely seen her cousin, Justine, who'd been sent off to boarding school at twelve. Lori's abiding memory of her now was from those last few months she'd spent in Northam during the summer holidays, at the end of year eleven. She'd been staying at her grandfather's and occasion-ally she'd catch glimpses of her cousin in the distance across the paddocks riding her horse.

'He asked for your address. Said he'd tried to contact you before but hadn't had much luck.'

'All right,' she said slowly.

'Listen, I didn't give your uncle any details about you. We don't do that. Of course, I have his details if you want to contact him.'

She nodded. 'So what do you want me to do here?' She could feel him looking at her, weighing things up.

'Help me look through his effects. See if we can find out anything more about him. Work. Girlfriend. Boyfriend. Whatever.'

'What about the neighbours?'

Levandi laughed. 'You sound like my boss. Neighbours have been contacted. We've left cards for some. I'll check them again when we're done here. Nothing back so far. But that's modern living for you, eh? No one knows their neighbours anymore.'

'I know mine,' she said, sounding unintentionally self-righteous.

He gave her a wry look. 'Impressive. I'm afraid to say I don't. I'm never home.' He sifted through the papers on the table, spreading them out. Bills for power and gas, a rates notice.

'Looks like he owns this place,' he said, pointing at the name on the rates notice.

'Really?' She hadn't expected that. 'He must have been working for a while, built up a bit of security.'

'Was there an inheritance?'

Money. Their money. It wasn't something she'd thought about for a long time. The trust was what her grandfather had called it. When you're twenty-five you can access it, he'd told her, and she'd wondered why on earth she would want to do that. It wasn't until later that she realised he had heart disease. That he'd known for quite some time that he may not last for long and the money he was talking about was his. She had a recollection of receiving a letter once (where exactly had she been living, she couldn't remember now) embossed with what looked like a solicitor's name, and pondering briefly how it had found its way to her before tearing it into small pieces and shoving it in the rubbish bin. Unopened. Undigested.

'We got a bit of money from our parents after they died,' she said finally. 'As for anything else, I really couldn't say. Maybe my grandfather's estate.'

She went to the drawers behind the dining table and pulled them out, one by one. Pencils, paper, notebooks. Daily detritus. But the bottom drawer contained something more substantial. A photo album. She recognised it straightaway. The worn blue vinyl cover. It had been a magnet for her when she was small. She'd often go to the cupboard where it was kept at home and pull it out onto the floor to look through it. Gaze at the images of her mother looking like a princess on her wedding day in her long white frock, a sheath of satin trimmed with lace at the sleeve and neckline. It surprised her that she could still remember most of the photos, their composition and their order on the pages. She hadn't thought about the album for years, yet without opening it she knew the first image was of her mother pinning a white carnation onto her father's lapel. Her parents were standing in the entrance hall at her grandparents' house, the scene framed under its heavy Victorian arch, the dark wooden stairs behind them. Her mother's face was fixed in concentration at the task. Her father gazed at her, an expression which, although it sounded cheesy, could only be described as one of adoration, an expression which Lori had seen in real-life moments between her parents, even in later years. They'd still had that connection. She remembered walking in on them a few days after Troy's death, their arms wrapped around each other in a way that made them look so insular, complete. Her heart had ached suddenly with loss, at the idea she could never have what they had, never be like them. Never be loved.

She took a deep breath. Behind her, she sensed that Daniel Levandi had stopped sorting through papers.

'You found something?' he asked.

'It's my parents' wedding album.' She bent down to get it and another plastic sleeve full of loose photos, and pulled them all onto the table.

'Do you mind?' He tilted his head to indicate he'd like to look at them.

She shrugged indecisively and pushed the album and sleeve along the table towards him, then turned back to the sideboard, grateful in a way that she didn't have to go through the photos just yet. It had taken her by surprise that Scott had the album. She hadn't expected to see photos of her parents, but then she realised there was no one else to take the stuff that had been their life. She wondered what else he had but didn't have the energy to even imagine what might be here, perhaps in some boxes in his spare room, or in a storage facility somewhere.

She hadn't imagined the books on Scott's shelves either. The way they duplicated what she'd read, or attempted to read, over the years. Herman Hesse, James Joyce, Virginia Woolf, Don DeLillo, David Foster Wallace. (A more blokey selection than hers, but a similar vein.) Lined up on the sideboard in front of her were works on Buddhism and comparative religion, sociology and anthropology. Had he gone to university? she wondered. Scanning their spines she noticed small clutches of envelopes pushed between titles. Then, further along the row, a lone letter: a thin envelope in a familiar hand, marked return to sender, which she pushed firmly back in place. She pulled the larger stashes off the shelves and inspected them. There were letters from charities, a superannuation fund; none appeared to have been opened. Clearly nothing that he'd deemed to be urgent. She turned and put them on the table.

Daniel Levandi, diverted from the photos, glanced at them and prodded the superannuation envelope. 'We'll be able to get his workplace through this.' He pushed it to the centre of the table, then motioned his head back to the album, a photo of her parents. 'Your mum and dad look nice.'

Nice. What a useless word that was. A word that said nothing, implied a glossing over. The enamel paint of language. How could nice go anywhere near to explaining who they were, what they were like, their foibles and quirks, their humour and passions? And yet after all this time she wasn't really sure she knew that herself. What they were in her head were pure constructs, half memory, half fabrication. Who they really were was most probably lost forever. Would she like them if she met them now? Would they be friends? Of course, it was ridiculous to think like that. She'd seen from Jason, from other people she knew, that parents were parents. They didn't have to uphold the same values, be anything like their children. They just had to be there for you, and she knew that without a doubt they would have been there for her if they'd had the chance.

'They were,' she replied after a beat. 'They were good people.'

Levandi had pulled photos out of the plastic sleeve and spread them across the table. 'You kids?' he asked.

There was Simon in their backyard, sitting on a banana lounge under an umbrella, reading a book. Next to that, Scott and Troy, bare-chested, arms around each other's shoulders, an unrecognisable car in the background. How heartbreakingly young they looked. Strangely different from the way she remembered them. More childlike, ingenuous, scarcely ready to begin their lives. Her eyes narrowed in on a shot of Scott standing at the table on the back deck cutting a cake, his expression half embarrassed, half attention-seeking. It was his eighteenth birthday party. She recalled how hot it had been that day; the beginning of autumn, but still no sense of respite from the summer heat. Her mum stood to Scott's right, smiling, her face so open and beautiful, so oblivious, as they all were, of what was to come. On his other side, Troy was leaning forward, eyes dark and glowing with mischief, his mouth open, mid-sentence. Was that what he was really like, she thought. Was this that boy?

Daniel put his finger on the photo of Scott and Troy. 'Who is that?'

'Troy Druitt.' She paused, unused to hearing the name, speaking the name. 'He was Scott's best friend.'

'The one who . . .'

'Yeah.'

Levandi looked at the photo for a few more seconds, then shuffled through more. Shots of the party, of her father playing golf. Of her parents at lunch with her grandfather. Faces she hadn't seen for twenty years, spread out like a deck of cards across a gaming table.

'You were close to your mum?' Daniel Levandi rested his fingertips on a photo of the two of them. It was from Scott's party and appeared to have been taken within a few seconds of the photo that she had kept. In this one she and her mother were standing together, but no longer touching. There was a momentum to them, as if they were about to part. They were looking at each other and laughing, something conspiratorial between them. The photographer was further from them now, the distance rendering them smaller in the frame, and she could see Troy in the background, perhaps alerted by the camera (who had been behind it? Simon?) pointed in their direction. She tried to remember. The photos, their provenance, their history. Had she seen this photo before? Had she discarded this one in favour of the one she had kept?

It took her a moment to notice that Daniel had glancingly touched her forearm. 'I apologise,' he said. 'This is clearly very hard for you.'

'Actually, I don't understand why I had to come here.' She was surprised at the sound of her own voice. Irritated, brittle, uncontrolled.

'The thing is, you are his next of kin. You just never know what we might find. You're the only person, it seems, who may be able to give us any clues.'

She turned and faced him, irritated now. 'You did your research. You know what happened to him. To us. You know that and you still want me to say something. I have nothing I can add. I don't know this man. This Scott Green. I haven't seen him for . . . for twenty years.' She moved past the table over to the couch where she had left her bag, and bent forward to pick it up.

'Please,' he spoke calmly, slowly, the way she imagined he'd been taught to deal with an armed offender at police training school, 'I'd really appreciate you waiting a few more minutes, just while I check the last of the drawers, and the spare room.'

She stopped, feeling the momentary heat leave her, and collapsed down on the couch, her back to the detective. She realised she was shaking. Shaking from the outburst, and because of it, because it had actually happened. She didn't do emotions, didn't lose her cool, especially not in front of strangers. A spark of rage, a flood of tears: these were things that made her feel out of control. But if she had been momentarily felled by her feelings, this fact seemed somehow to have gone unnoticed by Daniel Levandi. Behind her she could hear him opening drawers, shuffling through papers, then walking back through the kitchen, into the hallway and what she guessed was the spare room. She opened her bag and checked her phone. No missed calls. She clicked on her emails. Twelve of them. She could see at a glance at least two were to do with work. Work. She'd given it such little attention in the last few days. It had slipped well down the list of life's priorities.

After a minute she went out into the hall. She could hear noises from the far bedroom, shuffling steps, the scraping of cardboard. She stepped back through the door and around the table to the sideboard, where she gingerly picked out the envelope from its temporary hiding place. There it was, her address on the front. 'Return to sender' across it in her handwriting. She went back to the couch and slid it into her bag before making her way to the spare room.

'Detective Levandi,' she said, angling around the door to see him kneeling over a box, flicking through its contents.

He looked up at her distractedly, his concentration broken. 'Daniel.'

'Daniel?'

He smiled. 'Sorry, yes, please call me Daniel.'

'Okay. So, have you found anything?' She paused. 'Daniel.'

'Nothing obvious. There's a bit of paperwork I could go through. Nothing to indicate where he works. So much of that stuff, payslips, contracts, et cetera, is online now. But as I said, I can at least follow that up now with the super info.'

'Are you looking for something else, something more specific?'

He sat back on his haunches, steadied himself against a set of drawers. 'Apart from his work, or people he knows. Yeah, I'm thinking letters. Threats. Anything suspicious that might tie in with this incident.'

She frowned. 'I still don't understand how I can help.'

'It could be that you might recognise a name or something. Some artefact from the past.'

'Artefact from the past? What do you mean? Do you think this was deliberate? That this is tied up with what happened back then? I don't understand.'

'It could well be. We don't believe his injury was an accident.' There was uncertainty in his voice, as though he wasn't sure he should elaborate. 'Listen, a witness has come forward, someone who claims to have seen Scott being followed by a vehicle that night. He might have received a threat. Nothing's clear yet. Once the techs get to look at his computer I'm sure we'll have a few more answers.'

'But, really, this could be anything, couldn't it? It could be a coincidence or he could be involved in something. Some criminal activity. He might know anyone. He could be implicated in god knows what.' The words came out of her mouth in a rush, but as they did she doubted them, thought of the Buddhist images. (Was it stupid to think that Buddhism and criminality cancelled each other out?)

'Sure and, naturally, we will keep an open mind, look into it all.'

'I can't see why anyone would wait for twenty years to punish him all over again?'

'Could be opportunistic. Someone saw him somewhere out of the blue. Unexpected encounter.' He put his hands out in a no-idea gesture. 'You'd be surprised how things go.'

She raised her eyebrows. She felt fairly sure she knew how things went. To hell in a handcart on a routine basis, but this just seemed too left of field. 'Are you thinking it's the Druitts? I really don't believe that. I think they, well . . .' She shrugged. 'The only other people in the car were Josh and Melissa. The accident made her a paraplegic. That might have been a motive. Maybe she came across him and mowed him down in her wheelchair.'

Daniel gave her a stony look, a reaction to her poor taste.

'Really, I just don't think this is an angle. Not now.'

'What about Josh?'

'They were friends. They stayed friends afterwards. Well, for the time I was there. Scott managed to keep most of his friends. People liked him. He was the kind of guy people liked. You know, warm, funny, outgoing.'

'But you didn't stay friends?'

'No. Not us,' she said quietly. 'No, we went our separate ways.'

'So maybe there were other people who didn't stay friends either, after all that went down. Look, I ask these questions because we have to look at everything. It's what we do. It's our job. Sometimes that upsets people, sometimes it might seem stupid, redundant, but we can't not do it. I'm not trying to narrow down the options. I want to be able to rule things out.'

She felt suddenly tired. 'I know. I'm not trying . . . It's just . . .'

In the silence a muffled buzzing came from the living room.

'Your phone?' Daniel asked.

'You've got good hearing,' she said, walking back to her bag.

The voice at the other end of the line was immediately familiar. Rebecca, she said, from intensive care. 'I wasn't sure if you were coming in today.'

For a moment Lori could only hear a silent rebuke, the reminder that she hadn't been there over the weekend. It took several seconds to realise there was a different intent to the call. 'I was planning to come in soon. Is everything all right?'

'Good, good. Things are fine,' said Rebecca. 'I was ringing just in case you *weren't* coming in. I wanted to let you know that things have progressed. Your brother's condition has improved substantially.'

July 1993

Northam

On Monday morning Pam, failing to sleep well, had risen early and formed a firm decision. By just after eight she was driving down Main Street, making her way across town. It was a cool winter's day and a thin mist clung to the nearby hills. On any other occasion she might have noticed the beauty around her, the way the diffuse light rendered the town into a nineteenth century artwork, softened all colour to smudgy layers of monochrome. But today all she could see was the dark bitumen in front of her, preoccupied as she was with what was in her head. Rehearsing what she would say to Ray and Maxine.

She parked at the top of the street: a cul-de-sac with a dozen or so fairly new houses, five or six of them clustered around its generous turning circle and wide grass verge, giving it a faintly village-like atmosphere. 'A nice place to live,' Maxine had told her once. 'Safe,' she'd emphasised, as though she knew instinctively that something dangerous lurked on the other side of town. Pam hadn't been here for a long time. Even when the boys first knew each other there was only occasional dropping off and picking up to be done. Mostly they rode their bikes, they could even walk if they were desperate—it wasn't that far across town, just over a kilometre. But there had been a couple of times when she'd come to fetch Scott. She'd never been inside the house, just waited outside. It was usually dark and no one noticed. Not the Druitts. Not their neighbours. All of them safely walled up in their little compounds, involved in their evening routines.

But it wasn't dark now, and she was aware of her car being one of only a couple parked on the street. She wasn't sure why she had driven over when she did. She'd thought she was avoiding traffic (the local joke was that rush hour was between eight-twenty-five and eight-thirty) but perhaps she'd been avoiding thinking about what she was actually doing, acting on an impulse that might not hold. Now it felt too early to be here, to knock on the Druitts' door. She needed to wait until the morning was underway, breakfast over, she told herself; but the alternative meant that people coming and going might actually catch a glimpse of her, might have an idea who she was and know her purpose, or at least surmise it. She sat there aware of the last of the cars heading out. A throaty engine, a billowing exhaust, the clank of a garage door: all gave her enough warning to slump down in her seat, hope those cruising by wouldn't slow to a stop for a quick inspection.

Mick had declined to come with her, to put it politely. He had strenuously advised that she didn't do it, didn't go within a country mile of the place. She'd tried to convince him of the decency of it, but he wasn't persuaded that there was anything they could say that would do any good for anyone. 'Don't kick the hornet's nest,' he'd told her. 'You think the power of your charm's going to bring them around. You've got no idea. Just bloody well keep away.' Pam knew he was being sensible, if not a tad overdramatic. But something other than sense was compelling her to the Druitts. No matter what they might want to throw at her, she owed it to them to go. It was nothing to do with being charming. There was nothing else in all conscience she could do.

It was getting close to nine. Two kids on bikes rolled down the gentle incline, figure-eighting around each other, shouting a fractured conversation as they went, oblivious to her in the car, oblivious too, she was sure, to the family emotionally haemorrhaging at the end of their street. When they left there was silence, and after a few minutes she decided that it was finally time to move. The Druitts would be up, breakfast over (if they had been able to eat), yet it was also slightly early for visitors. It was the right time for her to slip in and say what she needed to say, slip away again before anyone else might happen to arrive. She opened the car door, clutching a small bunch of her camellias (plump and cream, framed in their shiny green foliage, from the same tree as those she brought Scott) and got out. The air was fresh after the fug of the car interior and she felt it on her face like a small slap. The click of the car door closing sonar-echoed between the houses.

She made her way along the street and paused for a moment next to the Druitts' letterbox, looking up the short concrete path to the sprawling pale-brick house. It seemed an abode of particular blandness to Pam. One side of it was dominated by a long concrete porch and two sets of large windows, bisected by a cream-painted wooden front door; the other side featured two huge roller doors. She'd never been inside and didn't know the layout, but she assumed that the living room lay to one side and the master bedroom to the other. Long net curtains obscured the interior from view, so which side was which she had no idea. She tried to imagine them, the family, inside, most probably in the kitchen, tight around the table, eating breakfast, drinking coffee or tea (she imagined they were coffee people, but you never could tell). It crossed her mind that Maxine might still be in bed, that she might not have left it since she'd had the news. But Ray would be up, she was sure of that. Only dire illness would see him confined to his room.

She smoothed her jacket, pulling it down around her hips, and inhaled deeply, trying to quell the insistent pounding of her heart in her chest. There was an eerie quietness around her; the house, the neighbourhood, felt like an architectural model, devoid of life. The sun, hidden behind the misty cloud cover, offered only a filtered, soft light. She walked up the concrete path, stepped onto the front porch and tentatively knocked at the door. For a moment there was no sign of a response, and she knocked again, a little louder. It took a few seconds before she heard the soft thud of footsteps from the interior and the door opened a crack. Pam saw the shock of bleached blond hair and anticipated a dishevelled Maxine, but instead it was Reggie whose face appeared around the edge of the door, skin pale and blotchy, eyes strangely vulnerable without their usual make-up. Pam had forgotten that Reggie lived next door; she wondered which house. They both seemed too large, too costly for a single mother and her son.

Reggie gave an audible gasp when she saw Pam. There was an odd mixture of surprise and dismay on her face, as though Pam was the last person that Reggie expected to see (which was probably the case) and the last person she wanted to see (equally true). But she seemed to regain her composure quickly enough, as though she'd secretly anticipated seeing her at some time or another, and leaned forward, her face set, her voice a low hiss. 'You can't be here. You really can't.'

'I had to come, Reggie. I have to tell them how—'

'Who's there?' Maxine's voice, brittle and wary, rang out from somewhere inside the house.

Reggie looked quickly over her shoulder. 'Go,' she murmured. 'Just fuck off now.'

'I just—'

Somewhere behind Reggie there were the sounds of activity. An approaching thumping stride, almost at a run. A male voice, loud but indistinct. Reggie turned her head and attempted to push the door closed but a meaty hand materialised out of nowhere and yanked it back. Ray, mountain-like in a rough workman's check shirt and khaki pants, stared out at her, his face reddened and unshaven, a faint trace of sweat as though he'd been doing something strenuous. Just as Reggie had been moments before, Ray too seemed momentarily stunned. He stared down at Pam, his eyes fixing on hers then flickering across her body, noting the flowers in her hand, the rising and falling of her chest, taking everything in, assessing the situation.

'Ray,' she said, her mouth so dry she could hardly speak.

'No, no,' muttered Reggie. It was unclear if she was talking to Pam or the universe in general.

'I don't believe it,' said Ray. His voice wavered oddly, its depth temporarily lost. It seemed as if he was slowing down somehow, concentrating his energy. 'What the hell are you doing here? And with those fucking flowers.' She'd never heard Ray swear before. He was one of those old-fashioned men (even though he was neither old, nor old-fashioned in general) who made a point of not swearing because his propriety allowed him some

186

kind of moral superiority. 'You think those flowers are going to do anything for us?' he went on.

'I only wanted to say—'

'Yeah, I bet you did. Well, too fucking late to say anything, isn't it? You might have tried a few words to your son a long time ago. Set him up on the right path to being a decent human being. But no, not you. Not you. No checks on you and your family. I knew right from the first time I met you that you were a piece of work. What a fucking hoity-toity bitch, a princess of the highest order. I said that to Max, she knew exactly what I meant. Sneers at us behind our backs, she said. Thinks she's better than us. Yeah, so much better that she doesn't even need rules.'

'What?' Pam felt stunned. It was hard to follow what he was saying. Hard not to be mesmerised by his gestures as he moved forward and over the threshold of the doorway, his eyes shining and his hand up, an index finger jabbing towards her. She took two quick steps back and wobbled as her foot went off the edge of the porch and twisted sideways. She thought she was going to tumble, but her toes found ground and her hand grabbed at one of the porch posts. A sharp pain shafted up her leg, but her attention was so drawn by Ray that she was transfixed, barely registering her own body. Ray, as if sensing blood, moved towards her again. They seemed to be engaged in some kind of predatory waltz: him pressing forward, she sliding back, away from him. Now he was on the front porch, she one step down on the path looking up at him.

'Your son. What he did to my boy. Even before . . .' He faltered for a moment. 'You know what? Troy changed when he was with him. I told him he should watch out, that your son would do no good by him, but he said that he knew better, had a right to choose his own friends. Well, that *friend*,' he spat the word out, 'got him doing things he would never have done. Drinking. Disrespecting his family. Not bothering with his schoolwork, falling further and further behind. You allowed all that. You tutored your son in selfishness, gave him a licence to do what the fuck he pleased. Never held him accountable. And you're going to do the same again, aren't you? You want him to get away with murder. A little gesture to the grieving family and you're away again. No price to pay. A few flowers and all is forgiven and forgotten. You'll probably run for bloody mayor next year. Keep it in the family. I hear your father was a corrupt old shit too.'

Suddenly Maxine appeared in the doorway. As though carried on the wind, she flew past Reggie and across the porch. She was wearing a pink fluffy dressing-gown and her hair stuck out from her head in wild tufts that reminded Pam in equal parts of Phyllis Diller and a screeching alien hatchling. Pam took another painful step back, thinking Maxine was going to launch herself at her, and in all likelihood she would have, but Ray turned and scooped her in his arms as she tried to get by. She collapsed then, running out of puff, sobbing harshly into Ray's chest while he stared back at Pam as if to say 'look what you did'.

'You truly are the scum of the earth. You know that? Did you think you could come and manipulate us with your fucking fake sympathy? Torture us?' Ray put on a singsong voice. 'My son's alive and yours is dead.' Then quiet, controlled. 'I have never known such cruelty, such arrogance. You are unbelievable.'

Thinking about those five minutes later, Pam asked herself over and over why she didn't bolt right away. All she could recall was a sense of being frozen, as though under a spell, unable to move. There was a power to it all, and a theatricality, that was completely riveting, that overrode her fear. Ray might have been practising, waiting for her to come, for the way he delivered his lines. It seemed to her that death demanded a stripping back, an honesty, but this was the opposite. This was a frightening elaboration. She had never seen anything like it.

'I only wanted to say how sorry—'

'Sorry!' Maxine looked up from Ray's arm. 'My baby is dead! My beautiful son. He's never coming back! Sorry won't do a thing. You can be as sorry as you like but I will never forgive Scott and I will never forgive your family.'

Reggie came then and put an arm around her sister, pulling her away from Ray. 'Come inside,' she said, giving Pam a sharp look. 'She'll be gone soon.' Maxine was hunched over sobbing, her energy spent. She staggered a little, leaning back into Reggie as they turned.

Ray, now alone on the stage that was their front porch, pulled himself straighter, towering over her. Under his gaze Pam felt tiny, utterly diminished, like Alice after imbibing the Drink Me potion. Lost in a foreign world with no sense of where she was going or what would happen. 'I don't want you or any of your family here ever again. Do you understand that? Don't come within cooee of any of us. If you see us in the street, piss off. If I see you, well, god knows what I might do. I am not the man I was. I will never be that man again. Once I tolerated you and your family, gave you the benefit of the doubt. But no longer. Because of you I have lost my son. I have no respect for you and any of yours.'

'I *am* sorry, Ray,' she said, not sure why she was continuing to speak. 'You have to know that we are hurting too. We will miss him too. It's . . .'

Ray shook his head and a strange animal sound escaped from his lips. His jaw jutted forward and he suddenly appeared far older than his thirty-eight years. 'Take those fucking flowers and go,' he said before turning and following Maxine and Reggie inside, leaving Pam standing alone on the front lawn.

Pam looked down at the flowers. Her knuckles where she clutched them were white and her hands numb. She wanted to throw them down on the grass, but she baulked at leaving them behind. They were hers, brought as an offering of condolence, but it would feel like some kind of defilement now to leave them on their territory. She desperately wanted to give the Druitts sympathy; that's why she had come, after all. But sympathy was the last thing she was feeling. Anger. Loathing. Hatred. These emotions all seemed more natural right now. She'd absorbed everything they'd cast at her and her only choice was to radiate it all back out towards them. She limped to the car feeling like she'd gone several bruising rounds with Mike Tyson. It was only twenty past nine, but it could have been midnight, the day already interminable.

Driving down the street she imagined the neighbours peering out from behind their curtains, perhaps with a little sympathy for her, but nonetheless thinking she deserved what she got, the stupid cow. The village-idiot glee of seeing her belittled, shunned. (She passed an instant of thanks that it was her left foot that she'd injured. She imagined the ignominy of having to hobble to a phone box and call for help because she couldn't press the accelerator pedal.) She drove, eyes stinging, stomach churning, until she found somewhere unobserved to stop, which turned out to be near the river, the small park next to the bridge, secluded from the road by a scrappy row of trees. As soon as she turned off the ignition she knew she couldn't get out of the car, even foot withstanding. The steering wheel loomed in her vision and she fell across it, starting first to cry, then to wail. Huge gut-wrenching howls, cries of pain and anger. Then she drew back and let fly with her fists, setting off the horn in small intermittent beeps, punching until her knuckles bled. When the last vestiges of energy were spent she threw open the car door, leaned out and vomited onto the gravel. As she straightened up again she caught sight of the camellias on the front seat beside her and hurled them out on top of the mucky mess. She sat numb then for a few moments, staring out at the rushing waters in front of her and wondering how the hell she came to be here. What on earth had she been thinking?

'Mick, Mick,' she murmured, a tear slithering down her cheek, wanting just to be held and be told everything would be all right.

When she got home Simon was at the table eating breakfast, his fair hair rough and spiky from sleep, his arm crooked defensively around his bowl, as if someone was about to snatch it from him.

'Did you sleep okay?' she asked from the doorway, her voice light, keeping her distance, not wanting him to see her state, smell her breath, notice her limp.

'Yeah.' He squinted at her behind his glasses, unease on his face. 'Are you all right? Where've you been?'

'Just had to pop out for a bit. Where's your father? His car's gone.'

Simon was frowning. 'He went to work.'

She felt a surge of annoyance. 'What? Why?'

'I don't know. I think he had a few things to fix up. He said he'd be back soon. He won't be gone all day.'

'Thank god for that. And Loren?'

'Still asleep, I think.'

In the bathroom Pam hardly recognised the face that looked back at her from the mirror. Ashen, drawn. This was what she would look like when she got old. Flesh pulled across bones like a saggy canvas tent. She thought of her mother's face when she was ill, going through chemo. There were days when she'd looked in her eighties, not her fifties. When she was young Pam had thought that deprivation seemed to sharpen features, make them more luminous. The opposite when you aged. Lack of sleep, the slightest illness soon reminded you of what was in store. Still, that was mortality and, like it or not, she had the privilege (or pain) of being able to face hers. It was what it was.

She washed her face and inspected her knuckles, swabbed them with Dettol and put two bandaids on the abrasions before brushing her teeth and running a comb through her hair. When she was done she walked across the hallway and opened Loren's door. The deep, even breathing told her that her daughter was still asleep and she wondered what time she had got off the night before. She had offered Loren a sleeping pill but she'd refused to take it, saying she didn't want to be drugged, that she hadn't liked feeling that way at the hospital and that she needed to be aware. Pam wondered why on earth she would want to be aware. Aware of what exactly? She felt the complete opposite herself. She wanted her awareness limited. If she could she would make herself numb around the clock, not just at bedtime. Awareness was hard.

Back in the kitchen, Simon was rinsing his breakfast dishes.

'You're a wonder,' said Pam flatly, patting his shoulder.

He wiped his bowl with a tea towel. 'Did you go to the Druitts'?' More of a statement in search of confirmation than a question.

'How did you know?'

'I heard you talking to Dad earlier. I heard him saying "don't go" and I thought, yeah, don't go.' Simon didn't really know the Druitts well, but he had had one memorable encounter with them. Once when he was home for the holidays a couple of years before, he'd picked Scott and Troy up from Troy's place to give them a lift to a party. When he'd knocked on the door he'd been given what Mick would call the third degree. Simon wasn't Scott. He was responsible, intense, focused, conservative. (His metal-rimmed glasses and striped polo shirt would have told any half-observant viewer that.) But what they did have in common was that they were both easygoing creatures, slow to offend. Simon came home that evening and told them that Ray had interrogated him at the door. '"Who are you?" "What do you do?" "Let me see your driver's licence." He treated me so harshly and, after it was all done, he just walked away like I didn't exist.'

'What?' Mick had said, adding insult to injury. 'You showed him your driver's licence? Should have told him to bugger off.'

Simon had looked doubly rueful. What was an eighteen-year-old to do in the face of an always challenging Ray Druitt? Surely his father should know that.

'I went,' said Pam, 'because I needed to say that we were sorry. To give our condolences. It felt right. You know, it was the right thing to do.'

'Oh.' He digested her statement. 'What did they say?'

'Say? Well, they . . . they are in a bad way. It's the worst pos-sible thing you can face as a parent.'

'Yeah. It must be pretty awful for them.' He put the tea towel in the cupboard under the sink. 'You know, when Dad rang me, I had a weird thought, just when he started to speak, that it was Scott. I kept thinking afterwards that it could have been him. What if it had been him? I still can't quite get it out of my mind.'

Pam gave her head a small affirmative shake. She too had had that thought, more than once, but it had been drowned out by the sorrow she felt at losing Troy, at the concern she had for Scott and Loren. Stark reality had eclipsed the merely possible. Thinking otherwise seemed little more than self-indulgent, but still its shadow loomed and even the hint of such loss filled her with a heavy dread.

'Dad said Scott might come out tomorrow.'

'Really? Where did he get that information?'

Simon shrugged.

'Only a few days more, I'm sure. It'll be good to have him home.' To have him close, she thought.

Outside the sun had broken out between the clouds and a patch of light hit the back decking.

'So what do you need me to do while I'm here?' asked Simon.

'Do? You don't have to do anything.'

'I feel I should make myself useful.'

She laughed. It was so Simon to think of being useful. She'd never hear the other two say such a thing. 'How long *will* you be here?'

'I guess I'll stay till after the funeral. I told work I might be away for the whole week. I wasn't sure when it would be.'

Simon had a job with an accounting firm over the mid-year break. They'd offered him a permanent place when he finished his degree. Only a few months away now, which seemed rather incredible to Pam.

'We won't be going to the funeral.'

'What? Why not?'

Pam stared at him for a moment as though she should be able to convey the reason by telepathy. 'The Druitts don't want us there.'

'God. They said that?'

She shrugged. She wasn't going to provide him with any details. She didn't even want to think about them. 'You should get back to work anyway. Maybe spend a day or two with Scott and head back. There's nothing more you can do really.'

'This feels weird. I mean it's horrible, but it's like—' He glanced downward, noticed the plasters on her hand. 'Did you get in a fight with them?'

She examined her knuckles briefly. 'No, of course not.' She realised she could well have. It had come close to that when Maxine had charged out onto the verandah. 'But I spoke to them and they made it very clear that we were to steer out of their way.'

'Wow,' he said slowly. 'Does that go for all of us? Not just Scott?'

'Well, definitely Scott, and definitely me. I suppose the rest of you could take your chances, but I wouldn't advise it.'

'Why you? I don't get it. Scott, yeah. But why you? Why us?'

'They think the family, this family, is the root of all evil. Scott was not formed in isolation. As such, I, his mother, made him the person he is, and he in turn corrupted Troy.' Pam could feel exhaustion flood through her, the sheer fatigue of having to exist in a world not of her making where she was forced to interpret herself through another lens. She leaned against the bench and Simon, not usually a hugger, bent forward and wrapped his arms around her.

'They are crazy, Mum,' he said to the top of her head. 'I mean, that's just insane.'

'They are grieving. I understand that. I do. Everyone copes in different ways. They are . . . he is rigid. He has to find a reason for what happened. Someone to blame.'

'Copes? That's not coping, is it?' He drew away from her so he could speak. 'I mean, like making up stuff about Troy's behaviour. I don't think he was that innocent. Kind of the opposite. I'm pretty sure he was like that when they first came here. I can remember him in year nine. God. He was always, not bad or anything, but you know . . .'

'A live wire?'

'He's got a personality.' Simon stumbled there, changed to the past tense. 'He did. He did have one. Oh shit. But what I mean is, it's like they're pretending he's something he wasn't.'

'Hmm.' She looked away for a moment, her eyes alighting on the dishcloth and she thought it needed a good rinse, perhaps a bleach. Strange brown stains covered its surface. 'No, I think they truly believe he was like that. They've never seen or wanted to see him in any other way. The only explanation for the changes they saw was that somehow other people influenced Troy's behaviour.'

Simon let out a long sigh. 'People are bloody weird.'

Outside there was the sound of a car pulling up. 'I hope that's your father,' said Pam. She didn't think she could bear to see anyone else today. Interactions with the outside world seemed horribly dangerous; she suddenly felt terribly fragile. Simon obligingly stepped into the dining room and craned his head to look out the front window. 'Yeah,' he said. 'Just Dad.'

The slam of a car door. Footsteps on the front porch, the rasp of the door being opened, the way the intrusion of air from outside changed the atmosphere within, like a vacuum being released. She thought about the sounds of the house, how they had grown into it, knew it all, every signal. Cracking floorboards, squeaking, rattling windows and doors. They'd been here for most of their married life. The kids had grown up here, never known another home. Pam felt a ridiculous attachment to the place, as though it was the fifth family member, existing autonomously yet symbiotically with them. She couldn't imagine living anywhere else. Those big open rooms, the northern aspect at the back on the deck. So many memories. If nothing else, it was where she felt safe. Her fortress. Her castle (Queen Pamela). This at least was her refuge.

April 2016

Melbourne

'When did you come to Melbourne?'

Lori wondered if Daniel Levandi was asking the question as a cop or as her new best friend. They were crossing the Yarra and she had been thinking that she didn't often get to glimpse the river, or the view of the city beyond. It always made her feel like a tourist, being a passenger and being able to look out and see it, as opposed to negotiating her way through it as a driver when the only things in her line of sight were boots, badges and tail-lights. 'I came here in the nineties,' she said at last. 'When I was seventeen.'

'Young.'

'I suppose. I didn't feel that young at the time.'

'No.' He gave out a small huh. 'I was the same age when I left home. Just staring straight ahead. That's all I remember. No idea about anything, which, in hindsight, was my greatest asset. No reflection, just getting ready for the big adventure.'

She glanced over at him, saw his sharp aquiline profile and wondered how old he was. Younger than her she was sure, but maybe not a lot. 'So what was your big adventure?'

'Well, I don't think it ever really eventuated. I didn't go down the Amazon or anything. But you know, at the time, just leaving my mum's house was a pretty big deal. I got a job at a fabricators, steel manufacturing. Doesn't sound that great, does it? But I was free. Free of school, free of my family. I lived with some other guys out near the hills and we did a lot of crazy things, and a lot of boring things, and drank way too much alcohol. Teenagers. Typical. It was a struggle to get to work some days. After a couple of years I could see that none of that was going anywhere. I was bored, to be frank, and I thought bugger this. But I didn't have any proper qualifications. Someone I knew had joined the police and said I might like it.'

'And the rest is history.'

'Yeah. Well, it opened my eyes. To a lot of things. And then one boss in particular said I had potential, encouraged me to go back to study. I had actually been okay at schoolwork, just never very good at applying myself. But I finished a degree in psychology. Now I'm doing law.'

'Wow. That boss must've really have seen something in you.'

'It wasn't just me. Management were always looking for people to take on further studies. Still, they must have seen something. Hard for me to know now. I look back on that kid and all I can see is ignorance and naiveté. Guess I improved.'

'Yeah, well, that goes with the territory, doesn't it?'

'What, the ignorance or the improvement?'

She laughed. 'You're ambitious, I guess.'

'You don't want to stay doing the same thing your whole life, do you?'

'Depends on who you are. For some people all that moving around is too much.'

'Most people, perhaps.'

'So head of Major Collision soon then?'

'Who knows. I'm open to all possibilities.'

She nodded, taking it all in, wondering at his energy. She'd often felt since the kids that her energy had drained down like a half-dead battery. Some days it felt like enough just to do the basics let alone plot a whole new career.

'So,' he said. 'What was your big adventure?'

'Adventure? I don't think that word was in my vocabulary. I didn't leave for adventure. Escape. That would be my noun, or is it verb, of choice.'

'Sorry,' he said. 'That sounded callous. Clearly things were very different for you.'

She shrugged. 'In some ways it was an adventure. Not one that I set out on intentionally, like you. After everything that happened, I needed to get away. I figured I could start a new life, be someone else. I came here with almost nothing. A bit of money from my parents. I just survived as best I could. No grand vision.'

'And did you get to be someone else?'

'I was never the same person again. Does that mean being someone else?' They were driving along Brunton Avenue, the MCG on one side overshadowing them, railway lines on the other, layers of city building ahead. Everywhere vast blocks of space, vertical and horizontal lines. You could lose yourself in this city, she thought. Hundreds of people went missing here each year. She could well have been one of them. She had been so alone when she first arrived, anonymous, even though she'd never thought of herself in that way, had always found people to hang out with. But if she'd died or been murdered or taken on a new identity, who would ever have known? Who would have noticed? How easy it might have been to disappear, become another statistic.

'Listen,' she said, 'I have to ask you something.'

'Yeah?' he sounded wary.

'What do you know about me?'

He glanced over at her, eyes narrowed a little, a small smile playing at his lips. 'That at some point things took a turn for the better.'

'Huh, well, things turning for the better took a while.' She stared at his profile, then at the dashboard, then back to him again. 'But what *do* you know? Do you, the police, I mean, have information about me? Am I on record somewhere?'

'Have you been convicted of anything?'

'No. Why?'

'Well, if you don't have a record, there won't be any information on you as such. I only know what the uniforms told me when they talked to you the other day and from our earlier conversation, and I've spoken to some people up at Northam about what happened. Historically, that is. I was looking for what could be relevant to your brother's accident. That's it. General stuff, but nothing specific to you.'

Hearing the word Northam, her mind danced to Des Robinson. Was he still alive? Certainly he was too old now to still be in the force. She wondered if Daniel had spoken to him, what he might have said. A flush of shame rose through her body, a physical reaction, as though her corporeal self knew what her mind did not, would not, accept. She stared ahead, trying to still her thoughts, and saw that they weren't far from the hospital now. A tram running down the centre of Victoria

Parade beside them clanged its bell and they stopped behind a stream of traffic. 'You know, I haven't talked to anyone about this before,' she said, wondering why, given the truth of her statement, she was saying this to him. A stranger. A cop.

Daniel had flicked the indicator on and was preparing to cross over the tram tracks. He was watching the car in front inch slowly forward. 'Come on,' he said. (Not nearly as impatient as Jason, she noted.) There was only enough room for two cars in the lane, but the vehicle ahead was taking up more than its share of the space. He moved up, as though glued to the other car's bumper, across the intersection ahead of a wave of oncoming traffic before turning into a side street. 'Sorry,' he said. 'Had to think about that one.'

'No, we don't want to all end up in intensive care,' she said, resigned then to him not having heard her, feeling a slight relief. There were so many reasons not to say anything more to this man.

But as it turned out he had heard her. 'What "about this" do you mean?' he said, now they were off the main road.

'Sorry?'

'You said you haven't spoken about this. Do you mean about your brother, or about what happened all those years ago?'

'Both. I've never told anyone about what happened to us.'

'No one at all?'

'I left Northam and I slammed the door closed.'

'But you're telling me.'

'Yeah, it seems so. But in a way not really because, actually, you already know.'

'But if I asked for details, you'd give them to me? You'd expand? I mean, I don't know much more than the outline.'

By now they had entered the car park. He pulled into a space and turned off the engine.

She took a long breath. 'Maybe. I don't know about the details, about what happened. That's a muscle that hasn't been used for a long time. I try not to even think about the past. I don't know what's left of it inside me anymore.' She could feel him looking at her now and she wondered if he believed her. (Why would that matter? Perhaps she didn't believe it herself. That might be more pertinent.)

'So you don't have anything to do with anyone you knew then?'

'No.'

'And no one you know now has any idea about your life before you came here?'

'Yep. That's right.'

'There's a real loneliness in that. That must have been hard— maybe it still is hard—to keep the door shut.'

She turned and looked at him then. 'You might not believe this, but that side of things, that's been quite easy, mostly. Much easier than the alternative, I believe.'

He stared back at her with an expression she found impossible to read. Pity or even scorn came to mind, but she thought they were probably her own projections. Cops were so good at playing neutral, you could read anything into that look. It was part of the logic. Let people catch themselves out with their own uncertainties, their own falsehoods reflected back to them. Just like psychoanalysis but with quicker results.

'Until something like this happens?' he said. 'You must at least have thought of the possibility of running into someone you knew, somewhere, sometime. It happens even when you're from out of town. That person you haven't seen since high school and there they are on the beach at Noosa. Or a family member decides to track you down.'

She shook her head. What had she thought back then? She couldn't really say anymore. You changed, adapted. Your new life quickly became a habit and soon it was your only life. Something you did without thinking. Like moving out of Darren's place and never seeing him again. Never seeing Rosie or Schiller once she'd settled in with Jason. Daniel was right. She hadn't put any thought into wondering about the past, and now she had to accept that it wasn't hers to control, that the past had a way of catching up with you, whether you liked it or not.

'You feeling all right about seeing your brother?'

She half shrugged. There was no 'yes' or 'no' response to that. It wasn't a simple question. She had already seen her brother, twice now. Each time she had readied herself for the shock of it. But neither experience had been as much of a shock as she'd expected. Given he'd been unconscious it had been, in a way, more like easing herself by increments into a cold sea rather than plunging headlong through the icy waters. Little by little she'd become used to him, in some way getting reacquainted without having to actually know him. Yet this was all deeper than just the fact of seeing him. There was also the question of her willingness to develop a relationship. That she still didn't know the answer to.

They went in silence from the car to the hospital entrance to the lift and up to the seventh floor. Lori thought she would have some sense of shame about exposing some of her inner self to this policeman, but somehow it felt oddly liberating. This must be what confession was like, she thought. What it did for you, cleansing your soul. This was the power of telling someone who was not an intimate. What she wasn't sure of was Daniel Levandi himself. She liked him, and he appeared to like her. But she wasn't certain on a human level, on a real and personal level, that he did. He was a cop. He was always looking for a way into people's heads. She knew that. He might be looking for something else entirely. Did he suspect her of running Scott over herself? He had asked her several questions about their relationship. Perhaps if she went home now she'd find forensics all over her car, rummaging through her studio. Or maybe he was secretly taping what she'd said and would use it to build a case against her.

They stood outside the door of ICU. She pushed the buzzer. While they waited for someone to come, Daniel went to the windows and looked out.

'Have you been up here before?' asked Lori.

'Yeah, once, a couple of years back.'

'I suppose you have to see a few people in hospital.'

'Sometimes. It's not usually ideal. Especially with head injuries. But then it's not easy dealing with people after accidents full stop. You'd know yourself from the other side of that exchange.'

The interviews she had endured had been eviscerating. No one realised how intrusive (in the deepest sense of the word) it was to be questioned in those circumstances, to be asked to expose the most profound, most delicate parts of your psyche: your grief and impotence, your guilt and shame. What were you doing at the time? Were you drinking? Wearing a seatbelt? How fast was the driver going? Did you attempt to warn him? The interviewers picked away at the scab of healing, took her repeatedly back into that night, made her relive it each time they questioned her, which in reality was only two or three times, but felt in her memory like a hundred. What they'd actually asked, and how she'd exactly responded she could no longer recall. Only the feeling of being interrogated by that horrible man, that out of town cop with his shiny lips and doughy body. Her mother in the background with a stony face sculpted by anger and pain.

Behind them the buzzer went off and the door clicked open. They went in and wiped their hands with antiseptic, walked past the nurses' desk and up to the room. The curtains were open and Lori could see Scott in bed, lying on his back, upper body slightly elevated.

'He looks like he's still out to it,' she said.

Daniel peered past her. 'He could be dopey for a while.'

'Dopey?'

'Not fully conscious. Depends on . . . well, a lot of things. They'll tell you, the staff. People don't just wake up and snap to, in my experience at least. Takes a bit of time, adjustment.'

Inside a new nurse was in attendance. He introduced himself as Malcolm and gave them a rundown of the morning's events: Scott's coming to, how responsive he'd been, improvements on the Glasgow Coma Scale, something she'd never heard of, never needed to know about, until four days ago.

'Not much good for me to talk to him then?' asked Daniel, after he'd explained who he was.

'I don't think so at this stage. He's still very disoriented. We'll just have to see how he goes. Physically, though, things seem relatively positive, so we're happy about that.'

'The neurologist said his responses from the beginning have been good,' said Lori.

Malcolm nodded 'Yeah. He's had a couple of longer periods of consciousness and he's responding to commands now, moving his limbs, his face is mobile. Of course we'll continue to monitor him, I expect to see some substantial changes over the next few days. We'll be looking at memory deficits, that kind of thing. There's always a continued risk of swelling, blood clots. We're not completely out of the woods.'

Lori moved to the bed and sat down next to her brother, put her hand on his arm. Saw his eyelids flutter.

'Scott?'

Daniel found another chair in the corner and pulled it to the other side of the bed. He was facing Lori now and he smiled fleetingly at her as if in encouragement. She was glad of his company. Glad that this had happened when she was with him and that he had decided to come along (paranoid speculation notwithstanding). It had been hard to see her brother alone. She wasn't sure of the depth of Daniel's knowledge about her, her family, but now any knowledge seemed better than none. His understanding her greatest gift.

Scott let out a low moan; not a cry of distress but something that she imagined approximated him re-emerging into the world. The kind of sound she'd heard her children emit as they woke in the morning, remembering their bodies again after a night of being physically untethered. She bent forward and watched as his eyes slowly opened and he stared up to the ceiling.

'Scott,' she said again.

The nurse came over, standing in front of him for a moment to check something, then moving back.

'Can you hear me?' Lori asked. She stood up and leaned over her brother, but he continued to gaze vacantly upwards. She sat again and placed her hand on his arm, felt him flinch reflexively, make a small noise. 'It's Lori,' she said. 'I'm here.' She glanced over at Daniel and shook her head.

'Tell him something. Tell him about life, or your work. Anything.'

She gave him a helpless look.

'What about when you were kids? Did you get on?'

'We were mates. We did a lot together, really.'

'What kind of things?'

She put her hands to her face, pressed her fingers into her cheeks. 'He was always into something—up to something—and I'd follow him. Blindly. Do whatever he did. When we were younger, he used to take his bike to the dirt road behind our house and ride it up and down. Practise snap turns, wheelies. I had a little bike, a little pink thing, and I'd go out after him. He was really good, but I was always falling off, skinning my knees, elbows. Skateboards later, until he banned me because he just wanted to be with his mates and having your kid sister tagging along was seriously uncool.'

Scott made a sound then that was more like a word than a grunt. She leaned towards him, surprised at her reflexes. 'It's okay. I'm here.' His eyes seemed to slide towards her then and focus momentarily on her face. 'I'm here,' she repeated, and he blinked and looked away as if it had all been too much, closed his eyes again. She sat still for a while watching him, waiting to see what he would do.

'That might be it for now,' said Malcolm.

'When will he wake again do you think?' said Lori.

'Could be an hour. Tonight. Tomorrow. There's no real knowing. Take a break for a while.'

'Want to get a coffee downstairs?' asked Daniel.

In the quarter-full hospital cafeteria they got coffee and water and sat at a white laminex table by the window with a view of the courtyard.

'This must be the quietest café in Fitzroy,' said Daniel.

'There's a lot of competition around here.'

He raised an eyebrow, as if to say he didn't think the competition would make much difference, and took a sip of coffee, made a face. 'You said you hadn't had contact with your brother for years. When was it exactly that you saw him last?'

'Just before he went to gaol.'

'Did you blame him? Is that why you didn't see him again.'

'Oh,' she said, surprised by his question and feeling the sudden heat of being seen as the perpetrator of an injustice. But he didn't seem to notice her unease and took another sip of his coffee while he waited for her to answer. She glanced away through the windows, noted hospital staff sitting at the tables outside. Some talking, a couple reading papers, others looking at their phones. A few were smoking. 'I wouldn't have described it like that then. It was something very physical. I couldn't bear to look at him. I was so angry. I guess I did blame him, but I didn't consciously think that. It seems impossible to explain now, but at the time I couldn't go near Scott. I think it was everything he represented. He and Troy were so close, it was hard to look at him and not see Troy. Expect to see Troy. It was terrible. I mean, it must have been awful for my parents. They had enough to handle as it was, and then me behaving like that.'

'Did you get counselling?'

'Counselling wasn't something people did in Northam twenty years ago. I guess they could have sent me somewhere—Shepparton or Wangaratta or down here. There were places, but it wasn't seen as a priority. I think they thought time would heal the wounds.' She let out a small snort.

'I think now you might be diagnosed with PTSD. Certainly because of what happened later, if not then.'

'You're probably right.' Lori closed her eyes briefly and thought about what Schiller had said. 'I used to cry in my sleep, apparently. Having the kids, I had a lot of anxiety before and after their births, I don't know if that was normal. I missed my mother so much then. But, in a way, having them changed everything for me. Someone else to live for, have a future for. I guess I got to transform some of that negative energy into something positive, but I might not have been able to do that by myself.'

He shrugged.

'I don't know. I might just be talking a pile of crap. Do you have kids?'

'No,' he said, then added, 'not sure I ever will.'

'Why not?'

Daniel looked surprised. Not even his mother had asked him that question. He cocked an eyebrow as if to say 'what a cheek' but answered anyway. 'My job. It can take me to some dark places. Doesn't always make me feel so positive about bringing kids into the world.'

'I understand that. I think if it hadn't been for Jason—my husband—I wouldn't have either.' She put her hands on the table in front of her and examined them for a moment. Her hands were a lot like her mother's, neither broad nor delicate, but with long tapering fingers that gave them a certain elegance. 'You know, it was hard for me to like myself for a long time. Even when I met Jason, I still didn't really. One day he said to me that he thought I had great hands—I don't mean he never complimented me, but this was kind of different, he made me see them differently. I've always been an artist, a designer. These hands are the tools of my trade, they enable me to make beautiful things and to earn a living. They remind me of what I can hold onto, touch. And they remind me of my mum. I can see her hands when I look at mine.'

'Does that help you make sense of it?'

'It helps me to see the connections. The wonder of being a child. Being a parent. This thing that links us. I'm glad of my children for that bond. It's worth the risk to have that intensity.'

'Sure,' he said. 'I get that.' Behind them, two people left the café. The door glided shut. He glanced around and then back at her. 'Do you want to talk about it? The accident?'

She narrowed her eyes. 'Why do you want to know? You'd have the reports.'

'You said you'd never talked to anyone about it. I thought perhaps now you'd like to.'

'Get some practice in, you reckon?'

'You worry about telling your husband?'

She sat quietly for a little while, staring out the windows, not wanting to think about Jason. 'I gave some statements to the police. The last one for sentencing. That's the last time I ever talked about the crash.'

'What about your parents?'

'They left me alone with it. I can't explain how angry I was. It wasn't just aimed at Scott. I mean I was angry with the world. With myself. Talking about what happened was the last thing I wanted to do, so they didn't either. And they were concerned about Scott. About him going to gaol. And about other stuff that was happening to them at the time. But I was a sixteen-year-old who had no idea.' She looked across the table at him and had an urge to reach over and brush his hair back, to kiss him. A kind of transference, she knew that, knew she had to let it wash over her, not take hold. She looked down at her hands again and hoped he hadn't noticed. She'd never been good at recognising what kind of signals she gave out.

'When the car crashed, it flipped, I don't know how many times. One minute Troy was sitting next to me. Saying things. Laughing. And then all of a sudden, there's stuff everywhere, everything is falling and he's gone. Disappeared. The car comes to rest on its wheels and I'm still there in the back, piled next to Josh. The door on Troy's side is wide open and all I can hear is Melissa crying in the front seat and I think Scott moaning and there is some hissing sound. Everything's dark, but there was this strange, spooky really, pale light from the headlights. Somehow they're still on.' She turned her head towards the window again and paused.

'I don't know why I wasn't hurt. Why Josh wasn't hurt. I don't know how that could have happened, but it did. I found Troy where he'd been thrown against a tree. Not far away. Just slumped down.' Her fingers felt for the glass of water in front of her and she put it to her lips, took a small sip. 'I could hear him. I could hear him . . . gurgling. Rasping. It was loud and weird and I think I knew what it meant, even then, but you know. I'll never forget that sound.' She put her hand to her mouth, looked across at Daniel silently for a few seconds. 'You must have seen a fair few accidents yourself. Your job.'

'The uniforms or CFA are generally the first responders. I saw more as a rookie cop than I do now. My team are often there after the worst of it. The aftermath. Looking at the wreck, tyre marks, working out how the accident happened, interviewing people.' He shook his head quickly as if he knew it wasn't the same. 'There's a lot of follow-up. That said, I've seen some pretty terrible things.'

They were both quiet for a while.

'No one I know has ever had the same experience, been in an accident like that. None of them had to deal with it. At least you know.' She looked away from him and down at her cup. 'I remember I put my arms around Troy and I said all the sort of shit that you say when you want everything to be okay. I couldn't see his face clearly. But I could hear that sound he was making, and then it stopped. Josh told me later that he called for me to help him with the others, but I didn't hear. Sometime later people came, someone pulled me off the ground.

'Memory is a funny thing. I don't know if it was because I was out of it that night. Even before the accident. I don't recall much about what went down—the party or the drive. Then later the hospital. My parents coming in. I think the doctor gave me some sedative. Maybe that stuffed me up too? When I look back, I feel like a spotlight fell on those few terrible moments and the rest was just swept away. And, even now, I don't know if those things I remember are real. I found out later that Josh pretty much kept Melissa alive and maybe Scott too in that time till the ambos came. I guess I found it hard to forgive myself for that. I was AWOL.'

'It would have been extremely difficult to witness what you did. You were with someone in their dying moments. I think you were very hard on yourself to imagine that you could leap up and start tending to others.' He paused delicately. 'Were you together? Boyfriend, girlfriend?'

Lori bit her lip. 'There was something just starting. I'd known him for years. He was my brother's friend, but he was mine too. I thought I was in love with him. I don't know how true that was. I was a child. But I did believe that for a long time, and that he loved me too. What was and what might have been. You know, when you lose someone like that you don't just lose them but all the possibilities. I felt as though I'd lost my future. Your first love. The intensity, the purity. I thought for a long time after that I was cursed. You know, that Scott and I both were. For us to live through all that, to have survived everything. It was too much. We could never be happy. We didn't deserve to be happy.'

'I can see why you thought that. You had an enormous amount to endure in the end. It must have taken grit to survive.'

She shrugged dismissively. 'But people do survive, don't they? People can lose everything. In war they lose their homes and families, their communities. They watch unspeakable acts. They are forced into bravery or abasement. They lose their dignity. But they go on. It's been part of the human cycle for millennia. It's the history of the human race.'

'Is this how you see that period? As war?'

She gave him a crooked smile. 'Well, it turned out to be that way, didn't it? I mean, I didn't think that at the time. I didn't say, "I'm in a war zone." But in many ways I was.'

The cafeteria was completely empty by then. Outside, too, the tables had cleared. It was just the two of them against the light of the glass, black figures in a sea of white. Around them the sounds of pots being scraped and cleaned, an indecipherable comment from someone in the kitchen. A peal of laughter. Lori checked her watch. She'd have to get back to pick up the kids soon. One last chance to see her brother. Daniel was already rising from the table having taken the cue. She shut her eyes for a second and thought of Jason. Imagined him across from her. Imagined that she had just told him what she'd told Daniel Levandi. And the rest as well. How would he be? Would he lean towards her, concerned, surprised, alarmed? Would he be angry that she'd never told him, feel betrayed? She thought she knew him, but when she thought about marrying her past with the present all she could see was a huge black hole. She had no idea how he would react.

August 1993

Northham

The telephone rang in the hallway four times before the answering machine clicked in and carried the message stealthily away from earshot. Pam knew now how many rings there were because she had reset the machine, reduced the number down from six to the minimum four (why four, for god's sake, why not zero?). It had become something of a ritual for her now, counting the rings, listening to see if a message would be left, waiting for the final beep of the machine. Whether she replayed the messages straightaway depended on how she felt at the time, if she was strong, was up to the assault. Mostly she wasn't.

The calls had started days after the accident. Some, she was sure, were kids. Lots of deep breathing and laughter, the odd ghostly 'ooooo' thrown in for effect. Once a wavering voice saying, 'I'm Troy and I am here to take my revenge.' Amateur and silly, sure, but deeply upsetting too, if only for their button-pushing callousness. Then there were the more menacing calls that featured either panting breaths or silence. More latterly, someone had taken to whispering the word 'killer' over and over. Pam found it hard to listen to these—even when she only gave them a couple of seconds, the knowledge of them coming in was enough—and she certainly didn't want Scott or Loren to hear them. Or even Mick half the time. (A problem shared, she believed, was not a problem halved but in their case one mutually stewed on.) Hence, she'd became the guardian of the answering machine, the chief bile absorber, checking each message, deleting those that were offensive or abusive and, when she was up to it, answering the merely routine.

Most of these calls came through at night. She, or Mick, had taken to pulling the phone cord from its socket after nine pm. Let the phone ring on in the ether, not allowing the hate to connect to its target. When the barrage had started, she'd gone to Des Robinson straightaway and he'd traced them. The majority were made from the town's three telephone boxes—by whom, who knew—with the others coming, she'd later found out, from the home of a year ten Northam High student. She'd speculated that it might have been a friend of Kyle Druitt. Des didn't provide details about that but assured her that whoever it was wouldn't call again. The laughing and ghostly voices dropped out of the mix, but the silences, heavy breathing and the whispered accusations continued unabated, no doubt from the round of phone boxes. Of course, while nothing could be proved, she was sure that these calls originated from the Druitts. Possibly executed by a number of people—extended family, friends—but that was a mere technicality. It was most certainly Ray's doing. To what end Pam couldn't be sure: revenge, rough justice, a way to make them feel as dreadful as they felt themselves? She attempted to put herself in their shoes but, try as she might, she couldn't imagine making trips to the local phone box and picking up the handset and breathing hard. She'd like to think she wouldn't do that if she'd been faced with the same situation, no matter how much grief and bitterness she might have harboured. If nothing else it was ridiculous. Like something from a B-grade movie, mobs with pitchforks and burning torches. Yet somehow she wouldn't be surprised to see one at her doorstep sometime soon, feel the sharp tips of the prongs on her skin, the heat against her face. Fantasy translated into reality.

Pam and Mick had heard from their friend Gary Alderson, who also happened to be Ray's boss, that Ray hadn't come back to work. He hadn't resigned. He simply hadn't been in. Gary told them that he'd gone to the funeral and given the Druitts his heartfelt condolences and that Ray had looked right through him. 'I didn't take it as a snub,' Gary said. 'He's an odd guy at the best of times, and he seemed to be like that with everyone. Like a zombie.'

Gary's wife, Karen, had said that Maxine seemed little better. 'I've never seen a funeral like it,' she'd told Pam the following weekend. 'Honestly, doll, it was good you didn't go. The eulogy was awful. Done by the minister. No one from the family could speak. Half of the church was wailing and the other half catatonic.'

Gary and Karen had come over for lunch. In fact they had brought most of lunch (salad, salami, pickles, a big crusty loaf from the bakery, a couple of coffee scrolls) and invited themselves in. Pam had known them since she was a kid. Their families had all been friendly when they were growing up. Alderson's car dealership (emblematic of the times, it was Ford in the old days, Toyota now) had been started by Gary's father in the 1940s. Karen's dad had been the town's accountant. Gary liked a drink, or two. Or three. He brought a bottle of Scotch with him to lunch, which Pam found to be an odd gesture. Karen made an apologetic face at Pam as if to say 'what a hick I married'.

'I've got wine in the fridge,' said Pam.

'For the ladies,' added Karen, glancing over her shoulder at Gary.

'I'll have one too,' said Mick.

'Never met anyone less ladylike than you, mate,' said Gary.

Pam thought it might have been the first time she'd laughed since the accident. Eight days. Was that too soon?

Gary and Karen brought the story of the funeral and the missing mechanic. It was understandable, Karen had pronounced, that Ray Druitt wouldn't go back to work for a while. Who on earth would, given what happened.

'I'll say one thing about him,' said Gary. 'He's a bloody hard worker. Good at what he does. And that means I really need someone to replace him—even a couple of blokes. Right now I don't know if he'll be back in a week or never. Going to have to sort something.'

Pam had marvelled at Gary's nonchalance. Thinking that a bereaved father would only take one week off work seemed highly unlikely. Gary had four children of his own, surely he could use his imagination. 'Did you go back to the house after?' she asked.

Karen shook her head. 'Invitations weren't extended. We said a few words at the church. I don't think they took much in.'

'Did you know many people?'

'Not really. There were a lot of kids,' said Gary. 'Half the high school, I'd say. Otherwise, family, by the look. Out of towners.'

'What about the bikies?' said Karen.

'Oh yeah, the bikies.' Gary laughed. 'Don't know if they were family or friends.'

Pam looked over at Mick. His eyes were fixed on Gary, probably thinking the same thing as she was: bikies were nothing to laugh about.

'I heard he used to be in some gang when he was young,' Karen piped up. 'Reformed now. Got religion or something.'

'Don't know about that,' said Gary. 'Might have reformed from religion as well. I think he's one of those people who likes rules, but prefers to make them himself. Not really a joiner, if you know what I mean.'

Pam suddenly felt exhausted. She'd been sleeping poorly all week, and drugging herself intermittently with sleeping pills hadn't seemed to help a great deal. She wondered if having people over had been a good idea. Not that she'd had much say in the matter, given they'd invited themselves.

Karen's voice came at her from left field. 'Are you all right, sweetheart?'

'Oh Karen,' she said, turning to her friend. 'Do you really want an answer to that question?'

'I do.' Karen waggled her head towards the back door. 'Come on, I need a ciggie.'

Outside, Pam had told Karen in a quiet voice about meeting the Druitts earlier in the week before the funeral. Then she told her about the phone calls.

'What does Des Robinson say?' asked Karen. She offered a smoke to Pam, who didn't smoke and simply shook her head, rendered mute out of astonishment that Karen, her friend for over thirty years, had either forgotten this fact or was trying to convert her.

'He's keeping an eye on things. There's not a lot he can do if we can't prove it's them. And even then. I'm hoping that it will quieten down soon. They can get rid of some of that anger.'

'That could take a while,' Karen said bluntly.

'You think so?'

'Gary says Ray is like a dog with a bone. Obsessive. He tracked down some guy they used to work with because he took a tool with him that wasn't his. Wasn't Ray's either, just belonged to the workshop. He drove down to Melbourne to get it back. Who does that sort of thing? Imagine being confronted with a big lunk like him. What was it? A monkey wrench. All I'm saying is that someone like him might not let this go. Especially if he decides not to come back to work. He'll just be there, at home, stewing away.'

Pam couldn't think of Ray as a big lunk. Lunk made him sound stupid, and he was far from that. 'God, I don't imagine he could keep doing it. Really? I think I'd want distraction after a while. Not to have to keep thinking the same thoughts over and over.'

'Yeah, but you're not him, are you? Gary also says he has a chip on his shoulder.'

'That's true, he does,' said Pam.

'Not a good combination then, is it?'

'Jesus, Kaz, you're supposed to be my friend.' Pam let out a small laugh.

'I'm being your friend, doll. You need to keep an eye on that bloke.'

'How?'

'Keep calling Des. Write everything down. Tell everyone you know what's going on. Look, it might all drop away, like you say, but it's terrible to put you through this. He shouldn't be allowed to get away with it.'

'Maybe it's not him. Them.'

'God, who else would it be?' Karen took a long drag on her cigarette and blew a waft of smoke out in front of them. They watched it slowly disperse into the cool afternoon air.

Pam thought about that conversation now as she listened to the phone ring, wondering who might be on the other end. Karen had been right. More than a month it had been and still the calls kept coming. If anything there were more of them, and, to Pam at least, they seemed more targeted. They often came in the daytime when she was home alone. The days when she wasn't at work and the kids (for all intents and purposes) were at school. They were full of unbelievable obscenities and the last few had included vague but menacing threats. The voice was muffled and it was almost impossible to tell if it was male or female, or even if it was always the same person. More recently excrement of unknown provenance (looks like dog shit, smells like dog shit, Mick had said) had been left on their front steps during the night, and her car egged twice. Suddenly it all felt too much and something rose up in her. An unbridled anger. She'd felt sympathy for the Druitts for weeks, turned the other cheek and allowed them their venom without reproach because it felt morally reprehensible to do otherwise, but today, standing here in the cool darkened hallway, she saw the absurdity of it all. Their attempts to shame and cower her, her family. 'Fuck you!' she said to the phone.

When she answered it, primed already to deliver a fusillade of expletives (very un-Pam but, hey, she was in the mood now), it turned out to be Cathy. 'Just wondering if you are coming down this afternoon?' she asked, referring to their yoga class.

Pam swallowed. She wouldn't have said this was a good day, a strong day. She could easily have gone back to bed and curled up in the foetal position, but in the end what good would that do? When would there ever be a right time for her to go out and face the world, start breathing again? Why not go to yoga? Breathing was something they did a lot of there.

'Yeah,' she said finally, 'I will come.'

'Sure?' asked Cathy.

'Don't ask me that,' said Pam. 'Ever.' They both laughed.

For the first week after the accident Pam had scarcely left the house. Apart from visiting Scott she had largely stayed indoors, sending Simon out on errands and occasionally Mick. After ten days she had gone back to work, dipping her toes in the world of small-town interactions and beginning some kind of normal routine. She knew sooner or later she would run into someone from the Druitt clan, and when that happened it would simply be a stroke of ill luck. But going to yoga was different. Reggie was a stalwart there. She and Janice had been the first people to take up Aurora's classes. Pam had to be prepared for whatever might come her way when she returned. A couple of weeks before, Cathy had told her that Reggie had taken a couple of weeks off too. Neither she nor Janice had turned up, said Cathy optimistically.

'I thought you liked them,' said Pam.

'God, Pam. I don't like them if they stop you from coming. If they behave like arseholes.'

Pam had shrugged. 'Well, that was Ray and Maxine. Reggie might be fine. She might just ignore me.'

'Yeah,' said Cathy, 'who knows how she'll be. She's a funny one.'

Then, two weeks later, Cathy announced that they had rejoined the class, wordlessly slipped in slightly late, then left again before the others were off their mats. 'It was weird. They were quiet. There was no eye contact,' said Cathy.

'Perhaps they were wondering if I'd be there,' said Pam. 'They might feel safe and think I'm not coming back.'

'Yeah. Or perhaps they were easing themselves back in. Well, Reggie. Perhaps she didn't want to have to deal with, you know, sympathy, curiosity. Questions.'

That's what Pam thought too as she drove down to the town hall, that she was going to ease herself in. She didn't want to have to deal with sympathy or curiosity or questions either. The curse of small-town living. Virtually everybody knew about the accident. Virtually everybody would have some kind of opinion, want to say something. Above her, strangely emblematic, the sky was full of fat dark clouds that had brought sporadic skiffs of rain. As she'd set off, drizzle had covered her windscreen and blurred her view, but by the time she got to the car park it was hosing down. There were half a dozen cars outside. She had to park twenty metres from the door and make a run for the building with the yoga mat held over her head.

Inside, ten or so people had occupied the usual spaces, quietly talking, laying their mats out. Pam stood at the front for a moment, damp, errant drips sliding down her body onto the wooden floor. Her eyes deliberately skimmed over the group until they alighted on Cathy's waving hand. She didn't register anyone else as she made her journey in squeaking damp shoes to the place Cathy had saved for her until a figure that she instantly recognised as Reggie leaned out of the group towards her, hissing, 'What the fuck are you doing here?'

Behind her she could hear Aurora's voice, sharply school-marmish. 'Is everything all right?'

Pam kept moving, stepping behind the group. She could sense Reggie's body twist, her laser stare follow her. 'No, everything is not all right. I want to know what she's doing in this class.'

Pam looked up then and saw Cathy in front of her, like a beacon of hope standing on her blue mat, a strange look of urgency on her face. She put her hand out as though she was going to save Pam from drowning.

'This class is open to everyone, Reggie,' said Aurora firmly.

Reggie's voice boomed out. 'I don't think you should let murderers in.'

Pam turned then, took in the whole group from her vantage point at the back corner. Heads swivelled between Reggie and Aurora. A couple glanced her way, then back again as though they were watching a footy ball being punted down a field. Someone murmured something that Pam couldn't hear. Friend or foe. Pam felt her stomach lurch at the hint of division.

'Reggie,' said Aurora, 'if you have a problem with anyone in this class, please deal with it outside. This is a place to relax and de-stress. I'd just—'

'That's right. So she shouldn't be here. You know I can't be here with her. I'm not going to de-stress if she's around. Get her out.'

Pam could feel Cathy step closer to her, her body leaning forward, on alert, hostile. 'Pam has as much right to be here as anyone,' she said loudly.

'You think? Don't you have any conscience?' Reggie swung around and was staring at Pam now, her voice fragmenting. 'You should just leave. I should be able to enjoy this class without the woman who is responsible for my nephew's death standing right behind me.'

Pam was still holding her mat. She looked across at Aurora. 'I'm sorry,' she said. 'I didn't realise . . .'

'That's your catchcry, isn't it?' shouted Reggie. 'Just like Ray says. Always playing the innocent. The victim.'

'I think you should bugger off,' said Cathy sharply. 'Pam hasn't done anything.'

'What would you know?' shouted Janice.

'What would *you* know?' Cathy shouted back.

'Ladies!' Aurora yelled, her voice somewhere between crowd control and terror. 'Please. Let's—'

'If you let her stay,' Reggie said, turning back to Aurora, 'you're siding with them. And I will leave this bloody class and never come back.'

'I'm going to go,' said Pam, who was now thinking that she had been blind, over-ambitious, naïve and plain stupid to have come here. She had imagined it might be uncomfortable, but she hadn't envisaged a slanging match, spitting hatred. What an idiot. Why wouldn't she get that, after everything else that had been sent her way? Would she never learn? She took a step to her right, around the back of Cathy. Not the most direct route out of the room, but the one farthest away from Reggie.

'No,' said Aurora, holding up her hand. 'You stay put, Pam. Reggie, this has nothing to do with me or this group. This is between you and Pam. And while you are here, you need to put that on hold, because this space is for all of us.'

Reggie, mouth downturned, stared from Aurora to Pam and shook her head. 'I knew this would happen. There's a closed circle in this town, one that we don't get to belong to. People like you don't have to answer for anything. You are always protected.'

'No one is protecting anyone,' said Aurora looking at Reggie, but still holding her hand up to Pam.

Reggie laughed. 'You just can't see it, can you?'

'Reggie, you are a valued part of this class, but I can't deny someone else a space because you have issues with them.'

'Issues!' Reggie screamed the word. 'You've got to be joking. Someone died. That's not an issue. That's a bloody tragedy.'

'Pam wasn't there,' shouted Cathy.

'She's responsible for that little scumbag.'

Pam took a few more steps towards the door, but Cathy caught her by the arm. 'No, don't let her push you out.' Then she looked around the room and said, 'Who thinks Pam should be expelled from this class?'

'God, Cathy, no,' said Pam, feeling the weight of judgement falling around her. A quiet murmur went up and Pam slid from Cathy's grip, but she couldn't avoid Aurora who stood firmly in her way.

'You're not leaving,' she said. 'I refuse to be bullied and black-mailed into letting you go.'

'Well, it's clear then, isn't it, whose side you are on,' said Reggie. She bent and picked up her mat and Janice followed suit, walking then to the bench and shoving their clothes into bags. Reggie pulled on her coat but carried her shoes and socks, not in any mood to spend time putting them on. 'You will regret this,' she spat at Aurora as she marched past. 'I thought you were decent. But you're just the bloody same as them. Shame on you. Just watch your classes go tits up now.'

At the door, Janice turned and surveyed the room. 'No one want to come with us?' She let out a strange little laugh, like something from a pantomime, before disappearing though the door with Reggie. Pam wondered for a moment if Janice was the full quid. What the hell had she just seen?

Aurora put her hand to her forehead, looking like she'd been stricken by a terrible headache. A couple of the other women in the class stepped forward. One put her arm around Aurora's shoulder, another asked her if she was all right. Others turned to Pam saying roughly the same thing, radiating sympathy, a shared indignation. Cathy at her side whispered, 'Jesus, Pammy. I'm so, so sorry. I should never have . . . I just didn't imagine . . . That was horrible.'

Aurora put her head back and looked up at the ceiling. 'I really don't think I handled that very well.'

'It wasn't your job to handle it,' said Pam. 'I shouldn't have come. It was stupid. My fault.'

One of the women next to her, an older woman called Bev with a head of white hair and a mildly cynical look on her face, said, 'You can't do anything with someone like her. I'll tell you something for nothing, she's a troublemaker. If I had to choose I'd have you any day. Good riddance, I say.'

'That's only because you've known me since I was knee-high.'

'Exactly,' said Bev. 'I know who you are, where you come from, and I have no idea who she is. And, what's more, I have no desire to know who she is. Someone who behaves like that.' She shook her head. 'Terrible. Terrible.'

'But she, her family, they have gone through some awful stuff.'

Bev's eye's widened. 'Darling, you're not responsible for that. They want to blame someone. That's how some people are.'

Aurora closed the door left open by Janice and took her place at the head of the group again. 'Apologies to you all for that disruption. If anyone wants to go, I'll completely understand. But for those who want to stay, I hope you'll be able to get into the class and, well, get some benefit from it.'

Murmurs ran around the room, but no one made a move to leave. Pam wasn't sure whether to read this as an act of solidarity or of resignation (what had happened had happened). Either way, no one had shunned her. Surely that was a good enough outcome. 'You start, I just need a moment,' she said, pointing vaguely outside.

When she went out into the corridor she saw the main door was open, left like that by Reggie and Janice as they stormed out. She peered gingerly outside before she closed it. It was still raining, and muddy pools had formed in the worn, potholed areas of the car park. She wasn't sure if any cars were missing. She didn't want to look too closely, try to remember what kind of cars they drove. Blue Commodore? Green Laser? Perhaps Reggie and Janice had gone, or perhaps they were sitting in one of the cars, one that she couldn't see so clearly through the misty rain, planning some act of sabotage or fuelling each other's anger. At least there was no sign of them. She closed the door, snibbing the lock for good measure. She didn't imagine anyone else would be coming in now. And bugger it if they did.

In the toilet she splashed water over her face, checking in the mirror for drips without actually looking at herself. She was becoming expert at that. Looking but not seeing. A few minutes before she'd thought she would be sick, but the urge had passed and she was left only with a sense of exhaustion, fragility. She wasn't sure how she'd go with fifty minutes of bending, stretching, balancing. But she knew she'd be glad of the company if nothing else. She certainly couldn't imagine walking back out into the drizzle now and driving home.

Almost an hour later and the class had finished. Pam lay still, on the mat, eyes firmly closed. She felt exhausted. It had been a while since she had done anything physical. She attempted to send out a psychic message to her fellow classmates to disappear, but her abilities in that department were clearly deficient as she could hear them all loitering, clustered in little groups and quietly conversing. Did they usually do this after a class? The dynamic had changed since she had last come along; there were a lot more attendees in these last few weeks. Contrary to predictions, Aurora's classes had become quite a hit.

'Pam,' she heard someone say above her. She looked up to see Bev. She hauled herself to sitting and Bev told her to have a good week and said she'd look forward to seeing her next Saturday. A procession of women followed, variously smiling, nodding and sharing a kind word or two. Pam sat there on her mat looking up at them as they passed, smiling and nodding back, feeling a little like the Dalai Lama, in exalted humble pose, giving audience. She only wished she had his wit and wisdom. What would he say, she wondered, about her situation? Was she paying for a transgression in another incarnation? Or was this simply the cut and thrust of the here and now, part of the vagaries of life, the randomness of existence?

Finally the room emptied and Aurora sat down next to her. 'How are you?' she asked.

Pam shook her head. 'Do you think this is how it is now? That it's always going to be about the Greens and the Druitts . . . avoiding each other? I was going to say hating each other, but I don't hate them, not really.'

'I wouldn't blame you if you did.'

Pam shook her head slowly. 'What I hate is being so hated by other human beings.'

'Bit like being a politician, getting crap thrown at you every time you go out in public,' said Cathy.

'Except that politicians choose their lives. They might not like it, but they know being abused is part of the job. Me, I don't know how the hell this happened. I'm not sure why they seem to hate me even more than they hate Scott. As if I'm the one who's ultimately responsible.'

'The sins of the mother,' mused Aurora.

'The worst thing is that a part of me thinks they're right,' said Pam.

'What on earth do you mean?'

'That it *was* ultimately my fault. That I should have been better at being a parent.'

'Don't be ridiculous,' said Cathy. 'You know you have three beautiful, good children. If you want to take that attitude then there's been no sin committed. Quite the opposite. Triumphs of the mother, I would say.'

'Just one of them made a terrible mistake.' Pam hugged her knees to her chest, inhaled. 'Does sin have to be intentional? I don't know. Well, I suppose the law would say not.'

'I'm not sure breaking the law and sinning are the same thing,' said Aurora.

'Most of the time they are,' Pam returned.

No one spoke for a little while, then Pam continued, 'Aurora, I want to say thank you for batting for me. I feel awful that I brought this all down on you.'

Aurora let out a small, unexpected laugh. 'Honestly, I had to struggle to be polite. I wanted to tell Reggie to fuck off straight up. Excuse my language, but there's been a bit of it around today. Look, it's not that I don't understand how she feels, but she made me choose. It wasn't that I wanted her to go. Those two have been quite supportive of me and they've brought a few students to my classes. But they're also hard work. Well, Reggie. Reggie's hard work. She's one of those people who only exist in two modes: either adores you or despises you. Frankly, it would have only been a matter of time until I slipped up, got moved from the good books to the bad. It happens when you get put on a pedestal. I never like that feeling.'

'Guess we'll see how many people turn up next week.' Cathy sighed. 'You might be cursing us then.'

'Never,' said Aurora, a defiant look on her face. 'I don't think Reggie will drum up too much support. But I hate all that agitation. Hate that I couldn't have seen some way around it all. I only hope Reggie—all of them—can find some peace.'

'Peace. That's an elusive concept,' said Pam. 'My family is a mess too.'

'Time,' said Aurora, putting her hand on Pam's shoulder. 'That's all you can give it.'

'But it feels like such a *waste* of time. All those good years we could have had, squandered in grief and anger and recrimination. Imprisonment. So much lost. So much we'll never get back. Sometimes it feels too hard to bear.'

'Bloody hell,' said Cathy. 'Pammy, life *is* tough at the moment, I won't deny it, but you have friends. We'll stand up with you, and for you. As you have seen. Things will get better. You just have to focus on the positive.'

'And then everything will be okay?'

'No. Of course not.' Cathy looked slightly put out. 'But you do have a lot on your side. Including us. Well, unless *that's* a problem?'

Pam laughed then, a tender acknowledgement of Cathy's earnestness, her desire for everything to be all right, to be able to magic away problems; her loyalty. 'I am grateful to have you on my side,' she said, and she was grateful, but in her heart she thought that company could only come so far with her on this journey. In the end she was going to have to walk the road alone, and no one else could ever know what that was like.

September 1993

Northam

The back door slammed, reverberating through the house. Pam was in the bedroom, making the bed. 'Scott?' she called. She could hear the clomp of footsteps up the hallway to his bedroom, the door being closed. She continued what she'd been doing, pulling up the quilt, plumping the pillows, folding clothes that had been left on the chair from the day before. When she finished she went down to the kitchen, passing Scott's room, noting the silence. She asked him once what he did in his room during the day, the times he was closed in there, and he told her, with an odd little grin, that he was practising for prison. She wasn't sure if that was an attempt at humour but she didn't find it the least bit funny. It made her want to throw something at him, hit him and wipe that smile off his stupid, beautiful face.

It was a Thursday, one of her two weekdays off, Monday being the other. Thursday was her designated shopping day. She'd never liked Mondays for shopping. They were too busy, too many people in the supermarket aisles catching up from the weekend. Shoppers shopping, staff unpacking. Thursdays were easier days, quieter and more sedate. Plenty of time to browse and plenty of space in which to do it. These days, post-accident, that also meant less chance of being jumped unexpectedly by people she didn't know very well wanting to ask her how she was going or even, as had happened on one occasion, Druitt sympathisers who might eyeball her, hiss a little warning, mention Scott's name loudly as they passed her by.

On any other Thursday she'd be heading out by now to the supermarket in town, or the Fruit Barn on the highway, but this morning she was thrown off balance. Scott's presence in the house, having been home for weeks, almost eight now, refusing to go to school, spending inordinate amounts of time in his room, was strange enough, but now there were his absences as well. He'd taken to leaving the house and not returning for a night or a day, not telling her where he was going or where he'd been. When she'd asked he'd simply ignored her or sidestepped her questions, and she hadn't pressed him. After all, he wasn't a child anymore, he was free to come and go. But it was more than the sum of these small parts. It felt to her as if something essential had broken. A delicate thread that had once encircled her family had been severed, transforming them from a single unit into free-floating bodies, like astronauts walking in space cut loose from the mother ship. If she had to describe the change she'd say that in two short months her world had gone from 'pretty good, thanks' to 'bloody nightmare'. Or in another version: 'I know my family, I've got a good idea what's going on' had become 'I have no idea about anything at all'.

Scott had spent a week in hospital after the accident. She and Mick had driven to Belandra to pick him up the following Sunday. It had been a rigmarole to take him out in the wheelchair, bundle him into the car, store the crutches on the back-seat floor. Scott reminded her of a newborn foal, unused to his new dimensions, his unsteady, clumsy limbs. It made him, the most sturdy, physically adept of her children, seem strangely, forebodingly vulnerable. She expected that he'd be happy about coming back, but instead he seemed more morose than he had been all week and sat silently in the car on the way home. He hadn't asked, when they came up to get him, if Loren was coming. He knew now that she wouldn't venture near the hospital. Pam had told him that she couldn't face it, but that was only her surmising. In truth Loren hadn't said anything at all except that she didn't want to go. 'No, no and no' had been her continued responses to the repeated question about whether she was coming to the hospital with them each day.

It was the second week of the holidays by then. Mike and Josh became frequent visitors to their house along with a few other kids Pam didn't know quite as well, including a girl called Deanna, who claimed she was there to help Scott with his maths homework and stayed in his room until late in the evening after the others had left. Loren, on the other hand, went out, avoiding these comings and goings as much as possible, instead spending time with Katie and Leah, or so she told Pam. At home she crept about like a lizard, rarely speaking to anyone, least of all Scott, her bedroom door implacably closed against them all.

'They just need some time to settle in,' Mick had said when Pam expressed her dismay at the lack of social cohesion in their house, the wall of doors closed in the hallway.

'They used to be best buddies,' replied Pam.

Mick sounded exasperated. 'Give it time. You of all people should know how hard it's been.'

'What do you mean me of all people?'

'You've taken it pretty hard yourself.'

'Well, we all have, haven't we?'

Mick inclined his head and made a grunting sound that could be read as agreement.

'You think I'm over the top about this, don't you?'

'I just think there's only so much we can do. Sometimes you've just got to let things take their course.'

Mick thought that about the dumped animal corpses and phone calls too. Everything in his estimation would pass and all would be fine. Maybe he was right, that she had taken it harder than him, but she'd also been at the front line, dealing with the Druitts, the messages, the children when he was off at work. She wasn't sure he really understood the scope of it all, the raw pain she'd endured. But perhaps she was exaggerating her part and underestimating his?

At the end of the holidays Scott had refused to go back to school, and this unexpected eventuality had shocked Pam. He hadn't indicated he wouldn't return, just didn't get up on the Monday morning. When she went in to wake him, assuming he'd overslept his alarm, he spoke to her from under the bedcovers and told her simply that he wasn't going back. She'd agreed, not concerned then, thinking she could talk him around in a few days, but in the end there was no budging him. At some point she'd wondered if it was the cast and offered to pick up homework from his teachers to save him from having to front up to school.

'No, I'm done,' was all he said.

'But—'

He held his palm up. 'I'm not going to talk about it again. I'm not going back. Ever. Okay?'

Accordingly she didn't bring it up again, well, not with him at least, but every time a friend came over she'd quietly take them aside and ask them to intercede. Only Deanna told her straight up that it was a waste of time.

'But you were helping him with maths,' said Pam, who felt like an idiot as soon as the words were out of her mouth.

Deanna smiled, not unkindly, carried on the fiction. 'That was before he'd talked to the lawyer.'

'The lawyer? You mean Hugh?'

'Don't know. Whoever it was, he said Scott could get years in prison. Like twenty or something. The cops were going to go for the harshest penalty.'

'No,' said Pam, wondering when that conversation had happened, how she'd been kept out of the loop. 'No, he'd never get that much.'

Deanna shrugged. 'He doesn't think school's worth it now. You need to let him make that decision. Hassling him only makes him feel worse.'

Pam had to restrain herself from telling this overconfident young interloper to bugger off. What the hell would she know? But she realised this was all new territory. The rules had changed. Maybe Scott had to use an intermediary now to express himself. She just hoped it wasn't the other way around, that the intermediary wasn't putting words into Scott's mouth. 'Does he think I'm hassling him?' she said at last.

Deanna shrugged again. 'He feels pressured. By everyone.'

Pam had gone to talk to Hugh after that. 'It's a possibility,' he'd said. 'He was a P-plater with a high level of blood alcohol. That alone will ensure he doesn't get minimum. But I've recommended that he plead guilty when the time comes. Show remorse. He clearly is remorseful. There could be other factors. We'll have to look at the witness statements.'

Until then she'd avoided thinking about sentencing. After all, Scott hadn't even been charged yet.

Hugh tilted his head as if to say expect the unexpected. 'Once he is charged it could all happen quite quickly,' he told her. 'He could be put into remand. Although chances are he'll be bailed until the sentencing. If he pleads guilty.'

'What if he doesn't?'

'Well, Scott has indicated he doesn't want to do that—plead not guilty. And there would have to be extenuating circumstances really to override the other factors. And I haven't seen anything in the witness statements that give me hope. But, if he did, same deal. I can't see him getting anything non-custodial.'

'So he'll go to prison. Sooner or later. One way or another.' She barely phrased it as a question.

'Undoubtedly,' had been his response.

Questions about the future were on Pam's mind this morning as she wrote out her shopping list at the table. Today or tomorrow or in another couple of months there would be a knock on the door and a cop would be standing there telling Scott that he was being charged with whatever offences they had decided to charge him with. There were a few to choose from apparently. Culpable driving causing death would most certainly be one of them. Driving under the influence of alcohol would be another. She woke often at night, even sometimes on the nights that she dosed up on sleeping pills (perhaps not heavily enough), thinking about this eventuality, and beyond. His future. Their future. Her mind circled obsessively around and around the idea of how her son would fare in gaol, of where his life might go after that. It was exhausting, all that speculation. Fear of the unknown Mick called it, as if she was going to feel better after Scott had been paraded in front of the judge and sentenced to ten years in an institution on the other side of the state. Feel better knowing he was at the mercy of burly gang members, psychopathic murderers, sadistic prison guards.

'Hey, Mum.'

Pam swivelled to see Scott in the doorway behind her. 'Oh, I thought you'd gone to bed.'

'Nup. I'm up.' He traipsed past her and she noticed that now his cast was gone his jeans seemed to be inordinately baggy, almost falling off him.

'Have you had breakfast?'

He sat down, put his elbows on the tabletop and rested his head on one hand. He appeared as weary as she felt. 'I'm okay,' he muttered. 'I ate something before.'

'Before? Where were you?' She made it sound as casual as she could, not sure if she'd get a reply.

'At Deanna's. Her mum made me some toast.'

'Oh, okay. Well, that's good.'

He looked up and gave her a half smile. 'Good I wasn't sleeping under a bridge.'

'Don't know of any decent bridges around here.' Without thinking she stretched her hand across the table and he glanced up at her for a second before covering it with his own. The warmth of it made her want to cry.

'I'm sorry, Mum,' he said.

'What? What for?'

'All of this.' He looked up at the ceiling for a moment. 'Jeez, what aren't I sorry for?'

'Sweetheart.' She turned her hand upward and squeezed his, said the line, or a variation of the line, she'd been trotting out now for weeks. The line of last resort, she'd come to think of it as. The line that plugged the yawning gap of having nothing better, more useful, to say. 'You know we love you.'

'Yeah.'

The room was quiet except for the ticking of the wall clock behind them. Somewhere, not far away, a dog barked. It was surprising how tranquil it could be up here on the Hill at times. Although she wasn't sure this felt like tranquillity. It was more desolate than that.

'So, things getting serious with Deanna?'

'Hah! Maybe. I don't know. I can't tell anything about anything anymore.'

'Her parents are all right . . .'

'With me? It's just her mum. She's fine.'

Pam had resisted asking a lot about Deanna as part of the not hassling deal and knew little about her, mostly just what she'd observed herself. Under normal circumstances she would have had a roll of questions about who her mother was, what she did, where she lived. These days she mostly waited to be told. 'Do you want her to stay here? I mean, she can anytime, you know.'

'What?' Scott looked surprised at this, almost puzzled. 'Oh,' he said after a few seconds. 'No. No. I like to . . .'

'Get away?'

'Yeah, I guess.' He ran his fingers through his hair. It was long and straggly now, brushing his shoulders. He looked like a beach bum in his ragged t-shirt and the too big jeans. 'Speaking of which, I wanted to talk to you about something.'

Pam almost stopped breathing. A dozen scenarios ran through her mind. She must have looked stricken because he let out a small laugh.

'I'm not doing a runner if that's what you're thinking. Not that I'd tell you anyway. But ah, no. I was going to say, how would you feel if I went to stay at Grandpa's?'

Pam blinked. It was the last thing she was expecting. 'Dad's? Really?'

'Look,' Scott leaned forward, 'things aren't good here. Obviously. So much crap happening—which I've brought on. I thought it would be good for me and Loz not to have to be around each other.'

Pam tried to digest everything he was saying but only got as far as him moving to her father's. 'Why Dad's? It's out of town and you don't have a car.'

'We get on all right. And I'm going to do some work up there for him. There's an old bike I can fix up so I can get around. Pa said I could borrow his car if I need to in the meantime. It makes sense, don't you think?'

Pam stared at her son. How deeply he'd thought about their situation, seen the way in which they had all been affected, and he'd come up with a solution perhaps not worse than any other. 'Maybe,' she said at last.

'You think Loz and I are going to work this stuff out, don't you? But I don't know about that, not soon anyway. I don't want more bad vibes. It feels too hard right now.'

'Okay,' said Pam. She picked up the pen and scribbled a meaningless line under the last item on her list. 'I understand all that. But I'm not sure about this. I mean the Druitts. They might start targeting Grandpa. It's isolated up there. I really wouldn't trust them.'

'Him,' said Scott. 'Ray. It's only him.'

Pam frowned. 'Why do you say that? You don't know.'

'I do. I've talked to Kyle.'

'What? When?'

'A few times.'

'How on earth did you do that?'

'On the way home from school. I just waited for him one day, told him I was really sorry and I wanted to let his family know. At first he kind of blocked me. But later we talked and he was okay. Said it could just as easily have been Troy driving and me dead. He told me he was never going to pass on my messages though because he reckons his old man would bash him if he knew we'd been talking.'

'Bash him?'

Scott gave her a flat-mouthed look as if to say he didn't know the truth of it.

'Did he bash Troy?'

'Not that I ever heard. Troy was like the . . . Well, the sun shone out of his arse, you know.'

'What about Maxine?'

Scott's face told her that it had never occurred to him that Maxine might be the victim of Ray's fists. 'Troy didn't tell me about anything like that. Just some of the bullshit he'd have to tell his old man sometimes so he would let him go out. Or to get money. His family weren't high on the list of things to talk about. I just know his dad was, is, a hard man. Used to hang out with bikies when he was young. He's got this code of honour stuff going on. I think Kyle was just freaking out, that's all. He said his dad has gone kind of psycho since the accident. He can't really cope.'

'What does that mean?'

Scott shrugged.

'So how do you know it's just him making the calls?'

'Kyle said.'

'But not Maxine?'

'He said his mum keeps telling his dad to stop. He said she's worried he'll get caught and go to gaol—like me.'

'So there aren't any bikies involved?'

Scott looked at her blankly. 'No. They're from when he used to live in Wang, like I said, when he was young. I don't think he even sees them anymore.'

'Karen and Gary said they were at the funeral.'

'Wow.' Scott considered this for a moment.

'So you haven't seen them?'

'Nup.'

'Do you get harassed when you're out?'

'What the hell, Mum? This is worse than those bloody police interviews.'

'I'm sorry, sweetheart.' She gave him a long look. 'I don't get to talk to you much anymore. I don't know what you have to deal with. You don't tell me anything.'

He shook his head. 'Nothing to tell. No one says much. It's not like I'm out on the streets. Usually just at Mike's or Deanna's. Everyone's busy with school. I don't go to parties or anything.'

'So how does Kyle know it's his dad?'

Scott sighed. 'I didn't ask that. But it makes sense, doesn't it? It takes energy to make those calls, leave roadkill around.

You have to think about it a lot. Who else is going to be bothered? Ray's the only one.'

For a moment Pam had a flash of pity for Ray. Understood again that the pain of his loss could drive him to such acts. She tried not to think about Troy, tried not to evoke his image, his voice, his laugh. But every now and then something would remind her of his former presence in their house, of the part he played in their lives. 'You must miss him,' she said quietly.

Scott looked across the table at her and she saw his eyes were glassy. 'I'm going back to bed,' he said.

It was unusually quiet at the supermarket. Pam grabbed a trolley inside the door and pushed it down one empty aisle and into another. It was only when she reached the tea, coffee and biscuit section that she saw another shopper, Mary Robinson as it turned out, her glasses perched on the end of her long nose, peering at a package. Pam was never quite sure how to deal with Mary. She wasn't someone with whom she had an easy rapport, which wasn't to say she didn't like her; it was more that they had never clicked, felt that ease. There was a directness about her that she found slightly unnerving. Des and Mary were not much older than her but, for some reason, Pam always thought of them as being more like her parents. Perhaps because Des and her father had had so much to do with each other in the early days, when her father was the mayor, and Des, the new young constable in town, was sent out by old Sergeant Todd in a fever of 1970s social engagement to represent the police in the community. Law-enforcement gravitas, city-slicker glamour, Des and Mary had something about them that made them seem so much more mature, more grown up than most of the twenty-somethings Pam knew. Even after she got married herself, had her children, the impression remained, bolstered in some way because she never really got to know them well, especially Mary. Despite the fact they lived on the Hill, only a few streets away, Mary's churchgoing, her childlessness, meant they moved in different spheres.

Mary was looking for sponge finger biscuits to make tiramisu, she told Pam, but she wasn't sure she was going to find them here. 'I'm wondering if these will do instead.' She held up a product that Pam couldn't readily identify. Pam shrugged. She was a home cook and didn't buy biscuits too often. Mary said she didn't either, which was proving to be a problem for her now in sorting out what she needed.

'I'm sure you could make them yourself,' said Pam.

'Perhaps,' Mary said. 'Although that would seem like a lot of trouble to go to.'

'Would a regular sponge do?' Pam creased her face into a look of possibility. She had no idea what a tiramisu was.

They stood awkwardly for a moment, then Mary said, 'How is everything going for you?'

Pam had discovered in the last months that people were mostly general in their inquiries about her and her family. They might ask how life was going, but there was a blankness to their faces, an eagerness to move the conversation along that betrayed their reluctance to really know, or at least to go too deep. But Pam sensed Mary was different. She already knew about their life, what they had had to endure. She genuinely wanted to know how Pam was being affected and Pam suddenly and inexplicably wanted to tell her.

'I have to say that life is not wonderful.'

Mary nodded. 'I can imagine. A lot to deal with. Your son's doing his last year of school, isn't he?'

'Actually, he didn't go back. Doesn't think there's any point. So, no.'

Mary considered this momentarily. 'Is he working?'

'He's . . . Well, he's about to do some work for his grandfather.'

'It's a good thing to work,' said Mary. 'I mean to have something to occupy you. And your daughter? Loren?'

'She is back at school and . . . she's very quiet. She's finding life pretty tough.'

'I know you were getting some harassment. That wouldn't help the situation.'

'Well, some harassment continues. I try not to let the kids be too aware of it. But it still affects us, I suppose.'

'Have you talked to Des?'

'Not for a while.'

Mary frowned at this. 'Keep him up to date. It's his job to keep you safe.'

Pam spoke matter of factly. 'I don't know about keeping us safe. I mean, he wasn't able to track the perpetrator before. I can't see how that will change.'

Two shoppers walked past in opposite directions and Pam swivelled her trolley towards the shelf to allow them by.

Mary was close to her now, her voice quiet. 'But you do know who it is, don't you? Aren't you afraid for your safety?'

'Frankly, it's disturbing, but I don't really feel unsafe. Mostly I think he's a manipulator. He wants us to feel what he feels. And it's his way of doing that.'

'So you do know who it is?'

Pam smiled wearily. 'We can't prove anything. It could be anyone making the calls. Des couldn't connect them to the Druitts' home phone. Only phone boxes. Calls made from different boxes at random times. The police don't have the time or money to stake them out.'

Mary nodded. 'How is Mick going with all this? He must find it frustrating.'

'There has been some improvement. We don't have as many unwanted gifts on the front path now, which is what he used to see, getting up in the morning to go to work. I'm the one who usually gets the phone calls—the ones I don't manage to avoid.'

Mary tucked her chin, arched her eyebrows. 'You mean you don't tell him?'

'I don't want him to worry.'

'Really? That's a lot to carry.'

'I feel that it's worse when we both get involved. Especially if neither of us can do anything.'

Mary looked sympathetic. 'Des tells me that too. He doesn't always talk a lot about his work. About the worst of it. He says he feels better if I don't know the details. That I can be a sort of neutral territory.'

'But you still do know, don't you? You're his wife.'

'There are some things you can't avoid. It's hard to know if your imaginings are worse than the truth. But, on balance, I think I'm happy that he keeps some things back.'

'There you go then.'

Mary leaned forward, gripped the side of the trolley. 'But it's not the same. What he keeps back are things that disturb him, not those that threaten us.'

Pam felt her heart beat a little harder. 'You think I should tell Mick about every single call? Would that really help?'

'Well, of course, that's your choice. But if I were you, I'd keep complaining. That man should not be able to get away with this behaviour. No matter what has led up to this. There is absolutely no excuse for it—to my mind anyway. It worries me, it really does. He's a bully.'

'I think it will peter out, in the end. He'll go back to work and . . .'

'That will be that?'

'Essentially.'

Mary lifted an eyebrow sceptically. 'Go and talk to Des again. Even if he can't prove Ray Druitt has been making the calls, he can give him a talking to. You don't need to put up with this.'

April 2016

Melbourne

The morning opened black and rainy. Jason left before dawn and Lori, who'd woken as the front door closed, lay in bed listening to the downpour and wishing she could go back to sleep. At seven she roused and went to the kitchen, made sandwiches for the kids and put the cereal, fruit and milk out on the table ready for breakfast. She took a quick shower, dressed and got the kids up. The weather had eased a little by then, but the forecast was for intermittent rain and thunderstorms. She'd probably have to drive them to school, a prospect she wasn't keen on. Walking in the morning was the best start to the day. Driving in the rain made her nervous.

The three of them ate together, mostly in silence. A shiny curtain of water outside the window rendered the back garden in shades of soft grey-green.

'Where does all the water come from?' Cody asked.

'The clouds,' said Lori, who had illustrated the water cycle several times now.

'Clouds are fluffy.'

'The fluff is made up of tiny drops of water.'

He shook his head in disbelief. 'It's not strong enough to hold all that water,' he replied.

'Exactly,' she said, getting up to collect the bowls. 'That is why it all falls down to the ground again.'

A frown flickered across Cody's face. She could see he was itching to ask more, clear this up, but she needed to get them moving. 'Come on,' she said. 'Clothes. Teeth. Five minutes.' She always said five minutes but in reality she allowed them more like fifteen. She hoped she wasn't permanently warping their sense of time, failing to familiarise them to their need to keep on a proper schedule.

She stacked the dishwasher then went to check on them. Sophie had brushed her teeth and was in their bedroom, pulling her school t-shirt over her head. Cody was sitting on his bed, still in his pyjamas, looking at a book. 'What's he saying?' he asked, pointing to the text underneath the pictures.

'He's saying, "It's time for school, Mr Fox."'

He looked up at her blankly. When was it, she thought, that humour kicked in? She was sure Sophie had already twigged by this age. 'Come on, bud,' she said, ruffling his hair then picking up his uniform from the chair and placing it next to him. He looked at it for a moment as if he had no idea what it was. Such a dreamer. Had she been like that as a kid? She suspected so, but who would know? Back then, kids were idiosyncratic. All sorts of behaviour was considered normal in the broadest sense. Now too much mental drifting and you were booked in for tests with the psychologist.

She took their bags into the kitchen and put their lunch boxes inside. The rain seemed to have slowed again, but she didn't trust they could walk. In the hallway she nabbed Cody, pointing him in the direction of the bathroom. 'Teeth,' she said.

Soon enough they were out of the house and getting into the car, shoes wet from the grass verge. Warm bodies and respiration fogging up the windscreen. The last time they'd driven to school was the day the police came. Only last Thursday, less than a week before, but it seemed like a lifetime. Even the weather had changed wildly since then.

The traffic to school was better than she'd thought and they managed to park reasonably close. She walked them in, the three of them huddled under the giant golf umbrella she kept in the boot of the car. No gathering in the playground on wet days, just straight into class. As she ran back towards her car she saw Anselma standing under the oak tree at the front gate.

'Hey, we meet at last,' she said as Lori reached her. 'Everything okay?'

Lori squinted out into the rain. 'Yes. And no.'

'You want to talk?'

Lori laughed lightly. 'Yes and no. I need to go home and do some work. I'm so behind.' She turned her face to Anselma. 'In a few days?'

'Sure.' Anselma gave her a searching look, as though she already had a good idea about the very thing that she hadn't been told, and Lori felt a spasm of guilt. She wished she could say then that in those few days her life had turned into something that she didn't quite recognise. But there was no nutshell to this story, no way she could simply throw the bare bones at her friend and rush off into the sunset. No way either that she could speak to her before Jason.

At home again, she stared at the pile of papers on her desk. All had been ignored for days now and she wasn't sure where to start. (Where had she left off?) It was hard to concentrate, but she knew she only had a limited amount of time before she headed back to Fitzroy. She rang the editor she'd been dealing with and told her that her brother had been in an accident and was in hospital and that this had disrupted her work. She had to choke back the sensation that she was telling a lie. The editor was sympathetic enough, and at least grateful to have had some word. She didn't know Lori well enough to say that she didn't know Lori had a brother. She didn't know her well enough to offer more than the usual murmurings of compassion. It was a relief to be free of scrutiny.

Lori set to work then, three pages sketched out by lunchtime. The shape of the book settled again in her head. She put her pen down and passed through the house, pulling the beds to a semblance of made, throwing the toys into boxes and kicking shoes under the beds. In the kitchen she assembled a quick sandwich with bread from the freezer and the depleted stocks in the fridge. She thought about dinner. The perennial question. A trip to the shops for something to put on pasta or rice would be required at some point.

She picked up her phone and dialled Jason. She didn't often call him at work, his work day so busy that contact was perfunctory.

'Hey,' she said when he answered. 'I'm wondering what time you'll be home tonight.'

'Why?' he said sharply, uncharacteristically. 'Do you need to go out?'

'No,' she replied, trying to keep annoyance out of her voice. 'I was thinking that if you were going to come home early I might get some fish.'

'Sure,' he said, distant now. 'Sorry, I'm in the middle of something. I'll ring you back a bit later, okay?'

'Yeah. Okay.'

She stood at the bench and looked out to the garden. The rain had transformed it, given it intensity, definition, painted the concrete path a dark grey, the weeds a lush green, the yellowed leaves of the pear tree a rich red-gold. She'd never doubted Jason, Jason's love. She wasn't sure why. Most people seemed to doubt their partners sometime or other. Even his late nights didn't prompt her to think he was having an affair or just didn't want to spend time with her. When he was with her, he was all hers. He could be tired, grumpy, irritable, but she was always his focus.

'He adores you, that man,' Anselma had commented one day. 'You think?'

'I know. Ross was never like that.' Ross was Anselma's former partner, father of Sasha. 'To think you've been together all these years and his eyes still light up when you walk into the room.'

In those moments on the phone, she thought she'd noted a change, something subtle and new, as though she was no longer that important person; that something else mattered more than her. Then she thought about her own preoccupation these last days and wondered if he was feeling the same thing. She added her plate and cup to the dishwasher and put it on. Grabbed her bag and keys and headed for the car.

—

In intensive care she went through the same ritual that she had on previous days, greeting staff, donning the gown, applying the antiseptic handwash. The curtains were only partially drawn and from her position outside the door she could see that there was no nurse in the room, that when she entered it would just be her and Scott. He was lying half propped up on his bed, his eyes closed, and whether he was conscious or not was impossible to tell. She fought down the queasy feeling in her stomach and slid the door back. When she turned to close it again she felt, as she had each time, that she'd passed through an airlock, was entering a foreign, unexplored world where anything might happen.

The room was quiet, just a small whirr of something electrical in the background. She walked to the bed and looked at her brother. As if on cue he opened his eyes and stared back at her.

'Hello,' she said.

A slow smile.

'Can you speak?'

He opened his mouth and a small croaky sound came forth like a false start, then, 'Think so.'

Lori put her fingers to her lips, thinking that she hadn't heard her brother's voice in all this time, his slow country accent. She couldn't tell if he still had that from those two blurred words but the tone was there. He sounded like Mick; even though she hadn't been able to remember Mick's voice, she could recognise it now. She looked around for the chair and pulled it up, hoping he wouldn't fade back to sleep, unconsciousness, whatever it was, wherever he was, before she settled. But he remained awake, eyes wide open.

She had a moment of doubt. 'You know who I am, don't you?'

His nod was accompanied by a small sound. He was still gazing at her as though she was an apparition, the second coming, but also an object of affection. A friend long unseen.

'I don't know what to say. This feels very strange. I think you already know a bit about me. If you can remember. I know nothing about you.'

'Nothing,' said Scott, 'to know.'

'I doubt that very much.' She scanned his bedside table. There was a small cup with a straw. She motioned her head towards it and said, 'Want some water?'

'Mmm.'

She took the cup and positioned the straw towards his mouth. She noticed that his lips were dry, flaking and slightly cracked. He took a sip then put his hands up to the cup, his fingers brushing hers.

'Enough?'

'Mmm,' he said again.

'Do you remember me coming in before?'

'Today?'

'No. Other days.'

He shook his head. 'Feel you've been . . . don't remember.' He paused for a moment as if he had to catch his breath. 'Sorry you had to come.'

'The police found my address at your place.'

He opened his mouth to speak, then faltered. 'Shouldn't have . . .'

'You don't have anyone in your life?'

'You won't . . . be stuck.'

A feeling overtook her then that she couldn't quiet identify. Pride. Wilfulness. 'You think I'd be standing here now if that was a consideration?'

Behind them the door slid open and Malcolm came in. 'Good afternoon. How are we?'

Lori turned in her seat. 'It's incredible. Scott is speaking.'

'And it's not Mandarin,' said Malcolm, hovering at the monitor for a moment before coming to inspect Scott more closely. 'How are you feeling right now, Mr Green? Any blurred vision, head-ache, nausea? Anything else we need to know about?'

'Head. Ache.'

'We can get you something for that. What would you give it out of ten?'

'Five.'

Malcolm pursed his lips slightly then returned to the computer, keying in a few words. 'Orrighty. I'll be back in a moment with something for that pain.'

Scott closed his eyes, tilted his head back into the pillow.

Scott?' she said, lightly touching his hand and feeling, with his lack of response, a bubble of impatience that immediately made her feel guilty. All she wanted was to talk to him. So long without contact, without looking for contact, and now her only desire was to talk and talk and talk. To listen, to know. But being here wasn't about her, it was about him. He needed time to recover and heal and she had to wait. There was testament in how far he still had to go in the dark circles under his eyes and the yellowed skin that stretched tight from cheekbone to jaw. It was the face of someone who'd been stripped of the few reserves he'd had.

Even the tan she'd noted when she'd first seen him seemed to have faded, making the small dark lines on his arm—just visible under the sleeve of his hospital gown—more obvious than they might have otherwise been. She looked at them, mentally piecing together an image from the little she could see and what she could remember; willing the entire shape of it into being.

They had driven to Shepparton that night—she, Scott, Troy, Mike and Josh—to that crumby tattoo parlour with the bleaching fluorescent light and the plastic chairs and the laminated prints of tattoo designs and photos of wild horses and trees and flowers covering the walls. That was the night she had realised there was something happening with Troy; something more than him indulging his friend's sister, something more than her tolerating her brother's friend. She, Mike and Troy had squeezed into the back seat of Scott's car, and all she could think of was the sensation of Troy beside her, his thigh pressed hard against her thigh, his breath on her cheek when he turned to speak.

It had been Troy who'd wanted the tattoo, a decision both spontaneous and deliberate. He'd been thinking about it for a long time, making drawings, accumulating designs. Loren had seen some of them in passing as he'd tried to convince Scott (and perhaps shore himself up in the process) of the beauty of getting one himself. Scott had been ambivalent, simultaneously attracted to the idea and repelled by the reality. 'Tattoos are forever,' he'd said uncertainly.

Troy had laughed hard and replied that that was the point. 'I want this on my arm forever. To remind me,' he had declared as they'd walked to the car. 'Of now. Of who I am right now. When I'm old and my skin is saggy and wrinkled I'm going to look at it and remember this.'

Lori leaned forward now and delicately lifted the sleeve of Scott's gown. There it was, the whole image. A sweet plump swallow, as good as you'd see on any sailor, faded to a washed-out indigo, an empty scroll in its beak. She recalled that the tattooist was a burly guy who looked like he rode a Harley Davidson and smoked piles of weed. What did he want him to write in the space, he'd asked Scott in a jaded voice, and Scott, who'd seemed to have sobered up after being subjected to the needle for twenty minutes, had said he wasn't sure. He was going to leave it until he was. She had known in that instant he'd regretted doing it. It wasn't him. But, of course, now it was. Now, whenever he'd look at this, he'd remember that moment. And so many more. She wasn't surprised to see he'd never filled the scroll in. What would he have to add? Live and learn. Life is suffering. Ink is destiny.

The door slid open and Malcolm returned holding a small medicine cup in his hand. 'Here we go,' he said.

Scott opened his eyes then. He wore a stunned expression, the kind that people have when they've woken from a long and deep sleep. Malcolm spoke to him, asked him a couple of perfunctory questions before giving him the liquid painkillers.

Lori sat down again. 'Do you want me to do anything? Call your work? Or anyone who needs to know.'

Scott squinted up at her. 'Lambeth Lincoln.'

'Lambeth Lincoln,' she repeated. 'Who's that?'

'Work.'

'What do you do?'

'Chippie.'

'Wow.' She considered this. 'I always thought you'd be working with machines or cars.'

'No cars.' His eyes rolled up to the ceiling in a way that might have been voluntary or involuntary.

She put her other hand on his hand then, feeling the roughness of it. 'Is that why you were on a bike?'

He looked at her as though the question made no sense.

'Do you remember?'

'A bike.'

'I mean what happened. The accident.'

'No.' He pressed his head back against the pillow and closed his eyes.

She waited for a minute for him to connect again, but he seemed to have fallen back to sleep. She looked over to Malcolm at the monitor, where he stood clicking away at the keyboard. 'Shall I go?' she asked quietly.

He inclined his head, smiled sympathetically. 'That was a lot of chat. It's exhausting for them when they come round, have to start processing. Good to take a break.'

She waited a little longer before getting up and going downstairs where she called Daniel Levandi from the café, sitting at the same table she'd been sitting with him the day before. 'He's pretty with it,' she said after telling him where she was and what she'd been doing. 'Surprisingly so. I really didn't know what to expect.'

'Good enough for me to talk to?'

'He's had it for today. I burned him out. Sorry. But he did tell me that he didn't remember the accident.'

Daniel didn't reply immediately. 'Okay. I'll talk to him tomorrow then. Probably be better anyway, stuff can come back over time.'

'You need to call the hospital first. They might be doing some more tests sometime tomorrow.'

'Right.' He sounded a little distracted, as though he was reading something or writing something down while they were talking. She'd noticed he often did that. Multitasking. It made him sound vague, unfocused, when experience had shown her he was far from it.

'Oh, almost forgot. He also gave me his employer's name. Some building firm, by the sound of it, called Lambeth Lincoln.'

'Okay. That's excellent. I was waiting on a call back from someone at the super fund. Don't need to worry about that now.' There was a momentary pause. 'Must have been something to talk to him. You all right?'

She smiled on her end of the phone. 'I am. It's strange, but I was really glad to talk to him. I amazed myself.' She could feel a sting behind her eyes, emotion threatening to overtake her.

'I'm happy to hear that.'

'Are you really?'

'It might surprise you to know that cops like good outcomes from their cases. It's not all about solve rates.' It was hard to tell if he was being serious or teasing.

She laughed, cleared her throat. 'Sorry, it's been a long day, I'm feeling a bit emotional. Got to go and pick up my children. Pull myself together.'

'Well, you do that, get some rest. I will continue with this trail, see what I can find. Thank you.'

'Thank *you*,' she said, putting the emphasis on the last word.

'Just part of the job,' he said. 'Just what I do.'

October 1993

Northam

D es hadn't been to the Druitt house for five weeks. And, five weeks before that, which had taken him back to the night in question. The night of the accident. Normally he would have felt somewhat ashamed about this state of affairs, but he'd had enough contact from the Druitts not to feel he needed to visit more regularly to keep them updated. Ray or Maxine rang him to see when charges were being laid, when an arrest would be made. They rang him to complain that they weren't being taken seriously. They rang him to say they'd seen Scott Green driving around town and that he shouldn't still have his licence. Des tried to explain the way it went. The complaints about Scott driving were pointless (he hadn't used that exact word, that would have been a red rag) as he had to be charged first with an offence and charges weren't, strictly speaking, coming from him. The police in Wangaratta would be dealing with this because one of their units, Major Traffic, had dealt with the accident. When this was about to be set in motion, Des might be given a slight advance warning and, if so, he in turn would tell Ray and Maxine, but he couldn't say definitively when that would be.

A few weeks ago Ray Druitt had come in, stood over his desk and declared it was an open and shut case and there was no reason for delay. All Des could do was shrug mildly, invite him to sit down. He understood Ray's pain, didn't want to seem dismissive or cause him any more hurt than he'd already endured, but there was no getting around the sad reality of it. 'These things can take a while to process, Ray,' was all he could say, and Ray had looked at him in that contemptuous way he had, curled his lip and turned and walked out. Ray was a man who believed that he had to fight for everything in life—in fact that nothing was worth anything without a damn good tussle, a show of force. Des also had a feeling that Ray was a man who believed in conspiracies. In his mind, responsibility for his son's death would never be shouldered. If he was to have any satisfaction he would have to fight for it because people in this town didn't want to let one of their precious boys take the blame. As far as he was concerned, Scott Green would never truly pay the price unless he was made to. Ray was out to make a point.

Most recently Maxine had rung Des to say that her sister Regina had been verbally attacked by Pam Green at the town hall on the weekend. 'I want a restraining order against that woman,' Maxine had brayed down the phone at Des, who for a moment had wished he had a restraining order against her. He held the receiver out from his head and his young constable, John Ryan, had turned in his chair and stared at him wide-eyed before uttering a small snigger and returning to his paperwork.

Des had already heard about the supposed verbal assault incident. Lorna Crew's daughter had been at the yoga class (quite popular these days apparently) and reported back to Lorna who had reported to Mary. Mary had also told him about running into Pam in the supermarket and Pam's reluctance to let him know about her family's continuing harassment. He had gone to visit Pam after that, but she was adamant that the drama would abate. Things were improving. She said she didn't want to make any kind of formal complaint. From his vantage point, he could see the way it played out: Pam trying to dampen down the situation by ignoring it if she could, while the Druitts, feeling disregarded, fobbed off, were keen to beat a drum of discontent—in plain sight, or by stealth. There was no winning this one. And, while he didn't have the resources to stake out the town's phone boxes, he certainly could have a little chat.

Des got into the station's one unmarked car and drove across to the estate. When he'd first come to Northam, the estate didn't exist. It was farmland then. A dairy property that belonged to the Ungers. He had an abiding memory of Mr Unger, although he couldn't quite recall his first name after all this time (was it Cyril?) standing on the grass strip next to the road complaining that young hoons had broken one of his gates, allowing his cattle to get out. Des had examined the gate in question and sympathised with Unger but had told the old man that they had little hope of catching whoever did it. Unger had looked at him in a way that was reminiscent of Ray now—half contempt, half anger—and declared that it was virtually useless to have police presence in the town if they were never going to catch any wrongdoers. Des had felt, not for the first time, nor the last time, a sense of quiet frustration with the way that people didn't understand how the world worked, the way they wanted someone to come along and fix the unfixable. Like children. And he the parent. Which he had to admit to himself is what he'd signed on for all those years ago. What else was a cop but one of the parents? For better or for worse (there certainly were egregious examples) for all concerned.

Unger's farm sat right across the river from town. Prime real estate that no one except wily old Jim Temple, ever aware of possibilities for development and growth, had ever thought could be anything other than a home for cows. Unger had died in the late seventies, but his wife lived on another ten years, running the farm for a time and then gradually reducing the herd, selling off the equipment. Jim Temple had the land rezoned by the time Mrs Unger died and the farm, inherited by a son who'd long moved away, was sold off, subdivided. Here it was now, a tract of sinuous wide streets, long, low houses, some small trees still not grown to maturity. Although, happily, a few old oaks still dotted about. Des couldn't quite marry this manicured suburbia—especially here in Northam—with the wide sloping green hills he'd first seen all those years ago. Whenever he came up here, he always tried to locate the house, the sheds, fences. Only the big exotic trees gave him any sense of place, markers in what seemed now to be a foreign landscape, which he was, half a decade later, only just growing used to.

Des parked the car one street back from the cul-de-sac and got out. He leaned on the bonnet and lit up a cigarette. Standing in the tepid sunshine with the eucalypt-scented breeze wafting down on him, he thought, not for the first time, that he really needed to give up the fags. He didn't know how Mary put up with him. She'd smoked for a while herself, years ago, as a kind of bonding exercise he'd figured at the time. But smoking didn't suit her and she'd stopped after a year or two. Lucky her. It would be no easy thing for him, having been hard at it for thirty-five years. His parents had smoked too. He should have taken note, both of them addictive personalities dying from the gaspers in one way or another. He stubbed the smoke out and got back into the car. Took a peppermint from the roll in his pocket and put it into his mouth, then drove around the corner.

The little street was deathly quiet. He remembered coming here the night of the accident. In the darkness you had no idea of the landscape of the place; that behind the houses a small band of grass melted slowly upward into the bush, giving the impression that the environment was cradling the estate, holding it close. He could imagine when the world ended that the bush would slowly spread downward again and take over everything man-made below. Maybe that wouldn't be such a bad thing, he thought. Peace. It would happen one day, when they were all long gone. The world put to rights again.

Des stood on the front verandah clutching a manila folder that was more for show than anything else and feeling faintly nauseous. He hadn't rung the Druitts earlier because he knew it would only have provoked a barrage of questions, which would have led to a query about why he was really coming. And the reason for his coming was something that needed to be dealt with face to face. He knocked on the door and within seconds a wary-looking Maxine opened it. He wondered if she'd glimpsed him through the window first as she didn't seem surprised.

'I hope you've got some good news for us,' she said as she opened the door.

He kept his face neutral. 'Is Ray here?'

'He's in the garage. I'll get him.' She pointed into the living room. 'Sit down.'

He'd sat in this room with Ray on the night he'd come from the accident with the news. He'd never felt so wretched, and he'd felt pretty wretched on many occasions before. That night Ray hadn't woken Maxine, but she'd heard them at some point. Heard Ray sobbing, Des believed, and she'd come out and when she realised what had happened she'd run into the kitchen and retched into the sink. With the focus on Ray and Maxine, the pain of the situation, he hadn't noticed that night how impeccably tidy the house was. It was only when he'd come back last month that he'd seen it. He wondered if it had always been like this or if it was a reaction to Troy's death. He noticed it again today, the minimalism, the lack of clutter, the lack of colour or, indeed, any kind of personality. No books, few trinkets. One family photo on the sideboard. It looked like a hotel. Some people liked that, he supposed.

Ray appeared before him in trackpants and an old shirt. Not too grubby for being in the garage, but Des figured he'd probably been wearing overalls and had scraped them off.

As if reading his mind, Ray said, 'Want to come into the kitchen? I'm a bit dirty to sit down here.'

Des thought about the night of the accident and how Des had been rain sodden. He'd supposed given the terrible events no one was going to care too much about the puddles, tracked in grit from the road. Maxine would have spent the next morning between jagged despair and cleaning the carpet. The only consolation was that it might have given her some distraction in those early hours of grief.

In the kitchen Maxine put on the kettle. Des was surprised by that, thought she'd want him gone. But then she hadn't heard what he had to say yet. He might find himself doused in hot Nescafe in a couple of minutes.

Ray sat across the table from Des and leaned forward. 'So what do you have to tell us?'

Des hadn't been so close up to Ray for a while. He noted his unshaven chin and bloodshot eyes and wondered. He'd never heard that Ray drank, but there was something about him now, a little dishevelled, unfocused. Ray had always been meticulous about his appearance. They both had, he and Maxine. But she seemed as neat as ever, only her colour palette a little more subdued. 'I'm sorry, I still don't have news on the charges . . .'

Ray let out a low groan. 'Ah, jeez.'

'I really wanted to talk to you about the Greens.'

It was as if a static charge had been let off. Ray and Maxine both tensed at once. Ray's face turned stony.

'What about that restraining order?' Maxine spat.

'I believe that it was your sister with that problem,' said Des. 'If she wants to take one out, she'll have to come into the station and fill out a form and give us a good reason for her concerns.'

Maxine's face contorted a little, as if holding something back. Behind her the kettle stared to whistle. 'Tea or coffee?'

'Coffee, thanks. Bit of milk. No sugar.'

Maxine turned to the bench and Ray said flatly, 'What's this about the Greens?'

'Well, I was hoping you might be able to help me.'

Ray leaned back in his chair, arms crossed, his expression contemptuous.

'Someone has been harassing them.'

Des heard Maxine let out a small, almost jubilant guffaw.

Des continued. 'We have no idea who's behind the incidents, but I was wondering if you might know anything. Maybe put in a word to stop what's going on.'

'You must think I'm a moron, Mr, sorry, Sergeant Robinson,' said Ray.

'In what way?'

'You pretty clearly think this is me. Well, I can tell you right now, I couldn't care less about the Greens. Wouldn't cross the road to spit on them, fire or no fire. If someone's harassing them, bloody good job. But don't look at me.'

'So you don't want to help us put a stop to this?'

'How could I do that?'

'Put the word out.'

Ray scoffed. 'There'll be a stop when justice is done.'

Justice, thought Des, and rubbed the side of his face with his palm. 'So you have some idea who might be responsible then?'

'No. No I don't.' Ray's jaw set hard. 'What did they do, anyway?'

Des felt the weight of farce on his shoulders. Telling Ray what he already knew. It was like watching a fire alongside the arsonist who'd lit it. He recounted the phone calls, roadkill and car eggings. Ray sat immobile, unmoved for all intents and purposes. Maxine put a coffee down in front of Des and he looked up into her eyes and she glanced away across to her husband, who fractionally softened. Des saw a complicity that, if he was a paranoid type, might make him wonder if Maxine had spiked his coffee. Especially when he realised she hadn't made anything for herself, or Ray.

'So they complained, did they?' said Ray. 'Reckoned it was me?'

'No, actually, they didn't. This came to my notice in another way.'

'Really.'

Maxine sat down next to Ray. He could see the exhaustion in her face, grief settling into fine etched lines around her eyes and mouth. 'Sergeant. It's impossible to tell you how much this has affected us. Those people took so much away from us. You can't expect us to have any sympathy for them.'

'So what you are saying is that if you did know who was doing this, you wouldn't do anything about it.'

Ray stared at Des. Maxine looked across the kitchen. 'If anyone is doing anything, they're doing it for us,' she said, a proud note to her voice.

'It's just that these things don't tend to play out too well in court,' said Des. 'They can make judges more sympathetic to the accused, end up in a lighter sentence.'

Ray's face remained impassive, but Des could see the muscles in his jaw work just a little. 'I wouldn't think you'd want Green to get a heavy sentence.'

'Sentencing is not what I do,' said Des.

'Ah, but you are part of something here though, aren't you?'

'I'm a part of the Northam community, I hope, Ray. A broad church.'

Ray shook his head. 'You reckon there's such a thing as the Northam community? Well, not one that I'm a part of. No one from this community has come to me to say they're sorry. To lend a hand. Just a coupla old mates from years back. Family. They're the only ones who've been around. But they don't live here. No one who does live here could care less.'

Des wanted to say that Pam Green had come, had offered her condolences (he'd heard a simple version of that story from her when she first told him about the harassment), but he held his tongue. 'I'm sorry to hear that. I suppose you haven't been here too long.'

'Not by the standards of this town, no.'

Des took a sip of his coffee and thought about Mary, how hard she'd worked to find a place here, make a new life. He had a role to play, didn't need to find a niche, but she didn't have any conventional way to make inroads and had to find ways to connect. He didn't imagine Ray had got out and networked too hard, volunteered, made himself available. He wasn't sure about Maxine, didn't know if she'd had a job before all of this, had town connections. She did have her sister, who he'd heard, funnily enough, was more like Ray than Maxine. Black and white, and full of righteous wrath. A kind of comfort, he supposed, that outraged certitude.

'Still no word from Wangaratta?' said Ray.

'Not as yet. I'll let you know as soon as I hear.'

'What happens after they arrest him?' said Maxine. 'Will he be gone then?'

'Gone? You mean to gaol? He might go to remand, but I'm fairly sure a judge will give him bail. Which means he'll be around until the trial, or sentencing. You haven't spoken to a lawyer?'

She shook her head.

'We don't need a lawyer,' said Ray. 'We just need that little shit locked up. Justice done. Judges never seem to do the right thing these days, do they?'

'Look, you may not need a lawyer for yourselves. But one could help you understand what's going on.'

Ray sparked up, his voice agitated. 'I think we can work that out for ourselves. As long as you keep us informed. We don't need to be paying some money-grubbing bastard for nothing.'

'You might want to make an impact statement. When it's time for sentencing. Let the court know how this has affected you. It's a reasonably new thing, allows the judges to take your suffering into consideration. A lawyer will certainly help with that.'

Maxine shook her head as if to say the very idea of it seemed too much, but Des knew ultimately she would want to do it. Most people did.

Ray, his face slipping from fatigue to irritation, slapped his hand firmly down on the table and looked Des in the eye. 'You know, don't you, Sergeant, that the only justice we will ever get is from God. No judge will do the right thing by us. Even the system. It's so bloody slow. The longer I wait the longer I wonder if anything will ever happen.'

Des wondered if he was meaning the kind of god who sent down a lightning strike, or the kind of god who got a helping hand from his disciples on Earth. 'I know it's hard—'

'Do you? Lost any kids of your own lately?'

Des tilted his head back. There was never any point in answering these provocations, especially with a man like Ray Druitt, who wasn't interested in an answer, only making a point. 'I will do my best to keep you informed. I can only ask for your patience.'

Ray looked at him and contorted his face into something that was somewhere between a laugh and a sneer. Des realised it was the first time he'd ever seen Ray's teeth. He wasn't someone who was big on expression. What had happened to make Ray the man he was? Des wondered. He'd not known him before the accident and had only seen the grieving tortured soul he saw now, but he'd heard he'd been a tough, proud man.

Proud of the quality of his work, proud of his family. But a little fixed, rigid. That's how someone had described him. Not a bad person, but just not accommodating to difference.

As he was leaving the house, Des saw Kyle walking up the road back from school. Kyle gave him a furtive look and Des wondered for a moment if he'd been wrong about Ray. Had he been covering all along?

'How's it going, Kyle?' Des was a man who couldn't use the word mate like many men he knew. Especially with a kid like Kyle, who clearly was not his mate, almost young enough to be his grandchild—if he'd had children exceptionally early on. Des knew he was always going to sound like a cop, a bit stilted and awkward, so he wasn't sure that Kyle would stop for him and was surprised when he did.

'I'm okay,' said Kyle, coming to a halt about two metres away. He regarded Des squarely but without any hint of menace. 'How are you?'

'Oh, you know,' said Des, slightly taken aback at this enquiry coming from—what was he?—a fifteen-year-old. 'Getting along. Just been talking to your mum and dad about the Greens. Don't know if you've heard, someone's been leaving them nasty gifts of late.'

An expression that Des couldn't read crossed Kyle's face. Fear, guilt, frustration. 'No.' He shook his head unconvincingly.

'Just asking them if they had any idea who was behind it. But no luck.'

Kyle stared at the carryall he was holding in front of him and kicked the asphalt with his shoe. Strange, Des thought, how the Druitts all looked so different from each other. The kids.

The parents. Kyle had straight nut-brown hair that flopped forward over his face, a fringe half covering his eyes, olive skin marginally less nut-brown than his hair, touched at the cheeks with reddish blotches of acne. He was teenage awkward now, and not as fine-featured as his brother had been, but he would grow into a good-enough looking man in a few years. Des felt a sudden twinge of sadness on his part. The loss of his brother, their past and future together. Des understood that, what it was to lose a brother. Especially when there were only two of you and one of you was the apple of your parents' eye.

Kyle swayed a little as he hauled his bag over his shoulder then looked directly at Des again, his face set in anger, but a different kind of anger than that of his parents, something simmering, subterranean. 'It wasn't me, if that's what you're thinking.'

'I wasn't suggesting—'

'It's despicable,' Kyle cut in acidly. His word choice surprised Des. 'It's bad enough, everything that's happened. I really don't get it at all, and I would never do it. I just want to forget.'

'No idea who might?'

Kyle, looking down again, shook his head, his fringe flicking across his face, and grunted in a way that seemed to translate as a 'no'.

'All right then, well, thanks for your time,' said Des.

Kyle looked up briefly and for a moment Des thought he was going to say something, but instead he nodded curtly and said goodbye. Des watched him as he walked away, up to the house and along the side path to the back, and he wondered if Maxine was behind the curtain watching him and if she would interrogate Kyle when he went inside. What would she ask him? Would she even care? Was there anything that Kyle could possibly say that would make a difference? After a few moments, Des made his way back to his car and returned to the station, only stopping off for a few minutes along the way at the park by the river to have a cigarette and clear his head.

November 1993

Northam

November was a month that could go either way in Northam. Intense dry heat, a harbinger of summer, or freezing tempestuous storms that descended, slashing and spitting like invading hordes rolling over the top of the mountains. Changes so quick that you couldn't remember which season you were supposed to be in from one day to the next. Pam surveyed the sky now, late in the morning, and hoped the unblemished blue would hold. The weather forecast hadn't been hopeful, but the weather forecast in these parts could never fully be relied upon, each valley up here its own micro-climate, its own conditions. In the end the weather wasn't so important. It was probably too ambitious to think about eating outdoors tonight anyway, given it wasn't summer yet and the cold came in quickly once the sun was behind the hills.

Despite this minor uncertainty, Pam felt a twinge of something that she recognised as excitement, the anticipation of a get-together, albeit one that once upon a time would barely have rated a mention. There had been a change for her in the past few weeks, a leavening. The coming of summer, a sense of future and possibilities, the passing of time extracting a little of the sting from their grief. Scott's long-term prospects caused her anxiety, but in the short term the move to her father's had been for the best. A positive. To everyone's surprise he seemed to enjoy farm life, using his time to fix all manner of equipment and to help Peter on occasion with his sheep and cattle (what a strange duo they made). Pam missed him, but he came for dinner once a week, neatly avoiding Loren who managed to be busy or staying with a friend on those nights. This space, odd and sometimes difficult as it was in many ways, had been good for her too. With Scott gone from home she emerged from her room more often, conversed with her parents, had even been seen to laugh from time to time. Pam wasn't happy that her children still didn't speak. She wondered if there was something neither of them was telling her or the police about the accident, but Loren said there was nothing else to tell. Why then had she frozen Scott out, Pam had demanded, to which Loren had responded with an icy stare that declared her disbelief that her mother could not possibly know, followed by a dramatic exit with a slammed door. But to Pam, this break gave her hope for healing. She felt optimistic that the situation would improve with time off. Tonight would test that theory.

Simon had arrived from Melbourne for the long weekend. He was a graduate now, almost. And he had a job. Pam could hardly believe it. It wasn't simply that he had completed his degree but that her firstborn had actually left the nest. When he was a student his weekend visits allowed her to pretend to herself that he was still living with them. But now he truly lived somewhere else, had employment with an accounting firm, the kind of start in adult life that would hold him in good stead. Somehow, though, this transition seemed bizarrely instantaneous to her, even though it patently hadn't been. She still needed time to adjust, move her mind into the new (emptier, but freer) space.

Simon had brought his bag in from the car and dumped it in his bedroom (old bedroom, former bedroom, she corrected herself). Now, having perambulated the property, he had materialised in the kitchen.

'We should have some lunch, I suppose. You hungry?' she said.

'Always.'

She opened the fridge door and looked inside. 'Do you know where Mick is? Did I hear you talking to him before?'

'He was in the garage. Looking in boxes. Didn't really talk. Just said hi. You know Dad, he was pretty engrossed in whatever it was he was doing.'

'What?' said Pam, turning her head to look at Simon. 'What boxes?'

'I don't know. I didn't ask. He didn't say.'

'Can you get the bread out and some chutney from the cupboard up there? Cheese and tomato be okay?'

'Sure.'

'I'll do something a bit more interesting for dinner, promise. Dad's going to put on the barbecue and I thought I'd make a potato salad and coleslaw and beans and I don't know.'

'Uh huh,' said Simon.

'You don't care, do you? As long as it's food.'

'Ah well, I'm thinking about becoming a vegetarian.'

Pam delivered butter, cheese and tomatoes to the bread board on the table. 'Just hold off till tomorrow then, all right? We have a carnivore's delight in the fridge right now.' Simon face contorted and Pam looked at him in exaggerated surprise. 'Gosh, you're not serious, are you?'

He opened his mouth to speak when he glanced beyond her to the door, smiled. 'Hiya,' he said.

Loren appeared, chalky faced and puffy-eyed from sleep. 'Not serious about what?' she asked, reaching up to the cupboard for a glass and filling it with water.

'Simon says he's going to become a vegetarian,' said Pam.

'Oh . . . okay.' She turned and rested her lower back against the sink, put the glass of water to her forehead. 'It's warm already.'

'Yeah. Let's hope it lasts. Want some lunch? Or going for breakfast first?'

Loren leaned forward and eyed what had been put on the table. 'Don't know just yet.'

'Oh well.' Pam threw her hands up in the air, then looked to Simon. 'At least *that* is vegetarian. Shouldn't be any quibbles from anyone. Just grab some plates and cutlery.'

Pam headed out the door to the garage, just a few metres off to the left of the back of the house, at the end of what was once a side path but had now been covered over for a carport. The garage was an old structure from the twenties or thirties, built at the same time or a little later than the house. Weatherboard, white with a red tin roof, but unlined and raw on the inside. It was one of the things that had attracted Pam to the property when they'd first inspected it more than twenty years ago. It reminded her of the garage at her parents' place, where she'd spent much time as a child in the company of her father's Pontiac, then Dodge. Sitting behind the wheel pretending to drive. (She'd left home by the time he started buying Fords.) This garage, however, was too small and too inconvenient a space to house a car, unless you owned a Model T or a Mini Minor, and was much more useful as a storage shed. Mick had, for a while, been keen on the idea of it being a toolshed, but he wasn't really very handy and the tools that eventually made their way inside were mostly of the gardening variety, a domain that largely belonged to her, apart from the lawnmower. Otherwise there was just boxes of stuff that went back twenty years and were rarely if ever looked at. Sometimes Pam thought she should just take it all to the tip, but that was something they needed to do together. Sort and sift. Discern and discard. She couldn't make a unilateral decision. Mick would go off his nut.

'Mick,' she said, peering into the dim interior. The double doors faced south and Mick had only opened one half, but she could hear him inside, the sound of grit scraping on the concrete floor and intermittent guttural grunts. She stepped in and saw that he was pulling a hefty box across the floor. 'Why didn't you turn the light on?'

'It's daytime.' A reply that at face value sounded logical.

'Need a hand?' she asked.

'Nah.' He stopped and slowly stood up.

'What's that?

'Dad's tools.'

'Oh.' She stood with her hands on her hips and waited for him to expand.

'Thought Scott might like them. He's been doing some carpentry up at Jim's. Could come in handy.' He got up and hauled open the other half of the door so there was more light, then pulled back the top of the box where the flaps had been folded in on themselves.

'That looks like something from before the war,' said Pam, eyebrows arched.

'Definitely pre-electric,' said Mick holding up a hand drill. 'Beautiful, isn't it?'

Mick's dad had died not long after Mick and Pam had married. Pam barely knew him. He'd always seemed nice enough, a quiet, unassuming soul. But she'd really only met him a handful of times before he'd suffered a catastrophic heart attack while she was pregnant with Simon. When Mick's mother moved up to Coffs Harbour a few years ago to live with his sister, she'd cleared out the house and Mick had taken his father's tools. Pam had wondered at the time why of all the keepsakes he could have chosen it had been those. His father had never really used them to her knowledge, he hadn't been a builder but a labourer, an odd-jobber most of his life. Mick told her that his dad had harboured hopes of being apprenticed. But the war broke out and he went off to New Guinea where he endured three and a half years of pursuing the Japanese over its densely forested slopes and suffered a bout of dengue fever, neither of which he ever properly recovered from. When he returned, his dream of becoming a chippie never eventuated and the tools he'd bought prewar were relegated to the shed (or various sheds, given the family's tendency to move). They became a symbol of his life's disappointments. The perfect keepsake given that his life seemed to be made up of disappointments.

'I don't know if Scott will use them,' Pam said dubiously, trying to imagine him putting in the time and effort to master these mechanical devices, considering if he would see the same beauty in them as his father did.

'Well, I'm not going to force them on him. He can play around with them if he wants to.'

'He probably won't have that much time now.'

281

'He can bring them back anytime.'

What was it that fathers wanted to give their sons? What had Mick's father given him? Nothing that Pam could tell. Years of childhood poverty and a sense of rootlessness. What did Mick want to give Scott? A sense of belonging, a lineage, a chance to rewrite the past in some small way? The week before Scott had been charged and bailed. A committal hearing had been scheduled for March. They, he, had four months, maybe more, depending on the vagaries of proceedings: the plea, the police, the judge. Four months until Scott's future would be cemented. After that he would have a criminal record, he would be in prison, and after that he would have been in prison. An ex-con.

Pam put her hand on Mick's forearm. 'It's nice,' she said. 'It's a nice thought.' She knew it was hard for him, even if he didn't say much. Hard for him, just as it was for her, to see a way forward, work out what he should do, needed to do.

Mick pushed the box out into the sunlight and they looked again at what was inside. Braces, chisels, drills and drill bits, a plane, a file, a hammer, a tack hammer. 'You know, it makes me sad looking at these.'

Pam was surprised at this pronouncement. Sad wasn't a word Mick used; he wasn't given to nostalgia, overt emotion, talking feelings. 'Why did you take them from your mum then? Why keep them?' she asked.

He stared down at the box as though the contents would provide an answer. 'He wanted me to have a better life than he did. These tools. They remind me of him, his life. Highs and lows. He never had a great deal. And there was a lot that he never got to do. Things that circumstances didn't allow. We—us, our generation—grew up in better times, we had more chances at life. Which as you well know I have wasted for the most part. He'd have been disappointed in me if he'd lived long enough. That I hadn't grabbed the opportunities he didn't get. Just let things happen to me.'

Pam who had been shaking her head as Mick was speaking, let out a long sigh. 'I think that was your mother. She was the disappointed one. I reckon your Dad would have liked you to be happy.'

Mick looked up at her, stretched his mouth flat. 'You know, you might be onto something. Mum only got excited when I married you because she thought I'd married into money.'

Pam snorted. She and Mick's mother had never really hit it off. She'd speculated over the years that Mick's mother had probably never really hit it off with anyone. She felt sorry for his sister, saddled with her in her dotage, although Mick always maintained they had a good enough relationship. She wasn't sure what he really knew about that. His sister never looked particularly happy to her. Perhaps though that was just projection on her part. 'So what do you mean you just let things happen?' she said finally.

'Well, that's me, isn't it? Never been known for my driving ambition.'

'Ambition? There are other things in life besides getting ahead. We do well enough. And now you have an accountant for a son. That's something, isn't it?'

He gave her a sharp look and the unspoken words filled the air between them. They had more than one child. 'I don't know. I've always cursed my old man, but I'm not any better.'

Pam put her hands on his shoulders. 'We're both in this child-rearing enterprise together you realise, don't you?'

He put a hand up to one of hers and gripped it tight. 'I worry about him. About the future.'

Pam turned her hand over and squeezed his back. 'Listen, lunch is on the table. Maybe it's time to come in and eat. You can sort this lot later. Were you going to give them to him tonight?'

'Yeah. I thought tonight'd be a good time. Don't know why. It's not as if we're not going to see him again. Guess it was on my mind.' He glanced into the garage. 'The shed needs a good clear-out.'

Pam laughed. 'Go for it. Just don't touch anything of mine.'

———

After lunch, Mick went back to the shed and Pam cleaned up and went to yoga. It had been weeks now since the confrontation with Reggie, but each time she braced herself for a further appearance. It wasn't just at yoga that she became apprehensive, although that was the worst, which was ridiculous really when she was surrounded by such support there and it was fairly unlikely that Reggie would ever venture back. She was wary wherever she went into Northam, despite having only caught sight of Maxine once in all this time—in the chemist a month or so ago, and she had quickly backed out before she'd been seen. Her fear, her caution, had made everyday life more circumscribed than before. It wasn't as though she was under house arrest, but she'd found herself hyperconscious of herself in public places and had developed a kind of disassociation that meant she was continually looking at herself from the outside as she moved about, running a constant imaginary surveillance. Between home and work there was shopping to be done, petrol to be put in the car, bills to be paid, visits to be made to doctor and dentist, accountant and mechanic. Now none of those were made automatically or taken for granted. Every entry or exit from car or building came with the fear of running into Ray or Maxine or Reggie, or perhaps even Kyle (she wasn't really sure about him, about where he stood) or some other crony, who may or may not exist.

After yoga Pam stayed for a few minutes talking to Aurora and Cathy. She was planning to leave swiftly so she could get home to make the salads. It was already past four. But Aurora, with an excited little hip-height beckoning hand wave at the end of the class, had signalled she wanted to talk.

'What are you two up to now?' she asked.

'Not a lot,' said Cathy. 'Got some ideas?'

Aurora laughed and looked at Pam. 'And you?'

'I've got to get home. The kids are all around for a barbecue. Dad's coming too.'

'Nice,' said Cathy. 'You'll all be together.'

'I'm a little nervous to tell the truth. But, you know.' She looked to Aurora. 'But *did* you want to do something? Maybe we could next weekend. Nothing planned. We could have dinner at my place—all of us.'

'I wasn't angling for a dinner invitation. Although that would be very nice. I just wanted a moment of your time now to tell you both something.'

Cathy's face went rigid. 'You're leaving!'

Aurora put her hand up. 'No, nothing like that.'

'What then?' said Pam.

'It's nothing bad. Relax.'

Cathy and Pam, getting the feeling they were being teased, stood looking at her while a small smile twitched at Aurora's lips.

'I'm pregnant,' she said.

There was half a second of silence before Cathy lunged forward, arms outstretched. 'Oh my god! Oh my god!'

Pam smiled at Aurora who was looking at her over Cathy's shoulder, pleased for Aurora, happy that Cathy had taken it well too. 'That's wonderful, sweetheart. Amazing. I have to say though that I'm a bit astounded. I didn't know a baby was on the agenda.'

'I didn't either,' said Aurora. 'I didn't think I could have kids. We'd tried for ages and then figured it was never going to happen.'

'It's the mountain air,' said Cathy, releasing Aurora from her grip.

'You'd expect the population of Northam would be larger if that was the case,' said Pam, taking her turn for a hug.

'I don't know what it is but it's a miracle.'

'I'm really, really happy for you,' said Pam. 'But does this mean you're going to give up teaching?'

'No way,' said Aurora. 'I plan to keep going for a as long as I can and come back as quickly as I can after.'

'And you will,' said Cathy. 'Super woman. Super bendy woman.'

'Noel is very supportive of my career. He's going to take time off, do the weekend shift.'

Pam smiled, nodded. That what's he says now, she thought, picturing Noel, lover of downtime and the great outdoors, with his hiking gear, his cross-country skis. She thought of Mick when she was pregnant with Simon. 'I don't have to come to the birth, do I?' he'd said to her. While she'd been horrified, her mother had told her it was a good thing. 'Men don't want to see that.' Pam didn't know what *that* meant until she'd gone through it, and when she had she thought she hadn't wanted to see it either, but there she was. She insisted Mick come to Scott and Lauren's births, even suspected he had a few puffs on the gas when no one was looking. But then he got to see the moment of birth (the thing that she missed out on, really, her head being at the wrong end of her body), the moment when a new life came into the world, when you got to see what you'd produced. That was something. It really was.

When she got home Pam felt a strange subdued sense of joy. Perhaps it was Aurora's news, but it was almost as though some miniscule weight had lifted. It reminded her of some of the ideas Aurora had talked about in her yoga sessions. What was it called again. *Anicca?* Impermanence. Nothing stays forever, good swept away by bad, bad swept away by good. Life swept away by death, death by life. She went into the living room, surveyed Mick's record collection and put on the Beatles, *Sergeant Pepper's*. Good music to make salads to. While she'd been out, Simon had joined his father in the shed and was doing his bidding, sorting the wanted and the unwanted into piles. Pam hoped they wouldn't be distracted mid-task and leave her with an untidy assortment of boxes. At least now, even if they were useless and took up space, they were neatly stacked. Almost out of sight, almost out of mind.

Loren had retreated to her room again and Pam had knocked gingerly on her door and asked if she'd be joining them for dinner, to which Loren had replied with a terse 'yes'. Pam wanted to ask her to come out and help, but she feared the next reply would be a terse 'no'. How had it come to this, she wondered, this trepidation. What was it about? They should all have gone to counselling. All they had done since the accident was to look perpetually forward. She'd seen the pain inflicted on Loren by the interviews with the police and she didn't want to make her daughter suffer any more. Silence had seemed to be the easiest option, a way to avoid more agony.

The sky, hazy now in the late afternoon, was beginning to lose its colour when the phone rang. Pam put down her knife, wiped her hands and walked into the hall, approaching the phone as she always did now, with a sensation of queasiness in her stomach. He (she still hadn't given the caller a name, even though she knew what his name was) didn't usually call on a Saturday, but there was no reason to think he wouldn't. When she answered the phone she was relieved momentarily to hear Scott's voice on the end of the line, then dismayed because he wouldn't have made the call unless there was a problem.

'Something's wrong with Grandad's car,' Scott blurted. He sounded like he'd been running. 'It might take a while to get it fixed.'

'Can't you borrow Peter's? Or Janet's?'

'Yeah, I went over, but they seem to have gone out. Anyway, I reckon I can get on top this. But it might take an extra hour or so.'

'Oh, okay. We'll wait for you. It's still early. Ish.'

'You sure? You can start and we can just eat something when we get there.'

'No! Look, if it doesn't seem likely, Simon can go out and pick you up in half an hour or so.'

'Okay, I'll let you know in a while.'

Pam went out to the shed and looked in at Simon and Mick.

'Do you want me to light the barbie?' asked Mick.

'No hurry yet. Dad and Scott are going to be late. There's something wrong with the car.' She ran through the phone call she'd just had because she knew Mick would say all the same things she'd just said and she'd have to repeat the whole thing for his benefit.

'Should have told them to bring the trailer down,' said Mick, casting an eye towards the pile of junk, both boxed and unboxed, he'd amassed in the middle of the garage floor.

'A trip to the tip.'

'Yeah. Haven't made one of those for quite some time.'

'Not since the last fridge,' said Pam.

Simon dragged a box from the shelf and prised open the flaps. 'God, what's this?' he said.

Pam stepped over to where he stood and looked inside. 'Baby things,' she said in a soft voice. She leaned in and pulled open a plastic bag that sat at the top, picking a small knitted jacket from inside. 'Look at that!'

'Mine?' said Simon.

'I think you all wore this.'

'Mine really though? I was the first.'

Pam laughed. 'I suppose so.'

She wanted to say then that Aurora was pregnant, but for some reason she couldn't. There was an obvious connection (baby clothes, pregnancy), but one that was also a segue, a diversion into someone else's life that didn't sit with the moment. Instead she said, 'You're not proposing throwing those out, are you? Because they are non-negotiable.'

'Wouldn't have dared,' said Mick, poker-faced.

Back inside, Pam put the salads on the table. The beef sat on a plate on the bench, beside it the chicken marinated in soy and honey and ginger. The sun was rapidly disappearing behind the hills and there was slight chill to the air already. Too cool now, she supposed, to eat outside. She checked the fridge for beer and went into the living room to retrieve the gin from the drinks cabinet. The Beatles had finished and she didn't feel like side B. She flicked through the shelf of records below the turntable and found an Ella Fitzgerald and Louis Armstrong album. In a moment the strains of Ella's sultry voice, the tinkle of piano rose up from the speakers and accompanied Pam as she stepped into the dining room. From the top drawer of the walnut sideboard she took out one of her mother's beautiful lace-edged tablecloths, one of the many things she had claimed from her father after her mother's death, and shook it out, watching it levitate then settle on the table. From another drawer she lifted out the good silver, setting five places and wondering as she did why she was bothering with her best tableware when it was only a barbecue. But somehow it felt right. The food might be simple, but the occasion not so much. It struck her briefly that this was the first time they'd had dinner in this room since the night of the accident, and her chest tightened around the thought. She gazed down the table and saw herself in residence, presiding over the events, enabling the unfolding of it all, drink in hand. Laughing. Always bloody laughing. A person could laugh too much, she thought, laugh so much that they didn't see what was going on around them.

She took paused for a moment, bringing her mind back to the evening and surveyed the table with a different eye. She went to the sideboard and pulled open the drawer where she kept the placemats, pulling out three different boxes and inspecting them. Two were hers—one depicting native flowers that she'd had for years, and the other something vaguely abstract and colourful that she'd bought on sale at David Jones on a trip down to Melbourne two summers ago. The third had been her mother's—an old set from the 1950s that depicted various British royal castles in subdued sepia tones. Just when she'd felt dubious about Mick's choice of memorabilia she was confronted with her own, her mother's ironic sense of connection to royalty. As if Marjorie would have ever passed muster. Less than a mere commoner, a colonial with an errant chain-dragging ancestor. (If you could trace your ancestry back to the 1800s, chances were high.) Still, Pam liked these placemats. They were hardy and delightfully old-fashioned. Just like her mother. She remembered loving them as a child, always opting for the view of Windsor Castle from across the Thames for herself when she set the table for dinner. She wondered if her father would recognise them when he sat down to eat. If they would make him feel nostalgic. Or if he wouldn't notice them at all. He'd never been much of a noticer.

Outside she became aware of raised voices, something amiss. She didn't have the music up high, but it was loud enough to distract from outside sounds, render them less distinct. It wasn't like Mick and Simon to argue. She upstretched her head, like a little prairie animal, alert, sensing. Baffled at first then quickly alarmed. She had little time to work out what was happening, what the shouts (if indeed they were shouts) might represent, when she heard a blast, like an explosion so close that she could feel the vibration of it through the house. An awful screaming followed and another great boom, as though she'd suddenly found herself in a war zone. She knew that sound, the sound of a shotgun. She'd heard it often enough growing up on the farm, rabbiting with her father and Peter, even learning how to use one herself, getting used to the kickback of the gun butt against her shoulder. While it might have been familiar, it was completely out of place. A shotgun was not a weapon that they kept in this house.

She rose to her feet, her body suffused with adrenaline, blood pounding through her head, drowning out music or extraneous noises. She felt oddly light, incapable of rational thought, only simple reaction. She had no idea whether to go forward or backward, or sideways, and instead ran aimlessly (like the chickens she had seen dispatched by her grandfather in her childhood, headless, blood spurting skyward with every heartbeat) past the end of the table and into the kitchen at the exact same time the back door swung violently open. In front of her, Ray Druitt appeared like a terrible apparition, a gun half raised in her direction. She stopped abruptly, facing him, feeling like she knew in that split second all there was to know, that the last four months had come to this. That life had been distilled into this tiny aperture.

'Where is he?' Ray said in a voice so measured she couldn't see the connection between it and the tortured expression on his face.

Pam tried to speak, but her throat was dry, her vocal chords reluctant.

'Where?' he repeated, louder this time.

'He's not here,' she rasped. 'He doesn't live here now.'

'Tell me where he is.' Ray stared at her with dull eyes, not able to register an answer that he didn't expect.

She shook her head frantically. 'What have you done? Where's Mick? Simon? What did you do?'

Behind them in the hall, the telephone began to ring, its urgent trills mingled with the silky-voiced Ella, a tinkling piano and soft jazz trumpet.

'What did I do? Fuck you. What did *you* do? You took away everything. Everything.' Ray's voice was a barely contained sob in one breath, a statement of steely rationalism in the next. 'Now I'm evening things up, taking it all away from you. That's only fair, isn't it?'

Ray lifted the shotgun higher, moved his arm unsteadily to take aim. Pam could not register what she was seeing. Instead visions of Loren filled her head, morphing snapshots of a tiny tot, taking her first steps across the kitchen floor—the place where Ray was standing now—a ten-year-old, proud as punch, holding a netball trophy high above her head with two hands, like a wild child gladiator. And then, inexplicably, a moment, or perhaps an amalgam of them, of the two of them in town in the days when it was still okay for Loren to be seen with her mother, and the pure joy on her face as she pointed something out as they passed a shop window and then turned to Pam, eyes shining, cheeks wide with excitement. 'Look at that, Mum! Look!'

Every fibre of Pam's being fought the urge to call out her daughter's name, warn her. But not alert him. She took a step backwards and bumped into the wall behind her. There was no more room for her to move. She knew she had run out of space. And time.

April 2016

Melbourne

T here were things he never talked about. Artefacts from
the past, to borrow a phrase from Daniel Levandi, that
he held close and didn't share. Jason's first girlfriend was called
Marissa. He went out with her for ten years, from the age of
sixteen to twenty-six. It had been an intense relationship from
all accounts, at least in the beginning, but not one that Lori
knew a lot about. It had been over for more than three years
when they met, and he'd had a few dalliances in its wake. Apart
from a brief rundown in the first weeks, he only ever mentioned
her again in the context of his own general history, as though
she hadn't been that important at all.

Lori tried not to think about Marissa in the early days of
their relationship. Was she the jealous type, she asked herself?
She'd never thought of herself that way. Perhaps the opposite, avoiding relationships rather than holding onto them, not
worried about control, or at least control over others. But, of
course, Jason was different. Everything about him, for her,
was different. Almost from the first moment she met him she
couldn't imagine life without him. Yet he'd had a life like this
with someone else—a girl he'd known since schooldays, had

gone through university with, the early years of working life. Until something happened. What exactly, he'd never properly explained. Sometimes it had driven her crazy, this lack of information. But, most of the time, she wasn't sure if she'd wanted to know.

To know or not to know. It was a delicate balance of preservation. Whenever she thought about his past, she thought about hers. To question and probe would only be to invite the same response from him. A minefield of reciprocity. It was the price she had paid, she told herself, in a vain attempt to prop herself up, create an equilibrium, excuse herself from never having told him the entire truth. But in the end she was fairly certain he'd never lied to her—by deliberation or by omission—and therein lay the real difference between them.

Jason had promised to come home early. It was a rarity on a weeknight, but she'd called him in the afternoon as she'd left the hospital and told him that she needed to talk to him about something. When she heard the note of concern in his voice, she assured him it was nothing dire like disease or divorce. 'Just something to think about for the future,' she'd said lightly. Enough to mildly warn him, but not enough to set off panic.

The kids were still up when he came in. They'd had their dinner already, and after some initial excitement at seeing their father went off to read their books in the living room. Cody was only just starting to decipher words and usually it was Lori who would sit patiently with him and help him along, but tonight he looked up and insisted that Jason took over that job. Jason had only just uncapped a beer and he gave her a small eye roll before heading to the couch, bottle in hand. She turned back to the stove, her stomach tight now with hunger and nerves.

After the reading he returned to the kitchen, grabbing another beer on the way. Drinking during the week was as unusual as him being home early.

'Everything okay?' she asked.

'I'm supposed to be asking you that question, aren't I?'

She turned off the stovetop and wiped her hands on a hand towel. 'Let's get the kids off to bed, shall we? Talk later.' Her voice sounded odd and stilted in her ears, but he didn't seem to notice.

Children settled, she served dinner, wondering why she'd decided on having this conversation over food. She took a beer out of the fridge for herself and gulped down half the bottle before she'd even sat down.

'How was work?' she said, not quite willing to begin what she had to say.

Jason put his elbow on the table and rested his head in his fingers. 'Well, if we're on the subject of me, I'm thinking of quitting.'

'What?' Her stomach seemed to do a little flip. 'Why? I mean . . . I know you've had some hassles but . . .'

'Because I don't know if I can keep going. The harassment. Threats.'

'Threats? God, Jason. You didn't tell me there were threats.'

'Yeah, well. There was no reason to have to drag you through it.' Suddenly his preoccupied demeanour had a different kind of context.

'Until now?'

'Yeah, 'cause now I think it's bad enough for me to leave.'

'How bad?' she asked tentatively.

'You want the unvarnished truth?' He made a small sharp sound. 'I've just been offered a truckload of money to look the other way on some pretty dubious shit. If I do that, I'm fucked. They'll own me, and I might still have to answer for an over-budget project. But if I don't knuckle under there's a good chance that their theft will look like my mismanagement. I either resign before I'm sacked, or I do what they want and they'll make me their bitch and this will happen over and over. For bloody ever.'

'What? Who is "they"?'

'A bunch of pretty powerful guys, I believe. I don't know who they all are. Some of them work on the site. They have connections to gangs, corrupt unions. Apparently.' He put his hands up in the air. 'It's a long story, and I don't think I know half of it.'

She looked across the table at him for a few seconds trying to take in what he was saying, interest in food lost. 'I can't believe those are the only choices—leave or knuckle under. What if you go to the company management? Tell them what's happened? Or the police?'

'Part of my job is to get on top of these bastards. And, besides, I just don't have any real proof.'

'But this is so bad. Crooked. Totally illegal. You can't be expected to stand up to them by yourself. It doesn't seem right. There must be a way to expose them?'

'There was a guy at work who had my back, and he was going to help me, but he's pissed off. I'm pretty sure they got to him. Bought him off, or threatened him. Without him I have no proof. It all just looks like incompetence on my part.'

'That Mike guy?'

'Yeah.'

'Where did he go?'

Jason shook his head despairingly. 'I thought about tracking him down, but I don't know just yet. It'd be hard. Fuck.'

'This is . . . it's just awful.'

'If I go I'll lose my completion money. So no paying off the renovations for a while.'

'I don't care about the bloody money. I only care that you're safe.'

He shrugged and took a long swig of beer, emptying the bottle, the bowl of pasta in front of him cold now. 'It could be worse. I don't know if I'm cut out for this shit. Managing these sorts of sites. Maybe it's for the best. I can just quit, go back and finish that degree. Do something else.'

She got up and put her arms around him. Then she sat on the chair next to his and he turned towards her, his face blurred with what looked to her like despair. He had always had such an open face, so much that could be read on it. He might be right, she thought, about not being cut out for that kind of a job. The stress of managing projects, then the stress of dealing with crooks. He wasn't a hard man. Not hard at all.

She said, 'You do what you have to do. Whatever that is.'

He nodded, picked up a fork and nudged his pasta.

'Cold,' she said, grabbing the bowl and taking it to the microwave.

He retrieved it a minute later and ate quickly, and in silence. She didn't bother to reheat her own, and after nibbling a few rubbery strands put it aside. When they finished, he looked up to the ceiling for a little while before getting up and clearing the plates away, stacking the dishwasher. She put the kettle on, spooned tea into the pot. He talked about Cody's reading and she started to think that perhaps he'd forgotten why he'd agreed to come home early and she felt a certain relief. His own news was momentous enough. No wonder Niels had asked her if she was worried. She felt like a fool now, not having read between the lines (even on the lines). This had been going on long before Scott had reappeared—she'd somehow failed to notice Jason's preoccupation for weeks or possibly months.

She poured the tea and they took their mugs and sat on the couch, and Jason smiled and said, 'I was going to watch the footy show, but you had something to talk to me about, didn't you?'

'Oh, we don't have to do that,' she said. 'I don't want to make today worse. You should just chill for a while.'

He looked a little surprised, perhaps remembering her earlier reassurances on the phone. 'It's not that bad, is it?'

'No. I don't know. It's . . .'

'Spill. I'm a big boy. I can deal with whatever.' He looked to her and smiled. 'One thing I know is that you're not pregnant because you had beer with dinner.'

She sighed. 'Okay. You remember on the weekend you said Sophie told you about the police coming? And I said they'd got it wrong.'

His eyes narrowed. 'They didn't?'

'Well, it is true that my brother died. My brother Simon. But the police didn't come about him. I had two brothers. The other one is called Scott and he is alive.'

He looked at her blankly. Seconds passed. 'Did you know? I . . .'

'That he was still alive? Yes, I knew. But when I met you I hadn't seen him for ten or twelve years. To me, he was dead. As good as.'

She could see Jason trying to process this information. 'Why wouldn't you see him?'

'Oh, why?' Seconds passed. 'I suppose because I thought he was responsible for my parents' and my brother's deaths. I was angry with him.'

'He was driving the car?'

She bit her lower lip, felt a small sharp pain. 'He was driving the car. But not *that* car.'

'I'm not following.'

'I'm not sure I can tell you everything right now.'

'Okay.' He blinked, as though he had something in his eye, then put his hand on her forearm. 'Can we talk about him? Can you tell me something?'

She nodded slowly. 'Yeah.'

'Why did the police come to see you?'

'He'd been in an accident. He's in hospital.'

'You've seen him?'

She nodded again.

'Is he all right?'

'I think he will be. He was unconscious, but he's coming round. I don't really know.'

'Jesus Christ. Why didn't you tell me?' He sounded bewildered. 'I don't get it. I mean, why *not* tell me? More than that, lie to me the other night.'

She looked across to the windows, saw their shapes reflected in the window. Jason half turned towards her, she looking straight ahead, eyes wide. 'When I first met you, my brother didn't feature in my life. Going into the past—any of it—was too hard. And, later, not talking about it became the way things were. A habit that got more and more entrenched. When the cops came I . . . I didn't know what was going to happen, if I'd see him, see him again. I had to wait to know.'

'Shit. So even on Saturday, you'd seen him but you didn't know if you'd go back?'

'It wasn't, isn't, that straightforward.' She rubbed her forehead. 'It's hard to explain. So many things going on. So much that happened.'

I thought you were a little strange on the weekend.'

'Really?'

'I've always known there was something,' he said suddenly. 'I just figured that losing your family so young, that it made you kind of self-contained. There was that vein of sadness.'

'Sadness?'

'I don't know. I can't describe it. It's really subtle.'

'Is that all?'

He looked at her, reflecting. 'You want to be something else? Something more dramatic? Is that what you're saying?'

She shook her head quickly. 'No. No. I want to know if I *am* something else. Crazy? Unstable?'

'You're asking me this now?' He considered his words. 'All I can say is that I don't know what you're thinking sometimes. That I guess I'm not that surprised about your brother on one level because you keep things in. Insular. That's the word for it, I guess. But I have known you a while now. I'm kind of used to that.'

'I'm sorry,' she said. 'I never wanted to lie.'

'I've never thought you were a liar. I've always trusted you completely.' A look of doubt shimmied across his face. 'Yet now I'm thinking that there was all this stuff you didn't trust me with.'

'It wasn't you I didn't trust. It was me.' Her voice wavered. 'My way to stop things getting away from me. And now I have no idea.'

He slid along the couch and put his arms around her, holding her close. 'Hey, it'll be okay. We'll work it out.'

'But there are still things you don't know.'

'Okay,' he said slowly. 'Things that will affect me and the kids?'

She pulled away from him, looked into his eyes. 'It's all my shit. Just mine. Nothing can hurt you guys.'

'Look, this is all weird and hard to process, that's for sure. But I love you and we will work it out, whatever it is that happened.'

'All right,' she said meekly.

He rubbed his eyes with his fingers, then drew them down his cheeks. 'I don't want to leave it here, god knows, but I need to get to bed, I'm completely bushed and, for now, work goes on.'

'Yeah, it's getting late.'

'When are you seeing your brother again?'

'Tomorrow.'

He considered this for a moment. 'You want me to come?' he asked.

'You've got work. And your own things to sort out.'

'Might be good for you to have someone there. Could be good for me, too. I can take a few hours, maybe later in the day.'

She pulled away from him and searched his face. 'I don't know. I feel like I've hardly got used to the idea myself.'

'I want to be there for you. Take some of that weight.'

She thought for a moment, unsure. 'Let's talk about it in the morning.'

After Jason went to bed, Lori walked into her office and took a book from her shelf. It was the book that contained the photo of her mother and, since Monday, the letter she had retrieved from Scott's apartment had also been sitting between its pages. She sat at her desk and inspected the envelope for a moment, as if she'd been wondering if it really had been addressed to her. It had arrived a couple of years earlier and she remembered looking at it for a long time, recognising the handwriting but resisting the recognition. There was no name on the back. Just the return address, a post-office box in South Yarra. She'd sent it back without knowing for sure, only sensing it was from him. Then she'd put it out of her mind. She held it in her hand now, feeling its weight before slitting the top and sliding out its contents: two handwritten sheets.

Dear Loren,

It's a long time since we had contact. I'm writing to you now because I have bought a little place not so far from where you live, and I wanted to let you know that you might just run into me one day. I bought it with the trust money from Grandpa's estate. I realise you haven't taken yours and I understand why, I guess. I was the same for a while. I didn't want to use it because it felt wrong somehow. But now, I figure, there's no point in letting it sit there and I need a roof over my head. The lawyers tried a few times to find you without luck apparently to let you know that the money was available. They didn't try hard enough in my opinion, because I managed it, with a little help. But maybe you'll ignore me too.

*I know you don't want to ever see me, and that's all
right. I'm not asking for anything from you, only to
remind you of what is yours. Uncle Peter has information too if you want to know anything about the estate
but don't want to talk to me. I enclose his address in
Queensland, and an address for the lawyers.*

Godspeed, sis. You are always in my thoughts.
Scott

After a few moments she got up, leaving the letter on her
desk, and went down to the bathroom and scrubbed her teeth,
locked the back door, checked the kids in their beds. In the
bedroom she changed in the half dark and then climbed into
bed. The streetlight crept in around the edges of the curtains,
giving form to the room. She still found it hard to sleep in the
dark, hated not to be able to see.

'You okay?' Jason's voice surprised her.

'Still awake?'

'Couldn't sleep.'

She turned to him and put her arm over his chest. 'You're
not going to have an easy time getting up in the morning.'

'I'm not going in, I decided.'

'Wow. That's radical.'

'Ain't it just.'

She ran the back of her fingers across his cheek, feeling the
sandpapery texture of his day-long growth.

'Talk to me,' he said. 'I'm not going to get to sleep anytime
soon. Tell me what you can. I want to know.'

She turned onto her back and looked up at the ceiling,
exhaled slowly. 'Even if it shocks you?'

'Will it shock me?'

'Yesterday I spoke to a policeman about what happened. He was the first person I've talked to since I left Northam. Since I was seventeen. And I talked to him because he knew already. And because he didn't care. About me, I mean.'

Jason pulled the sheets up higher around his shoulders. 'Was he investigating the accident?'

'Yeah, well, he doesn't think it was one.'

'Wow. Has this got something to do with back then? Is that why?'

'It's possible. But I don't really think so. I don't know. It's complicated, I guess, but it doesn't make sense really.'

A moment of silence. 'So what did happen back then? I don't need details, just tell me the bones.'

'The bones,' she said. She inhaled and exhaled slowly, trying to still her churning gut. 'Two things happened. The first was that Scott was in a car accident. He was driving and his best friend was killed.'

'Shit.' Jason turned to face her, put his hand on her arm. 'That must have been devastating? Was he drunk?'

'We all were.'

'We?'

'It was devastating for all of us.'

'How old were you then?'

'Sixteen.'

'Did you know that friend?'

She was quiet for a time, then she said, 'That wasn't the end of it. Something else happened. A while later. Maybe six months after the accident, his friend's father came to our house . . .'

A small sob escaped from her and Jason moved his arm across

her body, as though she needed bracing, and she placed her hand on his. She started to shake, the words came out in a jagged spurt. 'He murdered my family.'

'What?' Jason upturned his hand, gripping hers so tightly she thought her fingers might break. She could feel him rigid next to her. 'No. Jesus. No.'

'It's all right. I've had a bit of time to get used to it.'

'What? Half that time you've been with me. Fuck, how could I not know? I've been oblivious. I let you suffer by yourself.'

'No, Jase. It had nothing to do with you. I had to do it like that. I couldn't see any other way.'

He sat up and turned, leaned towards her, his features half in shadow reminding her of those block shadow portraits popular in the 1960s. Che Guevara, but without the beard, or the beret. 'I can't understand why I didn't know about your family. You know, put stuff together. Something like that? I don't even remember it. You'd think I'd remember it on the news or something.'

'People don't,' she said. 'It's surprising, but people just don't. Or they remember something vague. But not names or places. It was a long time ago. Even when I met you, it had been eleven years before.'

'Someone must. I reckon Mum would have. She was always a bit obsessed about those gory murders . . . Shit, shit. I'm sorry.' He lay back down, rolled towards her.

'Just hold me,' she said, turning her back to him. He moved in close, pushed his body tight against hers, his arm over hers, the warmth of him seeping into her skin.

'It explains a few things,' he said.

'Like what?' she asked, not sure if she wanted to know the answer.

'Just like I said. Being distant sometimes. Those nightmares.'

'Nightmares?'

'Well, you don't really seem to get them anymore. But you used to a bit. You haven't forgotten, have you?'

The night around them was quiet in the way that only cities can be quiet. The hum of cars on distant Brighton Road, a train coming into the station, the blast of a car horn in the next street.

'You always make everything all right,' she said softly. 'Just don't leave me, will you?'

He pressed her harder. 'Why the hell would I do that?'

'I'm really sorry. So, so sorry. I had this life before and I never told you.'

'Don't worry,' he said. 'Don't worry about that. I'm not going anywhere.'

November 1993

Northam

Wen Des Robinson retired more than a decade after what became known locally as the tragedy on the Hill, he gave a speech to a group of old and new officers over dinner at the newly refurbished Saltram Hotel in the centre of town. He'd always liked the Saltram. Even before the refurbishment it was a grand kind of place, a little frayed at the edges, but beautiful and dignified. It made him feel he was on a 1930s movie set, that Busby Berkeley dancers were about to descend down its curved staircase and tap their way into its front bar. At dinner he was glad to see that the hotel's tarting up hadn't been to its detriment. Although perhaps it had been to the local community's, given the prices had risen appreciably. The fresh look was set to attract a new clientele, a growing group of alpine tourists who were making their way with increasing eagerness to the region each year, and to provide them with more options than the current tents and cabins or homely B&Bs.

The speech Des gave that evening had nothing to do with the architecture of the hotel, but there was a connection nonetheless. Jim Temple. He'd been a stalwart here for years. Barely a week would go by when Jim wouldn't come down from his farm in the hills and have lunch in the dining room. Always an excuse for him to meet someone. Des had had his fair share of lunches with Jim when he'd done the police community liaison work early in his time in Northam, when Jim had been mayor. The only thing Des hadn't liked about it was that he had to pay his own way. He couldn't accept Jim paying for him when it was police business and the police wouldn't pay for more than a sandwich in the park. 'Dammit,' he'd said on more than one occasion to Mary when he'd got off the phone with Jim. When Jim's term as mayor came to an end, Des was more than a little relieved not to have to spend those extra dollars each month.

Des didn't mention Jim's name in his speech. He was long dead by then, had passed away less than a year after his daughter, and none of the younger officers would have known who he was, while all of the older ones remembered him, as Des did, like it was yesterday. He used the setting of the hotel's dining room not so much as an example about the need to keep a line drawn in the sand, even in a small inland town like Northam where there was little sand to be had, but as a way to examine what rural police really do. At the age of forty-nine he thought he'd seen everything there was to see. But when he was called to Jim's daughter's house that night, he was unprepared for what lay before him. Not only were all the victims known to him but he had played an ongoing role in the situation that had unfolded that night. Both before and after. There is always trauma attached to violent crime, he told the group in front of him. The victims, the witnesses and those who have to clean it up afterward all suffer. But when you live among the community where something like this occurs, or perhaps, worse still, are responsible for policing that community, there is an added layer of complexity to deal with. Des didn't use the word guilt. He wasn't even sure if that was the concept he had in the back of his mind. But he wanted his audience to reflect on their roles not just in looking after their communities but in looking after themselves. Understand the complications that they all faced.

Of course, Des didn't regale his fellow police with the details of that night. He'd lived them over and over in his mind, and then in the last few years sought private counselling to try to deal with what his own readings suggested were the symptoms of PTSD. The police then, in the 1990s and even beyond, weren't sympathetic to the idea of its members suffering from post-traumatic stress. In the eyes of both the hierarchy and the rank and file there were only two kinds of officers: the weak and the strong. Mental illness was weakness, nothing more. On that measure, Des wasn't really sure where he stood. Somewhere in between, he suspected, perhaps like most people in his situa-tion. After what he'd gone through he'd manage to hobble on for the last few years, survive in his post. But only just. (What would he have done without Mary?) People on the front line have to be looked after, he told his audience. We can't pretend we're not human, that we have no connection to what we do.

———

Des had been at home that evening in November 1993. It was only just past six and the smells of lamb and rosemary wafted out from the kitchen to the family room (the trendy name coined for these informal areas back in the sixties) where he was sitting in his armchair, Scotch on the table next to him, cigarette clamped between his fingers, reading the magazine from the Saturday paper. He heard the sound of a shotgun, two blasts in quick succession, but didn't give it a lot of thought. Where they lived, their prime spot on the Hill, was close to the edge of town. It was quite possible that someone was out rabbiting or some kid was practising hitting tin cans off the top of a fence post. Nonetheless, he noted the shots, felt a moment of awareness that he later thought was somewhat prescient. Five minutes after he heard another boom and, alerted now, waited for more. But none came.

He had squashed his cigarette into the ashtray and risen from his chair, glass in hand, when a fierce knocking started at the front of the house. As he went to answer it the phone rang in the kitchen and he heard Mary take the call as he opened the door. It was a woman he knew only by sight, a neighbour of Pam and Mick Green's, her face a sea of distress. Behind him Mary's voice was urgent. 'Des, it's the station. There's been a shooting.'

Des instructed the officer at the station, a young constable named Ryan, to bring his firearm down when he came. By the time he'd raced around the corner on foot, having only taken the time it took to discard his slippers and haul on his boots, Ryan was pulling up in the patrol car. It was twilight and the sky was streaked with an improbable pink. Des waited while Ryan retrieved his gun and they went onto the property together.

Des loved silence. As he grew older he found it more and more of a consolation. But there were times when he knew silence to be the most foreboding of sensations, a vacuum to which any sound became a counterpoint. That is how he felt as he and his constable walked across the front garden and down the side path, the sounds of their feet crunching lightly onto the gravel and the distant barks of a dog further along the hill echoing through the stillness. By the time he reached the end of the carport he could see, past the two cars parked bumper to bumper, the doors of the old garage open in front of him, the soft light of a single globe illuminating a mess of boxes and objects. As he came closer he saw a man he immediately recognised as Mick Green lying on his back across a box, his arms outstretched, Christ-like, a bloody mess where his stomach should have been. To his right another body, slumped sideways on the floor, his head in shadow.

Des, a few steps ahead of Ryan, put his arm out sideways to denote caution, and to signal that the constable should take care to guard in the direction of the back lawn and back door. 'Police,' he declared, half surprised he could make his voice work, before stepping into the garage, his gun drawn, but there was no one apart from the two men inside. He stepped towards the younger man and saw that half of his head had been blasted away, his face now obscured. He'd seen that kind of injury before on suicides, but it didn't make the seeing of it again any easier. He took a quick, sharp breath and looked to Mick, surprised to hear a groan rising up out of him.

'Mick,' he said, falling to his knees next to the sprawled figure. 'It's Des. I'm here. We've got you.' He took Mick's hand and thought he saw a flicker of eye movement. He turned back to Ryan who was standing in the doorway staring at the scene, face milk white. 'I came here that night of the accident,' he said flatly. 'Got them out of bed.'

Des stood up, focused on Ryan. He didn't want him zoning out on him. 'Did you call for an ambulance before you left?'

'Yeah.'

'Okay.' Des looked at his watch. How long would it take? Another twenty minutes? 'Call Doctor Fry. Now.'

Ryan scurried back down the drive while Des surveyed what he could of the back of the house. A light from the kitchen window illuminated the deck, but the garden beyond was in deep shadow, the trees in the far back corner completely obscured by a vine-covered fence. There wasn't time to secure it, but he doubted very much that there'd be anyone lurking there. If there had been, he'd probably already have taken a shot at Des. What Des feared more than being shot at was what he was going to see inside. If anyone had been left alive, there wouldn't be this kind of silence. He stepped up onto the deck and pushed open the slightly ajar kitchen door. Pam Green was sitting oddly upright against the far wall, near the door that led to the dining room. She was looking at him, her eyes wide and staring, her mouth a little open as though she were mid-sentence, a bloom of bloody slush across her chest at the level of her heart. Des gave the surrounding area a quick scan and strode over to her, kneeling down and searching for a pulse, knowing he wouldn't find one. 'Oh Pam,' he said. He wanted to close her eyes, but he knew he had to leave everything as intact as possible for the investigators, and he was already contaminating the house with his shoes. He got up, stepped past Pam, head and heart thumping in sickening unison, and walked through the dining room and into the living room. His hands shook as he clutched the gun in front of him, in a way he'd only ever done in police training drills, trying to remember how many people should or might be in the house, how many bedrooms there were. He turned left at the hall, crossed into the office and flicked on the light. Nothing. Hearing the back door again, he turned and called out sharply, 'Ryan?'

'Yes, sir,' came the response. 'Kytie and Paul are here now. Kytie's attending to Mr Green.' He was talking about the other two cops from their station.

Des was standing by the door to the kitchen. He found the light switch and turned on the hall light. 'We need to check these rooms. I don't know if anyone else was here.' He took the left side, Ryan the right.

The door to the first room was open, as were the curtains, providing just enough light to see inside. It had the stark, tidy look of a space that was no longer inhabited. A few old music posters featuring posturing young men in black pinned to the walls. Twin beds neatly made up, an unopened travel bag on one. He bent down and looked underneath, already knowing the bases were too close to the floor to afford a grown man a hiding place. Flicking on the light he checked the wardrobe, saw mostly coathangers, a few old shirts.

The door to the next bedroom was also open, but the curtains were pulled across. He entered gingerly, groping for the light switch as he again called out, 'Police.' This was clearly Loren's room, half bedroom, half studio, with large windows that looked out onto the front garden. The furniture here was different from the previous room, feminine but sparse. The wardrobe an open rail, the drawers a high tallboy. Her bed was Edwardian-style with a plain wooden slatted headboard. A thick red rug on the floor. Opposite, closer to the light, an easel, a small table with paints and papers. A chair.

He was about to crouch to look under the bed when he noticed a rivulet of liquid on the polished wooden floorboards. He took a step back, saw that it was clear, or near enough to.

'Loren?' he said quietly.

He could hear Ryan in the hallway, opening and closing a door.

'Loren? It's Des Robinson, Loren.'

A small whimper came in reply.

'Loren, I'm going to get down on the floor and help you out. All right?'

Outside he heard the strains of a distant siren. The ambulance finally arriving. He put his gun on the bed, knelt down and flicked back the cover that hung over the side. He knelt down and leaned forward, his jacket skimming the cold urine, a whiff of ammonia hitting his nose. He reached a hand towards Loren's indistinct form and after a moment's hesitation felt her grip on his wrist.

'Come,' he said simply.

She eased her way out, wriggling, sobbing, grunting; sounding more animal than human at that moment. He had a flash of her that morning months ago in the hospital with her parents and thought that no one should have to go through something like this once, let alone twice, especially not a kid. What would that do to you? She collapsed back against the bed as though she was unable to support herself and looked at him, her lips pressed together, glossy red-rimmed eyes. Her hair was matted and her left side was wet with piss and encrusted with dust from the floor.

'Are you all right?' he said, for want of anything more sensible to say, casting a quick eye over her, looking for injury but not seeing anything obvious. She didn't reply for a while but stared away from him to a point past his shoulder. He could see her lips quivering now. She was in shock. He glanced up from where they sat on the floor, looking for a blanket or something to wrap around her. There was a throw at the end of her bed and he raised himself on his haunches to get it.

'He killed them, didn't he?' she said quietly.

He lowered himself back down to her eye level. 'I'm so sorry,' he said, trying to keep his voice even. 'So, so sorry.'

'Are they all dead?'

'Your father is still alive.'

Her eyes became suddenly alert. 'Dad! I have to see him.' She tried to push herself up, but Des leaned forward and placed a hand on her shoulder.

'He's not conscious,' he said. 'We'll have to wait. There's nothing you can do.'

'I just want to see him.'

'Not right now, Loren. Not yet. It's not . . . It wouldn't be good for you to see anything out there. The ambos are here now. Doctor Fry. They'll look after him.'

She slumped back against the bed and made small jagged sounds, crying without tears. He got up, grabbed the throw and draped it over her shoulders, then crouched down again, put his hand on her arm. He wasn't sure she even noticed what he was doing; she didn't seem conscious of him, the external world. But he needed to bring her back, talk her into it.

'Loren, you said *he* killed them. Did you see or hear anything? Do you know who it was?'

For a moment she was completely still, as if all her energy was concentrating on one point. 'It was Troy's dad. I heard him in the house. His voice. Him and Mum. There was the shot and then he turned off the music and walked down here and opened all the doors. It was so quiet. I could hear him breathing.' Her whole body began to shake then, her eyes were wide.

'Did he say anything?'

'No. He just stood there. He didn't come in. I don't know what he did. Just breathing. I was under the bed by then. I heard him walk away. I should have done something and I hid.' She looked at him, eyes shining. 'I hid.'

'There was nothing you could do. You did the exact right thing.'

'No,' she sobbed. 'I haven't done the right thing.'

'Shh,' said Des. 'You don't need to say anything else right now.'

After a moment she said in a flat voice, 'Is he out there too?'

'No,' said Des. 'He's gone. It's okay.'

'I don't want him to die in our house. I don't want him here.'

'No, it's okay. Really, it is.'

The ambulance and another police car had pulled up outside. Des could see their lights flashing muted red and blue through the curtains and he stared at them, thinking about how he could get her out of the house without her seeing any of the carnage.

Ryan came in from his search of the other rooms and gaped when he saw them on the floor. 'Nothing here, sir,' he said, indicating the rest of the house with a flick of his head.

'Good. Listen, can you close the kitchen door for me, please?' He saw a frown, then a look of comprehension cross the constable's face.

When Ryan had disappeared, Des eased himself to standing, then gave Loren his hand and pulled her shakily to her feet.

'Constable?' he called over his shoulder.

'Secured, sir.'

'We're coming out now.'

'I don't want to leave,' Loren said quietly. 'I don't . . .'

'I know,' Des replied.

Their eyes met for second and she nodded, defeated. The safest place in the world no longer a refuge.

Des half walked, half carried Loren along the hall, past the closed kitchen door and around towards the front of the house. At the front door, which was now wide open to the night, he stopped momentarily, surprised by the light and movement in front of him. Police cars, ambulances, another car he assumed belonged to Doctor Fry. No suits yet, but they'd be making their way here soon, along the highway from Wangaratta, ahead of the big guns who'd come up later from Melbourne. Ryan appeared from the living room beside them and helped him guide Loren down the front steps and across the lawn. Two medics came forward and bundled her into an ambulance. Des followed them around and then stood and watched her as they laid her down on the gurney.

'I'll see you soon,' he called to her, not really knowing what he meant or what she'd expect from the words. He shut his eyes for a moment and rubbed his temples with his fingertips. His head felt like a pinball machine, a million thoughts swirling and colliding, discordant sounds assaulting his brain. The welfare of Mick Green, the whereabouts of Ray Druitt. He walked back up the gravel driveway ready to bark orders and found one young man, a constable from Belandra, sitting huddled under a tree by the carport, clearly overcome. In the garage just ahead of him, Doctor Fry and another ambo were huddled over Mick Green, Kytie watching on.

He caught Kytie's eye. 'How's he going?'

Kytie, otherwise known as Sergeant Geoff Kyte, stepped away from the group. 'Touch and go, I reckon.' He looked around. 'What a fucking mess.'

'We have to find Ray Druitt,' said Des.

'You know it was him?'

'Yep, according to Loren Green.'

'Ryan said you'd found her. Christ. Poor kid.'

'Poor kid indeed. Listen, we need someone up at his house, pronto. Send Paul and Ryan. We need a lookout for his car. Get these Belandra bodies onto a doorknock around the neighbourhood. Backup should be here soon. Has anyone checked the garden?'

Kytie's eyebrow went up.

'Almighty god!' Des stormed down to the patrol car and got a torch from the back seat and ran back up the drive and past the garage. He shone the torch's wide beam over the veggie patch, then along by the clothesline and across to the fruit trees in the far corner. They were partially obscured there by a trellis planted with passionfruit, so he had to step around that to get a good look through the trees. Kytie had materialised now next to him with a torch of his own. 'Fuck,' he said as his beam intersected with Des's close to the back fence. 'Fuck. Fuck.'

Ray hadn't chosen to end it with a gun but a short piece of green nylon rope. A stepladder lay on its side below his feet. Des pointed his torch to the ground. Kytie followed suit. The sight of the man in the eerie light was too much to take in, made him feel like puking. In the darkness he became aware of the isolated sounds in the silence again. His and Kytie's slow and laboured dissonant breathing. The ambos organising Mick's transfer onto a stretcher. More cars pulling up out the front. That dog barking again in the distance. Raised voices nearby, perhaps at the front of the house. Was anyone else taking charge, he wondered, or was it all still up to him?

'Do we take him down?' asked Kytie.

Des sighed, thinking Kytie should know better. 'This is a crime scene, Geoff. We don't touch a bloody thing now until the dees get here.'

'Just thought seeing as he's killed himself. And it's so bloody grim.'

'No. No.'

'Sir?' Ryan called from down near the shed.

'Yeah?'

'Scott Green is here. The Belandra boys are trying to restrain him.'

Des could hear him then, the raised voices now screams of rage. He ran back down to the front of the house to see that one of the Belandra officers had handcuffed Scott to the front fence. Scott looked to Des as he emerged, his face tear-stained. He started yelling so loudly that it took Des a moment to realise that his grandfather, Jim, was standing behind him, small and diminished in the strange glow of the emergency service lights.

Des approached Scott as if he was a wild animal. Hand outstretched, voice calm, soothing. He cast a sideways glance at one of the officers and hissed, 'Where are the keys?' As he glanced over at Jim he realised that the other ambulance had gone, that Loren had already been taken away.

'This is a crime scene, we can't let you in. Scott, can you promise me to stay here?'

Scott made a terrible guttural sound that Des took as a 'yes' but was more probably a sign of being overcome, overwhelmed.

Jim, his usual confidence absent, his voice wavering with shock, said, 'What happened, Des? Are they gone?'

Des wasn't sure what kind of gone Jim was talking about, not dealing in euphemisms himself. He shook his head and waited until Scott's handcuffs were unlocked. He didn't know how he was going to say this except bluntly. 'I'm very sorry to have to tell you that Pam and another person, a young male who I believe is your brother, Simon, are both deceased.'

Scott, who was staring at the ground, murmured, 'No, no, that's not possible. No. This is my fault. Oh god.'

'And the others?' ventured Jim.

'Loren is unharmed but has been taken to hospital for observation, and your son-in-law, Mick, is, well, he's badly wounded. The ambos have spent some time stabilising him.'

Voices came then from the direction of the house and they turned to see the ambos making their way down the driveway, balancing a stretcher.

'Dad!' called Scott, shrugging Jim off and staggering towards the group.

'Hold on. He can't respond, son,' said one of the carriers gently as Scott approached. 'You need to stop right there. We need you to give us a bit of space. Orrighty?'

Scott did as he was told, stepping back, standing numbly while they loaded Mick into the ambulance and watched as they drove off. As the red light receded down the street he turned to Des, his face unreadable in the shadow. 'Where's Mum?'

Des put a hand on Scott's arm. 'I can't let you up there, Scott. And you don't want to go. You don't want to see her like this.'

Scott leaned forward, resting his hands on the front of his thighs, and let out a sob. 'What do we do now?' The question seemed as open-ended as his life. He tilted his head up to look at Des. 'What?'

Jim took Scott's arm. 'We'll go to the hospital. See your sister and Mick.' Then he looked at Des. 'It was that Druitt who did this, wasn't it?'

'Yeah. I'm afraid so.'

'Has he been caught?'

'Mr Druitt is now deceased.'

Jim opened his mouth to say something but closed it again. He looked up towards the house and then back at Des, who nodded. He saw the defeated look on Jim's face and wondered how he'd survive this. This nuggetty, indefatigable man, who'd seemed to him when they'd first met to be someone who would never give up, overcome any obstacle. But there were obstacles that provided challenges and obstacles that could crush your very soul, and this was one of the latter.

In the clean-up that ensued, it took Des a long time to check back in on Jim and Scott, but they had left by then, gone to the hospital, he assumed. It was close to midnight when the detectives arrived from Melbourne and Des found himself standing in the same spot on the front lawn, briefing them on what had happened. They had brought equipment with them, floodlights, technicians. They were in the process of examining the place with a fine-tooth comb. Not that it mattered, he thought. There was nothing essential that they would discover. They were here simply to verify, document. All that could be known was already known. Only the fallout remained.

April 2016

Melbourne

It felt strange to make the trip to the hospital with Jason. As though two distinct parts of the world had collided, over-laying two disparate realities together, like a double-printed negative. Jason sitting next to her in the car, while she drove that newly familiar route, seemed wrong on so many counts. The fact she was driving, the fact he wasn't at work, the fact he now knew that for the past six days she'd been living a double life centred around not telling him about Scott.

They had woken late. Jason, who was good at pulling on old clothes and rushing out the door, did just that and got the kids off to school in quick-smart time. Lori lay dozing until he returned, stupefied from the night before, the sleeplessness, the upheaval, didn't believe she could do anything with alacrity. Only the coffee he made on his return helped in some way to wake her up. He sat on the edge of the bed with her, his face expectant, and she didn't know what to say. She'd thought the night before that the morning would bring clarity, but it hadn't. Instead she felt exhausted, not up to conversation. Not up to the detail that had been glossed over thus far.

'What time do you want to leave?' he asked.

'Are you sure you want to come?'

'Are you sure you want me to?'

She sucked in her lower lip. What was the point in putting this off? Uncomfortable now or uncomfortable later, those were the choices. 'Yeah, I'm sure.'

When they got to intensive care it was Lori who stepped into the room first. Rebecca, at the monitor, turned and greeted her. 'Improving in leaps and bounds,' she said cheerfully, tilting her head towards Scott who lay on his bed, eyes closed.

'Asleep?' asked Lori quietly.

'Perhaps. He was talking a few minutes ago, but he might have nodded off.'

Jason had walked in behind her and Lori was aware that he had stopped suddenly and was looking over at the bed. There was a strange stillness about him, perhaps the astonishment of seeing her brother for the first time, a family resemblance that she couldn't imagine herself, the idea of a relationship that he'd never thought he would have. Brother-in-law. She turned to see him step around to the other side of the bed and bend down towards Scott.

'Mike?' he said. He looked up at Lori, a plaintive expression on his face, as though the sight of her brother was something more painful than he could have imagined.

'His name's Scott, honey.'

For a moment he continued to stare at her, a strange, serious look on his face, his mouth turned downward. The night before, even this morning, had taken its toll. He hadn't been angry, he said he hadn't felt betrayed, yet she could tell he was deeply shocked. Shocked at this hitherto hidden part of her life, shocked at bewilderment that would not soon recede, she knew that. It was the nature of shock, a pressure pad between experience and understanding, coming to terms. She would have to be patient and allow him to adjust. And with herself as well. Adjustment would be their key term for the foreseeable future.

As Rebecca updated her, she glanced cautiously back at Jason. He had sat down in the chair next to Scott and was regarding him intently. He looked up again when Rebecca left the room but didn't speak. She stepped closer to the bed, looking from her husband to her brother and back, wondering at Jason's expression.

'I know him,' said Jason.

'What? No, you can't. How?'

'He's Mike. He was working with me.'

'No. Scott said he worked for someone else. Someone called . . .' She looked heavenward for inspiration. 'Lincolns. Or something like that.'

Jason nodded. 'Lambeth Lincoln.'

'Yes. That's it.'

'They're a labour hire firm. We get a lot of our people through them.'

'Oh.' She stared at Scott. 'You're sure?'

Jason made a small laughing sound, his mouth twisted up at one corner. 'Yeah. Totally sure.'

'I can't believe it. God, as if this wasn't all bizarre enough.'

Jason raised his eyebrows.

'Do you think he knew who you were?' Lori asked.

'He must have. Why else the false name?'

'What name?'

'Mike Green.'

'That's his middle name. He's Scott *Michael* Green.'

'You can ask me.' Scott's voice rose up between them.

Lori started. She put a hand on his arm. 'You're awake.'

Scott's eyes slid from Lori to Jason. 'I have a state. I am in a state of . . .'

'Mate,' said Jason, his voice suffused with emotion. 'What the hell is going on? You're not making sense.'

'Jase, he has a head injury.'

'It's okay,' said Scott. 'I know what's . . . on. Pretty much.'

'Yeah, but we have to take things slowly,' said Lori. 'Not let you get overloaded.'

'I was fucking worried about you,' said Jason. He looked across to Lori but pointed to the bed. 'Mike. Scott. This guy. He was the one I told you disappeared. My right-hand man.'

Lori and Jason exchanged glances, thoughts transmitted wordlessly.

'You need to talk to the police, Jase,' said Lori. 'You might be able to help them.'

'Of course. Whatever I can do, I'll do.'

Scott smiled woozily at Jason. 'It's good to see you.'

'You too, bro. Bro-in-law.' He laughed abruptly. 'Wow. This is unexpected.'

Scott kept smiling, a lopsided grin that in any other circumstances would make him appear like a drunkard or an imbecile. Lori hadn't quite got used to his tentative animation after days of watching him lying corpse-like on his back.

'What happened? Do you remember anything?' Jason asked. Lori had told him in the car that her brother had no recollection of the accident, but it seemed he'd forgotten that now, in the heat of the moment.

Scott closed his eyes. Seconds ticked by and he didn't respond.

'This is what happens,' she said. 'He just kind of tunes out. Sleeps. I'm not sure. The nurses said he gets super tired.'

Jason was nodding, but he seemed to have tuned out too. Lori saw that his face was pale and his eyes a little vacant. She thought that it was the way she had probably looked for the last few days too. He hadn't noticed because he didn't know what he should be looking for. She noticed because she knew exactly. 'I think I need to go,' he said.

'You want to get coffee or something to eat?'

'I don't know,' he said, and she felt something shift between them.

'It's too much, all this, isn't it?'

He was looking out the window. 'I just don't know what to make of any of this. I mean there's you, and there's him. It's fucking bizarre. You sure there's nothing else to know? No extra children or anything I haven't been told about?' There was a sharpness in Jason's voice. It made her stomach clench, left her speechless.

'Nothing, just the details, like I said.' She held her arms outward, as though giving a blessing. 'What the hell, Jason? Don't treat me like I orchestrated this. It's as much a shock to me as to you.'

He got up, pushing his chair back carelessly, looking at the floor rather than at her. 'I'm going to go out for a walk.'

'Go home if you want to,' she said to his back. 'I can make my own way.' She spoke gently so her words didn't sound angry, punitive.

'Don't be silly,' he said, stopping and turning. His face was soft again and he looked as though he was going to cry, and her instinct was to go to him, but she remained in her chair. 'I'm not going home,' he added. 'I just need a little time.'

After he closed the door she sat leaning forward, her arms resting at the edge of the bed, for what felt like an eternity.

'What were you up to, Scotty?' she said. 'Playing at being someone else? Or just . . .'

When he didn't reply she got up and walked to the window, looked out without seeing and turned around, surveying the room. 'I'll be back soon too,' she announced with no idea if he'd heard her or not.

In the café downstairs she texted Jason to tell him where she was in case he returned and didn't find her. She rang Daniel Levandi and, when he didn't answer, she left him a message to call her. After fifteen minutes and a horrible milky, weak coffee, she returned upstairs to find Jason sitting with Scott. He turned his head towards her and smiled as she came in.

'Has he said anything else?' she asked.

'Nothing that makes a lot of sense.'

She sat down in the opposite chair. 'The doctors said it could take weeks or months for him to stabilise. He could have deficits. They don't know how it will be.'

'Head injuries are a bastard. I had a friend at school who was in a car accident. It took him a long time to come good.'

She nodded, gave him a long look. 'How are *you*?'

Jason smiled wanly at her across the bed. 'I'm all right. I'm sorry if I sounded shitty. God, my part in all of this is minor. I don't have any right to be angry when you two have gone through so much.'

'He has. He has gone through so much crap.' She looked at him, lying still again, peaceful. 'And I treated him so badly.

For so long. There in my own bundle of pain, all I could do was blame him for everything.'

Scott's eyes opened and he looked to Jason. 'Did you get them?' he asked.

'Who?'

'Fricker and Walt . . . Cash.'

'Did they do this?' Jason's voice was urgent.

'What's he talking about?' interjected Lori.

'The guys I told you about at work,' Jason replied, then addressing Scott he said, 'I need you to tell me what you saw and heard. What happened to you.'

'Photos,' he said. 'On phone. And other . . .'

'Where's his phone?' Jason's voice was sharp.

'I don't know. The police?'

She got up and walked outside Scott's room looking for one of the nurses, saw Rebecca exiting another room and beckoned to her. Rebecca confirmed the police would have taken all Scott's effects, although she couldn't say exactly what they might have been. Lori made her way back to Scott's room and mimed 'phone call' through the glass to Jason before heading back out, through the open area by the nurses' station, down the short corridor to the exit door and out into the waiting room beyond. As if on cue, when she took her phone out of her pocket it rang. Daniel Levandi's number, which she recognised now, flashed up in front of her.

'I think I know who knocked Scott down,' she said.

'You do? Who?' He sounded neither surprised nor sceptical, as if he'd been expecting some kind of case breakthrough from her all along.

'Scott had been working on my husband's worksite. They were having problems with pilfering. Some kind of a racket.'

There was a second of silence. 'Ah. That's, um, a strange coincidence he ended up there.'

'I don't know about that. Jason knew him as Mike. He used his middle name. I imagine to obscure any possible connection to me. It might have been a coincidence, or he might have been . . . Well, I guess we'll have to wait and see what he says when he's better.'

'Who could blame him for changing his name though, eh? You changed yours, didn't you? Everyone wants a break from the past, don't they?'

'Yeah,' she said after brief consideration. 'I didn't think that . . . But, I guess I did.'

'So you think it was these blokes from his workplace?'

'Do you have his phone?'

'Why?'

'Apparently he took photos.'

'Hm, hold on. I don't think we do, but I'll double-check that.' She heard him rustling through papers again, had a vision, not for the first time, of his desk piled high with files and folders. Somehow she couldn't imagine that he was tidy. 'No, there's no phone in the inventory. Just clothes, wallet, keys, bike helmet, backpack with a thermos. That's it.'

'Shit. He said he'd taken photos of the guys doing something incriminating, I guess. They must have realised and taken his phone.'

'Could be what this has all been about. Or the phone might have skittered into a drain when he got knocked down. Could have been left in a work locker.'

'How will we ever know?'

'I'm thinking your husband knows exactly who they are, these blokes. We might be able to put something together. The footage we have from CCTV. The vehicle. There's a chance. We also have Scott's computer. He might have been sensible and downloaded the photos. I'll try to get a hurry up on that. And finding his number. Might find the phone too if we get a fix on it. I feel pretty confident that if this is the case, we'll be able to get these guys, one way or another. Could be good news for your husband too.'

'God, I hope so.'

The waiting room was empty. She walked over to the door and buzzed to get back in but no one responded. It took a few minutes for an older woman she'd never seen before with a harried look on her face to front the small booth by the door. 'Our staff are all busy right now,' she said, as if being summonsed by the buzzer had been a deep imposition. 'I'm afraid you'll have to wait a little.'

'I was just in there a few minutes ago,' Lori said a little testily. 'I only came out to use the phone. My husband is inside with my brother. He's a patient.'

The woman's face softened. 'I'm very sorry but I still can't let you back in until we have enough staff free. There's a ratio. One of the patients is being prepared for emergency surgery.'

Lori returned to the waiting area and sat down. This place, the ICU and its waiting area, was nothing like the hospital at Belandra. It was nothing like the ICU at the Royal Melbourne either, where her father was taken by air ambulance after the accident and where he lay for two days, without ever regaining consciousness. This ICU was new and spacious, with floor-to-ceiling glass windows rimmed and crisscrossed with thick white steel tubing. Did it make any difference to the whole experience of attending the critically ill, she wondered, if the furniture was modern, the walls and floor new and unblemished, if there was a view? When she'd been in those places had she been looking? Had she cared? Not at the time. But when she thought back she saw that her memories were made up of those images. Drab, dark hallways. Grey linoleum. Overstuffed noticeboards. Ugly plastic chairs. Low ceilings clad with perforated tiles. When she thought of her time here later she might remember the curved orange and aqua couches and the views across the rooftops of the neighbouring buildings, the stretch of sky above. A better outcome. She could only hope.

The quiet of the waiting room was broken by sudden traffic. Simultaneously, an elderly woman and her daughter emerged to her left with a ding from the lift, while from the right the door from the ICU swung open. As the two women stepped towards reception, Jason dodged around them to her. For a moment she thought only that he'd come to get her and didn't register his expression, the urgency of his step. When she looked up she saw his face was pinched and she knew in that instant that there was something wrong.

'What's happened?' she asked. 'Why did the ward shut down?'

'Mike had a fit. A convulsion? I don't know what it was. Fucking frightening. Good that nurse was in there. She took over. Some more of them rushed in. Pushed me out of the room, closed the curtains. I waited for you—'

'I couldn't get back in. They wouldn't let me.'

'Then the nurse came out and said he had to be taken down to theatre and I should leave.'

'My bag's still in there,' said Lori.

Jason sat down beside her and took her hand and held it tenderly.

'I never thought it would be him they were taking to surgery,' she said. 'He was doing so well.'

'He was talking to me when it happened.'

'What was he saying?'

'I asked him if he was working with me to get to you. He said it was a coincidence initially—he'd been jobbing on building sites for a long time—but when he started with our company he recognised my name. He'd had a private detective track you down a few years back, knew we got married.'

'Huh, makes sense.'

'When I didn't cotton on to who he was, he realised that you hadn't told me about him. He said he'd been calling himself Mike since he got out of prison. No big cover-up, just wanted to go under the radar, I guess.'

'You got a lot out of him,' said Lori.

'He wasn't saying heaps, really. Mostly I pieced it together.' He squeezed her fingers gently. 'We've known each other a while now, me and Mike. You know, we really got along. He's a good guy.'

They sat, mostly silent, holding hands and staring out at the view. What was it about rooftops that was so restful, she wondered. The sight of buildings against the sky. When the unit reopened they got up, following the woman and her daughter along the short corridor to the central open area. Lori walked on to Scott's room and found her bag in the corner near the door where she had left it. The room was empty, and there was no sign of Rebecca anywhere on the ward. The one nurse they did see at the central desk had no firm details about Scott and could only tell them that she believed the operation was most probably to clear a blood clot and that there was nothing to do but wait. It would be hours until he was back out again.

Jason called Daniel from the hospital foyer, told him all he knew, gave him Scott's phone number. Lori heard him explain his work situation to Daniel, saw him nodding his head as he listened to what Daniel had to say. When he'd finished, he'd looked at Lori and let out a long breath. 'I feel really bad. Mike was helping me out. If it was those guys, well, I reckon I put him in harm's way.'

'He would have wanted to do the right thing. It wasn't your fault,' she responded. 'You didn't start this.'

They drove home in silence, Jason at the wheel this time, too tired to talk about what they knew about Scott (or Mike), to swap memories and knowledge, to try to create some kind of objective vision. That was a conversation that would require time and energy; that would come out in dribs and drabs over weeks and months. When they got back, he volunteered to pick up the kids while Lori lay down on the bed and rested for an hour or so. But she couldn't sleep. Only stare up at the ceiling, repeating the same mantra over and over: please god, please god, please god.

At dinnertime, as she was reheating last night's tomato sauce and boiling water for pasta, Malcolm called and said that Scott was returning to ICU. He had survived the operation but they wouldn't know the outcome for hours, days or possibly even weeks. The effects could play out in many ways. Time without sufficient oxygen could have been detrimental. Haematomas could recur.

'What does it mean for us?' she asked.

'It's like returning to square one,' he said. 'He might be fine. Or he might not be. Or any degree in between. I can't say anything else right now. Sorry.'

'No,' she said. 'I'm grateful you're being honest. That's all I want. I can work with that.'

She thought about something her mother told her once, not long after Troy was killed. It was about life being a matter of chance and luck. She wasn't sure why Pam had said that. It seemed insensitive, callous, at the time. Her mother knew how she felt about Troy. She was little more than a child who wanted to see sense in everything, some point in the pain she was going through. She didn't want to have to picture the object of her affection as a soldier in some army-of-life board game, being swept away by the indifferent hand of fate as though he and his life had no real meaning. It wasn't until much, much later, after everything else that happened in those few months and the time that ensued, that she saw the truth in Pam's statement. Every act having an effect, like the movement of the wings of a butterfly in the Amazon. Nothing truly controllable. Action, reaction, chance, luck. The only thing that could be governed to any degree were your own reactions. Others reactions could go any which way. She took a lesson from that, made a choice. If you could stop remembering, you could stop feeling. If you could stop feeling you could live.

The kids chattered at the dinner table. Squabbled and laughed. Lori and Jason exchanged looks that said they were grateful for the noise. For the affirmation of life. When Jason cleared the plates away she put her hand on his arm and looked into his eyes and he bent and put his lips to her forehead. 'We'll talk soon,' he said.

Lori stealthily kissed the kids goodnight as they watched TV. They barely noticed her as she picked up her car keys and headed for the front door. In a few moments she was making the drive back across town again, ready to begin a vigil, hoping for the best for her brother.

July 1993

Northam

They were standing outside Raki Parry's house, a dumpy little weatherboard not far from the river on the Flat. Raki lived with his mum and dad, but they had gone fishing for the weekend, down to Lake Eildon, and had left Raki and his brother, Jai, at home. Jai worked for some company in Wang, and he had money and lots of weed. According to Raki, Jai grew some of it himself in a secret location somewhere and sold it to a bunch of mobsters over the border. It was hard to know with those guys where fact and fantasy began and ended, but the weed was good and not too pricey, so no one was about to call them on what may or may not have been bullshit.

Loren leaned against one of the cars, hands deep in her coat. Julie Roth, seemingly impervious to the cold, sprawled on the bonnet next to her, laughing hysterically. 'Fuck, where are the stars tonight!' she said, taking a deep drag on a joint. 'I love looking at the stars when I'm stoned.'

Loren, looking closer to hand, could see the end of the joint glow bright orange, hear the paper crackle. She put her hand out. 'Don't hog it.'

Julie propped herself up. The bonnet of the car made a dull pop underneath her as she moved. 'Shit, I hope I haven't broken something.'

Loren grabbed the joint from Julie's hand and took a toke while Julie slithered down beside her and turned to check if she'd left a dent. 'All good,' she said, although Loren wasn't sure what she could see out here as the light was so faint. No moon tonight, lots of cloud. The nearest street lamp was fifty metres away.

Just then, the muted thud of the party inside the house broke into a sharp vignette of music and voices as someone opened the front door. Julie looked over and said, 'Oh god, it's the man of my dreams.' Loren looked up but she couldn't see who it was now the door was closed.

Seconds later she heard a voice. 'Lore?'

Loren straightened up, her heart beginning to pound as though she'd been caught out doing something.

'Lore?'

Beside her Julie giggled. 'Is that you, Troy-boy?'

'Jeez, Julie.' Troy appeared beside them. 'Who's got the spliff?'

'I have. Jai gave me two of them.'

'Jai wants to get into your pants,' Troy laughed, taking the joint from Julie's fingers.

'Ugh. Well, he's not going to.'

'Were you looking for me?' asked Loren as she watched Troy put the glowing embers to his mouth and inhale.

He paused for a moment, then exhaled slowly. 'Ah. I was looking for Scott, thought you might know where he is.'

'No idea,' she replied lazily. 'I am not my brother's keeper.'

Julie laughed and retrieved her can of beer from the bonnet of the car. 'What time is it? I have to be home by one.'

'This party's closing down anyway,' said Troy. 'I reckon we should head off.'

'Give me a lift,' said Julie in a little girl voice.'

'I'm too gone to drive,' said Troy. 'You'll have to find someone else.'

'You going to leave the ute here?' asked Loren.

'Scotty can give me a lift.' He was standing close to her now, almost touching her, swaying just a little.

'And me too?' said Julie, still using her girly voice.

The joint between Troy's fingers was down to a stub. 'You're going to burn yourself,' Loren said.

'Aw, shit.' He dropped it on the ground. 'You and your stumpy joints, Julie.'

'You've thrown away a good roach,' she said indignantly.

'Don't worry, you've got a lifeline to Jai.'

Julie sighed dramatically. 'There's only so much I can get for free.'

Troy let out a harsh laugh and leaned forward, his head resting on Loren's shoulder. 'Let's find your brother,' he murmured. He reached down and gripped her hand and yanked her forward, pulling her up the street and into the darkness away from Julie.

'What are you doing?' hissed Loren.

He put on an American backwoods accent. 'Just going up here a ways.'

Behind them Loren could hear Julie's annoyed, slurring voice. 'I see how it is, you two. Go on. Fuck off then.'

They were close to the river; the grass was longer here and Loren could feel the wet blades flick against her legs as Troy pulled her along towards the bank.

'What are we doing?' asked Loren uncertainly.

Troy came to a halt and, unable to see in the darkness, she piled into him. He must have turned at the same time because in the suddenness of it all she could feel his chest against her face, then his hands move to clasp the top of her shoulders. She looked up, seeing just a vague shadow, but could feel his hair brush across her eyes, his forehead touch hers, his nose against hers. A small twist to the side and his lips were on her lips. She could taste beer and tobacco, feel the pressure of his tongue against her teeth. His hands ran down her arms and around her back. Hers moved upward to his face. She could barely see anything in the gloom, but she could feel his skin, the jut of his cheekbone, the softness of his hair. Hear his rushed breathing.

A beam of light passed behind them. The headlights of a car. They pulled away from each other as the vehicle came to a halt at the end of the road close to where they stood. The lights went off and someone got out, slammed the door hard.

'Hey!' It was Scott. 'Been looking for you. Shit, it's dark here. Who's that?'

'Who's what?' Loren answered, thinking he'd been talking to her.

'It's you!' Scott sounded surprised to hear his sister's voice. 'Oh wow.' He laughed. 'Sorry. You two, I never thought. Shit.'

Troy stepped away from Loren, waded back through the grass to Scott and slapped him on the back. 'What's up?' he asked. Loren was suddenly unsure of what Troy would do. Was he going to pretend he hadn't been with her?

'I'm taking Mike home,' said Scott. 'You want to come? Go for a drive.'

'Yeah, sure,' said Troy. He turned to Loren who was just behind him now and grabbed her hand. 'That party was getting boring.'

'That why you two are out here, is it?' said Scott with a cynical little laugh as he opened his car door.

Back at the house the party was dispersing, just a few kids now milling around outside. Melissa and Josh were standing with Mike, passing a bottle of bourbon from one to another. Troy put his arm around Loren's shoulder, took the bottle from Mike and had a swig, offered it to Loren who shook her head.

'I'll throw up if I drink that,' she said, already feeling a little woozy from the dope and some liquid concoction she'd had earlier.

Scott was waiting by the car. 'Come on, passengers,' he said, his voice raised over its throaty purr. He was leaning in the space between the open door and the body of the car, his foot on the bottom of the door jamb, his arms spread across the roof, his hands drumming a slow tattoo. 'Tired of fucking waiting.'

'Keep your hair on,' said Josh, grabbing the bottle of bourbon and heading for the far side of the car.

Mike and Melissa jumped into the front seat, Melissa sitting on his knee. Troy and Loren went in the back next to Josh. Scott pumped up the music, Eddie Vedder's voice raging through the speakers. Beside Loren, Troy wound down the window and screamed a whoop as Scott hammered the accelerator and the car fishtailed up the street.

'Christ,' Melissa squealed, pulling the seatbelt across her and Mike. 'Wait up, you madman!'

Troy leaned forward to Scott, raised his voice. 'You can drop me off after Mike. Okay?'

'You don't want to get the ute?' Scott said.

'Nah, mate. Just drop me home. I'll get it tomorrow.'

Loren gripped Troy's leg above the knee and pushed her fingers in deep.

'Ow,' he said.

'I don't want you to go,' she hissed into his ear.

Josh passed the bourbon across to Troy and he gripped the neck and took a long swig. 'I can't be too late tonight. Dad'll be pissed off. Gotta pile of work to do for school. He's been fucking relentless about it.'

'What do you mean?' she asked him and watched as he took another long slug.

He whispered, 'He wants me to do business at uni. I won't get in.'

'You don't know.'

'Ha! Have to be a miracle. I'm too fucking dumb.'

'You're not dumb.'

Troy gulped down the last of the bottle. 'No more!' he declared loudly, tipping it up.

'You bastard,' said Josh.

'I've got a tinny,' said Mike, passing a can over the seat.

'You are *not* dumb,' Loren said again, close to Troy's ear so it was more of a tickle than a sentence.

He laughed and pushed his face into hers, biting her lips. His hand ran down her arm, his body constrained from turning further by the seatbelt.

Suddenly he pulled back, his body lurching in time to the music. 'Fuck yeah!' he yelled.

They were on one of the back roads now. Loren looked out through the windscreen in front of her and saw an avenue of ghost gums guarding the bitumen, their branches like great white arms bending forward, threatening to scoop up the car as it passed below.

'I need a piss,' Josh yelled after a few minutes.

'What the hell!' Melissa yelled as Scott slammed on the brakes and they slid to a halt. Black Sabbath blared into the night while they waited for Josh.

When he returned Mike said, 'Hey, what about my driving lesson?'

'Jesus H Christ,' said Scott. 'Timing, mate!'

'Yeah, come on,' Mike urged as Josh got in and slammed the door.

Scott laughed and opened his door and they swapped seats, necessitating Melissa to get in and out again as well, sitting on Scott's knee once the changes were made. She looked over the back of the seat and winked at Loren.

Loren wasn't surprised. She'd been wondering about that state of affairs. She didn't think Mike was really her type, but then what would she know. Melissa was in year twelve with the boys, she wasn't one of her friends.

Mike took off then, driving slowly down the road, turning into a farm driveway and then turning back. Scott cracked open another can of beer. 'Free!' he proclaimed. 'Free!' It wasn't clear what he was free of—maybe the tyranny of the steering wheel—but whatever it was he was enjoying it. Loren looked at Troy and he laughed. Scott turned the music up louder, a driving relentless throb filling the car.

Mike pulled off the road at the entrance to his house. He wouldn't drive down. His dad had to get up for milking in the morning; Mike wouldn't be popular if he woke him up. He waited until Scott came back around to the driver's side and leaned back into the car to say goodnight. No special treatment for Melissa, Loren noted. She also noted Scott lurch slightly as he climbed back in and the look on his face as he turned to Melissa. He wanted to impress her. She could see that now. What a strange pair they would make. The revhead and the netball queen. The only thing they had in common right now, Loren observed, was that they were both cactus.

Scott put his foot down on the accelerator and the car skittered up the road. 'Gonna take a long cut home,' he said to no one in particular. 'Scenic route.'

Loren placed her head on Troy's shoulder, inhaling the boozy, sharp smell of him, listening to him chorus along with Bon Jovi, feeling his voice vibrate through her body. She thumped him playfully on the arm and he bent his head and looked at her, grinning. Lori felt a mad symphonic swell of emotion inside her and thought that she had never truly known what happiness was until that moment; never understood that the future could hold such possibilities.

She glanced ahead. Scott had turned the corner into an old side road that wound its way down to Allens Road, another route back to town. It wouldn't be too long until they were dropping Troy at his house. She turned her face up towards his, hardly daring to believe the realness of him next to her. He leaned towards her, his eyes hooded. Deftly, she unclicked her belt, then reached over, running her hand across the front of his jeans as she did, and unclicked his. Suddenly they were free, their bodies liberated from constraint. He twisted fully towards her but just as his lips touched hers he pulled away momentarily and shouted to Scott, 'Can't this car go any faster, mate? Come on! You're too slow, too slow.'

Scott laughed, turned up the music and floored the accelerator, and the car surged forward, propelling them into the darkness ahead.

Acknowledgements

Thanks to everyone at Allen & Unwin, especially Jane Palfreyman for her enthusiasm for this book, Christa Munns for her editorial care and Simone Ford for her close reading and insightful editing.

I am deeply grateful for the encouragement and support I have received in my writing life, especially from Wendy Anderson, Barry Watts and Lee Walker. I would also like to acknowledge Varuna, The Writer's House, which not only provided me with a space in the early days of shaping the manuscript for this book but also gave me faith in its future prospects.

My heartfelt appreciation goes to Julie Wells and Greg Connolly for their generosity in reading and responding to the manuscript and, most especially, to Jenny Hellen who had belief from the beginning and without whose unflagging enthusiasm this book would not exist. Finally, all my love and thanks to Greg, Aidan and Madi Connolly: my nearest and dearest, and constant inspirations.